Soon To Be Born

SOON TO BE BORN

A NOVEL BY
OSCAR RYAN

NEW STAR BOOKS LTD.
Vancouver • Toronto

New Star Books Ltd.
2504 York Avenue
Vancouver, B.C. V6K 1E3

Canadian Cataloguing in Publication Data

Ryan, Oscar, 1904-
    Soon to be born

      ISBN 0-919888-28-3 bd.
      ISBN 0-919888-27-5 pa.

      I. Title.
    PS8585.Y36S6   C813'.54   C80-091184-9
    PR9199.3.R93S6

The author wishes to thank the Canada
Council for its assistance.

This book was published with the
support of the Canada Council.

For Toby
of the Thirties
and Sandy
of Today

Suddenly the Angelus sounds, and the flock
of bells suddenly springs into wakefulness.
It is the new dawn! Behind the sheer black
rises the golden glory of the invisible sun.
Almost falling Christophe at last reaches
the bank, and he says to the Child:
  "Here we are! How heavy thou wert! Child,
who art thou?"
  And the child answers:
"I am the day soon to be born."

Jean-Christophe
Romain Rolland

Mourn not the dead that in the cool earth lie—
      Dust unto dust—
The calm sweet earth that mothers all who die
      As all men must;

Mourn not your captive comrades who must dwell—
      Too strong to strive—
Within each steel-bound coffin of a cell,
      Buried alive;

But rather mourn the apathetic throng—
      The cowed and the meek—
Who see the world's great anguish and its wrong
      And dare not speak!

Mourn Not the Dead
Ralph Chaplin

PART ONE

1

1939. September.
Casualty of War.

PALE ROWS OF beds in perspectives of pain reach from the hospital's wards.

Walk to the end of the corridor, open this door, turn into the small, hushed room of immobile wraiths where Arthur lies.

Search his pale face below bullet-broken tissue and bruised bone.

"He's not stalling?" The detective—a tall, hard, handsome man of morose expression and dry voice—asks, "You're sure?"

The dying and the broken ones sleep. Occasionally they sigh in resignation, groan in their despair, cry out in panic. One of them tries to sit up, mutters and falls back. A youth whimpers and an old man weeps into his pillow. It is a place of fears and fevers. It is mostly quiet now and the chance neighbours share the night's obscurity, its heavy stillnesses.

The detective challenges the doctor, a short, bald fellow. "He's not pretending?" The big man's voice is toneless, the words flat. His head is long, the reddish hair brush-cut, the eyebrows bushy and the thin moustache neatly trimmed. On the left side of his face, from cheekbone to chin, is a nasty bruise from the night before.

Once more the detective demands, "Are you sure he's not pretending?" The lips, like a ventriloquist's, barely move. The green eyes are as expressionless as the voice.

"I'm sure," the doctor replies. He is in command here and his eyes search the stony face. What kind of man is this, gazing steadily back at him? "He's not pretending. He's not even conscious."

3

"I'll have to stay," the cop says.

"Sorry, not here, not in this room. You can sit outside on the bench at the far end near the office. There's a good view, you can see everything from there. He won't slip out. I'm sorry, nobody gets into this room without my permission." Briskly, authoritatively, he says, "Regulations," and adds, "You know, this man may die."

Arthur on the bed mutters random sounds, vague fragments that make no sense.

"How long before he wakes up?" the cop demands.

The doctor shrugs. "A day. Two. Maybe not at all."

A young nurse enters the room and the detective watches moodily as she goes about her duties. He wonders how this well-padded girl would look stripped and how she would then perform in bed. When the nurse has left he turns to the doctor. "How many patients altogether in here?"

"I don't know, I didn't count."

Smart-ass jerk, the dick reflects. I'd like to give him a swift kick in the crotch and teach him some respect. He knows goddam well how many patients. The Krauts know how to handle this kind.

Here on the bed and thirty-four years old is Arthur, his unshaven face hollow from hurt, his limbs inert under the bedclothes.

"This man's very sick. He's helpless," the doctor warns. "He won't run away. He can't. You'd better leave now."

The detective steps closer to the bed, skeptical, assessing. Abruptly he switches on the bed-lamp. The unconscious man on the cot stirs and mumbles meaningless sounds. The big cop adjusts the lamp until its beam washes across Arthur's face.

"I thought I saw his eyes open..." The words offer neither excuse nor concern. He doesn't have to apologize to this bald-headed little sawbones.

Angrily the doctor snaps off the lamp. He stares incredulously at the detective. "For God's sake, man! What in hell's your name, anyway?"

"Gilbert. Detective Gilbert."

"Well, you better go now, Mister Gilbert!"

The detective ignores him and turns again to the lean figure on the bed. Gilbert leans down and shakes the patient's shoulder. The doctor seizes the hand and flings it aside. "Do you want to kill him? You better get the hell out of here—fast—or..."

Gilbert glares at the chunky doctor whose face is white with anger. The detective, calm but taut as a trigger, shrugs and smiles. The doctor stares at him in disgust.

Gilbert, still skeptical, says, "It looked...I thought he moved."

"I told you he's unconscious!" the doctor shouts. "He's damn near dead. Are you trying to finish him off?"

"Aw, keep your shirt on, doc."

The doctor opens the door and waits for Gilbert to leave. "We'll let you know if he tries to run away."

One final look at the man on the bed, then the big detective stalks out of Intensive Care and makes for the bench at the end of the long hallway.

Last night, after the violence in the park, and again this morning, the blonde woman paced the hospital corridor. This evening Gabrielle is here again. Graceful, feminine, slender. And scared.

Others came. A blue-eyed, distraught little woman in her fifties, his mother. And the black-haired, defiant woman, eight years younger, her sister. But Arthur's friends dare not come—the elderly Martin Shaughnessy and his son Fred, the frail Miss Gillespie, John Kravchuk who fought in Spain, others who were with them in the park last night. And whoever it was who hurled that brick.

Gabrielle has to pass the detective's post at the bench near the office. Automatically he catalogues her parts—lips, neck, limbs, breasts, belly, buttocks, groin—all utterly feminine. She's the one who called him a murdering bastard last night. He should have slapped her around a bit, maybe arrested her. But there were witnesses. She hadn't tried to run away. She kept insisting she had to stay with her husband. She wouldn't leave. Stubborn bitch.

In the soft light of the hospital corridor her body is lithe and sensuous. She scowls at Gilbert and her eyes are filled with anguish and loathing. He stares back. Rape's too good for her, he thinks.

The doctor is beside Arthur and Gaby in the room. She pleads, "I don't trust that detective, he's a killer! I beg you, don't leave him alone with my husband! He'll murder him! If anything happens I'll hold you responsible." There are tears in her eyes and her face is flushed. She weeps, she trembles with anger and she is near collapse.

"He'll be all right. Don't worry," the doctor encourages. "We run a hospital, not a prison camp. We're not storm-troopers. We'll do everything possible for him. Don't worry."

"Sometimes," she protests wearily, "I think the police run everything."

The doctor takes her arm and leads her down the hall, past Gilbert, to the elevators. "We'll phone if there's any news. Don't worry. Get some rest."

Gilbert watches as the elevator door closes behind her. He mutters, "Communists. A French bitch and a Jewboy Red. Christ, if I ever ripped her pants off her she'd never forget me—if she lived, if she ever walked again."

*

Across the ocean, in Poland, a war broke out. A week ago?...Now here, in Montreal, a run-down Main Street park, the war has claimed its victim.

We who are about to die...

1905. Below Mount Royal.
The Years of Discovery.

This story is about Arthur and others. He was born into the fifth year of the new century and he first cried out his awareness of the world from the rented upstairs flat of a row house on St. Urbain Street.

This is about Arthur who played across the road from the awesome Hotel Dieu hospital and who explored the slopes of the mountain that gave the city its name.

He was the son of anxious immigrants who relinquished their birthplaces and came to the New World and reached out for its promises, most of which eluded them. Perhaps it was their own fault, perhaps they lacked the skills or the cunning or nerve or panache or luck or whatever it was, or perhaps they were just born losers, but the disenchantments and frustrations and mockeries and defeats eventually swamped and saddened and then soured them. The worst would come later, when the boy was sixteen, seventeen.

Right now they were both young and the child was discovering his own world, a vast region of infinite possibilities, welcomes and rebuffs, hungers and abundance, constrictions and freedoms, joys and agonies. His world would mould his thoughts and generate his fears.

But now, what marvellous things he saw and felt and learned those first revealing years!

Furiously clanging bells and sparks from clattering hooves as horse-drawn fire-reel wagons charged over cobblestones or brick...The pungent smell of sawdust on the floors of grocery stores with open barrels of broken biscuits, dill pickles or salt herring...Sticky, golden, candied popcorn chunks...And the wondrous machines in shop windows, pulling and twisting *latire* candy...The effervescent *biere d'epinette,* the spruce beer which was not a beer at all but a robust Quebec thirst-quencher so volatile that the bottle mouth had to be capped with a glass ball and a wire clamp...French-Canadian neighbours belting out their ancient habitant songs and thumping out rhythm in exuberant dance at all-night celebrations on the floor below or the flat above or in both places at once...The measles, the chicken pox, the mumps. Fried-onion poultices for earaches, vinegar-soaked flannel cloths for a headache, hot milk-butter-and-honey concoctions for sore throat. The chicken-soup panacea; the camphor bag strung from the neck to fend off foul contagions; the ghastly castor-oil ritual; the oddly flavoured cod liver oil, a viscous yet seductive tonic, with the picture of the fisherman in sou'wester and slicker and with a huge codfish slung over his back...

And always the horses. What horses! Everywhere horses: teams of gigantic draft animals hauling the huge, low-slung, barge-like sleighs piled high with great blocks of green ice from the St. Lawrence River; majestic brewery horses prancing and gleaming in leather and brass; a calm horse drawing a doctor's buggy; a sleepy milk-wagon horse; a sad, cadaverous horse whose junk-man moaned, "Reks, buddles..."; and a fly-plagued nag of the fruit peddler, who sang out, "Wodda-meh-lun! Mush-meh-lun! Ba-nan! Ripe! Swit!" And the scary thrill when a frightened runaway, nostrils distended, careered along the street in wild flight, trailing its riderless wagon...

The observation tram radiantly lit up at night for the grand sightseeing tour down Park Avenue along the mountain's base beside Fletcher's Field, with the roofless, tiered streetcar blazing in many-coloured illumination; and the oompah swell of music pumped into the night by uniformed bandsmen...Rides on the

creaky incline railway, hauled by cable up a steep, greased
scaffolding on the mountainside, and everyone nervous that the
little cab might snap its line and plunge to destruction...

The games kids played on warm summer evenings in their
sweltering sidestreets...Leap-frog. Tag, of course. Runcheeprun
which, he learned much later, was really run-sheep-run. Marbles
and tippee. Winding a hard, waxed string around the pear-shaped,
varnished wooden top with its steel point, and deftly throwing it to
the floor or the sidewalk to make it spin...

The night's wonder when you are very young. The magic of the
street names, the mysteries of the streets—St. Urbain, St.
Dominque, St. Denis and the other saints, and Cadieux, Hotel de
Ville, Henri Julien, Marie-Anne, Jeanne Mance, Laurier,
Maisonneuve, Villeneuve, Papineau, Lagauchetiere...

A puffing, snorting piston engine in the railway station when his
parents took him to meet an incoming uncle. The steam seeming to
freeze solid in the winter night. The heavy snows, the great
snowbanks six feet high bordering the scraped and icy sidewalks.
The snowmen with eyes of coal. The snowballs...

The fairy-tale ice palaces all lit up and sparkling below the
mountain at night...huge, gleaming structures of ice, medieval
turreted fortresses sparkling under the nightly fireworks in the
falling snow, people dancing on the frozen surfaces as the bands
played waltzes and songs from the operettas...

Sledding on the slopes of Mount Royal. Skating on the open-air
rinks. Sliding across Fletcher's Field on ice-crusted snow after a
thaw and a fast freeze-up. Trying to snowshoe on the softest of new
snow. Tobogganing in the steep ruts...

The somnolent Saturday afternoons of an icy Montreal winter,
bitter cold outside, chest-stabbing cold, but sleepy-warm in the
sheltered indoors...

Visiting a favourite old uncle and sitting in a corner, nibbling on
a piece of almond biscuit as he watched the bearded men seated
around a table in the lazy twilight, hats or skullcaps pushed back on
their heads, sipping hot tea from tumblers, squeezing slices of
lemon, holding cubed lumps of sugar between their teeth and
slurping tea through it or (during Passover) cracking chunks of
glistening sugar from a foot-high cone wrapped in black paper...

The boy Arthur would sit silent in his corner, sleepily aware of
their deep voices, drowsily sharing the comforting warmth of the

porcelain-faced kitchen coal range, savouring the fragrances from a pot simmering on the oven-top, lulled by the red glow of the small, round Quebec heater in the hallway...

And dozing off until it was time to go home and he was wakened...

*

Arthur loved to handle the snuff-boxes. On Sundays, when visitors came to his house, he was glad when old men were among them, for the old men often carried snuff-boxes. They would let him open the lid and sniff the aromatic stuff and even let him inhale a crumb or two into his nostril until he sneezed from the delicious tickle.

He liked the lacquered smoothness of the boxes' satiny wood, black or brown and sometimes decorated, pleasant to the eye and nice to touch. About the size of a pocket matchbox, they opened easily and sealed in their fragrances when closed—spicy, oriental scents rising from the moist and crumbly mixture inside, gracious and tantalizingly seductive aromas which persisted in the wood for years after the elderly owner had left the world.

*

When his mother came to Canada with her parents she was six. Rose was sent to school to learn English. Four years later she was yanked out. What did a girl need education for, anyway? She'd be married in six or seven years. Meanwhile she could earn a few dollars. There was a job in a cigar factory.

Rose remembered little of the Russian village except that it was near an army barracks and that her mother—a devout woman who wore the traditional centre-parted brown wig—sold illicit liquor to the soldiers. (It was the tsar's law, not God's.) Her father, in his youth a cantor and now a scholar, spent much of his time in the synagogue, studying, moralizing, praying, philosophizing, splitting hairs. He earned a few kopeks writing letters, giving advice, teaching Hebrew to little boys or coaching them for the bar mitzvah celebration of their thirteenth birthday, when they achieved (they were gravely informed) the state of manhood.

Rose remembered talk of pogroms and whispers about young relatives crippling a trigger finger to dodge the tsar's army. The

Russian underground had no roots in her village and she knew nothing about revolutionaries. There were none in her own family; you don't boast about such things. She had probably never heard, in Montreal, of the revolution in the year of Arthur's birth. Russia was behind her, far behind, for now she was a Canadian, married to a Canadian citizen, and mother of a son born in Canada.

The child's father, Max, came to Montreal when he was seventeen, an orphan. In Rumania, in Russian Bessarabia, he had found his haven in the cafes. Intelligent, well-dressed, fluently argumentative in Rumanian, French, English, Yiddish, but penniless, he had spent his evenings sipping strong Turkish coffees and smoking strong Turkish cigarettes. And talking, always talking. (Later, in Canada, much later, the words dried up.)

A marriage was arranged by Rose's parents and an aunt of Max's and a white-bearded marriage broker. Matchmaking was an efficient, respectable business, quite proper, and a gamble. Romance? Love? These things might come later. And if they didn't, well, you lived with it for the rest of your life.

Max was a bookkeeper of sorts. His penmanship was magnificent, with graceful tall letters and ornate curlicues. The bookkeeping petered out and he became a "country peddler." Smallwares, clothes, religious objects for the Quebecois: holy pictures, crucifixes, chapelets, medallions that he packed into a couple of suitcases and lugged from farm to farm, covering countless tedious miles on foot in the futile effort to earn a living.

What a humiliating fate for this poor, stooped Jew trying to hawk the Church's paraphernalia among the hostile Catholics! How isolated and alien he felt during the big public religious festivals (especially the year of the Eucharistic Congress) when his street was ornate with decoration, posters, flags, fleur-de-lis banners, paper-flowered arches and holy plaster statues, and his was the only house that did not celebrate... *maudit Juif. Accursed Jew.*

How great his unhappiness when the bells pealed and his neighbours trooped off to church, turning their faces and refusing to return his greeting, the same neighbours who had smiled on Saturday... *maudit Juif.*

How bitter he became when his small son was baited by snickering old men who loitered at the corner store. And how he despaired when the children with whom Arthur played all week snubbed him on the Sunday. . . *maudit Juif.*

But Max Meller was stubborn. He refused to hide in a Jewish ghetto, though shunned everywhere in his adopted land. He wanted his son accepted. The boy, after all, was a native of this country, this city, this mountainside. Some day Arthur would show them. His son would outshine them all. And they would come to apologize, all these scornful clods. They'd have to hail Max Meller's son, his magnificent son, his *maudit Juif* son.

He would mould and toughen his boy, instill the fevers of ambition, make him dominate the herd and grasp the spoils. But how? What kind of example was he himself providing? How can a country peddler raise the money for high school and university and pay for shoes and clothes and books and provide pocket money?

The flat on St. Urbain Street was neat and clean and sparsely furnished. The meals were frugal but flavoursome. On Friday nights and the traditional holidays and High Holy Days there was a little extra—chicken, even goose. Bread, honey cakes and butter-buns all had been baked in the kitchen coal range.

Toys were few and modest. Their clothes were cheap, clean, often homemade.

Security was illusive, elusive; their poverty haunted them persistently. This week's income, or next week's or next year's, could never catch up with last month's demands. If you have only a few dollars for a short while, how do you decide which emergency is to receive priority? And if you can't borrow. . .?

Yet Rose and Max Meller dreamed their son would some day go to college to be groomed for one of the more genteel professions. When he was only four they kept him apart from the lesser children of the street so that he might grow up to achieve distinction by always deporting himself properly. Little Arthur would be a perfect little gentleman. Refined, respected. And rewarded.

*

He would tire of playing alone on his St. Urbain Street doorstep. He would plead to be allowed to play with the neighbours' children. Sometimes his mother relented, but when he ran in later, dusty, excited and boisterous, she would scold and forbid him ever again to play with "these noisy little French brats." He would sit alone and forlorn in a corner on the kitchen floor, building a

domino fort, or staring from the frontroom window, mystified by
the Hotel Dieu hospital and the ghostly sisters floating in their
flowing black robes. Or he would look at the tall trees or at the
entrance through which the horse-drawn ambulances rattled, or
watch the other children running, shouting, roller-skating.

One afternoon, as timid little Rose day-dreamed in her kitchen,
Max came home and asked, "Where's Arthur?"

"In the frontroom, at the window."

"He's not there," said Max, then called out, "Come out
wherever you're hiding! Come out, Arthur! Come see what I got
for you!"

But Arthur didn't come to claim candies or some magical toy.
They failed to find him in any of the four rooms. Rose started to
cry. Max again put on his dark blue serge vest and his jacket, took
his cap from the hook and went out to search, Rose beside him,
pale and frightened.

An hour later, in the coffee store on Main Street—the redolent
tea-coffee-chicory-spices-crockery-toy shop—they found Arthur
contemplating the English penny in his fist, the worn two-cent
copper disk.

The shop was an enchanting new world, awesome and magical,
rich in delicious aromas, full of marvels on many shelves laden with
opulent dinnerware, enamelled pots and pans and fancy glassware.
Undreamed-of toys hung from the walls and ceiling and overflowed
the window displays and sprawled onto the floor and the counters
and in front of the counters and on both sides and on top of a long,
low counter that ran down the middle of the floor. What a
cornucopia! Wind-up trains, whistles, pop-guns, wagons,
ice-skates, wooden swords, roller-skates, pails decorated with
seashore scenes, kites, shining rubber balls brightly coloured,
bugles and drums and tops and dolls and rocking-horses and
penny-banks and music-boxes! And gum-drops, fruit candies,
suckers, chocolate candies!

A man was smiling down at him, telling him from a great height
that he'd need many more pennies to buy the sleek wagon, the one
with the bright-red wheels, and that he'd better start saving right
away. The man smiled and gave the child a bag of peanuts. He was
tall, like Arthur's father, but rugged and very, very British. For
years afterwards Arthur always thought coffee and spices, crockery
and toys came only from genial Englishmen who spoke funny and

sounded so unlike his parents.

As Arthur stood with his penny in one fist and the bag of nuts in the other, and said, "Thank you for the nuts," just as he had been taught at home, he saw his parents. Rose ran forward and caught him in her arms. Max was about to scold the boy but instead patted his head. The Englishman smiled in approval.

"Later, when you're bigger," Max said as they walked home, "I'll buy it for you," and added as a matter of principle, "If you're a good boy and don't do bad things like getting lost and always remember to stay near your mother." He wondered whether they could ever collect enough premium coupons. He wondered how many pounds of tea and coffee they would have to buy to get enough of the coloured coupon cards to trade in for the wagon. How long, O Lord!

*

His doting, black-eyed young aunt, his mother's younger sister, lived in a room in their flat and was paying out a second-hand piano on the instalment plan. One evening a week her friends came to visit.

There was a roly-poly young man who played the flute; a middle-aged violinist, stiff and fiercely moustached; a doctor too recently out of medical school to seem entirely professional; a mournful baritone; and a pale youth from the shipping-room of the cigar factory, touchingly earnest as he read his poems in a language not yet his own.

The violin joined the flute and blended with the baritone, and Arthur's aunt sat at the piano, a fervent contralto liberating the music. And the young doctor not singing or playing, just watching her, and the shipping-room poet lost in wonder at the sounds that flowed about him. In the kitchen, the flame turned low in the gas mantle, were Max and Rose, too shy to enter their own parlour, and listening, the mother sighing, the father silent, both of them lost in thought, near tears.

Arthur sat alone in the downstairs doorway, too innocent to distinguish between the secret souls of piano and violin, flute and human voice, yet lulled by it all, the arias and the sonatas and the sentimental songs, the occasional scraps of conversation and the quiet laughter and the happy handclaps of the artists applauding themselves like the beating wings of a flock of gulls taking off.

He stared at the great walls, the dark stone mass of the Hotel Dieu, the vague blur of trees, the heavy night shadows of the hospital grounds. Beyond, he knew, was the hump of Mount Royal, the giant mound, mysteriously big. And the stars, so many, so magical, so high, so low.

Dare he? He ventured onto the lawn and sat there. He lay back and suddenly it was all suspended above him and he was awed by the stars, the queer, winking points of light so numerous, the mountain's height so ominous, the hospital so huge, its windows so yellow with light, the music floating from the upstairs parlour and caressing him. He remembered sweet, meaty strawberries at suppertime, the coffee-store and the kindly coffee-man, the sounds of singing, the aroma of spices, the sound of the flute, his young aunt's melting eyes, her perfume, the red wagon.

He closed his eyes and opened them again and the stars were still there, many and miraculous. He closed his eyes again and all was peaceful, all euphoria, the breeze cool and silvery and gentle, like his mother, like the soft lap of his aunt.

When Max came down and lifted him gently and carried him indoors, the child snuggled in his father's arms, secure and protected. He was placed on his bed and covered, exquisitely sleepy like a pup after a strenuous day.

The sounds from the frontroom were distant and confused and he heard less and less and less as he sank into the sensuous, comforting darkness.

*

It was a rare treat for the Mellers to be invited to a wedding. Their social status was insignificant and their connections tenuous at best, but sometimes one of their few relatives was pricked by guilt or felt sorry for them or was warmed by the thought of the struggling young couple and their shy little boy.

Those turn-of-the-century weddings were naively happy celebrations, long before immigrant Jews were dragooned into America's opulent means of expressing joy, long before catered gluttony and catered ostentation when tuxedoed bartenders snub the guests and costly sweets tables outshine the costly hors d'oeuvres. It was long before the amused condescension of the

newly prosperous toward greenies, before full-colour wedding
photo albums, before slick city dance bands degraded the ancient
folk songs.

In those days the immigrant's memories were precious. They had
not yet been given price tags. In those days few synagogues boasted
architect-designed banquet halls, gleaming stainless-steel kitchens,
stained-glass windows, polished wooden pews, public-address
systems. Montreal's old synagogues, few in number, exuded a
medieval austerity. Their old stones and bricks frowned on the
flippancies of the newly successful. But the unaffecting shelter, the
down-to-earth plebeian place of worship might welcome its
congregation in someone's front parlour for Friday evening and
Saturday services and, on High Holy Days, in a vacant store rented
to accommodate the once-a-year, conscience-smitten, lonely and
homesick workingman and his family. Two dollars, perhaps three,
and they had seats for the services and the transient's right to pray
in God's cut-rate company.

The wedding, consecrated earlier in the synagogue, was later
celebrated in a rented hall, if the family could afford it, or more
likely, in the double-parlour of a somewhat more prosperous
relative or friend.

The women of the family toiled for days baking strudels and
honey-cakes, roasting chickens or geese or ducks, pickling tongues
or preparing knishes or corned beef briskets, simmering the
savoury soups, chopping beef liver into exquisite paste spiked with
hard-boiled egg and minced onion. Pickled cucumbers were
brought up from cool cellars and dill-pickled tomatoes streaked with
the pink of a suspended ripeness and pickled melons and
sauerkraut still covered with ice crystals and salt herring with boiled
potatoes and pickled herring with onions and carrots, and grapes,
oranges, pears, figs, nuts, raisins. And sweet homemade wines and
cream soda for the kids and spruce beer and seltzer water.

There was gaiety and good fellowship, bitter-sweet and
moist-eyed sentimentality, sudden warmth and spontaneous
compliments, honest congratulations and and and...A
skull-capped, brown-bearded old fiddler played the nostalgic
songs of the Old Country. And they danced: the old men and their
old women, hopping, stumbling, stomping, flushed and a little
high; the children flinging themselves around in fast and dizzy
circles and showing off their mastery of the new dance steps to

prove they were more Canadian than their parents; their sweating mothers and fathers swinging intensely but soon slowed by the first surfeit of food they have enjoyed in many months; the dreamy young couples oblivious to everything, closely clasped and remembering their own wedding night of only a few months before. Or looking forward to it.

People. Poor people. Poor Jews. Jews from Poland, Jews from Rumania, Jews from Russia, from the Ukraine, from White Russia, Hungary, Latvia, Lithuania. Workers in the needle trades, in men's wear, millinery, dresses, work-clothes, furs, knit goods, leather. Peddlers, petty merchants, cigarmakers, cigarette-makers, bakers, tailors, butchers, dressmakers and carpenters. And *luftmenshen,* pathetic little promoters living by their wits. And the jobless. The poor, the persecuted, the pathetic. Sholom Aleichem's transplanted ghettoes, the fraternity of poverty.

And the children, platoons of them, carnivorous little starvelings, now overfed for once in many lean months, stuffed at the feast, herded into a back room to sleep it off on beds piled high with blankets and coats, then wakened to be taken home, groggy sleepwalkers in the middle of a magnificent night.

*

The child grew into his fifth year and his sixth, poverty his playmate.

Arthur's parents, despairing of the present, reached for tomorrow and, on the morrow, for the day after that and for the worlds they built in their fantasies. The mansions they dreamed up for their child sustained them for a while. But the flimsy strands of hallucination could not close out the reality for long. The wife grew quieter, the husband mute.

*

At school his conscientious teachers offered affection, facts and doctrine to the gullible mind, and his parents knew that it was proper and desirable for their child to be sculpted and shaped and buffed like the other children of their new country, all subjects of an empire and its emperor, King Edward, majestic ruler over despised colonials who, at an early age, learned to brown-nose and to genuflect at the same time.

Copy-book maxims were engraved on the innocent brain both in school and at home: Be a good boy. To be good is all right, but it's better to be best. Don't cheat your superiors, don't envy them their possessions. Wash your hands often. Keep your nose clean. Don't do disgusting things. Don't interrupt, don't point, don't talk loud, avoid rudeness even to inferiors. Be polite, tip your cap to ladies. Don't use dirty words, remember to flush the toilet, be respectful to teachers, rabbis and policemen, do not offend the well-heeled and the influential. Avoid laziness, don't wet the toilet seat. Drink plenty of milk, but no milk until six hours after meat. Never grunt when you eat, learn to spell properly, master the art of counting money, save, write neatly, eat all the food on your plate and don't waste bread while others starve. Place your hand on your mouth when you yawn, don't burp or break wind in company. Don't swear, don't eat unkosher food like pig or oysters. Don't ever enter a church, don't light fires or cut things or work on the sabbath. Don't spit on the sidewalk. Remember that sex without a marriage licence is obscene, don't abuse yourself, don't abuse little girls. Put money in your purse, neither a borrower nor a lender be, to thine own self be true, honour your parents and those relatives who have money and are good to you. Honour the king and also God, but especially your boss if you're ever fated to work for one instead of becoming one.

When he was seven the Meller family travelled west, searching new roots. Arthur discovered his country from a train window as the farmlands of his native Quebec slipped away in the smoke of the pounding steam engine. He stared in apprehension at the turbulent green depths of Lake Superior steeply below the railroad grade and marvelled at the unending golds and greens flowing across the prairie. He watched mesmerized by the white peaks of the Rockies deceptively close in the bright sunlight, gasped at the wild valleys far down beneath him, and the threatening rocks of the Coastal Range high above, and the fierce white waters as the train roared closer to Vancouver and the Pacific Ocean.

The West held them for a year, then disowned them, sent them in flight eastward again, by day coach again, now to Calgary. His father had had his chance with the Vancouver variety store and had flopped. In Calgary, land of cattle kings, cowboys and cowed Indians, he opened a dry-goods store. They ate and slept in the backroom. Here, on the banks of the Bow River, they would launch their galleon, their gravy-boat, with patience and with faith. The vessel foundered and sank under the weight of its debts and the well-heeled hostility of the established, unbeatable department store a block away. Max Meller's German immigrant neighbours preferred the bargains of the big store. Max Meller went bankrupt, not profitably or cushioned by a tidy hidden cache, but ineptly, honestly, pennilessly broke.

Arthur returned to his old Montreal school, the aging school a few fields distant from its namesake Mount Royal.

*

When he was ten the war was well on its way, World War I.

During the winter, training trenches were dug on Fletcher's Field deep down through the hard snow and ice and into the frozen soil. A cousin (McGill, Engineering) was home on leave from Valcartier Camp. He slept on the hard floor of his father's house and scorned a flabby bed. Hearty, big-boned, raw and tough, he was a devoted soldier of the Empire, his Empire that first blackballed him and then blackmailed him into kowtowing to its slurs and made him feel somehow inadequate as a member of the armed forces because he could never never become a genuine Anglo-Saxon. But in the war, with their backs to the wall, they used any weapon at hand, they even used a Jew, though they didn't need to fraternize with him.

Another cousin, a Westerner, passed through from Winnipeg on his way overseas, nervously balancing a patriotic chip on his shoulder and safely berthed (since he was a salesman) in the Quartermaster Corps. A week after landing in France he was killed by a shellburst.

*

A boy in class heard you could get books for nothing from the government, shocking books but free of charge. You wrote to an address in Ottawa, marked the envelope O.H.M.S., and said you were a university student and would you please be sent a copy. The books described in vivid detail how the Huns bayonetted babies, raped the mothers and shot the grandparents.

To hell with the Huns! Kill the Kaiser!

*

When Elsie Flander came into his classroom in their final year of public school his childhood was nearly over.

Where had her family come from? Flanders, in whose fields the poppies blow?

She was a grey-eyed, mysterious presence, fiery, gentle and beautiful. She excited him and disturbed him. She was the promise of a woman to be—noble, haughty, charming, graceful and wise. She was all of thirteen years old.

2

1939. September.
Night. The Hospital.

"HE'S NOT A bad-looking man," the nurse decides. "He's got a pleasant face, nice cheekbones, his hair's dark and neat, the chin's nice too, clean-shaven, yesterday I guess. Slim, medium height, probably a good dancer. Poor fellow, he's hurt real bad. But he doesn't look like the violent kind...I wish that red-headed detective didn't eye me like I was naked."

Arthur mumbles unfathomable shavings of sound. The detective, permitted into the ward for a brief look, bends forward to listen. The voice from the pillow lapses abruptly like a radio unplugged. Arthur lies inert on the white bed.

"If he dies," the detective speculates, watching moodily, "it'll be the first civilian I ever killed. I wonder, will he die? Anyway, why did the crazy bastard have to get in the way?"

Gilbert walks out to his bench at the end of the corridor to await his relief.

"I'd like to get my hands on the son of a bitch that threw the brick..."

1918. Below Mount Royal.
Children No More.

A disturbing year, a time of crowding new senses, germinating passions, the spurs of rebelliousness, the first pulsing of youth. Arthur was thirteen.

When the final school term opened and in his new class, a few desks to the right and near the front row, he saw Elsie, he watched and took stock. Her mouth was small, her neck long, the ears small, her hair curly and blondish. Her laugh was confident, her voice throaty, she spoke with animation. She had long legs. Her chest, he thought, must be heavenly.

She was clever, everybody said. Would she race him for the scholarship? He mooned because she was so lovely; he felt inadequate because she had been heard to say she planned to marry brains—a professor, a surgeon or a statesman—and he was jealous already.

The girls noted that he often stared across the rows of desks at her. They would watch him and from him turn their attention to her.

She helped with their homework. She showed them how to hook rugs, how to embroider, play chess, read teacup leaves, make willow whistles, pirouette, curtsey for royalty. They all worshipped her. Because she knew so much more than they did, and said she had read all the Shakespeare plays and even the sonnets, and had the gift of fluent speech, they were flattered by her confidences and accepted her as their mentor.

When classes were over for the day and she walked home, an adoring coterie surrounded her: chubby, merry Nora; small and serious Eve gazing in awe; Mabel who took ballet; boy-crazy Bev; Maggie who would rather have been born a boy; Pearl, far too sexy at twelve; Annie the agnostic; Hilda who wrote love lyrics. The goddess glided gracefully, chattered wisely about Victor Hugo, Beethoven, Upton Sinclair, Keats, Wilfrid Laurier. And spoke knowingly about the arcane emotions and physical fevers of adult men and women.

Life was vanity, it was transient, life was to be lived to the full, it was God's mad folly, life was...who knows?

Casually she dispensed knowledge, or dramatically, or

enigmatically, or with bored resignation, but never less than entrancingly to her camp followers, her disciples, as she fervently defended passion and marshalled her joyous evidence. Chopin! George Sand! Shelley! Juliet! Byron! Madame de Bovary! Ellen Terry! Desdemona! Aphrodite!

The girls guarded Elsie, they formed a protective shield around her. They were quick to detect and appraise romantic overtures, real or suspected. When a boy tossed off amusing remarks in her presence, or lent her a book or merely chatted, the girls alerted each other.

When they observed Arthur mooning across the desks at her they whispered among themselves, they watched, they approved. They would not dare to mention it to her, for they had seen her temper flare before.

Elsie appeared to suspect nothing, neither the approval nor the curiosity of her friends nor the adoration of the boy. Engrossed in her studies, her nose in her books, her eyes on the teacher, she seemed unaware. Or was she? After school, when she walked home, the girls were consumed in speculation. What would she say, what would she do if she knew?

Arthur and Elsie exchanged few words in or out of class. He was a minor scholarship rival, that was all. She tended to snub him. He avoided her.

Once he had a dream. A professor, a surgeon and a statesman, each wearing a horribly striped kaftan and pink mortarboard, were filing their fingernails most fastidiously. Elsie hovered highfalutin' in a tree and swung her left leg like a pendulum, so that her dress flew up and exposed her thighs each time. The professor leered and the other men drooled. Her shoe came off and struck the statesman and knocked off his head. Arthur laughed to see the professor crumble and the surgeon disintegrate—pouf! Elsie floated down from the tree and took Arthur's hand and asked him whether he was old enough to be her lover. She offered magical candies, aphrodisiacs, passion-filled potions. He said yes, he was a great lover. She danced and cried out, "Oh, I knew it, I knew!" And now he was dressed in a magnificent wedding costume and a flamboyant, star-studded mortarboard and he was most elegantly polishing his fingernails and offering flowers to her. Elsie kissed him.

When he awoke to go to school he knew he was in love.

*

It was 1918. The enemy was collapsing. The war would soon be over.

Sweet smell of blood for the victors.

For the ravaged young and the desecrated old there were no cheers and no today.

God bless our cause and onward Christian soldiers. God bless our bank accounts, our real estate, our household goods, our household gods and generals and munitions makers. And our brand-new millionaires.

*

One morning on his way to school he met Nora, Elsie's friend, who asked, "Arthur, what do you think of Elsie Flander?"

He hesitated. "I guess she's pretty smart."

"Do you like her, Arthur, really like her?"

"I guess she's all right."

"Everybody says you love her."

He flushed but said nothing.

"Do you?" she pressed.

Helpless, he whispered, "Yes, I do, I do..."

"Then why don't you tell her?"

Unhappily, he pleaded, "How can I?"

"Would you like me to tell her, Arthur?"

"No, please don't, I'm not ready." His voice was low, his eyes troubled.

But Nora could not resist the temptation; she confided in Elsie. And Elsie, with a world-weary air, told her she ought not meddle in other people's personal affairs.

Next day during recess Elsie confronted him. Bitingly she declared, "I've got a bone to pick with you, young man."

"What's the matter?"

"Don't pretend you don't know," she snapped. "I'm very angry with you. I'm furious and disgusted. You have no right to discuss me with Nora or anybody else. You're just too conceited. I wouldn't love you if you were the last person on earth. I don't care for you at all."

Arthur, ashamed and hurt, said nothing. His eyes pleaded.

"I think you have a lot of nerve," she continued. "I think," and she paused for a more damning assessment, "I think it's scandalous, just downright shocking!"

They didn't speak to each other again after that. Sometimes, when he gazed unhappily across the rows of desks, she might look up, turn her head disdainfully and direct her attention to the blackboard.

One day in November he found her watching him, her grey eyes soft and revealing. The two students regarded each other, seeing themselves at last as more than children. Was there the hint of a sad smile in her eyes?

The bell rang for fire drill and the moment was lost.

*

Had it been spring or fall they might have been able to reach out to one another, but suddenly it was December; the winter graduating class was embroiled in final exams. For Arthur, for Elsie and for a few others there was the added burden of the scholarships.

Worried boys and girls crammed before breakfast, crammed in class, crammed during recess, rushed home after school to cram far into the night, pale and worried, and came back in the morning, pale and worried still, into the fevered classroom.

From time to time, when their eyes met, Elsie's were distant and poignant and his were distant and sad.

*

It was the fifth troubled winter since 1914 had ushered in a sequence of disasters and discontents. Rumours had been rife—defective rifles and rotten meat for the troops, corrupt contracts for war profiteers, demoralization and defiance in the ranks, senseless sacrifices of lives overseas. Ontario's Berlin had been renamed for Lord Kitchener. Among workers east and west there was an outcry for jobs, for pay raises, for the good life promised before they had gone off to make the world safe. You could hear the union rumblings long before the Winnipeg Strike. Men were jailed. More's *Utopia* was blacklisted. There were midnight raids. Bellamy's *Looking Backward* was banned.

Irish rebels died. French sailors mutinied. The German

Spartacus Bund rose up and was crushed. Gabriele D'Annunzio paved a lyrical path for Mussolini. The philosopher Bertrand Russell opposed the war and went to jail in England. The socialist Gene Debs led a railroad strike in America and was locked up. A few years earlier Joe Hill, a union balladeer, had been executed by firing squad in Utah.

In November 1917 Lenin and his people had seized power.

*

In 1919 the Spanish influenza swept over Canada. Some said the plague was caused by the fierce cold. Others thought the hunger in the eyes of the poor cast malicious spells. Some believed it drifted over from the stinking slums of North Africa and Spain. Others said it was bred by the bloated rats and the unburied bodies in the trenches of France and Belgium. The superstitious called it the vengeance of God.

Whole pages of the newspapers carried the relentless lists of the dead in crowded columns of small type. Ambulances coursed the streets day and night. Hearses followed. Scarcely a family was spared. In many homes all were stricken and the least sick tried to minister to the more gravely afflicted, or tried to comfort the widows, the orphans, the bereft parents.

Children carried camphor bags around their necks to ward off infections. Their parents wore protective white cloth masks over their mouths.

The scourge did not subside for some time. It flooded through the factories and seeped into the schools.

It reached Arthur's school and it found its way into his classroom. Arthur came down with the flu, and Elsie, and many others.

The scholarship competitors, sick and enfeebled, managed to stumble to school to write exams. They came wrapped in bulky layers of clothing. The blackboards swam before them, the sunlight dazzled them, the teacher's voice sounded far off and muffled.

*

Arthur stared across the room. He could see her, bent over her desk. She turned and glanced back at him, her cheeks pale, eyes troubled. Then she smiled, a wan smile.

*

His head throbbed and his bones ached all day Friday and the boy took to his bed when he returned from school. The doctor came late at night and ordered medicines. He seemed on the verge of collapse himself. Arthur's father walked the few blocks from their new flat on Hotel de Ville to the Main Street shop of the bald old pharmacist with the walrus moustache and grey stubble of whiskers. The high walls of the drugstore were covered with shelves up to the ceiling. Thousands of apothecary jars filled the shelves and were all carefully identified in black italic hand-lettering on faded labels. Long ladders reached the highest shelves. In the corners of the street window hung two glass urns, one ruby-red, the other a deep green. Up front in this display window sat a heavy mortar and pestle, little piles of medicinal herbs, roots, barks and pulverized chemicals heaped on small dishes. All the magic of the alchemist! On a miniature easel a diploma certified that Alcide Laberge, M.D., was qualified to practise medicine in the Province de Quebec. Max Meller envied him his store, his quiet solidity, his status, his prosperity.

Arthur remained under blankets all weekend. On Monday morning his parents hovered over his bed and asked whether he felt better, was he well enough to go to school, well enough to write the exam. He wanted desperately to sleep; he thought he would never recover and didn't care and just wanted to be left alone. But they looked so anxious and spoke so wistfully of his claim on the scholarship that he somehow crawled out of bed and dressed himself. He ate hot porridge and drank coffee with chicory and milk boiled in a saucepan over the gas burner until the drink bubbled and formed a skin. He allowed his mother to dress him with heavy sweaters and a thick scarf to cover his face. His father led him to school. The street wouldn't lie flat and the snow and ice played tricks on his awkward feet. The sun blinded him, stung his eyes.

*

Somehow the days passed, exams were finished and public school was ended. A graduation party was arranged.

What fun to go back on Friday night, not as a conscript but a guest, and through the main doors at that! He removed his cap, realized he didn't have to now, stuck it back on jauntily, but quickly took it off again when he heard voices from the kindergarten at the end of the hall.

How strange now blithely to enter this room that had awed him so long ago!

Young people were standing around self-consciously. A boy attempted a handstand and fell sprawling. Everybody laughed and the ice was broken; the party began to warm up. Boys wrestled and played leap-frog, girls danced with each other and played *Chopsticks* on the piano.

Miss Marriott, their teacher, wearing a silky white blouse and a long brown skirt, sat in a corner on a cushion on the floor and led a group of boys and girls singing sentimental ballads.

Everybody had brought something: cake and candies, chocolates and biscuits, raisins, nuts.

They played musical chairs; each time the music stopped they flung themselves into the nearest empty seat. Girls giggled and boys guffawed. Teacher joined in. Once she fell and her skirt slipped up above her knees.

They played postman and Arthur blushed when he had to kiss Miss Marriott. They played blind man's buff. They laughed. They ate sandwiches and drank hot chocolate.

Before the party broke up Miss Marriott called them to attention. She was sorry, she said, that she could not give them the official results until Monday but she would let them know the names of the two scholarship winners. She paused and told them: there were two, one for a girl, one for a boy. The children waited; they already knew that. Then she announced the names: Elsie Flander was first, she had the highest marks; it was a pity she couldn't be at the party, but she was sick in bed. Arthur Meller was the other winner. There was applause, a few cheers. A loser, his face tight, strode over to Arthur and shook hands. "You need it more than I do," he said. "My father can afford two hundred dollars. He has plenty of money."

Nora, Elsie's friend, congratulated him and then, impulsively, kissed his cheek. "I'll tell Elsie," she whispered.

Arthur's father was waiting in the school corridor to walk him home. "Well," Max asked his son, "any news?" The boy faced his father, smiled, waited a moment for effect, and said yes, he'd won. Max embraced him and kissed him on the forehead. Arthur hoped nobody was watching. Max spoke gravely as they hurried through the falling snow. "I want you to know I'm proud of you, very proud. You worked hard and you won. It's an honour for our family. Maybe you'll change our luck."

At home the parents beamed at the scholarship winner. His mother fussed happily. Arthur went to bed pleased with himself, lulled by soft white snowflakes floating down like fleece in the black night beyond his window. Smiling, he fell asleep to the contented murmuring of his parents as they dreamed aloud their kitchen fantasies of future good fortune.

On Saturday morning when he opened his eyes his parents were standing in the doorway. On his pillow, touching his cheek, lay a brown leather wallet. "Open it!" his father commanded. "You're a scholarship boy now," his mother said. "This is a little present for you," his father went on. "I hope it will always be filled."

In the wallet he found a one-dollar bill, a twenty-five-cent shinplaster, two quarters, ten dimes, five small nickels and two fifty-cent pieces. "Enjoy it," his father said.

*

First he would again explore the forbidden downtown streets. Later he might go to the vaudeville show on St. Catherine West. He wandered along run-down Craig and St. Antoine and past old churches on Dorchester, through the noisy and convivial Bonsecours Market, down to the railroad tracks and the waterfront and then northward along The Main again.

The sky had clouded up; the snow had turned to sleet on his face and slush underfoot. Quietly elated, he recalled how his father had taken him aside at the start of the school term and cautioned him, "You know, Arthur, if you work hard you can win that scholarship so you'll be able to go to high school and later, God willing, to college. Some day there'll be a brass plate beside your door, like a doctor or a notary public. It's up to you to be a success."

Now he had won, now he had won it, Arthur kept telling himself in amazement as he trudged along. Now he had done it, now he had won!

On The Main below St. Catherine he passed the penny arcades where, he had been told, you could see little pictures of naked girls dancing. He gawked uneasily at life-size posters outside the burlesque house. He cringed as passing adults seemingly accused him of unspeakable obscenities. His mouth was dry, he was filled with shame and self-loathing; old men smirked at him from doorways. Wretched and confused, he collided with a woman as he turned to face westward on St. Catherine. He touched his cap and blurted, "Oh, I beg your pardon!" She gave him a pat on the shoulder, smiled warmly and said it was all right. "It's been a pleasure, sonny," she said, laughed and walked on, turning once to wave. What a beautiful face, what a lush voice, what a lovely figure! How soft her skin, how sensuous her mouth! He loved her, he yearned for her.

He floated. Near Morgan's, across from Phillips Square, he heard his name. It was Nora, chubby Nora, Elsie's friend.

"Have you heard?" she asked.

"What?"

"About Elsie."

"Elsie? Was she glad about the scholarship? Did you see her?"

"Elsie's dead. She died today. At noon—only three hours after I spoke to her."

He leaned against a store window. "You're making it up, it's not true, it's a joke..."

But Nora's eyes, brimming, stopped him. She touched his arm. "Walk me home, Arthur," she begged. As they turned back and walked up Bleury and onto Park below the mountain, she spoke quietly. "Arthur, I didn't mean any harm when I told her what you said to me that time. I mean, I only wanted to help you both, I only wanted you to love each other. Is that bad? I guess I didn't handle it very well."

"It's all right, Nora. Anyway, it doesn't matter now, does it?"

When they parted she squeezed his hand and ran in tears into her house.

At home Arthur's mother told him the news. He said he'd heard. He ate his supper and read a comic paper; it wasn't funny at all, the type blurred, nothing registered. He said he had a headache. He lay down on the bed in his room. He was bored, empty, tied in an aching knot. His grief pushed a sob to the surface and the rest came out in a torrent. He closed his door and pressed his face to the pillow.

*

People stood in front of the Flander house on Sunday—neighbours, school children. The relatives were indoors. Out front, against the low fence that enclosed the snow-covered lawn, friends and classmates whispered. A white horse-drawn hearse waited nearby. Saturday's sleet had been replaced by heavy snow; the city was again soft and white; the sun struggled, retreated behind clouds, emerged, vanished. Heavy grey light oppressed the street and snow fell steadily.

When Nora saw Arthur standing alone on the other side of the street she went over to him. "Have you seen her?" she asked. When he shook his head she took him by the hand and led him across, past the groups at the door, into the house and into the room where Elsie lay.

For an agonizing moment he stared at the floor, at his boots. Then he gazed at her face, her blonde hair, an ear-lobe, her cheeks, her throat. He caught Nora's hand, turned, walked swiftly away, beyond the door and the snow-covered lawn and the fence, to the other side of the street, Nora beside him.

"I'm sorry, Nora, I can't help it."

"I know," she said, "I know."

He kicked at the snow. Nora came closer, her face white, eyes glistening.

"I saw her only a few hours before. I never knew she was going to die. I can't believe it, Arthur. Do you know what she said to me? She said she'd wanted you to win, no one but you. She said something else. She said, 'I want you to tell Arthur I love him.'"

"I wish I'd known," he said. "I wish I could have told her. I wanted to but never did. If only...."

*

The house door opened, the white box was carried out; it was placed in the hearse, the glass doors were closed, the horses moved slowly forward.

Arthur and Nora fell in near the end of the cortege, walked through the snow on the road together. He was afraid that he would cry.

At the end of the block he said, "Goodbye, Nora," turned from her and hurried home.

Monday he went to school to get his report card and receive his bronze medal. He heard Elsie's name read out, then his own. Her medal and report card were given to Nora to deliver to the Flander family.

At noon, when they were dismissed, he went to her desk and found a wooden pen-holder with her initials, "E.F." He took his report card and his medal and Elsie's pen-holder.

Public school was over for Arthur, for grey-eyed haughty eager Elsie. For all of them. Finished.

Children no more.

PART TWO

1

1939. September.
Intensive Care. Graveyard Shift.

RALPH GILBERT's relief is late.

"Frenchie's too goddam busy loving up somebody's wife," he groused to himself. "He never gets enough. Well, O.K., but not on my time."

Detective Gilbert is pooped. The lids lie wearily over the green eyes. He lapses into sleep, snores gutturally and wakes himself. The bruise lies ugly on his white cheek.

His partner Frenchie emerges from the elevator, hefts 237 hard pounds onto the bench beside Ralph, grins and winks at his red-headed partner.

A long night lies ahead, visiting hours have long expired.

Hollow corridor sounds accent the graveyard shift of orderlies, cleaners, nurses, interns, and the two vigilant sentinels, one off duty now and anticipating a thick steak and a night of love. But first a double scotch, no soda, no water.

Gabrielle has long ago gone, the last visitor to leave. She had earlier sent Arthur's mother home with his Aunt Laura.

In the hospital corridors and in the Intensive Care ward where Arthur lies unconscious it is quiet, and in the house where Rose and her sister Laura try vainly to sleep it is quiet, like the silence after a sigh.

In the silent house near the McGill campus Gabrielle paces her livingroom. She has been speaking on the phone to Arthur's aunt. "I'll be all right, Laura. No, I don't mind being alone. Tell Rose

33

not to worry. Yes, I'll call if there's any news. Thanks, Laura.''

She pours herself a brandy, sips it slowly, but remains cold sober. And very low.

1919. The Laurentians.
More War Casualties.

It was summer. The killing had ceased overseas.

In the village of La Macaza in the Laurentians, a hundred miles northwest of Montreal, Gabrielle stepped through the door of the painted pine farmhouse into the cool early morning air and stretched her young arms toward the mountains that brooded dark green, purple, black, waiting for the sun to penetrate the mists and make them shimmer and liberate the peaks in bursts of gold and violent blue and pink.

Madeleine Lajeunesse sat by herself on a bench beside the water, her eyes red from hours of sleeplessness and solitary weeping. The four younger children still slept. Gabrielle sat down beside her mother and embraced her.

The war was over, the armistice had been declared at eleven o'clock on the morning of November 11. Now it was June and there was no word about her father, no letter, official or otherwise, no notification, no document, no rumour.

What had pushed Dominique Lajeunesse into this war when as head of a family and as a farmer he was exempt from army service? Why did he join up? Why did he take an oath of allegiance in the English king's war? Why, indeed, when Quebec seethed with anti-conscription demonstrations, did this blue-eyed habitant wear that khaki uniform?

Did he really think General Sir Arthur Currie, Marechal Foch of France and the English Lord Kitchener would reward him for gambling his life? Did he hope to escape his lifelong drudgery of the farm and drift away like a hedonist on a sybaritic barge? Did he perhaps need to be a single man again? Did he really believe those impassioned slogans about saving the world for democracy? Did he visualize a great public ceremony where he would present his credentials and receive guarantees of freedom and long life for all his children as battalions of priests sang *Te Deums* and brass bands welcomed the conqueror-hero home and a grateful king patted him

on his straight back and filled his pockets with heavy gold coins and
the sun shone its rays into his eyes and the whole assembly suddenly
gasped as an angel flew down from heaven and kissed him on his
suntanned cheek and Dominique's tears of happiness and pride
turned to pearls and every living soul in La Macaza beamed
proudly and sang his praises?

Whatever the reasons he gave himself, Dominique volunteered.
He made all the necessary arrangements. His brother would run the
farm for him and split the proceeds with Madeleine.

"I'll be turning over most of my army pay to her. If anything
happens to me, you know, like a bullet with my number on it, well,
I'd like you to look after Madeleine and my kids."

"Don't worry, I'll keep an eye on them, the same like my own.
Good luck! And be careful!"

Dominique spent three days on odd jobs around his farm, in the
barn and the house. He visited baffled friends and relatives, said
goodbye to neighbours and the priest, kissed his wife and the five
children and took the train to Montreal. Within a week he was
learning to be a soldier at Valcartier Camp. In two months he was
on board a troopship steaming towards England. A month later he
was in France. It was 1916. He was thirty-five years old.

*

At the end of hostilities, as the killing was called, there was
unfinished business. It was a different enemy this time. The
Hohenzollern foe was crushed. Now there was a new foe, a greater
menace, a Red Russian Bolshevik Goliath; Marx's spectre of
communism was once more haunting Europe, a Red flood was
spilling over to the States and even into Canada.

The colonels called for harsher measures against A.W.O.L.
peasoup anarchists whose ancestors had migrated to Canada three,
four centuries ago and hadn't learned their place yet.

There was trouble in English-speaking units too. Shots were
fired. Insubordination, rebellion, subversion, sedition; they had to
be crushed. So round them up fast, court-martial them, kill the
Reds.

Army officers and military police strode into barracks, guns
drawn. Soldiers held meetings, violated regulations, slouched
before their superiors in dumb insolence, took off without passes

and straggled back to their quarters, drunk or defiant or mutinous. They demanded to be demobilized right away, they wanted passage home immediately, they wanted to be civilians again.

The war, however, was not quite finished. These Canadians might be needed for occupation in Germany or to kill Russians in Siberia or even the Reds at home.

Men were shot, men died. Among them was the farmer, Dominique Lajeunesse, father of Gaby and four younger children, husband of Madeleine. It was in the spring that he died.

In July the word filtered through that Private Lajeunesse of La Macaza had been accidentally killed during a riot at camp.

Gabrielle found her mother in the morning on the kitchen floor, an empty glass beside her head. Through the kitchen window glinted the first fires of the Laurentian sun on mountain rock.

*

At fourteen Gabrielle was a healthy farm girl who did her share of the hoeing, the milking, the churning. She helped in her uncle's home and looked after her brothers and sisters, who slept with her in her father's nearby house.

She was a cheerful sort. After her chores she liked to swim or to dance. She enjoyed reading. The family was fond of Gabrielle.

In September her uncle and aunt decided that she ought to attend a convent school. Grandfather Lesage came from the city and took her back to stay with him for a few days before she entered that austere institution in the east end of Montreal.

Ovide was a unique man, a Laurentian giant of a grandfather who, at seventy-five, enjoyed telling how as a farm boy earmarked for the priesthood he had kicked over the traces, shouted, "I won't be celibate!" and ran away to the city where he found work as a road labourer, saloon bouncer, longshoreman, and from that to deck-hand and first mate and later captain of a St. Lawrence River freighter. His wife had died and he lived alone on his savings and a pension.

He cultivated a backyard vegetable garden, developed skills from carpentry to metalwork, made heady homebrew and taught himself to play the guitar. He was a good cook. He was witty and shrewd, affectionate and impulsive. He had bushy white hair, the sailor's bronzed face and a voice like a foghorn. He entertained himself with short stories, novels, socialist pamphlets and the humorists and cartoonists in the Saturday *La Presse*. He liked the old songs and he was a generous host when friends visited.

When Gabrielle had been at the convent barely a year he asked her to come and live in his house. She could be his housekeeper and he would give her a weekly allowance. He would feed and clothe her and she would have a sunny room of her own. Her friends would be welcome to visit. She would attend a school with boys as well as girls and where there weren't so damned many rules.

Gaby agreed. He beamed with pleasure.

The old man wanted his daughter's child to have a warm home, a few material comforts, some affection and the freedom to develop as a normal young woman.

He was determined that neither her mind nor her soul would lack nourishment. Nourishment he very much doubted she would find either in La Macaza or at the convent. Gaby would learn to speak fluent English as well as French. She would discover the English poets, the novelists, the playwrights. She would be enriched by the great French writers forbidden by the Church blacklist. She would learn to think for herself, to question, to seek out alternatives. She would see, she would hear, she would live!

Gaby came to his narrow two-storey house on a downtown street around the corner from the McGill campus and Montreal High, where she would be enrolled in September.

Even in his youth Ovide Lesage had demanded explanations and reasons. Catechisms made him impatient, dogma riled him. "How do you know God isn't an atheist?" he once demanded of an exasperated Jesuit.

Gaby's grandfather in his travels had heard the socialist Jean Jaures in Paris, and the communist Tom Mann in Trafalgar Square. Their words were more deeply impressed on him when the clubs of Neapolitan militiamen beat his head bloody.

It was about this time that reading began to obsess him. He never stopped...Zola, France, Rolland, Barbusse.

He had left La Macaza far behind and he hoped his granddaughter would do the same.

2

1939. September.
In the Hospital.

DETECTIVE GILBERT sharpens the end of a match and picks his teeth. A fibre of steak is wedged between two teeth and it has been bothering him ever since he returned to take up his vigil again and replace his partner. Down the hall in Intensive Care lies his prisoner.

> *There he is, lying half-dead*
> *Like lead on a bed.*

Gilbert, picking at his teeth, reflects, "It rhymes."

> *Lying half-dead*
> *On a hospital bed*
> *He must be sick in the head.*

Gilbert is pleased. "I'm a poet and I don't know it." He prods, the meat comes loose, he examines it and flips it away into the air.

> *There he is, lying half-dead*
> *On the hospital bed*
> *And sick in the head*
> *Half-dead*
>
> *On a bed,*
> *Half-dead in the head.*
> *What was that the dead Red said,*
> *The dread Red?*

Nothing, Ralphie Gilbert, he didn't say anything, nothing at all, nothing bloody nothing, not a bloody thing.

Gilbert squirms on the bench. His pants are too tight.

*

Do you, Arthur Meller, remember anything that happened
yesterday, before this sombre sleuth with the bruised face sat
slouched in the hospital corridor in the suffering night?

Please note, Meller, anything you say may be used against you as
evidence in a court of law. Anything you ever said, you ever
thought, you ever did. Or anything you never said, thought, did.

1919. The Labour Force.
Application Rejected.

He lasted a day on his first job.

Arthur knew the summer was for vacation if your family was
well-to-do. But for most kids it was a time to earn. No more aimless
exploration of the back of Mount Royal and the Cote des Neiges
orchards any time your fancy moved you.

"He's fourteen," Max said. Rose washed her dishes. Arthur was
out front reading a British comic paper. Rose dried her dishes. Max
turned the pages of the *Star*. "Our Arthur isn't a baby any more,"
he said.

She glanced at him. What was he thinking about? "At fourteen
they're still babies," she said.

"At fourteen they start to be men. It'll do him good, just for a
month. Let him learn a little bit about the world. My father was
only nine when he went to work—not just for the summer. I myself
started when I was eleven. It never hurt me."

"I know, Max," she conceded. "I was only ten. But we're more
civilized now. He can wait a bit. I don't want him to work this
summer, not yet, Max."

"We're not millionaires. He has to start sometime."

"We can wait a year, just another year. So we'll be millionaires a
year later."

"You don't need to be sarcastic."

"I'm not."

"You are."

"His two, three dollars won't make any difference. Maybe you'll
earn a little more yourself, things will pick up."

"I can't, I'm doing all I can."

"I suppose so," Rose muttered.

"What do you mean by that?"

"I just said I guess so."

"You meant something else."

"All right, so I meant something, so I meant you should try more. Never mind Arthur, he's only a child, he can't make our living for us."

"You don't have to be nasty!"

"Oh, what's the use, Max!"

They retreated into silence. He rustled the pages, bitterly scanned the want ads and finally threw the paper to the floor.

"Rose," he pleaded, "it's not the money. He has to start, he has to learn, it'll make a man of him. We'll let him keep some for himself, give him pride. You'll make up nice lunches for him. He'll like it, you'll see. You'll be proud of your son. I'll open a bank account for him to save; we'll buy him new clothes, skates, even a bike. If something's left over we can get a new rug for the hall or a desk for his homework, and..."

Rose wrenched out the words, "And a new diningroom set and a mansion in Westmount. I forgot, an automobile too. The rest we'll give to charity!" She burst into tears.

Arthur started job-hunting. Every day he bought a paper for a penny, read the help-wanted, hurried to the address in the ad. The boss would come out, regard him with distaste, and snort that he was too damn slow, the job was already filled, an hour ago. "If you want to get ahead, sonny," he sneered, "you better get the lead out of your ass."

Arthur learned to wait early outside the newspaper building and shove and struggle with the crush of boys trying to grab the first *Star* on the street. He would force his way to the front and snatch a paper from the newsie, pay his money, break away from the mob and run panting from the solemn grey granite of avaricious St. James Street.

Flustered and hot after a fruitless week, he fought once again for the first *Star*, stopped and devoured the ads, the sweat streaking his face as a July sun scorched the street. There it was, that small one halfway down the second column. He started off when a stately gentleman (white moustache, silver-headed cane, white panama hat) who had watched the scrambling boys with kindly amusement, beckoned Arthur and gave him a dime. "Hurry," he urged, "take a streetcar, you'll beat the others. Get there first, my boy, get there first!"

Breathlessly Arthur thanked his benefactor and hurried off to
launch a Horatio Alger career.

The man watched the running boy, sighed and strolled back to
his office. At five o'clock he was chauffeured home. It had been a
good day. He felt physically fit. His investments were sound. And
he had helped a nice boy touch the first rung of The Ladder. What
the country needs are battalions of go-getting youngsters!

*

The man behind the soda fountain was hot and annoyed about
something. He frowned in disapproval at this nervous kid applying
for a job in his ice-cream parlour across from Dominion Square
near the Windsor Hotel. O.K., he told the boy, come back
tomorrow at noon. Three dollars a week. Bring lunch. There was
no briefing, no pep-talk about rising to the top, nothing about the
sacredness of ice-cream.

On Saturday he was nearly as nervous as on his very first day of
school among unfamiliar children and with a strange woman
demanding, "What's your name?" Now he was reporting for his
first job ever. The ice-cream boss frowned.

"What's your name?" the man asked.

"Meller, Arthur Meller."

"O.K., Art, go in the back and put this on." He tossed a white
cotton coat at the boy. "Then come back and get behind the tubs.
I'll tell you what to do."

Arthur hung his jacket on a nail, buttoned up the white coat and
walked out to face the ordeal.

The first thing he ever did for pay, the first job of his life—the
ritual initiation into the labour force—was to wash a tubful of
glasses, saucers and spoons. The boss demonstrated; he ran hot
water from the tap, poured liquid soap from a jar, plunged hairy
arms into the scalding mess and stirred up a lather.

"You see? That's how you do it. Don't let the dirty dishes pile
up. See? Wash 'em quick, dry 'em quick. See? Then you put 'em
here. Neat piles, see? Here's the towels, here's the soap. So get
busy, go ahead, work fast. If you get thirsty you can take a ginger
ale from the fountain. All you like. See? O.K., get to work."

Arthur dipped fingers into the suds and quickly yanked them
out.

"You'll get used to it." The boss laughed. "Blow on them, Art, blow them cool. Put in some cold water, not too much. See?"

He got used to it. By six o'clock he had washed and dried mountains of glass, glass-holders and plates. He had learned to mix fountain limeade, cola-and-lemon and ice-cream sodas and even fixed a few sundaes and banana splits.

Ice-cream parlours were forlorn places in wintertime, the boss sitting stoically, reading a paper behind the counter, bestirring himself only when the occasional couple came in for a hot chocolate with wafer. But summer, ah summer! The place came alive. Blessed be the hot winds, the humidity and the broiling sun! Waitresses were hired, women were brought in to polish the woodwork. The overhead fan blades were sent spinning and humming and glasses were polished and arrayed in formations on the shelves in front of the panels of mirrors. Lights burned low in the evening and striped awnings kept out the sun during the day. Cool drinks flowed into tall glasses. The weary were revived with ice-cream.

There was no lending library or magazine rack, no films to develop, no hot dogs or hamburgers and no souvenirs, no sunglasses, no books or magazines. It was the time of the ice-cream parlour pure and simple and delicious.

As the day dragged on his clothes became drenched. The overhead fans merely cooled the sweat. Arthur washed furiously, dried frantically, hurried to fill orders, scooped ice-cream, split bananas, spread nuts and crushed pineapple on sundaes and flushed soda into flavour syrups. He realized that he was developing a work rhythm, limiting his motions, conserving energy. He was proud. But the perspiration poured from him and he was near collapse when the boss finally told him during a lull, "O.K., Art, go eat supper in the back. You can take an ice-cream and pop. Don't be too long."

He sat for the first time in six hours, chewing a sandwich, when Marge the waitress came in. "Whew, what a day!" she called out. She removed her white smock and stood in panties and brassiere, combing her hair. Arthur reddened and lowered his eyes to his food, Marge laughed and changed casually into a mauve gingham dress. "All right, sonny, you can look up now. I'm all finished."

He said, "You're very beautiful."

Marge laughed again. She went over to him and kissed him on the mouth.

He repeated. "You're very beautiful."

She sat down beside him and impulsively pressed his head to her breast. She held the boy close and stroked his dark head. "I sure wish you were older." She sighed.

The door opened. The boss, grinning, shouted, "Hey Marge, he's too small, he's not ripe. What you doing, robbing the cradle? How about me? I could show you something big. I could make you holler 'Uncle!'"

"Your mouth is like a sewer," she shot back.

"You're no angel yourself, honey." The man grinned. "I bet you know how babies are made. Want to try?"

Marge slammed the door.

"Get back to your dishes, Mr. Oscar Wilde," the boss ordered. "No more monkey business. See? You're too small for nooky. Wait till you get bigger. Maybe Marge'll teach you how to do it. Later, when you're older. But not today, we're too busy. O.K.?"

The evening dragged, the humidity closed in, the fans rotated lazily, people kept coming in. Would the night ever end?

At midnight the boss said he could go now and come back Sunday at two in the afternoon. Arthur boarded the streetcar and arrived home with a headache. His father congratulated him; it was an important milestone in Arthur's life, his first day's work. Supper waited on the table. He ate ravenously. His head ached. He lurched into the bathroom and threw up.

"What's wrong, Arthur?" his mother cried out in alarm.

"I feel sick. I guess I'm sick, Ma. I have a headache." He felt faint. They undressed him and put him to bed. Rose flashed an angry look at Max. "Satisfied?" she demanded.

"It's all right," his father kept saying. "It's all right, Arthur, you'll stay home tomorrow, you'll take the day off. Maybe Monday you'll go back."

The mother interrupted, said flatly, "You won't go back, you won't go back at all."

He fell asleep and dreamed that he was stranded on the edge of a pit that bubbled over with boiling suds and that Marge the waitress was being attacked by the boss and was imploring Arthur to save her, but he was helpless and afraid. The boss swam around drooling and pawing the waitress and tearing off her clothes and throwing them in among the dishes in the steaming pool. And now Arthur was teetering on the brink and the boss reached out and pulled him down into the boiling whirlpool and Marge swam over

swiftly and clasped Arthur to herself and kissed and fondled him.
He pressed himself hard against her. It was a revelation, it was
something he had never before experienced, his body had acquired
a miraculous new manhood, he was full of strength and the ecstasy
flowed through him and demanded release. He woke spurting
semen. He was surprised and bewildered and proud, he was in love
with Marge and dreamed of her a few more times; he conjured up
uninhibited fantasies about making love to her. Would he ever see
her again? But he could never work up nerve to return to the
ice-cream parlour. Later he had dreams about other love goddesses
whom he could never approach except in fantasy.

3

1939. September Night.
In the Hospital.

TRY, ARTHUR, TRY to remember that you're still alive. Compel your
brain to wake and make your heartbeat strong again. Wake and sit
up, stand again. And remember, Fred, your good friend, would be
astir by now. Remember Fred. He's tough and gentle and alive and
wise and hard to kill.

Do you recall, Arthur, the first time you met Fred? The joyous
anger of this man must surely breathe new life into your flesh
again. His laughter creates life.

*

Fred is somewhere in hiding. They've been looking for him since
last night in the park. There are charges waiting to be laid by
Detective Gilbert and his knights of the Red Squad.

Sedition? Possibly. Unlawful assembly? Sure. Disorderly
conduct, causing a disturbance, rioting, violating various by-laws?
Yep. Plus dumb insolence for glaring contemptuously at
stool pigeons, informers and finks.

1919. Spring Day.
The Fishermen.

Early daylight hovered between green blind and white window sill in the upstairs flat on a plebeian street in downtown Montreal's Griffintown and spread a pale bar across the narrow wooden bed where the longshoreman slept. Lace curtains were stirred by a breeze.

The room also held a chest of drawers painted dark green, a scuffed metal-banded brown trunk, a wooden chair newly painted red, a reading lamp on the night table beside the bed. A grocery store's wall calendar featured a bouquet of red carnations. A framed homemade panel carried portraits (left to right) of Rabbie Burns, Kier Hardie, Karl Marx and Joan of Arc. On the floor beside his bed was an oval rug.

Hanging from a bracket, a wire cage sheltered a canary who warbled from time to time. On the night stand a few books rested, and a magazine, half a glass of water, a clothes brush, a pink denture soaking in an enamel cup, a tobacco pouch and a pipe and a box of wooden matches, an ashtray, a mouth organ, a clock.

At five the clock buzzed. Martin Shaughnessy reached over and silenced it. He sat up in bed and scratched his hairy chest, clasped the back of his neck with both hands and swung his head and torso slowly from side to side to loosen the tough muscles of his shoulders and back. He stared in bafflement at the clock and finally smiled. Of course, it was Sunday.

"I must have forgotten and set the alarm clock last night...Habit—like a horse plodding the treadmill...Bloody galley slave...Forty years old and I never get enough sleep..."

He reset the alarm for nine. Since he was already awake he wandered sleepily through his small, square hallway and into the sittingroom, taking stock of the comforting security of cushioned armchair, black mock-leather sofa with built-in headrest, a voiceless wind-up mahogany gramophone, the bulging bookcase, a scuffed fumed-oak desk with leaded stained-glass reading lamp suspended above it.

A framed sepia photograph of a woman, about thirty-five, head high and bold of eye, stood on a miniature easel on top of the bookcase. On a wall hung a photo of the dignified, droop-moustached Jim Connolly, once dubbed "the Irish Lenin" by a punning editor.

There was no oilcloth on the brown-painted floor, just a couple of rugs. The green slats of the outside shutters released feeble wafers of light.

Shaughnessy, in oversized pyjamas hanging loosely on his short, stocky frame, paused at the picture of his wife, sighed and returned to his lonely bed. The boy in the other room slept undisturbed.

At nine the clock rang again and Martin got out of bed, entered his son's room, shook the sleeping Fred and boomed, "Wake up! It's your birthday! Wake up and live!"

"Huh?..."

"Wake up! You're fifteen! Don't snore your life away! You're a man today!"

Fred sat up. "Thanks, Dad, but I was a man yesterday too. I've been a man for some time now." He laughed and swung out of bed.

"If you're actually awake," Martin said, "I've got something for you. In that package there." He pointed brusquely at the bed-table. Fred tore open the paper. Inside was a tackle box. He opened it, held up and admired fishing lines, hooks, leaders, sinkers, floats, a stringer, fishing knife and scaler.

"They're smart, Dad, real smart." His father responded with a gap-toothed grin, his grey-green eyes filled with pleasure. Fred embraced him.

Martin said, "How would you like to try out the new tackle? We'll pack a lunch, catch a train and go fishing. When we come home we'll eat a fish supper, our own fish."

Fred made the beds, tidied the rooms and washed the breakfast dishes while Martin scraped away with an old straight razor. Fred made salmon sandwiches and hard-boiled some eggs. Martin went out to dig for worms in the backyard.

On the train Martin read the Saturday *Star* and fell asleep to the pounding of the wheels. Fred shook him awake when the conductor called St. Jerome.

They walked to the river, rented a punt and were given a couple of bamboo fishing rods. Fred rowed. "Let's go near the other boats, where it's deeper."

"All right," Martin agreed, but dubiously. "We can try a while." But they got no nibbles. Every time they checked the lines they found the worms intact and turning paler. "Move over and give me the oars," Martin said. "I'm going to look for a better spot."

He rowed into a reed-covered bay. It was too shallow. He moved into deeper water where thick weeds reached within inches under the boat and broke above the surface. On the edge of this weed-bed, deep down in the clear water, they could make out a pile of masonry and lumber, perhaps part of an old dock or a diving raft crushed in the spring break-up. Good for bass, if they had leeches, which they didn't, or if there were any bass in this water, or any fish at all.

Martin eyed his motionless float on the smooth surface. Six feet below, the fresh worm wriggled on the hook. Martin smoked contentedly. Nothing happened and he considered moving again. He glanced over to Fred. "Take it easy, lad." He leaned his rod against an oar-lock, held it in place with his knee and refilled his pipe. The float started to bob, went down in a quick, short jerk, surfaced and sank violently again. He grabbed the pole and yanked and a flash of yellow sunfish, four inches long, danced on the end of his line. He freed the creature and it darted down below. He speared a new worm and waited, alert this time, as a green-grey foot-long fish approached the worm. Martin held his rod steady and waited for the striped fish to take the bait. Then he struck and whipped his rod back. The perch slapped into the punt, beating against the floorboards. Fred strung it through the mouth and a gill and tied the stringer to the anchor line. Martin exulted; it was a jumbo perch.

Fred peered into the water; it was swarming with perch. His father snapped the rod again and brought in another. Fred slowly lowered his bait into the water and teased the hungry school. He hardly needed to strike; they were just about hooking themselves. All he had to do was haul them in, unhook and string them. Martin smoked serenely and added to the catch.

The bait-can ran low; the Shaughnessys rationed themselves to quarter-inch lengths. It was impossible to miss the hungry fish. The fishermen became selective, keeping only the bigger ones. They hoped for bass, but the bass didn't bite.

"Bass are canny creatures," Martin reflected. "They're easily scared away. Let them taste the bait and don't strike too soon. Your hand's got to be as fast as your eye and your brain as fast as the fish."

"There's no more worms," Fred reported.

"We could cut up a small fish and use it as bait."

"They wouldn't eat their own," Fred protested.

"Why not? They don't know the difference." Martin sliced a perch and fixed a piece onto his hook and another on Fred's. The fish resumed biting.

"We could go on forever," Fred laughed. "Catch little perch to cut up to catch more perch to cut up to catch more to cut up to..."

"I think we better row back before you run amuk and scuttle us," Martin said. They dried their wet lines in the sun, packed away their tackle and counted thirty-two perch, all good-size keepers. Fred laid out the lunches and they ate hungrily in the shade of an overhanging willow. Their arms and faces were sun-reddened. They were tired and at peace with the day.

"A cold beer would go good now," said Martin. "There's a quart at home, but I forgot it."

Fred looked smugly toward his father; he pulled on a cord at the stern and fished a sock from the water. From it he removed a bottle. "It kept cool in the water," he said. "I thought you might like a beer."

"Perfect day, just bloody perfect," Martin sighed. He forced the cap off and handed the bottle to his son. "Have a sip, lad, down to there," and pointed to a spot halfway down. Fred gulped, the froth streaking his chin and his neck. Martin drank slowly, appreciatively. The beer gurgled in the long bottleneck and into his throat.

Fred hoisted anchor and moved slowly to shore.

When they left the train in Montreal the city was warm and dark. They scaled, cleaned and salted their catch and wrapped it in cheesecloth, packing it between blocks of ice in their ice-box. They were too tired to fry their fish and decided to have it the next day.

They washed up, knocked together a quick dinner of left-over boiled potatoes, cooked ham, tomatoes and cheddar cheese, drank a mug or two of tea and retired to their rooms, Fred with a mystery story, Martin with a weekend paper. They were dog-tired after their outing, their eyes drooped, they undressed and sought their beds.

Fred called out, "Dad...I just want to say thanks. It was a grand day."

"You're welcome, son...And goodnight. Goodnight, Fred... We'll eat fresh fish for supper tomorrow. Our own catch. How'd you like 'em? Fried, baked, a chowder?

Fred didn't answer. He was asleep and starting to snore.

*

Back to reality, 5 a.m. Monday, Martin silencing the alarm clock, Fred awake and guilt-ridden for hiding in bed while his father breaks his ass on the docks to give him an education fit for a snob.

He's got to get a summer job.

Sure, his old man is right; Fred needs schooling to learn the wonders of the world and to change its heartbeat, nothing less.

"Sunt lacrimae rerum." From *The Aeneid* by Virgilius Maro. Montreal High School Latin, fourth form. Mr. Christopher's simplified version: "There are tears for the state of things."

You have seen it all your young life; succeeding generations have grown accustomed to it. It has to be eternal. The rejected reject each other and themselves. We're failures, we're beneath contempt.

Some see the horror when their eyes focus for the first time. The commonplace becomes grotesque. You see every hard-edged detail; you feel every slap on the face, every violated raw nerve.

Worse than the affront to human flesh is the humiliation of the spirit.

In a grubby barbershop below St. Catherine and above the waterfront on St. Lawrence-Main a shoeshine kid of eleven or twelve smokes a cigarette and coughs up T.B. bugs, and he's too cocky to take the butt out of his mouth while he coughs. The old pimp getting the shine breathes through rotting teeth and boasts to the child about how many overheated broads he's laid, so many pounds of rancid meat. After he leaves, his greasy felt hat limp on his head, he leans against a post, sputters dirty invitations and makes obscene gestures to passing chippies. Children or old women? Who can tell the difference?

"Sunt lacrimae rerum." This barber cuts hair and shaves faces all day. When business slows he reads the *Racing Form.* All his years he's tried to pick a sure thing, but the nags cheat. Every week he drops two or three bucks into quicksand. When he doesn't dream about his dream horses he just stands at the door of the shop, seeing nothing. He could be fifty years old, sixty, seventy, ageless, lifeless. He has yet to beat the system.

"Sunt lacrimae rerum." "Where's the old Chinaman with the crooked mouth?" a customer asks. The smart shoeshine kid wisecracks, "He's pushing daisies. Squint-eye Susans for the Chink." The barber adds, "He got cancer." From the penny arcade a player-piano belches out a convulsion of noises. *"Requiescat in pace."*

"Sunt lacrimae rerum." Farther down the street an auctioneer barks out a rapid-fire spiel. "Fine gold watch fourteen-carat twenty-one jewels railroad engineers' favourite government inspected guaranteed for life how much am I offered how much? Do I hear five, gents? Five. Do I hear six? What's the matter? Cat got your tongue? Ain't there six bucks in the house? Tell you what, here's a genuine fourteen-carat gold chain. O.K., how about I throw in this beauty of a tiger-head watch-fob straight from the Humalasian Mountains? If you ever go there you can use it like a pass to let you in to the secret orgies of the Tiebeetian monks. Boy, they sure know their orgies! Who'll give me six bucks for the lot? It's a steal at ten. Thank you, sir, and good luck."

"Sunt lacrimae rerum." Men with glazed eyes. Women old at twenty-six. Streets where the sun fries the garbage. Rooms that smell of death. Winters when frost kills the starving. Streets without trees. Houses without paint. Tables without food. Evenings without rest. Despair without end. Children without a childhood.

Back to reality at 5 a.m. Monday. And I, Fred Shaughnessy, proletarian Irish slob hankering to have an education and lying luxurious in bed as Dad wolfs his breakfast to give him strength to make the daily quota of nails for his own coffin.

Five a.m. Monday, for Christ's sake, and I'm spouting Latin. *"Sunt* bloody *lacrimae rerum."* O parasite! O snob! O shit! I ought to hire a hall. Or shut up. Or get a job.

*

Down by the water the dockers walked out and set up their picket lines. By foot, by Ford, by Harley-Davidson and by horse came the cops, clubbing and arresting and succouring the State from subversion and collapse.

*

In a fourth-form class at Montreal High the history master, Major Stinson Steele, erstwhile British Army Intelligence, dispensed judgment on the Corn Laws and the Corn Law protests. He fully acquitted the Manchester gentry and praised the firm hand behind the Peterloo massacre of 1819.

Warming to the subject, he tore into *The Mask of Anarchy* and sneered it down as a vulgar outburst of doggerel propaganda by that great lover (a wink), that pretty pansy boy (a roll of the eyes), Percy Bysshe Shelley, who wore open-neck blouses (a flutter of the fingers) and had such long lashes (oo-la-la!).

Jesus, what a performer, mincing and prancing and limping his wrists!

Assuming a more sober and sincere mien, he now worked himself into a lurid diatribe against the anti-Christ conspiracy: Bernard Shaw, Lenin, Kaiser Bill, Louis Riel, Emma Goldman, Henri Barbusse, Upton Sinclair, Eamonn de Valera—foremost in a seditious crew.

Well launched, he exhorted his captive congregation in this cathedral of learning to eschew radical villainy. He extended the frontiers of pedagogy by stunning the minds of his students. He liberated logic. If, he argued, the fickle Manchester rabble had been so utterly confounded by freedoms it was not mature enough to handle, how could you expect the colonies to be more advanced than the very heart of the Empire? Canada, after all, has a long way to go and a lot to learn. It's not ready for freedom.

"Very well, *quod erat demonstrandum*. Let's be a little more specific. This flouting of authority, this anarchistic violence, this irresponsible nose-thumbing at the public weal, this godless challenge to the lifeblood of a prostrate city, this disruption of one of the great harbours of the world, this immoral strike by greedy self-seeking Bolshevik agitators, this sacrilege, this real sedition, this pestilence—it must be stopped here and now and without mercy. I'd line them up against a wall, every swinish rotter, every traitor and every rotten I.W.W. I-Won't-Work bum, and I'd shoot 'em all on the street without the nonsense of a trial, every manjack one of them!"

"Sir," said Fred Shaughnessy, "my father's one of those longshoremen. He's on strike. He's not a criminal. You have no right to insult him. If he doesn't get more money I guess I won't be able to come back here next year."

"You Irish," the major spat out, "have disturbed the peace for hundreds of years!"

"You, sir," Fred shot back, "are the shit we disturb."

Major Steele descended on the boy, hauled him by the collar to the front of the room and pushed him into a corner. The monitor was dispatched and soon came back with the strap.

"Speechifying scum!" Steele bit out as he struck with the leather. "Hun!" and he stung the left palm. "Bolshevik!" and he struck the right, "Anarchist!" and back to the left again. "Irish trash!" and swung at the right. And the left again, and the right again; in all, ten times.

While it was happening, Fred glared scornfully at the major. After the strapping he walked firmly to his seat, turned slowly to his classmates and held up his swollen palms for them to see the purple welts. He shrugged and sat down.

What tribal loyalties united these thirty-two boys behind their classmate? Half were from workers' homes, half from the homes of petty shopkeepers, a few from old families, but most were sons of immigrants from Eastern Europe and the British Isles. They resented the bigoted imperialist; they were offended by his bully-boy arrogance and admired any lad who had the guts to tell him off.

A boy applauded, then another, and another, until they were all clapping. A boy cheered and another took it up and they all cheered, until their teacher, their master, red-faced and humiliated, shouted that the whole damn class would be detained after school and that Fred Shaughnessy would be dealt with by the rector's office.

The rector regretted the embarrassment. This longshoreman's boy was a bright student who excelled in sports and studies. It was decided to give Fred another chance. All he would have to do is make a suitable apology before the class.

Fred refused. He was expelled. That was how, at fifteen, his formal education was terminated.

So, no more education, no door to opportunity. And no illusions.

What would his father say? "Bastards!" his father said, but managed a grin. "There's always books, lad. You don't need any bloody major's bloody permission to bloody-well read them!"

*

On Fred's last day of school Arthur Meller accompanied him across the university campus on their way to Sherbrooke Street, where Fred would cut down to St. Catherine and south to Dorchester and beyond until he reached home in the heart of Griffintown.

"My father," said Fred, "was in the post office in Dublin when the English soldiers smashed their way in. Dad was right beside Jim Connolly when Jim was wounded. Dad emptied his gun into the Black-and-Tans and escaped. He hid out until my uncle gave us the money to come to Canada." Fred paused. "My mother didn't make it. She was shot down, standing on her own doorstep.

"I guess the Black-and-Tans are everywhere, Canada too."

4

1939. September Night.
Hospital Blues.

THERE'S RALPH GILBERT the gunman, his face flawed by a brick or a stone. He is slumped on his ass on the corridor bench.

"Perhaps the stupid bugger's better off dead," the detective tells himself. "If he survives he'll end up in the pen or an internment camp. For the duration."

Here's the night nurse, checking the charts in Intensive Care. That Meller patient hasn't changed. "Poor man," she tells herself. She appears unhappy and tired. "His poor wife..." She moves to the next bed.

There you are, you barely stir. Lie quietly, Arthur, rest peacefully on your cot. You were sick before and it passed. You were sick a long time ago and it passed.

How old were you, four, five? Your hair had been cut short and your mother saved the curls, souvenirs of innocence. You caught cold and your father said it was the haircut. When you were bedded down and he came to say goodnight he showed you a small red case, something like a snuff-box. He pressed a button and the lid flew open but the case was empty. Then he closed it and opened it again and you found three satin candy cushions in different pastel colours. The crust was crisp and the filler soft and chewy. You were amazed to open this trick box and find it empty and then see your father make mysterious passes over it and solemnly return it for you to open again and find candies where there had been none before. Your father waited, hungry for approval, grateful that you were enchanted by his magic.

1921, 1922. Waters Roiled.
The Meller Family Blues.

Once late at night when Arthur was reading the *Freethinker* his father burst into the room and snatched the magazine from his hand. "I don't want this atheist garbage in my house!" Max shouted. Arthur got out of bed, but Max pushed him back and the boy fell, striking his head against the bed-rail. Rose came running. "It was an accident, it was his own fault," her husband explained. "I don't want him reading all this crank stuff, wasting his life. I'll burn every scrap he brings home." Turning on Arthur, he warned him, "You'll be a grumbler, a radical, a troublemaker! You'll be an outcast and a bum! Decent people will vomit when you come near. Like a plague! You'll never have anything, you'll never amount to anything, you'll have to beg for food! What will you be, an anarchist, a God-hater? You want to end up in jail, a murderer? What in hell's the matter with you? Why can't you be like other boys?"

"I'm nearly seventeen years old. I want to find out. What's wrong with having books? What's wrong with reading?" Arthur argued.

"I don't want my son reading against God—sewer garbage and atheism. That's what's wrong!"

"Why don't we all go to sleep?" Rose pleaded. "It's late."

*

Max was worried about his son. When prohibition failed he tried ridicule. "Your great men aren't gods. Even your Bernard Shaw eats sausages like everybody else. He's no saint, he isn't the Messiah."

"He never eats sausages," Arthur countered.

His father frowned. "How do you know?" he demanded. "And you don't have to be impudent."

"I know," Arthur replied slowly, relishing the thrust. "I know, because he's a vegetarian. And I'm not impudent."

The father glowered. Discussion died.

*

Why did his father insult him with sour prophecies? "Wait till you're older, you'll cool off, you'll learn that radicals are fools." But for the boy they were free spirits who rode rockets to the future, they were visionaries, probers, pioneers.

Why should his father hide among the "apathetic throng," Ralph Chaplin's "cowed and the meek who see the world's great anguish and its wrong and dare not speak"? Why was the man so old so soon? Why did he stifle the memory of his own youth? What had he left for himself except his jaded thoughts and threadbare words, the muddy shadows of his dead-end world? Had he ever been young? Ever questioned or dreamed? What did this failed man fear? What could he lose?

Every new day of his rebellious seventeenth year Arthur rediscovered the world. Now as he sat alone at night on a park bench at the base of Mount Royal, his head tilted back, he remembered himself as a child on the lawn across from the massive stone hospital on St. Urbain, remembered his wonder at the stars in the summer night and the music made by his beautiful aunt and her charmed friends. And now tonight the sky sang and the stars flashed and the breeze lifted him and the moon beckoned and he was airborne. The universe hummed and murmured and the sounds of its life swelled and his spirit soared.

He was strong now, could conquer anything, do everything, for he was part of all this, he was at its loving chanting roaring centre. He was creation and creator.

*

All the poor deluded innocents! Innocent or not, but hypnotized, drugged or warped! For how long must they eke out shrunken lives on the short rations of a wasteland? Is dry rot the only thing that's worth preserving?

Ask my father, it's his world.

*

Max was unwell. His legs hurt, his stomach hurt, his teeth hurt, his son hurt.

Max was irritable and impatient; he scolded Arthur and nagged Rose. He blamed his son for driving him to an early grave; Arthur for whom he had planned and slaved and trudged his feet off, Arthur who had no ambition, no respect, Arthur who didn't love him.

Rose pleaded with Max, wept, appealed to her son, lost her temper, scolded and wept and adored her foolish boy.

The poverty quickened, the table shrank, the clothes grew shoddy, the gloom oppressed.

Max would fly into a rage when his wife asked for money. Some days he merely looked at her and walked into the other room. He began to dole out a few cents every day instead of giving her the house allowance once a week. One day he left nothing at all and when Rose called after him he wrenched a quarter from his pocket and flung it on the table with a look of infinite grief. Or perhaps it was hatred.

During the Christmas holidays Arthur found a few weeks' work. A few weeks stretched into a few months. The schoolboy didn't go back to school; he was now a workingman. School days were over for him. Life had begun.

*

He dreaded getting out of bed on winter mornings.

He would wake too soon, disturbed by his mother making coffee in her kitchen, or his father groaning as he clutched his stomach.

What a pity it wasn't Sunday, when he could pull the blanket over his head and shut everything out. He heard the door close as Max shuffled out to peddle crucifixes and beads to the faithful. Rose tugged at her son's shoulder to wake him for work.

As he sat dressing with chilled fingers, the promise of the day
bore down on him: cold warehouse, stuffy front office, overfed
Aaron Turner, the routine of morning duties—unfastening back
doors, sweeping out the store, straightening stock, nailing cases,
sorting samples—all a senseless scurrying under the baleful eye of
pudgy, adenoidal, querulous Aaron Turner, rush-rush Turner,
squawking Turner, bitching Turner. Never a word of
encouragement. Ten hours six days every week Arthur packed or
unpacked heavy crates, shipped woolen socks to Nipigon, bulging
bales of underwear to Ansonville, wooden cases of mitts to North
Bay, cartons of overalls to Rocky Mountain House or Drumheller
or Glace Bay.

Fat Aaron stood at his elbow, checking his invoices,
complaining, whining, worrying, losing money, getting more
corpulent. The greasy pink face of the man, his high-pitched whine
and apoplectic temper, his petulancy, the homburg hat he wore
indoors on the back of his bald head, the Virginia Ovals he
smoked, his garish neckties—everything about this greaseball
outraged him. This creature, this lout, this Aaron gave him his
grudging sustenance, his right to live.

When for the second time in a week Aaron told him, ten minutes
before quitting time, "We're working tonight; you've got twenty
minutes to eat," and Arthur said, "I can't, I'm taking a night
course, a business course," he was fired on the spot.

Now he could sleep late. No need to hurry panting every morning
past the iron-barred doors and into Aaron Turner Registered. Now
he could sleep until ten, rise languidly from bed, warm himself
near the stove. After breakfast he could go downtown to look for
a job if he felt like it, come home for supper, visit a friend in the
evening and return to sleep. Then wake again, late, and walk the
streets again, all day, day after day. Walking and looking for work.

Ah, freedom! Ah, bliss! Ah, treadmill! Ah, horseshit!

*

Often when he came home now his mother was away, and his
father, home early, sat at the kitchen table, or by the coal range,
reading in the soiled light of a sunless winter day. Outside, the
heavy clouds were as grey as the February snows polluted by the
ceaseless traffic of horses, sleighs and motorcars. The kitchen

brooded around his father. Arthur wanted to cry out and shatter the leaden silence.

Max would hardly look up or greet him; his son was his enemy, they were all his enemies. His head throbbed from its ache and his nerves hurt. The whole world goaded his lacerated soul. On the table, in a tin basin of vinegar, a cloth soaked.

The father sat, elbows on the table, the wet rag held to his forehead, a book before him. The room was pungent with the smell of vinegar. Odd, thought the son, his father reads a book when he had never before looked at anything but a newspaper. Annoying that he should choose a depressing thing like Ibanez's *Four Horsemen of the Apocalypse.*

Why couldn't his father try to sell something besides beads and crucifixes? Why couldn't he peddle housewares, bedding, stuff like that? Others made a living. Why couldn't his father sell in a store? Why did he have to look like death warmed over? He couldn't be all that sick.

Max stayed home more often and read books and more books, anything to forget his misery. He didn't dare stop reading.

There were days when Arthur returned from downtown job-hunting and said hello, but all Max did was mutter an uneasy response. Arthur would pour himself a glass of milk, if there was milk in the house, and retire to the frontroom, where he too would read. "What's that you've got?" Max once asked. "Upton Sinclair, *The Brass Cheque,*" said Arthur. The father said, "Garbage!" and stomped into the bathroom.

Should Max talk to his son? And tell him...what? There was nothing they could say to each other. It was galling the way the boy sat there in the frontroom, like a visitor. ("Have a cool drink, Mr. Meller. Eat some cake, Mr. Meller. And how is your poor sick papa? Is he still living or did he die already?")

It was galling the way his wife had to run out of the house over to Cadieux Street to unburden herself to her sister every day. Rose hardly looked at him these days, just sat staring at the wall like a tragedienne in the Yiddish theatre, or she ran crying into the bathroom.

Some days Max didn't leave the house at all. Some days he left early but didn't take his merchandise, and came home late at night. Most of the time he sat near the stove and read. Where else could he go? To a hotel?

The days grew dark. Nobody bothered to light a lamp. They ate their supper in silence. If Arthur came home late for the meal, Max complained, "You don't show respect." Arthur would not bother to answer. Rose would start to cry and would leave the table. Arthur would leave the table. The father would eat alone.

Rose remembered suppers at her mother's house: steaming dishes, candlelight, laughter, affection, wine...

At times, when his father dozed over the kitchen table in the afternoon, his head on his arms, Arthur experienced a nagging pity. This unhappy man—what could he say to him?... "I'm sorry you're a failure, Max Meller, my father...It's my fault and I apologize because I've been a stubborn son...Forgive me for failing to respect your philistine code...You're dying and I don't want to die like you...Perhaps you should apologize to me instead..."

When Rose came home to prepare their supper, Arthur was relieved because he was no longer alone with his father.

And so the winter passed—the woman near hysteria, the man feeding on his own gall, the boy rebellious and distraught.

*

In the spring when the streets ran slimy with slush and the icicles dripped from the eaves like cold tears, Max's older brother was called to the house for an urgent Sunday conference. Henry and his family had not visited much of late; the meetings had been much too awkward.

When Henry Meller arrived it was plain to him that the three of them were tense with despair. He suspected that they blamed him. He had always helped, he told himself, he had been generous. He had to consider his own family, his wife, his two daughters, the three sons, but he had helped Max before, generously and more than once. Tough-luck Max had always been a loser. What did they want from him—a pension? He could visualize the three of them before some austere rabbinical court far away and long ago, accusing, demanding his excommunication, or chanting a Hebrew prayer in the synagogue on the Day of Atonement and shocking, exhorting, supplicating and wailing at the congregation:

"O my brother, my uncle, my brother-in-law, why hast thou abandoned us? How have we sinned? Have we blasphemed thy

name? Did we snicker at thy pompous banalities? Do not deny us
thy tender balm, O family godhead, for thou art well-heeled and
thy children and thy children's children and all their seed stuff their
bellies with sweetmeats and pomegranates and spit out the seeds
into our faces. Come across, O Uncle Henry Rockefeller-Meller-
Rothschild, Esquire. O your Excellency, give us our daily bread,
give us this day our cash, place money on our wounds as unguent to
heal them. Give, give, have mercy and give!''

Suppose he gave Max some more money. Would matters
improve? Would the money be frittered away? What then? More of
the same and nothing solved.

Max by this time didn't want anything but to get out and get
away, to be released from this trap. Henry, the grey eminence, had
been asked to preside, not to advise nor to help but to witness a
crisis, inspect a bankruptcy, justify abdication, certify his flight.

In her frontroom with its cracked marble collie propping the door
open, and stiff white lace curtains filtering the afternoon sun, she
sat below enlarged oval photos of her bewigged mother and her
bearded, skullcapped father.

Arthur stood behind her. She watched tensely as the brothers
faced each other. She sat in her own frontroom as though waiting
in the anteroom of a charity clinic. In her hallway a breeze
disturbed the portiere Max had once bartered for chapelets from a
farmer. Rose wondered how many hours it had taken the habitant
housewife to shape and paste those hundreds of wallpaper beads.
She was jolted back into reality by Henry's dry voice.

"So what are you going to do?" he asked.

"I don't know," said Max.

"What do you want me to do?" the older man asked.

"I don't know."

"And what about Rose? What about Arthur?" the brother
pressed.

"I don't know."

Uncle Henry was a wizened and phlegmatic little man. The
situation had impressed itself on him. He had seen such tragedies in
the Yiddish theatre at the Monument Nationale. He thought for a
moment and coughed. "It's a very delicatessen..." he fumbled,
searching for the right word. "It's a very delicate thing," he said.
"I'm very sorry. It's a delicate..."

The boy snickered and covered it with a nervous cough. His

mother turned her head away. Was she laughing at such a critical time? Arthur saw her face, blotched and agitated, and followed her when she rose and ran to the door. She tripped on the little marble dog and started to straighten it but kicked it instead and fled into her kitchen.

Max and Henry sat, waiting. Then Henry left. Then Max packed two valises and left.

At two o'clock in the morning the boy and his mother hauled the sewing machine down two flights of stairs, pushed it for two blocks and carried it up a flight of steps to his aunt's flat. Next day early he stole back alone to his father's deserted house and locked himself in. During the afternoon the doorbell rang. When he squinted through a crack in the blind he saw the landlord. The man rang and rapped insistently and eventually left.

Late at night, while the street slept, a horse and rig drove up. Arthur and the driver and his Uncle Norman, Laura's husband, carried down the furniture and the other household things and piled them on the wagon. Some neighbours, disturbed by the moving, watched from their windows. The fugitives lifted a trunk onto the rig and started to move off when a gesticulating man came running down the dark street.

"Wait! Wait!" he shouted, but the carter cracked his whip sharply, the horse reared and galloped off, and the landlord stood helpless like a fool, shouting, "Stop! Wait! I want my rent!" The absconders turned a corner and were gone.

A week passed. One evening Arthur saw his father dragging a wooden box to the door of a decrepit building on decaying downtown Clark Street. They saw each other at the same moment. The boy pretended he hadn't seen his father. He walked away. He turned and saw that Max was watching him, his box beside him on the pavement, his hand on the knob of a glassless door. The tall, stooped figure was like a derelict, a beaten old derelict, the remnants of a man.

His father entered the house. He pulled the wooden box in with him.

*

Max knew Arthur had seen him. He was upset because Arthur had seen him like this; he didn't want anyone to remind him. They had hurt him; why couldn't they leave him alone? He would never go back to them.

He climbed the narrow stairs to his attic room and lay down on the grey blanket, utterly drained. When it grew darker the lights were turned on across the alley and he could see into a room where another old man sat bent over something. Max stood in the dark by his window. The old man held a shirt over his knee and was sewing on a button.

Max was forty—how old he felt! He turned on his light and examined the battered wooden box he had found in a lane. He moved it to a corner. It would be useful for books and odds and ends. He would buy some thrillers in a second-hand shop, some detective stories and adventures. The box wobbled; he tried to fix it but he couldn't get it right. He sat on the bed, fretting. Across the alley the other old man still struggled with the button.

Max turned off his light and sat in the dark.

He put on his hat and left the house. He found a saloon where he ordered a glass of beer. He had never liked beer; beer was for bums. It tasted flat. The saloon was noisy; he had never been in one before. The air was foul with the smell of stale beer. He could find no peace in this place and sat alone at a table until he could stand it no more and walked out.

He walked down to St. Catherine. Where were all these fools rushing? He went into a movie theatre to get away from them. The picture made no sense. Why were those idiots laughing? He tried to doze, but they all cackled. He opened his eyes. A fanfare blasted from the pit orchestra. The vaudeville was starting. Vaudeville, well, sort of vaudeville-burlesque.

Six chorus girls in black tights and low-cut white blouses were leaning low, swinging low over the footlights, teasing with cleavage and tossing behinds. Their faces were stony. One—she must have been forty—heaved herself hard as she tried to match pace with the younger girls. The white scar of an old operation strained on her midriff. Perspiration glistened on her throat. She grinned and winked and giggled and from time to time whispered a hoarse "Wow!" but nobody as much as smiled because it was embarrassing to watch this middle-aged has-been hoofer. When the chorus number ended nobody applauded. They were waiting for the strip tease. They started to whistle. The air was damp and hot. Max was cursed and hooted as he slunk out in the middle of the stripper's grind, blocking the view and frustrating the prurience.

He wished desperately to find a cool spot free from this pestilential heat and the torrents of Rose's tears and Arthur's scorn pouring over him. He wanted to go away and sit near a quiet river where he would meet no one, to find rest from the fevers of his life, to make peace with himself, to escape from the sour jaundiced years.

He staggered through sidestreets, driven by fear, pursued by panic. Children had gone indoors, tired of play. Parents sat on their doorsteps. He raised his eyes and found himself on St. Urbain Street, near the hospital, the venerable Hotel Dieu, opposite the brick row house where Arthur was born. The dwelling hadn't changed at all, except for coloured curtains instead of white lace. There was the sound of someone laughing in there.

He was tempted to cross over and knock and say, "How do you do, I'm Mr. Meller, I used to live here a long time ago. Excuse me, I forgot something, I've come back to find my youth. There was fine music here, once...My son was born in this house."

He walked to Fletcher's Field, where he could hear the dark pulse of Mount Royal. He took a streetcar and transferred to the high and massive suburban tram. As it fled the city, it accelerated across the open countryside. When the car stopped in Cartierville Max got off. People were waiting for the return trip to the city.

They had been to Cartierville before, he and Rose and the child. Once they rented a boat for an hour. At night, when they returned, Rose rested her head on his shoulder like a schoolgirl, while Arthur slept on a seat beside them. They didn't talk during the long ride home; they sat back, absorbing the breeze from the open windows.

The big tram sped away. Max stood deep in thought, then turned and made his way towards the river. A drunk stopped him. Max gave him a dime. A dog ran at him and barked. He drove it off with a stick. A streetwalker offered him a good time. He said she was too late. Puzzled, she told him anyway to go to hell and spat at him.

He reached the shore and sat down on the grass and smoked a cigarette. When only a butt remained he threw it into the water and saw its glow expire.

He stretched out on the river bank. The sky caressed him. Here it was cool and far removed from the pestilence of heat and the festering anxieties. He lay beside the silent stream where he would see no enemy. He would here find release from drudgery and hunger and fear. He would find escape from the steel traps of his hopes and his failures.

He was free for the first time since he had walked away from Rose and Arthur. He sighed, his face was filled with wonder, he moaned softly.

He became silent and seemed to be sleeping. He sat up and stared at the black water. He closed his eyes and lay back again.

Slowly, deliberately, he rolled himself over to the edge of the river until it was too late to stop or to pull back. He fell into the water. He heard a splash, his own frightened cry, a brief commotion as he sank.

The surface was soon perfectly tranquil as the eddies died away.

The night was now hushed again. Except once or twice when the dismal signal of the tram expired on its last trip back to town.

PART THREE

1

1939. September.
Until the Day Break.

HER HOME IS a narrow unit in a row of attached two-storey houses. Four newly painted grey wooden steps lead abruptly from the sidewalk to the curtained green door with its shallow stained-glass transom. It is an old red brick house and it shows the street a modest face. The stairs are bordered by black iron handrails.

Gaby Lajeunesse has lived here for some twenty years—two with her grandfather, one year alone, seventeen with Arthur Meller.

When she was seventeen and Ovide Lesage was eighty he had sat one evening in his rocking-chair reading a mystery novel. "Soon," he had told Gaby, "I will know the solution. I think I can guess." He had smiled, had appeared to be puzzled, had fallen forward.

Relatives had arrived from La Macaza to comfort her and arrange for the funeral of the giant. The family had lavished sympathy, begged her to come back to the farm, urged her to live among her own people. But, no, she had been stubborn. "I love you all, but this is my home now; this is my life and I must stay here." How pleased Grandpa would have been with her refusal to sell the house he had left her, how proud that she had decided to live here and not return to the old life!

The uncles and aunts and cousins and brothers and sisters had kissed her an emotional goodbye and left sadly for home, wondering how a young girl alone would face the dangers and the ugliness—and worse, the city's unconcern.

That had been fifteen, sixteen years ago, no, eighteen. Now she sits in her livingroom alone again, as she sat alone on the night her grandfather died, as she sat alone after the funeral.

Now Arthur lies in the hospital. Who is his guard, slouching on the bench at the end of the corridor? That red-headed horror of a detective? Or is his massive partner on duty now? And do either of these two gorillas care much whether Gaby's husband lives or dies?

And tonight in this small house on a sidestreet near the high school she had attended and the ivied university buildings, she leans back in her grandfather's rocking-chair. It is very late on this September night in 1939 and she is too weary to weep and the day will be bleak when it breaks.

Then what?

*

Gabrielle, you have smiled. Are you remembering the letter? The one he sent you the day after you told him he could stay. What an idyllic night, dear Gabrielle, what a magical world for the two of you!

In his letter Arthur had written, "Sweet Gaby, after last night I want to whisper what Elizabeth Barrett wrote to Robert Browning, 'How do I love thee?' and to sing her manifesto, 'Let me count the ways. I love thee to the depth and breadth and height my soul can reach...'

"The poet who wrote *Song of Songs*—wasn't he singing for us too? Perhaps you know it best in French, but it's all the same: 'Behold, thou art fair, my love, behold thou art fair. Thou hast doves' eyes within thy locks...Thy lips are like a thread of scarlet and thy speech is comely...Thy two breasts are like two young roes that are twins, which feed among the lilies.'"

Do you smile now, Gabrielle, remembering him embarrassed by his own shy boldness? Can you picture him hesitating to put into words what his hands and his lips had told you?

"'Until the day break and the shadows flee away, I will get me to the mountain of myrrh and to the hill of frankincense...How much better is thy love than wine!...'

"Dear Gaby, I love you. Sweet Gabrielle, Gaby, Gabrielle, Gaby, Gaby!"

It Is 1922. I Am 18.
The City's My Home.

My name is Gaby, Gabrielle Lajeunesse. I must have a good look at myself and take stock now that Grandpa is dead and I have made my decision to stay in Montreal, a hundred miles from my family, from La Macaza. In four years I've become a city creature. It's not that I prefer the city's concrete to the gentle meadows of the north; cement is not kind to bare feet.

The city's heartbeat woke me up. My grandfather, Ovide Lesage, woke me up. He was the most alive person I ever knew. Now that he is gone I have to prove to myself that I too am not afraid to be alive and not afraid to be alone.

I could go back to the farm and they would all give me shelter and food and affection and advice and strength. I could watch the early sun kiss the mountains and I could splash around in the cool clear water on a hot summer day. I could eat the wild red berries where they grow and pick the wild yellow flowers at my feet. But I want to stay here in Montreal; this city is now my home.

I have just looked in the mirror, not out of vanity, not self-delusion. I try to be modest, and honest. Well, my eyes are blue, with a little green. My hair is fair, a sort of dull blonde, not peroxide, and I wear it medium short. The face isn't bad, I suppose, maybe a little serious, perhaps too private, but not austere and not standoffish. It's kind of oval and my cheekbones are high. Grandpa used to say there was a legend about his own grandmother, that she was part Mohawk. He said he was proud to be even a little bit Indian. My mouth isn't afraid to laugh or kiss. My teeth are good. My bones aren't big, but the farm made me strong, not muscular but strong. I am of average height and slim and my figure is nicely rounded. I mean, my chest isn't bony; firm but also soft. My health is good. I'm not a virgin; I haven't been for a year.

I like the touch of good cloth, but it has to be comfortable. I like people, most of them, and they like me. I like the company of men; I like being a woman. I like to read books, I like to listen to music and I can play the guitar a little; Grandpa taught me. I learned to sew; a nun showed me how.

I enjoy movies and stage shows and I like paintings and sculpture and parks and the harbour and skating and tennis. I sometimes go to public lectures. I've heard Scott Nearing and Captain Paxton Hibben, people like that, and socialists, anarchists, communists.

I like walking on Sherbrooke Street on a Sunday afternoon, and window-shopping on St. Catherine on Saturdays. I don't care to go to church; I haven't gone since I was at the convent five years ago. I like to keep busy. I get irritable when I'm bored. I can be nasty when I'm angry. I have no patience with fools or phonies.

I speak English with an accent, for which I make no excuse. I used to think all the Anglos here were impossible, and their conceit still offends me, but I have learned the difference between the moneybags who own my country and those other Britishers like Dickens, Shelley, Houseman and Hardy and Burns and Tom Payne. I learned from my grandfather that Moliere, Emile Zola and Anatole France were not faithless monsters.

I am not an intellectual; high school (in a foreign language at that) was my limit. But ideas mean a lot to me, ideas and, even more, feelings. I guess the farm gives you your human instincts and the city feeds your brain.

I don't know anything about politics; Grandpa used to say it was a trickster's business, suitable only for those with strong stomachs and little conscience. He said you had to be realistic and face up to it, like taking out the garbage, or getting seasick on a smelly ship in stormy weather.

Grandpa was very wise. He was also as strong as a horse. He had the laugh of a pagan and the temper of a bull, the soul of a poet and the tenderness of a saint. His wife, my grandmother, was a farm girl he met one summer when he unexpectedly came home to visit. He'd been working in the city and got homesick, so he came to La Macaza and surprised them all, with presents for the whole family. He met a girl, a neighbour's daughter, and two hours later they were in bed together. He used to say to me, quite seriously, "Gaby, we were fools to wait two whole hours."

They were soon married and he stayed to work on the farm. After my mother was born they went to live in Montreal, but Grandma and Mama returned home when he got work on the boats. When my mother grew up, she too married a farm boy.

*

La Macaza! Where my grandparents were born. And theirs too.

And my mother and father. And I.

The high mountains kept out the turbulent outside world. We lived in peace. Then the far bugles were heard by some of our young men and they never returned after the war. Four years ago.

Now it is very much as it was in the past. It's back to normal again, at peace and hard-working, at peace and confident.

"Come back to the farm," my uncle had urged after Grandpa died. "The city is full of hatred and war. Come home, Gaby. Here we have no soldiers, no armouries, no militarists, no cannons. Our mountains will keep them out. They won't dare come again. Never again. Never."

*

We did not find out what my father was supposed to have done or what exactly was done to him or in what far foreign place or how many bullets they had to use to stop his life or how many stabs with a bayonet or whether he was bludgeoned or strangled in pain or languished in God knows what agony or what his last words were or whether he cried out in English or in French or mumbled a Latin prayer or called on his wife or perhaps me or his other children or his mother or whether he died without a word or whether he at all realized he was going to die at the hands of strangers in a distant country or even by the guns of his countrymen.

I remember him as he grinned on the day he kissed us goodbye and left us. I remember I was disappointed because he had not yet been issued the khaki uniform—no peaked cap or puttees, no web belts or brass buttons or badges, no sword or lance, no horse, no rifle or revolver. When you're ten and thousands of miles from war, it's glorious.

I remember his arm around my shoulder as he said, "You're my oldest, Gaby. Keep an eye on them."

Then the train was snorting and tearing itself away and my father smiled and waved from its open window and called farewell, *au revoir,* goodbye, so long.

Then he was gone.

From the distance the moaning siren of the steam locomotive was like a keening chorus sung by the bitches of war.

*

Ah, the obscenity of the blade, the bullet, the bomb!

After official killing was concluded and official peace was duly
initialed in triplicate and quintuplicate by generals and diplomats,
and consecrated by holy men, the new rules warned that henceforth
it would be unlawful to take human life without written permit.
The penalty would be death.

But the killing continued and officials shrugged. Rebels,
disgruntled veterans, shell-shocked youths and homesick farmers,
like Dominique Lajeunesse my father, died after the war and
before the peace.

Drunk? Forgot to buff your buttons? Saluted with dumb
insolence? Turned Red?

Who knows?

The war was over for him.

The peace never began for him.

*

I had never met anyone quite like Gabrielle Lajeunesse.

Here I was turning on the formulas that rarely failed me before:
lambent words, self-deprecating modesty, boyish sincerity,
flattery, the slow smile and bedroom eyes, the romantic sigh, the
whisper, the rush of eloquence, the idolatry.

The hesitant touch of my hand on hers, my lips brushing her
cheek. Then, with abandon, my lips on hers, hands on her
shoulders, caressing, pleading, claiming...

I pause, I turn my head to hide anguish, I groan as my soul
surrenders, surrenders yet demands as it prostrates itself. My voice
breaks. I am now ready for the kill.

"Merde!" she says softly and laughs. "You know, Gordon,
you're one big phoney. Every word you speak sounds like it comes
out from a mask. What seducers' manual did you memorize? You
didn't think I'd fall for that line, did you? Never mind. Don't look
so unhappy. Let's start all over again. But not tonight. Let's be
good friends and never mind pretending eternal love. You know
you don't mean it. Let's be honest and nobody'll get hurt."

I used to think of myself as the undefeated amateur bedroom
champ. She hurt my pride, she made me look foolish in my own
eyes.

A week later, when I saw her again, she was charming. She responded warmly, she encouraged me but she took her time. It dawned on me that this was the first woman who ever made the rules for me. She humoured me, I guess, and it both flattered and disturbed me. For the first time in my life I actually felt embarrassed without my clothes. Here was a girl I tried to make who just smiled in amusement, led me on and then calmly took me to herself, in her own good time and on her own terms.

She wasn't aggressive or tough. On the contrary, she was gentle, feminine and ardent. Her skin was like velvet over a body as supple as a willow tree. She was like happy dance music and sparkling wine. She was all joy. But she was her own woman and even when she gave in—or when I thought she was giving in to me—I knew that I was really the one who had submitted.

Christ, what a beautiful creature, and only eighteen!

Later, as we lay smoking, she raised herself on her elbow and smiled. "Gordon," she said, "you're a son of a bitch but at least there's one thing you're really sincere about. While it lasts, anyway. Now get dressed. Be a good boy and please go home. I'm sleepy."

2

1939. September. Night.
The Hospital. And Gaby's.

THE NURSE AND the intern stand beside Detective Gilbert.

On the bed lies the man, unconscious and inert.

Gilbert bends over and listens. Arthur Meller dead? He is perfectly still and doesn't seem to breathe at all. Gilbert turns to the intern. "Is he dead?"

"No, he isn't dead. He's breathing."

He peers down at the patient and remarks, "He looks a goner." Gilbert and the intern leave Intensive Care. At the end of the corridor a phone buzzes. A nurse answers, "No, there's no change. No, he's not any worse, Mrs. Meller. We're doing everything we can; now we'll just have to wait. Yes, I'll phone. Goodnight, Mrs. Meller. Don't worry."

She replaces the receiver. "That was his wife again," she tells the intern. Gilbert returns to his post. Why, he wonders again, did that damn fool Meller have to butt in and get himself hurt?

At home Gaby pours herself a weak drink. She feels chilled although it is not cold. She builds a small fire and watches the flames darting among the logs. She sits staring into the livingroom fireplace. Impulsively she splashes the drink into the flames. The liquor ignites in blue-green-purple spurts. She refills her glass, right to the brim, sips thoughtfully in the dark room lit only by the fitful fire, sits staring, her eyes tear-filled, until the liquor and her exhaustion and the late hour subdue her and she sleeps.

Do you remember, Gabrielle, do you remember? How many years ago...eighteen? Do you remember? You were not then too much concerned about loneliness; you were strong. But now things are different, in 1939, and you too are different.

1922. Man of the Year.
And a Real Nice Guy.

Gordon Colman was twice my age, a bachelor who liked to think of himself as a man-about-nightclubs, man-about-art, man-about-books, man-about-women. You know the type: smooth, well-built, quite handsome, with thick blonde hair and a neat moustache. He was a smart dresser. He cultivated artistic types. He had once lived in France and tried to sound Parisian. His accent flattered a few local actresses into his bed. He wrote the occasional theatre review for the *Gazette.* He confided to me (and I'm sure to many others) that he was "scribbling" away at a novella (not a novel), but it wasn't quite finished (it was never finished, I'm sure). He rented space in the studio of a commercial artist on Beaver Hall Hill, where he turned out oil paintings of elongated cabbages and corkscrew bananas to which he gave human faces, claiming to be influenced greatly by Modigliani and El Greco.

Mostly he talked. He talked sculpture, poetry, painting, the dance (modern, of course), music and theatre. He mentioned Freud (with a knowing smile), adored Nietzsche and Schopenhauer (titans both), patronized O. Henry (ah, O. Henry), lauded Machiavelli (shrewd) and laughed at Lenin (a little oriental Jew, he scoffed).

Gordon Colman liked to talk. He talked and talked and talked. The more he was inspired, the more he enthused about culture, the closer he moved to me on the couch and the busier his hands became.

*

Such species as Gordon Colman flourish in a mulch of dollars from independent income, the increment from a rich relative's estate, the legacy of a grateful matron befriended in bed, the guaranteed annual income from a blackmailed patron's trust fund. He should have banked fortunes from astute forays into the market place, collected royalties for amazing inventions, tapped gushers of Hollywood gold for brilliant bestsellers.

Gordie Colman enjoyed none of the blessings of patronage, had few of the skills to grasp fame and none of the talents to generate a lot of instant cash. When he came home from the war, a lieutenant, he had no trade and no profession.

And so he sold. Mostly he sold himself: a nice guy, man's man, lady's man, jolly with kids, polite to elderly dames, a damned entertaining chap, rarely a nasty word about anyone, a real nice fellow.

He held exclusive territory (Montreal, Ottawa and Toronto) for a line of men's shirts, dressing gowns, smoking jackets, scarves, neckwear and quality accessories—smart, snooty, imported and expensive.

He did not earn big fat money, but it was fresh and green and enough for his bachelor comforts and bachelor sins.

There was scarcely a subject on which he could not offer a smattering of trivialities.

He kept up-to-date on the vital intelligence of the downtown cafes and he could gossip urbanely about the underworld and its racketeers, which politician was into what gravy, which dentist owned which whorehouse, which hockey forward was swish, the latest juicy domestic scandal simmering under the uppercrust. Always engagingly.

Among artists he might make an observation about Titian's pigments. To a violinist he would comment on Elman's bowing. He used words like bravura, tutti, panache, verve, elan, libido,

Weltschmerz, chiaroscuro, charisma.

He was subtle and versatile. He could say a woman was pregnant and make it sound variously dirty, clinical, matter-of-fact or divine, at a time when only married women dared to become pregnant and only their female relatives or their doctors would talk about it, mostly in private.

Charlatans were attracted to him, as he was to them. He operated airily in their world, he had an instinct for their games. In the company of pretenders, admiration and popularity came easily.

Among honest people he felt under some strain and proceeded more cautiously. It was easier to fool the phonies.

Still, he tried to be charming in both worlds. When his act did not succeed he smiled his little-boy-I-done-wrong smile.

To each woman he showed a different face: he was the fervent idealist, or the satyr, the epicure, the gay blade, the friendly uncle.

To Gaby he said, "I think I could fall in love with you."

*

Gaby drew the book from the shelf and propped it on her pillow. She kicked the slippers from her feet and lay on her bed, chin supported on a fist. She leafed through the book, skimmed the sonnets and stopped at the tenth:

> *For shame deny that thou bear'st love to any,*
> *Who for thyself art so improvident.*
> *Grant, if thou wilt, thou art beloved of many,*
> *But that thou none lovest is most evident.*

Gaby read the other ten lines but dismissed them and returned to the first four. She read aloud, repeating it aloud. She placed the book on the floor, turned out the bed-light and closed her eyes.

"...that thou none lovest..."

*

In the morning, in the lazy sunny Sunday morning, the music was like a laugh left over from a happy dream. It sparkled and danced in from somewhere in the neighbourhood, perhaps a child practising. On the floor lay the book.

"...that thou none lovest is most evident."

A distant phone rang and the music stopped abruptly. Gaby sighed, the piano came alive again and Gaby stretched her long legs and turned over on her side, listening, remembering...

On her tenth birthday her father had given her a golden spaniel pup with mournful brown eyes and wobbly legs. It had whimpered and piddled. She used to pick it up and hold it to her, stroking its silky long fur. She took charge of its feeding and training and it slept at the foot of her bed and sometimes on the blanket. The dog followed her everywhere.

She recalled summer evenings when she tired of games and listened to her parents beside the water.

She savoured the memory of cedar shavings, the night fragrance of nicotine flowers, the tart taste of gooseberries, the perfume of apple blossoms, the first light on the hills, butter forming in the churn, sleighbells at night.

And the breathless spring when she was becoming a woman.

*

Gordie has asked me to the Saturday night dinner-dance at Pointe Claire. His sales manager has invited him, a Mr. Cormack. Jeff Cormack. We're to be his table guests at the country club. Cormack will pick us up. He drives a Packard. We'll be back by 1 or 2 a.m., Gordie promised.

*

Big-boned Cormack, beefy, fiftyish and bald, arrived with a lady who was not his wife. Lorraine Hart was forty years old, a chesty blonde viking with a Mona Lisa half-smile and unfettered breasts.

So, it was going to be that kind of an evening—Lorraine for Jeff, Gaby for Gord. Or the other way around? Anyway, a chummy foursome ending up as Mr. and Mrs. Smith and Mr. and Mrs. Jones and shacking up for offbeat jollies in some discreet hotel or lodge.

Like hell! Gaby would tag along, up to a point, but no more. She'd eat the dinner and sip the drinks (slowly) and dance a bit with each of the men; she'd be pleasant but no more than that. To hell with them!

Cormack drove his Packard. When they arrived at the club they drank cool highballs in the lounge. Later they ate a splendid meal.

After dinner a band played and Cormack asked Gabrielle to dance.

He was agile, smooth and lecherous. Dancing with him was a rehearsal for rape.

He tried to lure her outside into the shadows, but the music stopped and she led him pleasantly but firmly back to their table. Drinks were poured.

Wearied of dancing and peevish because this teen-age flesh would not succumb and lie down under him after all his hospitality and masculine appeal (to say nothing of the money it was costing him), he sat at their table, *his* table, and sulked and drank.

Gordon, anxious to please the boss, hovered, grinned and generally danced attendance.

Peeved Lorraine and fed-up Gaby sat across the table from each other—enemies, allies, observers—and made desultory small talk.

Gordon tried to revive the party. He talked and flattered and chattered, but Jeff Cormack was drunk by now, and crabby. He told Gord to shut up, for God's sake.

"I'm sorry, Jeff," said Gord.

"I'm sorry, Jeff. I'm sorry, Jeff. I'm sorry, Jeff," Jeff mimicked. "What in hell kind of a man are you, anyway, with all that artsy-fartsy talk? And that little frozen-ass virgin you brought!" Jeff finished his drink and poured himself another, a double. "What the hell do you ever do except talk? Your sales aren't so hot, you know. When the hell did you ever use your fists? What the hell did you do in the war—push a pen, juggle bedpans? Did you ever spill blood, or would it make you fall down and swoon? Did you ever kill? Are you too goddam squeamish? Well, did you? You're just a bloody cream-puff. Come on, you fruit, you pansy, did you ever kill?"

Gordon took a gulp from his glass. "All right, Boss, I'll tell you. I'm just as tough as you. Yes, I was in the army. Four bloody years, and I mean *bloody*. I joined a private, ended up a lieutenant. I killed. I killed Huns. I killed my own men. You want to know why? O.K. After the Armistice we were waiting to be demobbed and the men wanted to go home, but the brass had other plans, other destinations, like Germany, Russia. The discipline just fell apart. Troublemakers moved in, anarchists, Reds, God knows what. You know what chaos looks like? We had it, every variety. One day a bunch in my company wouldn't take orders, wouldn't salute, wouldn't tidy their bunks. They bitched about the grub, they threw it on the floor, they told me to go to hell. I ordered them confined to barracks. They laughed and went A.W.O.L. I sent for the M.P.s and had my men locked up. They went berserk, they set fire to the guardhouse, they tried to burn their way out. We used the fire-hoses and it stopped them for a while; they lay on the floor in puddles like drowned dogs. Next day they broke out and demanded to be sent home. I ordered them back. They cursed and threw things. It was a mutiny; they behaved like Bolsheviks. We had to stop it. It was self-defence. We used our guns, we shot them, I shot them, we killed them.

"You asked me did I ever kill? Sure, Boss, sure, Mr. Cormack, I killed!"

*

I listened in horror as loverboy redeemed himself.

"And then, Gordie," I asked, "and then, Gordie, what did you do?"

"How do you mean, 'and then'?" he asked, frowning.

"And then, were you a hero? Did you win a medal?" I had ruined his story.

"You wouldn't understand," he complained. "You're a woman."

Jeff Cormack had been impressed. "For Christ's sake, girl!" he exploded, "you ought to be proud! He's a hero!"

"Who died, Gordie? Who died?" I demanded, I shouted, I screamed.

"What's the difference? Bums, farmers, frogs, Reds."

"Who were they, Gordie? Why did they die?"

"What's the difference? They had to."

"Who were they, Gordie? Why did they die?"

"They were bums and Bolsheviks, they mutinied."

"Where did they come from, Gordie, where?"

"Look, Gaby love, I'm not a bloody census-taker. They came from all over. What difference does it make? Montreal, Toronto, Halifax. There was even a hick from some place with a crazy name. Maklazaza, Krapaza, Makzaza, a funny name. What's it to you anyway?"

"Gordie Colman, you're a son of a bitch!"

He pleaded, "Why do you do this to me, Gaby? You know I love you!"

I stood up and threw my drink in his face. I heaved the table over onto the three of them, spilling the liquor, the ashtrays and coffee cups, the sugar and cream jugs. It was an awful mess.

"That hick...was his name Lajeunesse?" I screamed at him.

"My God..." Gord said, "my God!"

I ran across the dance floor and out and I ran until I fell. I ran across the golf links and along the country road until I couldn't run anymore. I sat down and hid in a ditch. I cried. I was angry and felt filthy and betrayed. I crawled out of the ditch and walked until I reached the little railway station.

It was 2 a.m. There wasn't a soul around. I sat on a bench in front of the building until daylight. When the Montreal train came through at last I got on and found a seat away from the others in the day-coach. I guess I looked like a chippie homeward-bound after a rough weekend.

Gordie phoned next day. I told him he made my skin crawl. I shouted for him never to phone me again. I said we were through.

I never saw him again.

At eighteen I learned the hard way.

3

1939. September. Night.
Tell Them All to Go to Hell!

YOU ARE THAT man on the bed, Arthur Meller.

Tissues have been torn by bullet, consciousness bludgeoned by pain.

Liquid stuff drips from a tube into a vein.

The morose son of a bitch stalking the corridor tried to kill you when you stepped out of line.

He pointed his gun at you and fired.

You are now an outlaw. Dead or alive.

What more can you lose now? Your life?

Tell them to go to hell: the fevered money-makers, their scowling bull-necked cops and tight-lipped financiers, their fatuous advertising image-makers, the brainwashers, hypnotists, mentors of infamy, and their suave engineers of death, their whore-masters, the whole bloody entourage of panderers, hatemongers, tormentors of harassed humanity.

Tell them—tell them—tell them all to go to hell.

Arthur, help us to survive!

*

Do you remember that summer, the summer's people?

The men and the lads in the basement dorm—one cot apiece, one locker each for the kitchen people, waiters, cleaners, and separate poky rooms for the chef and the club steward. For the chambermaids and waitresses there was an attic loft, out of bounds for the cellar crews.

Remember the others, the people of that other 1922 world, the club members: stockbrokers, lawyers, doctors, professors, politicians?

Remember the cop, the bootlegger, the sales manager, the whore?

And Georgina, round and pale, the girl with the worried smile...

*

Are you dreaming that in your hospital room tonight a pale nurse, now in her thirties, short and plump, approaches your bed, stares in sad recognition, her face pathetic in regret, and leans toward you, brushing tears from pallid cheeks? She moves closer and kisses you on the lips, removes her white clothes until she stands naked, with a worried smile and penitent. She moves under the covers beside you. She clings to you and breathes life into you so that you open your eyes at last.

She says, "Hello, Arthur, it's me, Georgie."

1922. Summer. Pointe Claire.
Country Club Syndrome.

Rose packed a suitcase for her son who was going to work at the club. He would be hobnobbing with the leisure class.

When he got there he reported to the chef, who briefed him:

"Stay out of the way of the members. Don't cross them. Don't give their women the eye. Keep yourself clean because you'll be handling food. Stay sober. Do your work well and some day you may become a chef like me, God forbid. Don't work any harder than you have to, nobody will thank you for it. Don't get into fist fights. Don't argue with your superiors. You have one day off every Thursday, all day. The staff eats at 7 a.m. Now go and mingle with the other slaves. Take care. And good luck."

Busboys, bellboys, waitresses, steward, engineer, maintenance men and chambermaids ate together in a crowded room, next to the pantry, where the chef, assistant chef, butcher, kitchen-boy and dishwasher had their meals.

At 8 a.m. began the frying of bacon, ham, sausages and eggs for the members and their guests.

The steward sat in his office phoning Montreal fish markets and butchers. He drove out every day to nearby farms for eggs and vegetables. He found ways to doctor the bills.

Vegetables, meats and stock were fed into huge pots to simmer all day and become consomme which was chilled and jelled overnight in the walk-in refrigerator room.

The assistant chef studied his *Racing Form*. The butcher had a hangover and sipped a raw egg in Worcestershire sauce. The old dishwasher sat waiting near his tubs.

For the new kitchen-boy there were potatoes to peel, peas to shell, corn to husk, and onions, stringbeans, carrots. Fish had to be scaled and cleaned, cream whipped. Later, over the steam-table, he would ladle soup into bowls for scurrying waitresses.

A whole summer of this, six days a week?

Shortly before noon each day the help wolfed a fast lunch. At long last, about three o'clock, after tidying up and mopping the floor, he was free until five-thirty, when the staff was fed quickly before the big effort of the day, the club dinner. Later he would help old Murray with the dishwashing. At nine the work-day ended and the large white kitchen was deserted, except for Arthur, who stood alone at a window, very tired and a little homesick.

When the door opened he turned and noticed a short girl, round-faced and pale, with glasses and coppery-brown hair. "Hello," she said, "I'm Georgie, Georgina Ross."

"I'm Arthur Meller, I'm the new kitchen-boy."

"I'm a chambermaid here. Some days I wait on table too."

They made awkward conversation and exchanged scraps of personal history. She had three older sisters and a brother in Hull. Her father was out of work. She heard the club was hiring, so she came.

"I hope you like it here," she said. "Don't work too hard...Well, I got to be going."

"Me too. I have to write home. It was nice meeting you."

"Wait a minute, I've got some nice letter paper, I'll fetch it, I'll be right back." At the door she turned, a hesitant smile warming her eyes. She returned soon, offering the paper and an envelope. "Would you like to go for a walk?" she asked. "It's a nice night. Let's. Write the letter tomorrow."

They crossed the fields to the road and into the village in twilight and returned in the dark. They spoke little. Georgina took his hand and led him to a tree beside a cedar-rail fence. They sat. His pulse began to pound. He could see her eyes pleading. He touched her cheek. They embraced. They lay back on the thick grass. They kissed. His eyes were closed, hers wide open. His heart hammered. He whispered, "You're beautiful," and pressed against her. He opened his eyes and she smiled. His limbs trembled and he clung to her. Georgie, soft and yielding, responded urgently. He backed away, afraid of her eagerness. He waited, the girl waited. Should he? Georgie stood up, straightened her clothes, looked down at him. "I'm going back," she said. "It's cold." She left him sitting on the grass, frustrated and ashamed of himself.

*

Saturday was to be a big day, with a tournament in the afternoon to be followed by the dinner-dance.

A whole salmon, poached and spiced and chilled and garnished with lemon slices and parsley, was laid out on a long wooden platter ensconced on a buffet just inside the diningroom entrance. Freshly cut flowers graced the tables and the window sills.

Outside on the links a cool-clad entourage followed the golfers in respectful silence, applauding as the whistling clubs cut swift, clean strokes, and cheering mildly when a player neatly dispatched the pock-marked white ball over manicured green lawn into its target hole. Then everybody trailed back for drinks.

The dinner was a triumph of smoked oysters, clam chowder, the cold poached salmon, sauces, crisp green salad, hot rolls wrapped in white linen, steamed vegetables, imported cheeses and marbled ice-cream and creamy coffee.

Elegantly they gorged themselves. Elegantly they sipped their wines and guzzled from their high-proof private liquor stocks released from bond in the club's cellars. Elegantly they excused themselves to hurry off to the washrooms to belch or break wind. Red-faced they returned, sweating but dignified, sat down at their tables under the whirring propellers of the overhead electric fans and cooled off for the next drink and the next dance.

They danced. How they danced, and with what flair! The lean and handsome predators, the smug and pudgy ones, the pompous men, the pushy ones, the wives, the lady-loves, the bed-bait debutantes!

How they danced! Manufacturers, merchants, magnates, mill-owners, managers, monopolists, mortgage-holders, million-aires, mine-owners, the masters of Montreal, the whole damned money-grubbing menagerie.

They danced and the sweat ran from their heads, wilted their clothes.

How they hated each other! The aging wives, nervous mistresses, tentative virgins and shrewd widows.

How anxiously they sweated! All the ice-cube souls on the make from mattress to matrimony, bed to bank, investment to bonanza.

The power and the glory. Horseflesh.

*

Sweating waiters and bone-tired girls stumbled from the kitchen, their trays laden with summer treats.

As the night began to grey, the crowd thinned out, the tempo slowed, the music petered out.

In the kitchen the younger chambermaids and waiters affected mock-elegant postures, pursed their lips and threw their heads back. Only a swinging door separated them from the blue-blood revellers, a door and established money, a door and a low place in the scheme of things.

"Snap out of it!" the steward barked as he charged in from the dance floor. "Stop it right now! You better smarten up! Get back on the job. You only work here, you don't own the place, goddam!"

*

Jeff Cormack was bored. This dame talked too much and kept him at arms' length as they danced. He pleaded a heart condition, smiled wanly ("just a murmur..."), excused himself and led her back to her husband's table, where he thanked her, nodded to the husband and left the dance floor. To hell with her, the bitch.

The husky man with the questing paunch was a loner tonight. Alma, his wife, would be meditating, she said, on a weekend retreat in a monastery cell. Buttocksy-busty Lorraine had been seduced by the ardour of a Westmount dentist and was not available. To hell with her too, the bitch.

Jeff had considered that amazing girl Gaby who, only the week before, had scorned his physical mass and loused up his evening with a one-woman riot. But he was embarrassed to ask his salesman for her phone number. To hell with her too, the little French bitch. To hell with her too.

He had driven out to the country club. Solo. Perhaps he could connect with some unattached bit of fluff, a waitress or a chambermaid. He would tease her with erotic hints and insinuations, lubricate her with liquor and take her to his bed, snorting over her like a yearling bull.

But, no, this was not to be his night, it seemed. Neither to howl nor to hump. So he drank. Angrily, steadily.

He staggered across the dance floor and through the swinging door into a kitchen where sullen kitchen help and waitresses stood frozen like statues as a furious club steward hollered at them, "You only work here, you don't own the place, goddam!"

"The hell I don't!" Jeff shouted. "Do you know who I am?" He didn't wait for an answer but lurched out through another door and down the stairs to the men's dorm. He flopped onto a cot and pressed his face to the cool pillow. It smelled of sweat and he threw up on it. He heaved his way up the steps and out to the club grounds. He stretched out on the bench, face up. Jesus, he was sick. He loosened his tie and threw up again. He slipped off the bench and lay swearing in the puke. He fell asleep, snored.

When Arthur came out to cool off he saw the bulky body, he saw a little blood where the bald head had been scraped by the stone chips of the walk.

He bent over the drunk and asked, "Are you all right, mister? Do you need help?"

Cormack sat up and grinned. "I'm just fine, boy. I like lying in my own vomit, I like it mixed with my own blood. Look, boy, get me a towel and a bowl of warm water, on the double. And for Christ's sake, don't call me mister. What are you, a Greek or a Dago or something?" Suspicious, he said, "You must be a Jew. When you address me, call me sir."

Sir? Sir what? Sir Vomit? Sir Blood?

When Arthur returned with water and towel Cormack was seated on the bench, pushing a silver-stippled flask into a rear pocket. The teen-age Arthur in the white kitchen jacket dabbed the wet warm towel hesitantly over the bloody bald head.

"Careful, you bugger," Cormack complained, "that hurts."

"I'm sorry," the boy said.

"The hell you are. You know damn well you're not. Who in hell asked you anyway, Buttinski? Leave me alone, for Jesus' sake. I don't need you, you skinny kike. What's your name, Isaac, Abie, Jake?"

Jeff thought that was kind of funny. He chuckled. Then he started to weep, great, heaving, blubbery, baritone sobs.

"Goddam Alma, goddam Lorraine, goddam Gaby!" he wailed. "What a hell of a way to spend Saturday night...Christ, I'm sick...I'm not a very happy man...Look, son, I'm sorry I shouted...Stay with me, don't leave..."

He hoisted himself up and fell down again. The steward came prowling. He helped Cormack to his feet and was socked on the jaw for his trouble.

"Get lost, you lousy headwaiter!" Jeff roared.

"Yes, sir," said the steward and withdrew into the clubhouse.

Jeff shoved the boy toward the parking lot. He ordered Arthur to crank the car and motioned him to sit in front with him. The big man took the wheel and the car went bombing down the driveway and out of the grounds. They ripped along at forty, fifty, sixty, weaving erratically, barely avoiding ditches and skidding on gravel. Suddenly a building rose before them. Cormack braked hard, the car skidded and they came to a shuddering halt against the brick wall.

A cop emerged on the run from the police station, hoisting wide suspenders over naked shoulders, fumbling with his fly and inserting buttons into the wrong buttonholes. Behind him, one hand hitching up her skirt, the other clutching at a gaping bodice, appeared the well-endowed Madame Angelique, visibly annoyed because her coupling with the chronically horny constable had been interrupted at the moment of truth. "*Merde!*" she exclaimed and, in the spirit of bilingualism, translated the protest.

Cormack, shaken almost sober, got out of the car and bowed to Angelique. "Good evening, madame, I am Jeffery Cormack, at your service," and added, "I hope." He leered. "At this moment you look like a madonna. Or even the Virgin Mary. You are magnificent." He shook the policeman's hand. "Good evening, chief, it's a pleasure."

The cop thought to himself: these wealthy buggers, you can recognize them from a distance. They have a way. It's how they stand; they walk with authority, they command, they wear expensive clothes, their bellies are larded. They have an aura of dollars. I better show respect. He made another effort to rearrange his fly and gave up.

"Stop playing with yourself," madame hissed, rearranging the blue polka-dot blouse over her bust.

"What can I do for you, sir?" the cop asked Jeff.

"Well, chief," said Cormack, "I regret if I interrupted anything."

"Hah!" Angelique snorted.

"Anyway, chief, I want you to arrest this little Jewboy. He slandered my wife, kicked me in the scrotum, stole my automobile, kidnapped me, broke the speed limit, damaged your wall and flatulated four times."

What can that fancy word mean? Was it some kind of sex, the cop wondered, something dirty?

"That boy's a menace," Jeff warned. "He drinks the blood of virgins. He violates Christian girls on Passover. He makes bootleg wine. By the way, I'm thirsty. How about you, my dear madame?"

He directed a warped, boyish grin at Angelique.

"What'll I do with the prisoner?" the policeman asked. "What's the charge, treason, sodomy, spitting on the floor, assault, rape?"

"No, no, no, I'm a fair man. Just book him for disorderly."

Firmly the cop grasped the outraged Arthur by the neck and led him into the police station. "You can't do those things in this town. Shame on you."

"I didn't do anything," Arthur protested. "I didn't break any law. I only tried to help him; he was drunk."

"Bloody little Jewboy liar," said Cormack.

"*Maudit Juif* bum," said the cop.

"I'm not a bum, I work at the country club," Arthur protested.

"I don't want to hear any more of your immoral dirt!" the cop shouted, pushing him. Arthur fell and the policeman kicked him in the back, leaned over and punched his head and neck. Cormack laughed and slapped him hard across the face. Arthur cried out in pain and protest. The two men subdued him and threw him into a cell.

The cop and madame and Cormack drank from Jeff's flask. When it ran dry the law officer phoned for more.

"Napoleon," said the cop when the bootlegger arrived, "is a very good man. He's my wife's cousin and Angelique's brother. He's a good sport. How's business, Napoleon?"

"As long as somebody's thirsty, I don't starve."

"He's a philosopher, that Napoleon," the cop said.

Angelique, keen on public relations, chimed in, "As long as men get bothered in the crotch, I too won't starve. I'm the best there is, the hottest, the biggest, I give satisfaction. Ask anybody in town—they've all screwed me—the best people, bigshots, members of parliament, judges. Try me out, I can wake the dead. I always deliver but I don't give credit, it's always cash on the line. In advance."

They killed one 25-ouncer, the four of them, then another.

"Let's have some fun with the Jew," the cop said. "Him and Angelique."

Arthur was led out of his cell and given the choice. He could rot in a cage or ride Angelique to freedom, provided he was able to overcome her.

"You make me sick!" he exclaimed, and puked over the now-stupefied lady. He was flung back into the cell.

"You have insulted a lady!" the constable roared. "You ain't no gentleman!"

Jeff raised his hand and called for order. "Me," he said, "I don't like to waste anything, especially a well-built lady like this," and staggered over and managed to mount the angelical throne. The lady, in a stupor, waved Jeff's five-dollar bill, then passed out. Jeff was not discouraged and proceeded to romance his unconscious paramour.

"Bravo!" Napoleon cried.

"God bless lovers!" the cop exclaimed.

"Oh boy!" Cormack puffed. "Hallelujah!"

"Onward Christian soldiers!" Arthur sang from his cell.

"Shut your dirty mouth!" the constable bellowed. "You goddam Christ-killer!"

*

After Jeff, Napoleon, Angelique and the cop had left the scene to find further carousal farther afield, Arthur was the sole occupant of the building. He was wounded, weary, indignant and confused. He fell into an uncomfortable half-sleep on the straw pallet, squirming, closing his eyes against the flickering light bulb in the ceiling of his cell.

*

Georgina, the chambermaid at the country club, had in her innocence offered and asked for love, but he had run away and brooded for days on end because he had denied her need, offended his self-respect and compounded loneliness for both of them.

And now tonight as he lay on his iron bed in this village jailhouse he was angry and humiliated because that stupid cow Angelique, who went to bed with anyone for money, had been thrust at him and he had been ordered to perform like a barnyard beast, and he had ended up contemptible in the eyes of a small-town cop, a metropolitan sales executive and a village bootlegger because he, Arthur Meller, the country club kitchen-boy, had not been man enough to ride the rolls of whorish blubber like some drunken freak and titillate three horny drunks.

As he lay in his cell, this young man, not quite eighteen years of

age, mourned his lost illusions. What had happened to all those
dreams about beautiful bodies in communion? The crude realities
left little room for loveliness.

He recalled how at the wholesale house he had overheard his boss
boasting of bedroom conquests. Aaron had confessed to moral
reservations; he despised the common whore and favoured young
widows, unmarried business ladies and divorcees. Yet he admitted
that on occasion he had been attracted to what he called the
"high-class professional," usually a perfect lady with all the social
graces, the freelancer whose good looks, lush figure and sexual
expertise excited his admiration as well as his libido.

Arthur thought uneasily of the fleshpots of The Main, in
particular the walkdown basement dance-hall in a factory building
occupied mainly by needle-trades shops across the street from the
dry-goods house where he used to work. It was a noisy hangout for
thrill-hungry youngsters and middle-aged sports and for the pimps
and whores and bootleggers who serviced them.

In a section near the back corridor were the washrooms, male and
female, separated only by head-high partitions. Assignations were
often arranged in the adjoining passageway. Aaron called it "the
bucket of blood and clap."

An elderly couple, stern and grey, operated the enterprise. The
woman sat at the cash and sold admissions. The old man prowled
the dance floor to enforce a decorum of sorts. The police were paid
off to stay away. The owners were a very devout pair; for High
Holy Days they suspended operations.

From this venereal shrine St. Lawrence Boulevard (which was
hardly a boulevard but just a shabby, shuffling street) oozed its
way south like a festering sore. Arthur shuddered as he recalled the
time he had opened a door near the foot of this street, climbed the
stairs, was greeted by a whore, and fled in fear and disgust.

Now exhausted and depressed, he twisted and turned on the hard
bed in his jailhouse cell until he fell asleep.

*

At the country club the surviving dancers stumbled into the
disintegrating night.

Waiters sweated, chambermaids wilted, the kitchen people
moved more and more like automatons.

*

On an immaculately cropped lawn, under yellow floodlights,
somnambulistic old gentlemen in white flannels and blue blazers
methodically bowled away their silent, slow-motion leisure.

4

**1939. September. Days of Fear.
A Small Room at Laura's.**

ROSE IS IN her bedroom. It is 2 a.m. and she cannot sleep. She has
been to the hospital to enquire about her son.

"He's getting the best possible attention. Don't worry, Mrs.
Meller, trust us."

Trust them?

She and her sister Laura were allowed to look at him for a
moment, two moments, and were then led out of Intensive Care by
a nurse, were guided down the corridor and hurried along past the
bench occupied (requisitioned?) by the red-headed detective, were
ushered to the exit by the friendly young nurse (whose parts were
again assessed by the sullen officer) and were wished a hearty
goodnight and again urged not to worry.

It is 2:30 a.m. and Rose sits in the dark on the hard edge of her
bed.

At fifty-eight years of age, she faces her sixth crisis. The first was
her wedding night, fear contesting with ardour, ardour with
propriety. Later came the pain and the fear and the hope of
Arthur's birth. Then the day when Max walked away from them,
the valises dragging him down, his eyes burdened with defeat, her
own eyes afraid for him. Then the day after his death, when they
took her to identify the body she had once lain with. And then the
summer of her ordeal. And now Arthur.

Again she is afraid.

*

That man on the hospital cot is my son. How pitifully white is my son's face.

*

That woman on the edge of her bed is your mother.
   How pitifully white is your mother's face.
   How pale the blue of the eyes.
   How grey the hair.

*

I groaned and wept...and I heaved and he was born...and then I sighed...I smiled when I heard his cry and saw his face.
   I gave him his life.
   He has to live, he must.
   You'll see, he will.
   You'll see.
   O God, he must.

1922. Summer. Days of Fear.
Blessed Are the Meek.

Life began again at forty. Rose Meller went back to the factory, to men's clothing, to the kind of job she quit when she married Max. Back to the crowded streetcars, early morning and late afternoon. Back to the bench, the sweat, the shop. Back to the sweatshop bench, the speed-up, the piecework, the machine. Back to the foreman and the boss.
   Start all over again. Meekly, modestly.
   Blessed are the modest meek. The meek...
   For they shall inherit...

5

1939. September. Night.
Weary Hospital Blues.

IN THE PROLONGED hush of the weary hospital night you have not
opened your eyes, not once.

They measure your pulse, take your temperature, adjust the
intravenous feeding rig and check its bottle.

Detective Gilbert fights off sleep all night on his rump-numbing
bench at the end of the corridor outside Intensive Care. Later he
will nod to the doctor on duty, ask about his prisoner's condition,
phone headquarters and wait for his relief to replace him.

Strangers telephone the hospital and ask about you. They write
fervent letters. Telegrams of concern travel thousands of miles
from people neither you nor Gaby ever knew.

*

Names and faces and days and places, vague fears and feelings and
uncomprehending pain drift through the haze of your pallid unconsciousness. Lost years chide you on your dead-white, dread-
white hospital bed.

Names and places and days and faces...

School days, remembered or forgotten days, dear old golden rule
days...Here's old Christopher, lanky presence of dour mien, and
sparse carrot-hair, military moustache precisely clipped, Scottish
burr, a sixtyish schoolmaster snapping "You Jews!" at a stubborn
boy, immediately despising himself but continuing the lesson, and
at the end of the period apologizing to the class, later the same day
taking the boy to dinner at the Christopher home...Here's
Christopher guiding you through *The Aeneid:*

"*Sunt lacrimae rerum...?*"

"The woes of the world bring tears to the eyes."

"*Et mentem mortalia tangunt...?*"

"And mankind's deep distress afflicts our souls."

Just tell it straight, Arthur. Skip the sad music and the grace
notes, pull the chain and flush the frills. Now what else do you

remember from Mr. Christopher's Latin at Montreal High? Or Mr. Lockwood's English—pale, black-haired Lockwood, slender and severe, with a face as sad as a death-mask and the poet's love of words. And those other teachers, who could inspire you—and did—and those others again who corroded the souls of boys and left them hollow.

"And slowly answered Arthur from the bilge. . ."

That should be barge, wise guy, barge. Now continue.

"The old order changeth, yielding place to new. . ."

Enunciate your Tennyson distinctly. It's order, not ordure. Ordure is for foreigners; British subjects merit more. Now, enunciate! Articulate! All right, go on, finish.

"And God fulfills himself in many ways. . ."

Right. Remember that. Always. And articulate. Always. Now sit down. Yes? What now, Meller?

"Just for a handful of silver he left us, just for a riband to stick in his coat. . ."

Sit down, smart-ass. And don't sneer. You merely manifest plebeian pique. To sneer is unbecoming a poet, whose language should be pure-distilled and elegantly buffed. Browning, understand, was galled because they didn't make him poet laureate. Resenting Wordsworth, as you know, had made him petulant.

Well, that's all for today. Go to the washroom, Meller, and purge yourself, and while you're there please memorize his *Pippa Passes*. And remember, always articulate.

"Sir, shouldn't that be *Papa Pisses*?"

*

They expect you to open your eyes and greet your friends gravely, after your shy fashion, to smile and assert with earnest conviction and deep feeling your personal and public revelation:

"The old order changeth, yielding place to new. . . to new. . . to new. . . to new. . ."

1922. Summer Night.
Jailhouse Blues. The Men.

This place is no plush lounge of private club for flush old boys, but if you closed your eyes to blur the shape of things, you could perhaps invoke the subdued murmurs of drowsing lords soothing their gullets with liqueurs after a trencherman input of gourmand meats.

Alas, this was no goddam affluent retreat for goddam overstuffed men filling goddam overstuffed chairs. Anyone could belong—the drunk and the declassed, the outcast, dispossessed, the bum and thief and even fools. Anyone could belong. Here was a democracy of the despised.

From one of the cells a tired voice droned in the dry, patient rhythm of such voices, and you listened not so much to the words as to their sound and the gravelly masculine timbre, until you were mesmerized by a huskiness borne gently like drowsy cargoes to your bewitched senses. Arthur Meller was reminded of an uncle, his mother's only brother, a cigarmaker, a small, poor man of creased face, furrowed forehead, sensuous full lips and the gentlest of black eyes, a smile of experience and infinite charity and a diction of utter weariness.

Now from the dark boxed-in cave in a corner of the gloomy cell-block the dry voice of a brittle old man recited a rambling string of reminiscences. His listeners cared little whether it was bull or fantasy or gospel truth; all they knew was that it helped them forget their boredom for a while.

They sprawled on their bunks soaking it all up—the wild lies and the savage wisdom and the old man's pride in his folly—and they hungered for more, like children begging for another bedtime story, yet gleefully heckling, laughing with pleasure, listening, awake but dreaming that they felt good as long as the thin, weather-beaten prisoner spoke truth or told lies to nourish their starved souls, and stared out of his pale and cynical old eyes into the night of the cells.

Now as he lay on his bunk he floated away to another place and time, up and out of his cell, up and away from the cell-block, up higher and freed from the jail's gravity pull, up and flying like a lone blue heron, angular wings flapping in awkward slow-motion westward across the prairies, gliding over the Rockies, low above the Georgia Strait, and swinging, dipping down, diving, swooping, landing abruptly on a sidewalk before the dowager Empress Hotel.

New Year's Eve in Victoria, and raining. Ring out, rain out the old!

He was on the friggin' lawn of the friggin' Empress, getting wet. On the other side of the clammy cold walls it was dry and warm and people clinked glasses and gorged while he hunted butts on the soggy grass. His feet were wet and his throat was dry and the rain soaked him to the bone. He felt faint from hunger and couldn't even find a weed to comfort him. Jesus, it was New Year's Eve, and here he was shooting snipes in the gutter in vain in this friggin' rain. Happy-crappy New Year, everybody!

Back in his cell in the cell-block in Quebec in the sultry summer night the rasping voice paused. "I thought I heard a whisper, like 'Hey there, wait.' He din't sound like no cop, he din't look like no cop. He was a guy maybe forty-five, fifty, wearin' a black coat with beaver collar and cuffs, a grey hat and grey gloves and a red silk scarf. His face was dead white, like his hands, like a corpse. When he come closer I could sniff the strong smell of money in his wallet. I din't mind that, there's worse things in life.

"'My good man,' he said, 'I wish to talk with you.' Christ Jesus, his good man! 'Why?' I asked. 'Because,' he said, 'you're down and out and you got nothin' to lose. I need to talk, I'm in trouble, I'm very unhappy and I got to talk to somebody even worse off than me. Tell me, have you ever been in love?'

"He acted nervous and started talkin' faster and louder. 'Mister,' I said, 'you don't need to shout, I ain't deaf. No, I never been in love; I don't hold with that crap, it's too risky.'

"Well, he shakes his head sadly and puts a hand on my shoulder. 'That's my problem, friend. I fell for the upstairs maid, you could say I made the maid. I knocked her up and she had an abortion and now she needs blood. Would you oblige?'

"I din't like this story one little bit. I could smell trouble, like police court and prison bars. I started to walk away, but he grabbed my arm with fingers like steel claws and begged me, 'Please, I'll pay good.' I just kept walkin'. He followed right behind and he was damn near cryin'. 'All right,' he says, 'I guess you don't believe me. I'll tell you the God's truth. It's my wife. She was jealous of my mistress and tried to commit suicide but she bungled the job and might croak if she don't get blood right away. It can be embarrassin' for a man in my position. Lookit, you don't need all that blood; I'm sure you can spare a few pints.'

"He kept on coaxin'. He said, 'Lookit, I have a fine home, it's warm and dry, the rugs are ankle-deep and I got every type liquor you can name, and then some, and every type grub you ever dreamed of, all ready cooked and sizzlin' with flavour.' "

(O comfort ye, my people!)

A voice called out, "Pass the caviar!" and another, "Pass the pate de fois gras!" and another, "Pass the friggin' gravy...Pass the lobster...Pass the steak!" A man belched and exclaimed, "What a bouquet, what a superb port wine, just right for the baloney!"

From his cage the old man resumed, "'Ask for anything,' the guy begged. 'You want girls? You can have any colour, skinny or plump, savage or shy, kinky or straight. Two together, three, four? They're yours. Just ask. Come to my house, give a little blood. Eat, drink, have your kicks. You name it, anythin'! Sleep, wake up and go on your way in the mornin' after a banquet of a breakfast. No obligation. You're no worse off, in fact a lot better, and twenty bucks ahead. All you do is give a little blood. You won't miss it.'

"So I go with this guy. He hails a cab and we wind up on a wide empty street full of trees and bushes. At the end of the street there's a high iron gate with spiked bars. He pulls a rope and clangs a bell and soon a butler opens the gate and we go in. The gate closes behind us and we walk down a driveway and into another world."

A man coughed, another snored, one broke wind.

"A mansion! You shoulda seen the insides: logs burnin' in a king-size fireplace, and one of those grand pianos with its lid held up on a stick, and hand-painted pictures, marble statues, long oak tables, a suit of armour, fat leather chairs, chandeliers, squawkin' birds in fancy cages, a spooky Siamese cat and a purple French poodle on cushions. In a pool sunk in the floor there was big fat goldfish swimmin' around. And that was only the parlour.

"This white-face guy told the butler to see I should have a hot shower with plenty of soap. He told him to get clean duds for me and throw out my old rags. After I got cleaned up and dressed I went back into this big room. Servants brought me hot soup and appetizers, just for starters. After smoke turkey and cranberries I et roast goose with pickled apples. For dessert there was ice-cream and strawberries out of season and a couple slugs cognac."

From the depths of the cell-block a prisoner pretended to gag.

"White-Face came in and offered me a Cuban cigar. While I blew smoke-rings he says to me, 'Lookit, I like you, so I'll level. It ain't the maid and it ain't my wife. It's my maw. She's a very sensitive dame, clean-livin' and very refined, like a nun, practically a virgin. She's in trouble. The butler did it and she had to have an abortion, poor Mum. You got to help her. She needs blood. Speakin' man to man, I beg you to help her!'

"The guy had class. But you know what I said? I said, 'Mister, don't give me none of that shit. What do you really want?' So he told me."

"What did he want, Dad?" a young voice sneered. "You?"

"Shut up, you little prick, don't interrupt. Anyways, he only wanted blood. Not for his maid or his wife or mistress or even his maw. Just for hisself. You see, boys, he was a vampire."

"What the hell's that, Pop?"

"Jesus, din't you learn nothin' in school?"

"Like Dracula, Pop? You mean to drink?"

"Yeah, he drinks it. Anyways, I give him blood. I was on the skids, I needed the cash. Besides, the house was warm, the grub was out of this world, the liquor flowed like a fountain. So I give him a quart. It was easy, din't hurt a bit. He just jabbed a needle in my arm and the blood came out through a tube into a quart bottle of genuine cut-glass. He said thank you, sleep well, and retired with his nightcap.

"The butler came over and said, 'Will there be anythin' else, sir?' and I settled down at the table and begun stuffin' my face all over again till I was damn near bustin' with steak and goulash and chop suey. I gorged like a friggin' king, then I guzzled booze like the world was runnin' dry.

"After I stopped burpin' the butler asked was that all. I said, 'Hell, no, I ain't started yet. The night's a pup. Bring the girls!'

"He took me upstairs on a little elevator into a room with soft lights and jazzy music playin' and silk cushions all over, and a bar stacked with booze.

"A naked girl run in and kissed me and another naked girl run in and undressed me and three other naked broads run in and flipped me onto a queen-size wall-to-wall bed and then the whole stark-naked gang, all five, they giggled and squealed and pushed theirselves over and under me like sex maniacs fresh out of solitary."

"Five dames, Dad? Only five?"

"Well, son, my name ain't Samson. I was wacked out. When I woke up in the mornin' I was weak like a kitten. And then this

Dracula guy tapped me for another quart. For his breakfast, I guess. He had a nice pink glow on his face now. He give me twenty bucks.

"But I ain't nobody's fool, so I says, 'Mister, I got to get back to my gramma in Moose Jaw and twenty bucks won't go far. Could I have an extra ten?' So he frowns and says, 'Very well.' Then I say, 'Could I have a signed paper, like a receipt, to show I ain't a bum if I get picked up for vag because I'm so pale now? Could you pack me a little lunch and a flask of something to wash it down?' So he smiles and says, 'Very well, I suppose we can do that,' and tears a page from a pad and writes:

"'Jan. 1—$30 worth of blood. Paid in full, cash. Plus food, drink, shelter, also entertainment. The donor is a gentleman and a scholar and nobody is under no obligation, not me, not him.'

"He signed it, walked me to the door, shook hands and said to call again sometime. His cook, a fat eunuch with tits, led me down the driveway and slammed the gate on my arse with a giggle and 'Good luck, sir!'

"I had thirty bucks blood-money and my receipt and a bag of cold chicken and sausage, a buttered bun, two tangerines and a deck of smokes, also a mickey of rum. I had a bitch of a hangover, a king-size head from the night before, but I was startin' New Year's Day with thirty dollars in my pants pocket, a real solid citizen. I was floatin' on a cloud, even with the missin' blood, maybe because of it.

"I crossed over to Vancouver the same day and when I got off the ferry I looked up a lady who lived in a old shack near the water. What did she do? She saved souls on skid road. You could say she was a kind of a missionary. I bought a gallon of wine from a bootlegger and we never left her place for a week, except to get a refill and some grub.

"Well, all good things got to end. One day she give me a mickey finn and when I woke up I was in the cooler again. All my money was gone. All I had left was a hangover. So when they finally sprung me a month later I hopped a freight. But in Moose Jaw a railroad dick bust my nose. I lost lots of blood. This time I din't get paid for it.

"Next mornin' before the blood was hardly dry on my face I was hauled into police court. I told them about the vampire. The magistrate said I gotta be some kind of tanked-up wino and maybe

I shoulda been drownded at birth. I showed him the receipt. He said it din't prove nothin' and din't tell who give who what. He said they'd check the Victoria end. Meantime they'd hold me for thirty days. Next time I was in court a Victoria gumshoe took the stand and told the beak how this vampire bugger told him I bummed him for a handout and how the man took pity—a real Christian gentleman—and give me a night's shelter, and then I paid him back by stealin' fifty bucks and other things. The blood? What blood? 'Oh that,' the vampire says, 'that was when this here sex maniac got drunk and tried to rape my mother. He cut himself on her garter.'

"So I got eight months in the clink. That was ten friggin' years ago."

The blurred eyes stared at the ceiling of the cell, the dry lips rested. Young Arthur Meller, in his own cell, leaned forward.

"They can't do that," he said, incredulous.

"The hell they can't," the old-timer mocked.

A key turned in a lock and a slippered night guard shuffled down the corridor, poking flashlight beams through bars onto faces suddenly asleep. "Garbage," he muttered, finished his rounds and slammed and locked the iron door of the cell-block.

The dry voice resumed its narrative. "Well, that son of a bitch of a vampire was rich and I made up my mind to take him for every goddam dollar I could get. When I finished my stretch I bummed my way back to Victoria and sued him for fifty thousand bucks' damages.

"My lawyer told the court I used to be a husky guy. 'Look at him now, your lordship, his health's been ruined!' The judge give me a glance like he was goin' to puke. He threw out the case. I got sore and hollered, 'Hell, judge, you can't do that!' So he fined me twenty-five smackers for contempt of court.

"I appealed the case. I lost again. I blew my top and called the judge a queer. I got thirty days. I said, 'You can't do that to me!' and got an extra month.

"I went right up to the Supreme Court and got screwed again. I screamed, 'You can't do that!' They just yawned.

"I decided I'd push my case right up to the Privy Council, that's the highest court in the whole friggin' Empire."

"Where'd you get all that money for all them lawyers?" a skeptic asked from the dark.

"Where? I sold my blood, gallons of blood. Hospitals, labs, anyplace I could peddle it. That's where I got the money. And that's the reason I always look so pale now, I can't afford my own blood.

"Anyways, they ruled my receipt was no friggin' good because it din't say the place or year and my name wasn't on it, and the receipt said, 'Paid in full,' and also, they couldn't tell who give who what, and was it pig, chicken or human blood, and besides, anybody could see I was a bum, and blood from a skid road bum wouldn't fetch more than maybe two-bits a quart. Finally, they said, this vampire bloodsucker wasn't no human bein' anyways, so the law couldn't touch him no ways."

The old convict stopped. He was finished and sleepy now.

"They can't do that," a man sneered.

"The hell they can't," said the ancient prisoner. He laughed a short bark of a laugh and the cell-block was silent for a while.

Arthur spoke softly from his cage in the dark. "They can do anything they like, can't they?"

"You better believe it," the old man said.

PART FOUR

1

1939. September.
Night-Shift Hospital Blues.

LOOK, ARTHUR, your nurse is weary, bone-weary. It's the middle of the night. She sighs heavily.

What's bothering her? She's tired, that's all. She's a little bit blue and would rather be home.

Just don't spoil the night for her, don't die during her shift.

She is young and vibrant and has not yet known the act of love.

She is young and vital and is not yet accustomed to the sight of death.

*

What do you want, girl, what do you dream?

Do you know our wells have been poisoned, their brackish waters warping your mind and making you believe you're nothing, driving you to fight stubbornly for mediocrity, and perpetuating your humiliation, breeding it into your daughters and granddaughters? And turning your sons into jocks who despise you?

*

Forty-nine daughters of Danaus, King of Argos, were doomed to draw water with sieves from a pool in the world of the dead.

No matter how steadfastly they scooped, they could never fill the vessels.

105

It was said that on command of the father, on her wedding night, each of the forty-nine sisters had murdered her husband.

And this was their punishment:

The Danaides would be forever tormented by conscience and frustration, condemned to labour eternally, never allowed to forget their crime, their father's crime.

Except once, when they hear the song of Orpheus searching and grieving in the Underworld for his lost Eurydice, and the sisters pause in their labour to listen to the lament of the bereft lover.

For a while they forget their own misfortune as they weep for Orpheus and his Eurydice.

Perhaps they are now able to weep for themselves.

1922. Summer Search.
The Women: Gaby.

One idle day when I happened to promenade past the gloomy old Fraser Library, downtown a little way below St. Catherine, I had an impulse to "look myself up." I went in. Of course I'm not so vain as to expect my name would be in the encyclopedia, like this:

"Lajeunesse, Gabrielle, b. 1904 La Macaza, Quebec, Canada, grandchild of Ovide Lesage, mariner, freethinker; daughter of Madeleine, widow, suicide; and of Dominique Lajeunesse, soldier, farmer, mutineer summarily killed in a post-war 'incident'; rebellious young woman, free spirit, seeker after happiness; passionate (very); affectionate, slender, blonde, blue-eyed, healthy, and so on."

No, it wasn't vanity or conceit or grandeur. What I looked for was something different. I searched the dictionaries under *W*. I thought if I learned something about *women* I would learn about myself, about Gaby Lajeunesse. That's me. I'm a woman, eighteen years old and curious. I had to know what the world thought about us—in general, officially, by definition on paper. Did I fit the type or didn't I?

So I looked myself up in the big *Webster,* the unabridged one, and this is what it said:

A woman is "an adult female of the human race, a full-grown female, as distinguished from a man, boy or child, and sometimes, but not as a rule, from a girl."

I discovered something else, that "the characteristic qualities of womankind" are "timidity, modesty, mildness, tenderness, etc.," that a man who is called womanish is "one who is effeminate, cowardly, emotional or weak," that "to play the woman" meant "to give way to unmanly emotion, to weep," that "a woman of the town" is a whore, but "a woman of the world" is "a woman skilled in the ways of the world; one engrossed in society or the fashionable life, a society woman."

Other characterizations informed me that a woman was "a female attendant, a paramour, mistress."

I looked up *female* and found her nature to be "tender, delicate, weak," and "tender, soft."

Then I checked *feminism* and the crabby old *Webster* editor frowned on me from a sepulchre and chanted a sing-song catechism:

"Feminism is a theory, cult or movement on the part of those who assert and advocate what they consider the rights of women, and who favour doing away with all social, economic and political restrictions on the sex."

So, maybe. And maybe I'm unlady-like and maybe immodest and maybe I'm indelicate and tough. But excuse me, please, *mon vieux,* if I cry *Merde!* (That's like your English word, but better.)

Anyway, towards the end of that summer I was getting restless. I was eighteen, after all, and I didn't see much of a future for an independent girl with no trade or profession, just working at odd jobs in factories or like a salesgirl in a store. I looked around and found an empty little place on a sidestreet off Sherbrooke, near the university, almost across the way from the main facade.

I started off cleaning the store, gave it a coat of paint to make it attractive. I displayed a bunch of second-hand novels and picture-books (my own) and hung up some art prints and laid out a bunch of wood carvings, pottery, costume jewelry and knick-knacks, a few hand-hooked floor-mats, leatherwork, things like that. The craftsmen let me have it on loan; if and when I sold their stuff I'd pay for it.

I hoped people would get to know my shop, people looking for gifts, tourists wanting souvenirs but not junk. I had a little money Grandpa had left me, enough to pay the rent for a while and buy some bread-and-butter stock like pens, pencils, notebooks and art supplies for the students. I even showed little jars of jam I'd put up myself and had a corner for potted plants I offered for sale.

Well, after Labour Day I was in business. I didn't do too badly, I got by, I was my own boss and my own woman. Of course, I warned myself, it mustn't take over my whole life, it's only a living.

The shop was where I first met Arthur.

1922. Summer Hell.
The Women: Rose.

You've lost your husband, your home and your domesticity. You're not a normal woman any more, Rose. You're in deep disgrace, Rose. You have become an object of pity. "How pathetic. That poor Mrs. Meller. He walked out on her. I wonder why. Imagine, he drowned himself. He must have had a reason."

Decent people will blame you, they will surely avoid you. Moralists will scorn you and hordes of the unctuous will hiss denunciation. You will be spat on when you try to shop at the Rachel market; the farm wives will blanch and cross themselves. You will be hated and hunted. The tarts will taunt you from every street corner. Little children will run from that wicked old witch; they'll call you Crazy Rosie.

It's all your fault, you were a bad wife, you managed poorly, you squandered, you were a rotten mother, you were selfish. Worst of all, you failed. You're a loser, a misfit, a cripple, a freak.

You're one of the wretched, the meek. You are not blessed and you will not inherit the earth.

*

The sun is low, but the clammy heat curdles my clothing, the starch has been sweated out of my yellow cotton dress, I am weak and drowning in my sweat.

I sit at the silent sewing machine and even though it has stopped clattering, and the humid work-day is finished, I simply haven't got the strength to get up and go home. There's a buzzing in my ears. I've almost forgotten where I live. Am I still in my own flat? Of course not, I live with Laura. Where's Arthur? Oh, he's away at the golf club. Well, anyway he's in the country, thank God. It'll be a nice summer for him, hobnobbing with the Four Hundred. They tip well. It could lead to a good job.

But I must go home now. That's it, punch the clock, my name's on the card, Rose Meller. Pick up my purse. Go out through the doorway, the factory door, down the stairs and into the street.

God, it's hot. I'd better get home to my flat and get into some fresh clothes, a housedress. Max will be waiting for supper. And Arthur. Growing boys eat a lot. It would be nice after supper to go to Cartierville on the big tram. Where it's cool, near the water, the three of us. I remember once, when Arthur was very small, we used to... No, not now, not any more, not for poor Max.

I'm confused. Who am I? How old am I? What year is it, which day, why is it so hot? Did it snow only yesterday? Where has it all gone?

Take hold of yourself. No hysteria. Please.

The factory, I remember it from long ago. Now or before or forever, it's still the factory.

Here's the park. I have to sit down, I don't feel good. I must sit down on that green wooden bench, under the tree, in the shade. Do trees feel, do they think? I'll feel better when I close my eyes. I'll rest a while.

I'm Rose Meller, forty, and back where I started. Only it's worse this time. How empty I am, how scared!

I wish my son were here on the bench beside me. I would talk to him. Would he understand? I hope they're not working him too hard. It must be cool at the country club. I guess they have big fans everywhere. He must remember to eat well and get enough sleep. I must write him not to pick up any bad habits. I hope one of these days he'll find a nice job, a really nice job in a nice store or an office, and work his way up. He's a bright boy, he's honest and polite and he's likeable. Good-looking too. We could have a nice home, nice furniture. On a nice street with nice neighbours.

My God, I'm so ashamed of myself.

Why, Max?

If only...

*

She sat on the bench, absorbing the green peace of trees, grass and flowers, raising her face to the faintest flutters of the breeze, yearning to touch the white cushions of cloud. Enviously Rose watched the passersby, beautiful women, fortunate women who have husbands and homes and household chores and happy chatter to share, and physical intimacies. Don't they realize their miraculous good fortune? Where is their ecstasy?

She will sit here a little longer, only a short while, to rest. She will stop at the market to pick up strawberries. Max likes berries, so does Arthur. After supper they will go to Laura's.

Laura? Who? Max? Who? Arthur? She's been day-dreaming of course. Nerves. A bad dream. It'll pass.

*

I see this girl moving along the path in the park, a few yards, slowly, looking over her shoulder. She is graceful and lovely in her youth.

A man follows, anonymous and impersonal; it's his job to keep the girls off the streets.

She has seen his eyes and she is afraid. Such men treat women like animals, like enemies; they do not court, they rape.

I watch the girl. She looks nervously at the detective. He draws his gun.

I run to help her and the man throws me to the ground and kicks and curses me. I am going to die. Help me, Max! Arthur, Mother, help me!

"I am the law," he intones. "I am life and death. Rose Meller, you've broken the law, for you have blue eyes and yellow hair. Get back to your machine, Rose Meller. Sweat and shiver!"

I am fingerprinted, stripped and searched, tried in court and sentenced to thirty years for gross indecency. The evidence is that I have no husband.

I am dying, the blood floods my eyes and I can't see. My cell is deep down under a putrid lake. Green slime drips from the walls. I am bleeding to death.

Max!

Who is the cadaver sprawled on my plank bed? She smiles and I recognize the sweet young girl of the park.

"My God, I'm so ashamed. I've never been in a jail before."

"You've been framed. You and me too."

"Framed? I don't understand."

"Framed. You know, tricked, conned, set up. Where have you

been all these years? You know, one way or another we're all
framed the minute we're born, all we women. That's all there is,
there ain't no more. That's life, sister. You better accept it and live
with it.''

                                    *

During the night every few hours a clock strikes and a procession of
grotesque figures comes lumbering in like golems. They circle my
cubicle and leave. None of these creatures speaks. There is the boss
and the straw-boss and a regiment of detectives. My God, they all
have Max's face. Yet they look at me imploringly.

What have they done to you, Max?

And you, Max, what have you done to me?

I'm thirsty. I see a tin cup on a chain. I must wash it thoroughly.
Who knows what pestilence it holds, what wretch last used it? Odd,
there's no tap. Where's the tap?

Max, get me a glass of water, please. I don't feel so good.

I keep forgetting. Max is dead, drowned at Cartierville. How can
I ever drink water again? Max dead?

Arthur, are you asleep? Please, son, get me a drink of water. Let
it run a while to cool. But I forget, Arthur isn't home, he's at
Pointe Claire, at the club. I hope he's all right.

I'm crying. Am I that unhappy? I'm behaving like a child, yet
I'm the mother of a young man of seventeen. Or is it eighteen?

I've never wanted more than other women, never to own more or
enjoy more or be more.

I must have fallen asleep. I'm slouched on a park bench. That's
undignified, like a tramp. I feel sick. I had better go home. Where?

Now I know. Opposite the Hotel Dieu on St. Urbain. The door
to my upstairs flat is locked and I can't get in; I must have lost
my key. Who took the curtain from the door-glass, my pretty ecru
lace? I'll ring the bell; Max will open the door, Arthur will kiss me.

I'm tired, my head throbs. I'd better ring the bell again. And
again. Once more. Can't they hear me?

Don't they want me?

Who are all these people? Why do they stare? Don't they know
me, their neighbour?

                                    *

Laura came to fetch her sister. She led her home, like a lost child. "You're tired, Rose. You'll have a nice bath. I'll make your bed. You won't go back to the shop. I'll look after you. When Arthur comes back you'll be well again."

She undressed her sister, sponged her body, bathed her and clad her in a fresh nightgown. She spread cool bedsheets and pillowslips. She filled a vase with fresh flowers.

A doctor came and ordered rest, tonics and sympathy, and no excitement.

Laura would sit at her bedside, speaking softly, patiently as to a child. She drew the blinds down during the day to keep out the heat but allow a little light, and at night she parted the curtains so that a breeze might enter, and starlight. She fed her sister and bathed her and hummed softly as though to a small daughter. She watched to detect any hint of change in the listless woman. It was as though Rose's mind had been shifted onto a siding and was waiting for something to happen, for a connection, but had forgotten what.

"She's been hurt terribly," Laura told her children. She hinted that Max was to blame. How could a dead man hurt anyone? they wondered.

Weeks passed. Rose began to leave her bed and sit by the window, little aware of what she saw, for she said nothing and seemed to move in a trance. Laura thought it would help if she took her outside. They walked below the mountain nearly every afternoon. She was happy that Rose slept more soundly now.

The doctor came by regularly and approved. All a matter of time, he said. Patient care, kindness, clean and cheerful surroundings—all the things she didn't have at the factory—that's the best medicine. She's obviously a sensitive woman and she's had her share of trouble. Sweatshops are hard on such people. It would take time, Laura would need patience.

"You know," he said, "they say patience..."

"I know, a virtue," she filled in with just a trace of impatience. She frowned.

The doctor smiled tentatively. "You've been under a great deal of pressure," he said kindly. "I can imagine your worries, but nerves won't help you or your sister, you know. Try to relax."

"I suppose so, doctor. I'll try."

"That's the good girl. Everything will turn out fine, you'll see. You're a good sister. I'm depending on you."

How could you be anything but a good sister to Rose? She watched the doctor's horse and buggy move sedately away. Such women as Rose are always victims. She sighed, then swore angrily.

Blessed are the meek, for they shall inherit... What?

*

How is it possible that in all my forty years you were never aware of me?

I am Rose, widow of Max.

My father was a devout man. You ought to remember him; he believed in you. Did you believe in him? Did he believe in you in vain?

When I was young I worked in men's clothing, and also recently.

I worked in sweatshops. Have you ever seen the inside of a sweatshop, dear God?

Then why have you forsaken me?

1922. And Summers Past.
The Women: Irma.

Your name? My name is Irma Gillespie.

Your age? I'm sixty-five.

Place of birth? Charlottetown.

Where is that? Prince Edward Island.

Father's occupation? He was a doctor.

Your mother? She was a minister's daughter.

Are your parents living? No, they're dead.

Any brothers or sisters? None.

Race? White.

Nationality? Canadian.

Parents' country of origin? Both born here, in New Brunswick, that is.

Grandparents? Two were from Scotland, two from England.

Religion of grandparents? On my father's side Presbyterian, on my mother's Anglican.

*

I used to love the sea. I suppose I still do, but it's more than forty-five years since I left my home and I have never gone back. My father once told me that the Micmac Indians called our province *Abegweit*. I think it means a house on the waves or cradled on the waves. Father said Jacques Cartier landed there in 1534 and France ruled us for 200 years, then England ruled us, then she let us withdraw from Nova Scotia, to which we belonged, and we became a separate colony. We finally joined Canada about fifty years ago.

At home I often went to the waterfront with my school chums and we'd look at the big ships and wonder about the strange little puffed-up squids floating like tiny toy umbrellas near the deep harbour wall. I'd watch the dark water for hours and listen to the gulls crying and throw them bits of bread and watch them dive.

When visitors came "from away," from the mainland, they were always amazed to see our soil; it looked so odd to them, so red under the city grass, so very red under the green of the farms, so rust-red everywhere.

In the warm weather, on our holidays, we'd travel to the north shore and walk barefoot across the miles of sand, and gather scores of seashells, and climb the shifting dunes behind the beaches, and pick the wild flowers clinging to the dunes.

And my God! The ocean rolling in forever! And the sun kissing the sky and warming our bodies! The salt water whitecaps tumbling, the land soft and sensual underfoot, the wind caressing!

The summer I was twelve we spent two weeks wandering around Covehead Bay and Rustico Bay and their fishing villages with their boats and weathered old sheds and stacks of lobster traps. We dug clams for chowder and we boiled lobsters and fried thick cod steaks in newly churned butter.

I'd sit on an overturned dory and watch the big herons standing like slate-coloured statues on one long stick of a leg in the wet sand. They didn't seem to mind me staring from the dock. They just stared back.

A fishing captain agreed to take us to the mackerel grounds. We sailed out twenty miles or so. Stretching away to the north and east of us was the Gulf of St. Lawrence, and east beyond that the Atlantic, thousands of miles of it, and beyond that the rest of the world.

Father showed me how to use wafer-thin squares of mackerel,

mostly skin, about half an inch, which we stuck on a hook at the end of a hand-held line. The hook showed, but it didn't matter, the fish bit anyway and got caught when you jerked the line a little.

Have you ever seen a school of mackerel scudding beyond your bow on a fine summer day, fluttering the sea, moving towards you as you lie at anchor? They swim just below the surface, thousands of them, and agitate the water and make it tremble, and the sea sparkles in the sun, and then they're gone, scurrying. Suddenly they're taking your bait, and you haul in your line, and nearly every time there's a fish on the hook. You shake it off and throw it into a box or a barrel, and dip your line again, and before you know it, if it's a good day, the box is full.

We fished other summers, but after I left the island perhaps seven or eight years later, when I was nineteen, I never went back and I never saw Rustico or Covehead or the beaches again or the place where I was born sixty-five years ago.

*

When she was only nineteen, in 1876, Irma Gillespie was already teaching school. She liked her work and she was good with children. She was fond of books and music, of pictures and of poems.

She was a small girl, thin, with straight, auburn hair and large hazel eyes in a friendly face. She was shy in the presence of men, around some of whom, quite unknown to them, she secretly spun fantasies before she fell asleep. She tried to imagine falling in love and having a man romance her. She floated in day-dreams about chance meetings that led to awesome infatuations and flared into passion and abandon. Happily she blushed, anticipating that first sea-borne, sky-borne ecstasy. He would surely be the perfect lover, eloquent and gentle, for he would not hurt her either the first time or ever afterwards. They would cling to each other and give themselves totally to one another for the rest of their lives. All their days they would wait spellbound until the night united and liberated them.

*

The man paused as she sat reading beside a tree. He tipped his hat. It was a beautiful day, he murmured. Hesitantly he asked: Did she mind terribly if he stopped to chat? He was exhausted, he'd walked miles admiring the land and had spoken to hardly a soul all day. Could he sit down? Goodness, what a heap of books! Were they all hers? Indeed? Was she (and he smiled) a lady writer? Oh, a teacher. What a happy coincidence, his sister is a teacher too, in Halifax. "A pretty girl. She rather resembles you, if I may venture to say so." Oh yes, he's a Maritimer. In Charlottetown on business. For the government. But too boring for her pretty ears.

He had an open, easy smile. He was athletically built and handsome, his voice low and cultured, words well-chosen, manner relaxed.

Must she leave so soon? Well, all good things have to end. He smiled. May he escort her part of the way? May he carry her books? No trouble at all. On the contrary. He smiled. It has been a most stimulating conversation. One meets so few young ladies who have both brains and handsome looks. He smiled, she blushed.

As they strolled by a wooded stretch beside the footpath, he dropped the bundle of books. Still smiling, he dropped the charm.

"Look, my dear," he said, "I want you. Right now. Will you be sensible?" He reached for her and she ran. He caught her easily and slapped her head. His smile was tight. She struggled and screamed, but no one could hear her. He struck at her until she was helpless. She fell on her face and lay whimpering. He turned her over on her back and threw himself on her. Grunting, he gored in, snorting and heaving and pumping pain into her until his fever and his hate exploded and poured like a sewer's overflow.

He lay spent, hot and sweating over the girl, and then rose unsteadily to his feet and buttoned his fly.

Why couldn't she cooperate? Why did she have to fight me? What in hell's the matter with her?

He took a silver coin from his pocket and stood over her, smiling. He placed it on her bare navel. After some reflection he moved it lower. That was really funny. He hesitated, changed his mind, removed the silver and replaced it with a copper coin.

He walked away, smoothing his clothes, and smiling.

"Love conquers all," he said aloud.

*

What's your name? Irma.
  Do you live alone? Yes.
  Are you married? No.
  Were you ever married? No.
  Did you ever have a lover? No.
  Have you ever been in love? I suppose not.
  Are you a virgin? No.

*

When she regained her senses Irma picked up the books and
managed somehow to get home.

*

Your name? Irma Gillespie.
  Any children? None.
  Were you ever a mother? Not quite.
  How old were you? I was almost twenty at the time.

*

My father gave me different medicines and I swallowed them all,
but they had no effect. My mother told me to jump and run and do
other violent exercise. It didn't work. Father said surgery was out
of the question. Abortion was a crime against man and God and
dangerous. I pleaded and he replied passionately that we were not
heathens, life was not cheap, this was 1876, not the Middle Ages,
we were a civilized people of high moral standards. We were
God-fearing and decent, we would bear our cross. With God's help
we would survive.
  Let us examine the situation calmly, dispassionately, he said.
Had anyone seen me in my bloodied clothes when I walked home? I
didn't think so. Well, thank goodness for that. My mother said we
had to keep it a secret. If people found out, they might say I had led
him on, that it was my own fault.
  They decided that I couldn't have my baby in Charlottetown; the
scandal would haunt us forever. "People are cruel," my father
said. "They'd crucify us, you'd always be the butt of gossip, the
townspeople would shun you. They wouldn't want you to teach

their children. You might as well be dead right now. Your mother would die of the shame. My own future as a physician would be compromised.''

I would have to go away, it would be best for everyone. He would take me to Montreal and set up a modest fund for my needs. Shortly before my confinement, Mother would come to stay with me. It was the only way. The child would be placed in a home and offered for adoption. I had better leave soon, before people began to notice.

So Father took me to Montreal, found respectable lodgings and completed the financial arrangements. He kissed me on the cheek and held my shoulders tightly and said goodbye. I looked up at him but I couldn't say anything to comfort him. His eyes filled with tears. He turned and left quickly. I lay on the bed and cried.

I spent a desperate week searching for help. Finally I found a midwife who agreed to an abortion. She was old, kind and gentle. The agony was short, the operation successful, but there were complications and I would never again be able to bear a child. I stayed in the woman's house, in a clean, comfortable room. For three days she fed me and fussed over me like a mother.

I decided to stay in Montreal. I wrote my parents and told them what I had done. They were horrified. I received a few more letters from them and I mailed a few in reply, but the exchange soured in recriminations. I got two notes, distressingly cool, one at Christmas, the other at Easter. I wept and waited, but the correspondence faltered and languished. Finally the letters stopped.

I never heard from them again, I never saw them again.

*

She taught school for many years in Montreal, lived frugally and alone, saved a little money, and quit work after inheriting a small legacy on her father's death. In 1920, when she was sixty-three years old, she discovered Jack London, John Reed, Carl Sandburg, Upton Sinclair. She decided she believed in socialism as much as she believed in God. She also believed in Emile Zola and Bernard Shaw.

Thin, small, grey-haired and spinsterish, Irma Gillespie dressed demurely in soft colours. Her manner was shy, her posture erect and dignified, her walk leisurely, her voice soft and her speech patient. She was a gentle, courteous woman who played a recorder in the privacy of her flat, listened to classical music disks on the Victrola, and read novels, poetry, some biography, radical tracts and socialist magazines.

She enjoyed lectures and political rallies. Parades and demonstrations thrilled her, but she watched nervously from the sidelines, reluctant to be swept into the action.

She made no intimate friendships and felt a great need for privacy. Nobody knew much about her except that she had been a schoolteacher, helped with door-to-door leaflets and contributed small amounts to various causes. She was a good soul, they all said.

She lived in a comfortable little apartment on the second-floor rear of an old house in a threadbare, respectable street on the lower middle-class fringe of affluent Westmount. She occupied a cosy bedsitting room, a small kitchen and her own bathroom, but what most pleased her was her balcony overlooking a large garden in which flourished lilacs and peonies, apple trees and berry bushes, roses and marigolds and petunias.

*

Your name is? Miss Gillespie.

How old are you? Sixty-five.

What do you do? I'm retired.

Any living relatives? None.

Are you an old maid? You mean, am I unmarried? Yes.

Are you unhappy? Sometimes I cry. But, yes, I think I'm happy now, most of the time.

Do you ever think of Prince Edward Island? Sometimes. Yes, often.

Will you ever return? Perhaps, some day before I die.

What do you hope to see? The rust-red soil and the moist green fields. The dunes. The beaches. And the colours of the sea.

1922. Summer Blues.
The Women: Veronica.

My Matthew enjoys work, he never watches the clock, takes pride in the job no matter what they give him to do. He's top producer, he makes good money, works longer than anybody, never complains.

He delivers the most. The man's not born can make him slow down. Matthew stops for nobody when there's work to do. My Matthew believes in a job well done, a fair day's work a fair day's pay. If it's worth doing at all, it's worth doing well.

Where is he now, you ask? How dare you ask! You ought to know. Doing his bit, he's no slacker—king and country—my Matthew he's working in the war, the shooting and all. No shirker, he works every day all day all year all at straight pay no piece rates no overtime pay. He saves it and sends it all home to me every penny of it for our future for the golden days salting away the banknotes the bank interest the victory bonds for our sunset years. Oh, it's a good job great promise it pays money and it's all gravy—a free bunk for sleeping and lots of fresh air outdoors free nice thick grey blankets free and the rest is gravy gratis free no charge for socks free underwear greatcoat cap belt free shirts gloves mitts free gasmask webbing free uniform free shoes boots laces free ointment for sores blisters rashes and free meals doctoring free travel free church free dentist! Oh, it's all gravy all free all absolutely free: surgery rifle cartridges free bayonet all positively free. God's on our side and God's free too.

My Matthew don't pay red cent not a dime not a nickel for anything not a penny. If he wants, he can have nice funeral free if he likes and nice cross with name carved free.

Proud of work! That's my Matthew, the best, a professional, a god, a giant at everything, at anything he touches. Oh, my beloved Matthew sweating in the shop and, oh, my sweet Matthew creating love in my bed and, oh, my brave Matthew bleeding on the battlefield. You work harder than anyone else, you love more gently than anyone else, you kill harder than all the rest, but gently, and the more you kill the longer you live. So don't stop killing!

My Matthew my provider my lover my hero my soldier-boy my angel my saint...My Matthew tells me that I am *all* woman.

*

I wish he'd come home for supper.
    It's getting cold.

*

Ralph rang the doorbell and waited.

Veronica Sawchuk cautiously moved the curtain behind the glass of her door to reveal her pale face, blonde hair and bright blue eyes peering suspiciously. Russian, Polack? Something like that. About forty years old, big, well-padded. She made no move to open her door and stared into his eyes.

He called, "Open up, lady, police."

She shoved the curtain back so that he couldn't see her at all.

He rattled the doorknob and rang the bell again. There was no response. Then she called through the letter-slot, "Who are you? What do you want?"

He stooped down on his side of the slot and called, "Police!"

"You can't be police, you have no uniform, no brass buttons!"

"I'm plainclothes."

"I don't want any clothes, I want the police."

"Mrs. Sawchuk, I'm a policeman without a uniform."

"Did you lose it someplace?"

"Lady, I don't need a uniform, all I need's a badge."

"It's against the law to walk around naked."

"Lookit, lady, I'm not naked."

"Naughty boy, you're flirting."

"Madam, I don't flirt on duty. What do you want?"

"Show me your badge."

Red in the face and hoarse from shouting into the slot, Ralph straightened up and held the metal shield at eye-level.

She studied it dubiously and shook her head. "You look like a crook or even a cop, I can't tell you apart. Did you find your badge in the pile of old clothes you stole? I'll tell my husband about you when he comes home."

"Madame, I haven't got the time to play games and stand on my knees all day talking into your keyhole."

"It's not a keyhole, it's a letter-box and you're no letter carrier because you're not wearing a uniform. Who are you, a slacker or something? Where's your uniform? Go away and get me a real policeman or a soldier."

"O.K., lady, but will you please phone the police station and ask if they sent me, ask my description, ask is my name Ralph Gilbert, ask if I got a mole on my back, ask anything."

"Wait," she ordered and withdrew. When she returned she opened the door. "Oh, there you are, hiding. Detectives always hide, don't they? There was an old Jew junkman trying to force my door before. Did he escape? He was a German spy, you know. I like your uniform, it's neat and conservative. My Matthew and I, we always voted Conservative, like the rich people in Westmount. They can't stop us just because we're poor. Come right in, officer. Sit in this nice comfortable chair. My husband always sits there but he won't be home for supper. He's at the war. So you're a policeman. Can you tell me, have you heard, will the war be finished soon? Before supper? My Matthew's there...Over there, over there...Like the song."

"Lady," Ralph said, his face expressionless, "the war's over, it stopped three years ago, give or take a few bodies."

She was puzzled. "It can't be, my husband isn't home yet."

"Mrs. Sawchuk," he said, "you phoned a complaint. That's why I'm here. What's your problem?"

"Spies. I'm scared. They're everywhere! They wear disguises, like beards and scary masks. They put things in my letter-box. They tell lies, they write against the war, they believe in free love and sex, dirty things like that. They want to steal my money and nationalize me; they're plotting to kill my Matthew and sell his body. They want to abolish the army. But we women won't let them, will we? We'll breed new soldiers. They'll slaughter everyone."

"Madame, I'd like to see this paper they put in your door."

"It was horrible. Worst of all was the part you couldn't see; it was all in invisible ink, filthy stuff, so I burned it. Now will you please tell me why you're here? Are you sure you have a mole?"

"Lady, I haven't got a mole."

"Now isn't that odd, neither have I. Would you be a good boy and undo these fasteners? Thank you. Now you see, I have no mole. No, silly boy, those aren't moles. I nearly forgot, you're the one not supposed to have a mole. You must be my husband, he has no mole either.

"You're taking your shoes off. That's thoughtful. You're always such a considerate lover, Matthew. But why are you so rough today? Are you unhappy, something I said?...I've been lonely, sad lonely, hurting lonely. All those nights...I'm happy now...But why are you dressing? Did I say something?...Where are you going? Back to the war? It won't ever end, will it?...Wait a minute, don't leave...Forgive me if I cry. I'm so sorry...Oh, dear God, stop the war, I beg you...Dear Matthew, I need you. Will you be home for supper?...Kiss me once before you go..."

*

Hours later, as he walked his beat on Sherbrooke near the university, the madwoman still haunted him. No female had ever affected him like this; no woman had ever given so much of herself. They had always fought him and he'd always savaged them. This one was eager and vital. She was strong and she was his match.

It was a lousy night, windy and wet. He paced his beat, waiting for the shift to end so he could go home.

*

Home? I'll return to her house. Will she let me in, will she remember me, will she call me her Matthew? I'll return to the hospitality of her warm bed, her firm full flesh, her uninhibited bigness.

I'll be doing her a favour, myself too.

Matthew, I salute you, rest in peace, for to you I dedicate my daily good Samaritan deed, my patriotic boy scout good turn, consoling her daily, making her happy twice a day. Pity the poor widow and help her forget. Meet your proxy husband, madame, Matthew's identical twin, even better than Matthew, who regrets he is unable to sleep with you in person, unavoidably detained under a mountain of mud and won't be home for supper. Asked me to carry on, comfort you, keep your feet warm, love you up. At your service, ma'am.

The poor dame, that poor unhappy Sawchuk dame...What a hell of a life, what a goddamed cockeyed manure-packed booby-hatch of a lousy world.

I'll go back to her after my shift. I wish this friggin' rain would stop. The poor crazy dame. I want her. Her loving makes me feel good; I never felt so good with a dame before, she's the best I ever had. I like her. I never felt this way before.

*

Gilbert wiped the rain from his face. He would be free soon and would go back to his woman.

There goes that scrawny biddy with the umbrella and the shopping bag. What does she keep in it? He shrugged, then remembered Veronica's spies, the villains in her letter-box.

"Just a minute, lady," he called, "I'll have a look in that bag."

"There's nothing there, officer, just knitting," said Miss Gillespie.

"I'll look anyway."

The bag contained a ball of wool and knitting needles.

"All right," Ralph said. "Go on home."

"Thank you, officer, and goodnight," the old woman said pleasantly as she walked away.

That was close! If he'd stopped her a few minutes earlier...But the leaflets had all been disposed of, distributed, circulated, planted like seeds, germinating, pleading...How obvious detectives are, how transparent, how easy it is to spot the snoopers a mile away, something in the way they walk, the stance, the expression, the bland hostility they radiate...If she'd been caught and taken to the station...

She hurried homewards to get into her nightgown and her bathrobe and slippers and to sit securely in her rocking-chair with a good story and a cup of tea.

1922. Summers Lost.
The Women: Laura.

Like her sister Rose, she had started work very young. Laura found a job in a cigar factory. Their parents didn't think working girls needed too much school. Go to work, bring money in, marry early, an ambitious, hard-working boy with prospects, from a nice respectable family, and start bearing children.

Both parents had died within months of each other, the mother at home, soaking blood onto the second-hand brass bed in her gaslit bedroom in the middle of the night after a terrifying stillbirth, with a doctor rushing in, reeking of liquor, his shirt collarless, arriving too late, when she was already dying.

The father, shocked and brooding and helpless with grief, walked the streets for hours, for weeks, months, climbing the mountain to its highest level, talking to himself, groaning, crying out, collapsing there, falling down as the blood flooded his brain, lying dead and muddied where the policeman found him.

Laura moved into the back bedroom on St. Urbain Street with her sister and brother-in-law Max.

When she was seventeen she wanted to become a singer. She found a voice teacher. High on excitement and ambition, she bought a used upright on the instalment plan and began to take piano lessons from the same teacher, the slow-moving, heavy Signor Arturo Minelli, his sallow face saddened by a drooping black moustache.

The week was long and tough in a workshop pungent with tobacco leaf: ten hours on each of the first five weekdays, six hours on Saturdays (the short day), thirty minutes to swallow the cold lunch she had packed the night before. As a learner she got no pay the first few weeks. She was not paid for days off sick, or on the High Holy Days or when she went to the funerals of her parents.

The boss offered condolences but docked her. He also docked for spoilages; otherwise a man could go bankrupt.

*

In the evening, after helping Rose with the dishes, you would have loved to lie down for a nap but you rubbed your eyes and pushed yourself awake, and for the second time that day you travelled by streetcar (and occasionally walked) down Park Avenue past Pine and Sherbrooke and onto St. Catherine westward only a block past your slumbering cigar loft.

In the walk-up third-floor studio apartment the stout and aging Signor Minelli, during your third lesson, made clumsy passes, failed to tempt your fresh young ardour, apologized profusely and resigned himself to instructing you solely in the art of song for voice and pianoforte.

At times avuncular, he reminisced wistfully of past successes, hinting at grand romances, and showed you yellowed newspaper accounts of long-ago triumphs as a tenor in Paris, Rome and Rio de Janeiro. He showed you faded wall-posters for long-forgotten recitals, flamboyant publicity photos of his younger days when he was handsomer, much more slender, somehow taller, clean-shaven.

Twice a week you reported to Professor Minelli, who listened to your scales and watched your hands, and four nights a week you practised vocal exercises and fingering at home.

What fine young musicians you met! What ardent music-lovers they were, what dear romantics, what beautiful friends!

Gradually the musical fun grew into an obsession. You began to want more, something better than the dreary cigar box of a factory and its drained and captive zombies. You would study harder, you would become known, you would sing on the stage, in recital, on tour, some day perhaps in opera. But for a start, for now, you were glad to have weddings, society concerts, bar mitzvahs, amateur nights, banquets, benefits, anything.

*

His first day on earth, I picked him up from Rose's bed and carried him into the parlour. I pressed his pink fist ever so gently against the piano keys and tapped out those first four warning notes of Beethoven's *Fifth*. Arthur howled.

Later, often, I sang him to sleep. Later still, he began to explore the sounds of the piano keys by himself. He was a sweet child.

My new friends took me to open-air band concerts. A few times we got reckless and actually bought tickets for the opera; we sat in the gods. I learned a lot about music from them and from my teacher.

On Sunday nights my friends came to visit and we'd sing and play music all evening.

What satisfying times we had! We talked and laughed and glowed in our warm dear friendship—the dreamy little man with the flute; the solid baritone who looked like a thug and sang like a saint; the violinist, older than all of us but warm and relaxed; the pale young doctor just out of medical school who couldn't sing or play a note but listened and smiled whenever our eyes met; my own contralto; and the young fellow from the shipping-room, lost in wonder at the wonderful sounds, bravely reading his own fervent poems in heavily accented English.

In the kitchen, with the gas-mantle turned low, my sister Rose and her husband Max listened. And on the doorstep down below sat my little nephew, hypnotized by the sounds until he dozed off to sleep under the low stars, and Max finding him, picking him up, carrying him upstairs, and Rose undressing her child and putting him to bed.

Other nights my friends and I walked the dirt road that climbed and circled Mount Royal. Once the young doctor kissed me, and once it was the young poet. They'd all walk me home in a body and say goodnight and drift off dreamily to their own places. It was a happy time and we were all happy then, all very happy.

I'm thirty-five now, twice the age I was when Arthur was born. I have two young children. Norman is in prison and I have to go out to work. Sometimes I play the piano in movie houses, sometimes I sing at affairs, but I've never had a recital.

*

She was in her early twenties, an intense, dark girl when she married Norm Nelson, the big sport.

She had been booked to play the piano and lead a sing-song at a social club. When she entered the hall she realized she was the only woman among all those males, who whistled and cheered and called out as she sat at the back waiting for the man who had hired her.

They were all drinking and snacking and smoking at a table loaded with cheese and pretzels, bread and delicatessen meats and pickles, and crowding a bar heavy with tubs full of quarts of beer on ice, and clusters of glass tumblers at the ready beside rows of liquor bottles already well-launched by the jostling celebrants, and free cigarettes and cigars.

Laura waited apprehensively among the boisterous drunks. As a side door opened it revealed a roomful of women, seven or eight of them, all heavily made up, most of them smoking and drinking, none wearing much more than a slip or a transparent dressing-gown. Were *they* on the program too? Dancers? Actresses? They didn't look like elocutionists or liedersingers.

A man approached her, a friendly fellow. "I'm Norm Nelson. I'm the only sober committee member." He grinned widely, showed gleaming teeth, bright eyes. She smiled uneasily. "Are you ready for your number?" he asked, and she mounted a platform. "Give the little lady a big hand!" he shouted. She started to sing, "'Tis the last rose of summer," and had hardly gotten out the first few nervous words when they started to holler, "Take it off! Come on, sister, jiggle 'em! Strip, strip, show us what you got!"

Poor Laura turned and ran to the door and out, with Norm right behind, pleading that it was all a mistake, the boys thought they

were going to see a stripper, somebody on the committee had
loused things up, the jerk. They were bums, all of them. It's like
singing for pigs; they weren't fit to meet a real lady. He hoped she
would accept his personal apology, O.K.?

"I'm real sorry. Please, can I see you home, pay for your cab?
How about supper at Childs?"

*

Good Lord, how long ago was that? Ten, fifteen years? I thought I
knew what I wanted, and nothing, nothing was going to stop me.

How do you explain it? I knew where I was going. How did I get
sidetracked so soon, so easily? Boom, right away, quick!...One
baby, then the other. Interruptions. Housework, laundry, sewing,
cooking meals. And two pregnancies. Vocal lessons shuffled,
postponed, cancelled, finally terminated. The piano stood
deserted, sourly accusing, dusty and untuned.

No, I haven't given up; don't say I have. I must wait a bit. I'll
find my way back, you'll see. Nothing is going to stop me.

Nothing?

Nothing.

Norman was all the right things, popular, generous, cheerful and
amusing. He was an outdoors man, fished and boated in summer,
skated and snowshoed in winter. He was an indoors man, played
cards, danced, enjoyed musical comedies.

He bought big boxes of chocolates and marzipan for Laura, a
pop-gun for Arthur. He praised Rose's cooking and Max's
homemade wine.

He dressed smartly, smoked good cigars, spoke an easy English,
conversed interestingly, exuded material success and ambition.

He gave her tickets for the opera, for concerts, because she liked
that sort of stuff. For himself he preferred burlesque and
vaudeville.

On Sundays he hired a horse and buggy and took Laura around
the mountain, sometimes with little Arthur.

The courtship was memorable, the wedding was memorable. It
was small and intimate (he had few relatives in Montreal, a sister, a
cousin) but it was festive and even merry, with fine food and drink
and goodwill.

Laura's dear friends, her musical friends, masked their secret

disappointments but wished her heartfelt good fortune. The poet of
the cigar-shop shipping-room read lines he had composed for her.
Rose cried.

After a New York honeymoon (where else?) the young couple
moved into a good neighbourhood and furnished their flat with
nice new things, everything new, even the piano, a baby grand.
Laura quit her job at the cigars. She continued with the music
lessons.

Norm was his own boss. Nobody was going to tell him what to do
or how hard to work. "Anybody wants to be a workhorse on a
treadmill, let him, but count me out," he told Laura. "When a man
lives by his hands his whole body gets worn out like his hands. But
not Norm Nelson," he assured her. "I use the brain the good Lord
gave me."

During their first year of marriage he seemed to prosper—real
estate, insurance and vague promotional ventures which he avoided
mentioning to her—but his bright self-confidence faltered when he
was outsmarted and lost heavily in a series of questionable deals.

He told Laura that conditions were bad; they'd have to
economize until business improved. He asked her to be patient, to
have faith in him. Hadn't he been a good provider?

He bought into a tired little cigar factory. Laura had worked in
one herself; she would help until the baby came. But the enterprise
fizzled and he pulled out. He became part owner of a restaurant in
Verdun; it went broke. He bought a share in a tavern, worked every
afternoon and every night except Sunday. When after six months
he demanded an accounting he was told he was not really a partner.
When he made a scene and started to fight he was beaten up and
evicted.

He gambled on the ponies and lost. He started to drink. The
worse things got, the more he drank. When he couldn't buy gin he
bought cheap wine. The breezy winner had become a loser.

He fumed, he vowed, "I'll show the bastards, I'll break them!"

He drank away, gambled away, pissed away the grocery money,
the phone money, the rent money. They moved into a cheaper
place.

Now he was into the rackets: enforcer for a loan shark, racetrack
tout, bootlegger's messenger, arsonist, pimp.

On a busy noontime he strolled into a bank, puffing nervously
on a black stogie. He pointed a dummy pistol at the girl behind the

cash. She threw a fistful of quarters; some cleared the grill and struck his face. She shrieked and fainted, he turned and ran to the street. The alarm bells rang, a rookie cop tripped him and clubbed him over the head and handcuffed him. The young constable received a commendation and Norm spent the next three years in Kingston Pen.

*

When Laura visited her husband he didn't look much like a man-about-town. In his prison garb he was no longer the sport nor one of the boys.

He smiled bitterly and complained, "I'm the original hardluck kid. If I found a million dollars, they'd be counterfeit. If I was an undertaker, people would stop dying."

Alone at night in his cell he was overcome with anxiety. He saw himself, toiling in greasy overalls, with a road gang in the scorching heat, enduring twelve-hour shifts behind the counter of a cigar-store, or washing dishes in a greasy-spoon cafe.

"I want you to promise me," Laura broke into his pessimism, "I want you to promise you'll never touch dirty money again."

"Do you know any other kind?" he demanded.

"You know what I mean, Norman. We can't live that way."

"Clean or dirty, what's the difference? Kid gloves or brass knuckles, it's all the same. Guys like me have no choice."

"You ought to think of your family."

"I'm thinking of you and the kids. Look, Laura, when I get out of here we'll start a new life. I've been thinking hard, I've been planning. I've got some real solid ideas. Leave it to me, Laura. We'll make it, Laura. We'll be sitting on top of the world."

It sounded like the same old self-assured Norman until she looked again at the grey face and bleak eyes of a beaten little man she didn't love or even pity.

*

Whatever induced me to marry him? We had little in common, he didn't care for music, opera made him gag. He was good to the kids but he also screamed at them, and at me.

Why did I marry him? His good looks? His charm,

self-confidence, virility? His love? I think he loved me at first. I think I loved him but I'm not too sure now.

I'm not that unhappy; I have the children.

When I think of myself now...and at nineteen...

How many summers I've lost...how many!

1922. Jailhouse Blues.
Arthur's Women.

Arthur mourned at his own funeral in the middle of the uneasy night in his dark cell in the sleeping jailhouse at Pointe Claire.

He dreamed that he was looking down at the face of the young man on the bier and he was shocked to recognize his own face.

In his dream he saw them grieving his life's end; all the women he had known and not known, those he had loved and not loved, the briefly cherished and the soon-forgotten ones, and those he had created out of his dreams and his need.

His mother, who had carried him for nine anxious months in her own body, stood stunned and silent, then turned to him and gestured towards the body in the coffin, "He was mine, you know, my only child."

Her sister, his Aunt Laura, was there. She used to sing for him when he was a baby, read poems for him when he was growing up, and on his sixteenth birthday earnestly assured him, "You'll discover ecstasy one day soon, I hope. You'll be a gentle lover, a sweet lover." She turned to his mother now, saying, "He was mine too, you know."

School teachers, women young and old, stood moist-eyed. "He was mine, you know," they murmured in unison.

Schoolgirls, classmates, paid their respects. "He was ours."

Elsie, herself dead, touched his cheek with her lips. "And mine."

The waitress, Marge, impulsively pressing his face to her breast in the backroom of the ice-cream parlour on Peel Street on his first day at work. She mourned, "Mine also."

And Georgie, at the country club, offering, waiting. "Even mine."

And crowding forward, the fleshy Angelique, twitching at the rustle of a dollar bill. "Any man is mine for money."

Absent was the missing girl he hadn't met. Would she claim him too, offering poetry and light, a soul on fire, a body radiant, eyes glowing with the wisdom of a thousand years, a mouth laughing joyously?

Would he recognize her?

PART FIVE

1

1939. End of Summer.
The Hospital. Night Watch.

RALPH GILBERT LOCKS himself into the stall in the hospital washroom, lowers the lid onto the seat, loosens his collar, sits down and leans back with a sigh, his head cool against the tiled lavatory wall.

From a deep inside jacket pocket he draws his leather-coated flask, unscrews the cap and drinks happily, savouring the golden Benedictine, rolling it in his mouth, stirring the sticky liqueur with his tongue, letting the piquant viscosity trickle drop by drop down his throat. He closes his eyes. This is the very essence of pleasure, to take what he wants when he wants it.

He returns the flask to his pocket. A door slams as someone enters the washroom. He flushes the unused toilet bowl and returns to his post in the corridor.

On the bench, with an unobstructed view of the Intensive Care ward, he resumes the watch, alert in case the door should fly open and Arthur Meller escapes violent and crazed and has to be shot again.

Will his prisoner recover and live or will he die? If that Red bastard croaks, it could be a manslaughter rap, murder perhaps.

Hell, he knows the law, he's a good cop, he performs his duty, he has a clean record. There's nothing to worry about.

*

Ambition hasn't paid off. He's in a rut. Twenty years a cop, where has it got him? How come all those young punks outranked him? For twenty long years he's plugged away; he's dreamed of clippings in a scrapbook:

"Constable Gilbert's squad. A surprise raid by Detective Gilbert's men. Clues uncovered by Sgt. Ralph Gilbert. New arrests announced by Inspector Gilbert's office. Acting Police Chief Ralph (Tiger) Gilbert warns city's underworld. Knighthood conferred on Commissioner Gilbert. Sir Ralph uncovers Red network."

Meanwhile he books vags and floosies and drunks, pickpockets, perverts and pimps. He's not a popular cop, he isn't a leader of men, but he's always been a hard worker and a loyal public servant. He deserves better.

After adequate but undistinguished service in the provost corps, he had been routinely discharged from the army in 1919, a year after war's end. The war had dragged; the only shooting he saw was when a bunch ran amuk in camp and had to be fired on.

Red-headed, ruddy-faced and hawk-nosed, Ralph Gilbert is a handsome, masculine six-foot-two bruiser with neat flat ears, clipped red moustache, an oddly small steel-trap mouth, piercing green eyes under bushy red eyebrows. He is alert, built of tough sinew, bone and muscle honed by years on the beat. He has only a rudimentary education, having narrowly survived public school and flunked first-year high, and shows few of the softer impulses of other men.

Not once as a teen-age youth did he fall in love, and never as a mature man. Romance was for the bashful milquetoast and an utter waste of time. If a girl indicated interest, he could hardly wait to snatch off her pants. Preliminary wooing taxed his patience. He believed in the quick, mechanical feel, until at last they gave in gasping.

After the rumpus he might say amiably, "I'll be seeing you again some day; keep the oven hot," or "Keep your motor running; I might need a ride."

If the girl failed to cooperate, he would grab her face and snarl, "You cold little bitch, who do you think you are to hold out on me?"

*

Gilbert's family back home were delinquents who didn't give a damn about their immortal souls, mistrusted their Catholic neighbours, loathed the Jews though they had never seen one, quoted hearsay to despise the blacks and mimic orientals, told dirty stories about priests and nuns, snickered at the Virgin Mary and read *The Confessions of Maria Monk* as gospel truth.

Ralph's haphazard contact with his large and quarrelsome clan was impatient and abrasive. He disliked his mother; he considered her a cow.

At fifteen he was insulting his father and getting away with it. The father grinned foolishly from toothless gums.

Two younger brothers fitfully worked the farm when they didn't bootleg, steal chickens or fight each other.

Their sister was a tart. Grandpa corroded his liver and his brain with his own illicit rotgut and sat for hours ranting to himself in the outhouse, its privy door wide open.

Only Ralph ever made it to the big city. The others hated or were scared of cities and city people even more than they hated farms and farm people. They were mired on their wretched potato farm marooned many miles from Moncton in a deeply depressed, deeply distressed New Brunswick marginal backwoods wasteland.

For his one abortive year of high school he lived with his mother's brother in Montreal as a means of liquidating the uncle's $50 family debt. Ralph's mother wrote her brother that the boy would be company for the lonely widower and help with the chores. What chores, the man asked himself, what chores? She didn't come right out and say that Ralphie wasn't wanted at home.

When the war broke out Gilbert enlisted to fight Kaiser Bill and also to be free of his guardian's growlings and the back-home brawls. He was sixteen but big and miserable, passing for eighteen and a welcome addition to the military police.

Never once in twenty years, he recalls now as he holds watch from the bench in the hospital corridor, has he missed his family or felt the slightest desire to visit home since that first post-war reunion.

*

Another twenty years on the force and he'll be pensioned off. Then what? Hotel dick, industrial snoop, divorce peeper? His own agency?...Gilbert Services, the Gilbert Undercover Co., Sure-Fire Investigations?

In his forties, he lives alone in an apartment on Guy near Sherbrooke. In the livingroom are a plum-coloured easy-chair, a green-covered continental bed and a large desk with shaded lamp. On a coffee table lie some girlie magazines. The only pictures on the walls are a photo of himself in army uniform and a bank calendar.

Stored in the kitchenette fridge are ice-cube trays, a couple of frozen pork chops, a thick steak, a package of minced beef and a half-pound folder of back bacon, as well as a tray of eggs, some butter, Oka cheese, Polish salami and six quart bottles of lager beer.

On a shelf stand a started bottle of brandy, a forty-ouncer of Canadian rye whiskey, half a crock of Holland gin and a large-size Benedictine. From the window he can see a piece of the mountain if he raises the blind, but it is seldom raised.

Usually deadpan, he does not laugh easily. He is a sullen man without one goddam person he can call his friend.

*

After the war when Ralph came home from overseas and visited the weather-beaten old farmhouse to collect his belongings, his father got drunk and so did his mother, the sister and the brothers and Ralph too, all made numb from distilled swampsweat (nicknamed pantherpiss).

Ralphie poured beer over Ma's venerable grey head, fought with his brothers, urinated into a bag of flour, overturned the outhouse and chased the chickens out of the yard. Grandma and Grandpa, drunk behind the barn, escaped Ralph's rage.

He staggered away from his birthplace and never again returned to the house, not even for the old man's funeral; he never sent as much as a Christmas card, never bothered to answer a diminishing trickle of begging letters from his mother. He didn't owe any of them a bloody thing.

*

Ralph derives little satisfaction from books; reading is a restless way to pass the time. He doesn't have the patience to fish; the countryside bores him; he'd had enough of nature as a kid. In the wintertime he sits in the noisy ice arena on occasional nights off and watches hockey, keyed up by the violence, a solitary stone-faced man in the crowd.

Sometimes he skates in the darkened rink on Fletcher's Field just east of Park at the base of Mount Royal, late at night and alone, after everyone has left.

He plays cards in the staffroom with other off-duty cops, gambles on the nags and slips into restaurants on The Main to wolf the tantalizing smoked-meat sandwiches and dill pickles of the Rumanian Jews and to eavesdrop on hyped-up communists eating and laughing and jawing happily in an adjacent booth after a meeting and not realizing (simpletons!) that he is monitoring their contraband euphoria, his brain absorbing every nuance of their sedition...If he had his way—just five no-holds-barred minutes—they wouldn't laugh.

He favours a blue pinstripe suit with vest, a neat checked shirt, maroon tie and socks, brown shoes with grey spats and a grey fur-felt hat for winter. He prefers a dove-grey tropical-weight two-piece suit in summer, with navy-blue tie and socks, white shoes, a creamy panama hat, white cotton shirt.

He enjoys rare steaks, heavy stews, thick soups and gravies, heaps of hash-brown potatoes. He eats with total concentration.

He has no tolerance for long-term emotional attachments. "I want variety." He grins at the girl, briefly and hard. "I want first of all to please myself, so don't hold back on me. There's no next time."

Years back, in the early Twenties, he had been strangely drawn to the widow, the unhappy madwoman. Vera? No, Veronica. She thought he was her husband. The poor bugger, if she was to be believed, had been blown apart and buried in mud in the first war, but she kept calling Gilbert her Matthew. More than once as her bed quaked he had wanted to shout, "For Christ's sake, woman, stop calling me Matthew! He's dead, but I'm alive! He's no use to you! I'm alive, I'm here, I'm lots better than he ever was! Forget him!"

Would she have clawed his chest, kicked and shrieked?

As the dead Matthew's surrogate he had to remember to restrain his bullish onslaughts and to approach her with some gentleness and even to offer some awkward tenderness. The poor woman would cling to him and sigh, "Matthew, Matthew..."

What if in sudden clarity she saw not Matthew but the stranger in her bed and screamed for help?

One afternoon she started to cry and pushed him away. "Don't, Matthew, don't touch me, go away and never come back. You have another woman. I can tell because you never say you love me."

Now, seventeen years later, he can scarcely remember the name or the face.

She was the only woman he had ever liked, really liked.

1922. End of Summer.
The Art Critic.

"You got a licence to sell this?"

He had to be a detective—his size, walk, brooding go-to-hell air. He had walked into her shop, a new store on his beat, off Sherbrooke below the campus, with hardly a hello, his hand gesturing at the shelves and display tables.

He gave scant attention to the art things, the gift stuff; his glance dismissed them with contempt as though they were some kind of perversion. He strode over to a bookstall and leafed through a dozen volumes, pausing over a book of colour plates, amused because the lavishly fleshed nudes had such incongruously small breasts, and puzzled by photos of statues that showed muscled male giants no better endowed with private parts than little boys.

"Yes, I have a licence," said Gaby.

"You shouldn't sell dirty books," he snapped.

"I don't. They're not dirty. You can buy them at Morgan's, the same books. If you're looking for nudes, go to the Art Gallery."

"Don't tell me what to do."

"Suit yourself. But it's good for the soul."

He glowered, assessing the parts of this self-assured young woman who tossed her English at him with a touch of French-accented insolence.

"Just be careful," he warned, and left.

"Sure," she said. She wasn't afraid of this red-headed hulk in his dove-grey suit and panama hat. To hell with him. The book stayed.

2

1939. Summer's End.
All Night the Screaming.

THE NURSE AT her night station in Intensive Care keeps watch over patients lost in limbo.

Arthur lies as though sound asleep or dead.

"He's the one they shot," she tells the intern. "He doesn't look like a wild one to me."

"They don't look crazy when they sleep. I've seen lots of them at the asylum, before I came here. They want me to go back, but I turned it down, it's too hard on my nerves. Maybe after the war. I'm joining up in the Army Medical Corps. You get a commission right off, they say."

"At the Verdun asylum they scream all night. My sister works there. I don't think I could stand it, I'd crack up."

"You get used to it. You get used to everything."

"I don't think I could be a war nurse. Can you imagine the wounds, the screaming? Like a million lunatic asylums."

1922. End of Summer.
Foreigner Assimilating.

It was the fourth bewildering year since the war, scarcely five after the shock of the Russian Revolution, only three since the Winnipeg Strike.

Only a year before, an uncle of Arthur's had come east on business. He was a prospering Winnipeg furrier, a decent sort but caught in family conflicts, marital irritations, a fear of failure and the uneasy suspicion that his sons and daughters were ashamed of his foreign accent and awkward etiquette.

If approached, he could be expected to help a poverty-pinched relative and derive some satisfaction from the deed, but he would not be pushed. He seethed with indignation when his eighteen workers (like himself all more or less green immigrants) had forced him to sign a union contract.

Alexander was grateful that his Montreal sisters-in-law were hospitable and asked for nothing. He brought fruit, nuts, a box of chocolates. Tired after trudging around all day pushing his line to the big buyers, he liked to come home to the sisters and remove his tie, his jacket, his shoes, eat their good home cooking and later, in the cosy parlour, sit back contentedly and chat through the evening, exchanging family gossip, telling them his troubles, boasting about his big house in Winnipeg and his smart youngsters, but complaining, though secretly proud, that they refused to speak Yiddish to him or his wife, and grousing that his workers, about whom he worried like a father, were ungrateful wretches who persecuted a fellow-Jew.

The sisters, Laura and Rose, nodded sympathetically, forgetting for the moment, in a surge of loyalty, their own detested bosses.

Encouraged, he poured out a bitter tirade against the General Strike, that horrible 1919 nightmare with all those crazy red-eyed socialists turning the city upside down. "Imagine!" he stormed, "dirty foreign bums, lazy kikes, anarchist ignoramuses! Imagine, to tell me how much I should pay them, what hours I should hold my shop open! Cossacks! Anti-semites! Bolsheviks! Dirty teefs!"

"Your blood pressure, Alec, don't work yourself up. Have a little schnapps." Laura ran into the kitchen, returned with a bottle, filled a wineglass. She touched his arm. "Drink," she urged. Rose murmured sympathy, "Eat some cake, Alec."

Not so many years earlier, in 1905, only fourteen years before the big strike, he had run, a young Odessa radical, in headlong panic from the sword of a charging cavalryman and escaped into an alley and down a cellar stairs. In 1919 in Winnipeg, enrolled in the Citizens' Committee, he had marched up and down in army drill halls, neck stiff, eyes front, shoulders back and paunch tight, and learned to form fours, salute, swing a wooden club and shoot bullets from a real gun.

He felt proud to be at last accepted, at last fulfilled, proud to be patronized by the same neighbours who so recently had snubbed this unwanted outsider, their strange next-door neighbour-foreigner-Jew.

Arthur listened to his uncle's story and said nothing. You must never offend prosperous relatives.

3

1939. Wartime.
In Praise of Fred.

YES, FRED, I know you wouldn't be lying like this, helpless in a hospital.

Being shot is new to me. I'm not used to it, like you.

If I were you, I'd be awake by now, demanding something to eat and kidding the nurses.

If I know you, Fred, you'd be making a pass, even before breakfast.

You could be wrapped in a plaster cast from head to toe but you'd try, you'd find a way. You'd mean·no harm, you'd just want to be friendly and sleep with her.

And if I know you, she'd probably fall for you, right into your bed.

1922. The Bleak Time.
Fred Shaughnessy's Summer.

Fred Shaughnessy at eighteen had not forgotten the Dublin Easter shootings of six years ago, and his mother falling on her own doorstep, but he and Martin spoke less and less about the Old Country. Canada claimed them now and Ireland's villains had their counterparts in Montreal: factory bosses, shipping bosses, political bosses, cops.

In 1922 some nine million people were spread thin across an epic land-and-water mass but settled thickly in the cities of Ontario and Quebec. Most were descendants of Frenchmen and Englishmen, and of Scots, Irishmen, Welshmen, followed later by immigrants from the Ukraine, Russia, Germany, Finland, and from Poland, Sweden, Italy, and also from India, China, Africa and many other hungry places.

Those who had been here long before the strangers came, the first Canadians, who had lived here in the beginning, they were now the outsiders. Their descendants—the misnamed Eskimos and

Indians—were the forgotten ones, shunned and ostracized.

In 1922 we were a country of workers and farmers, peddlers and shopkeepers, people in the professions and students at school. And of aggressive financiers, promoters, employers of labour, big operators and speculators and high-born scoundrels. And also of visionaries and explorers, rebels and reformers, good men and women who were mostly anonymous.

In 1922, a harsh year, a hungry year, Canadians by the thousands pushed westward on low-fare excursion trains for harvest jobs—the only work they would have that year—labouring from dismal dawn to dismal dark, choked by the dust, drenched in sweat, collapsing in sleep on the dank straw of a barn loft.

Fred was out of work, Martin worked part-time at the harbourfront. Harvesting offered a stake for the winter; it would be a chance for Fred to see the country. He was browned-off with the classified help-wanted ads and the hours of daily door-to-door job hunting that ended in blind alleys. He was restless and bored with the park-bench futility and the sleazy bottom stretch of St. Lawrence-Main's penny arcades and cheap movies.

He would wander off, out of inertia, to Park Avenue at Pine, or in well-heeled Outremont, idly watching the cars as they rolled by, all with their distinctive radiator shapes and brand-name crests. Under his breath he checked them out:

"Packard. Marmon. Willys-Knight. Hupmobile and Dort and Star. Nash and Moon and Duesenberg. Lexington, Pierce-Arrow, Paige. Overland, McLaughlin, Stutz. A Liberty, a Chevrolet. And Franklin, Chalmers, Chandler, Ford. A Dupont, a Columbia. Essex, Auburn and Durant. Here comes a Rolls-Royce!"

There were limits to how many hours you could tinker with a crystal set, squeaky warning of the booming radios soon to fill the air.

Fishing was fine, but train fare and the boat cost money. Dominion Park band concerts (Creatore! Sousa!) were fun, and so were the carnival side shows, but expensive if you're out of work.

Books offered relief: novels of adventure and romance, the short stories of O. Henry, the muckraking exposures of Lincoln Steffens, the radical classics, Upton Sinclair, Jack London, John Reed. Books were beautiful, they opened up new worlds. Yet he felt a vague guilt that he was indulging himself, escaping into books and day-dreaming. He had to do more than read. He had to act, to move.

He had to face the fact of their poverty, their poor lodgings, the scant food in the ice-box, the sparse money in their pockets. You had to live, you had to, you had to be alive.

Fred wasn't sure he knew what he wanted. It would be good to have a trade, like electrician or auto mechanic, but right now there was no work for a young fellow anyplace except a few days here and there. Join the army? Hell, no, they killed his mother.

His father bolstered his confidence, kindled his dreams. Where would he be without the old man's dependable presence? It occurred to him also that Martin, under his tough self-assurance, needed his son's support. No, he couldn't leave Martin and go off harvesting; it would be like desertion. Still, would a few weeks away hurt, with a little time bumming around Vancouver, a week on a fishing boat, more cash for the grub-stake and an easier winter at home for both of them, new clothes, groceries, a crock for his dad?

Instead of the great western argosy, Fred found work close to home. A neighbour, chef in a country club, was looking for a kitchen-boy to replace a kid who'd gotten into trouble. The cook was in town on his day off; he would be in a tavern on St. Antoine in the afternoon. See him early, before he got oiled, Fred was told. He met the man, accepted a beer, and a second beer, and got the job.

Early next morning he travelled by train with his new boss to Pointe Claire. The chef had a hangover; he was subdued and shamefaced but friendly. Fred liked him.

"Stay out of the way of the guests," the man warned him. "They're a bunch of stuffed shirts with too much money, but otherwise they're not bad. They were born that way, they can't help it. They're not the worst you're likely to meet, lad. The real bastards are a couple of flunkies on the staff, like the steward, a real toady, a genuine Uriah Heep who creeps along on all fours smirking and sniffing at the guests for tips, but hell on wheels when he's barking at the rest of us. To hell with him, screw him! Anyway, lad, keep your nose clean, do your job and don't let nobody push you around."

At the golf club he was assigned a bed and a locker in the basement dorm and immediately went to work in the kitchen. The steward swept through, saw the newcomer, stopped and barked at the boy:

"Keep clean, boy, dress neat and watch your language. Be civil to the guests, don't eat more than your share, leave the girls alone. Just watch your step, that's all. The last kid showed lip, he's in the hoosegow now. Skinny little Jewboy. What's your name? Hmm, Irish. Well, don't let me catch you drinking. All right, get back to shelling your peas. Move smartly, Shaughnessy, don't talk back, don't malinger, don't sleep late, don't waste time, or out you go.''

The steward swept briskly through the swinging doors.

"Bugger him," said the chef.

"Bugger him," said Fred.

Cook raised his hand in the O.K. sign. Fred repeated the sign.

*

After work, after the dinner clean-up, Fred asked a chambermaid the way to the village. "Sure, I'll show you," she offered. On the way back she suggested a short-cut across a field.

"Let's sit here a while under this tree," he said, taking her hand. "You're not in a hurry to get back, are you?" She shook her head. "No, we're not far, anyway. I can see the lights."

They lay beside each other. "So many stars," she said. Then, "I can't see any at all now, you're blocking my view," and then, "Who cares now?" and later, "You don't close your eyes, do you?"

Much later, five minutes later she said, "I like you."

And Fred asked, "What's your name?"

"Georgina."

"Mine's Fred."

"I like you, Fred. You're fun. I like the way you laugh...and everything."

"I like you too, Georgie. You were great, really great."

As they followed the lights back to the club he asked, "What happened with the other fellow, the one before me? What did he do?"

"You sure ask queer questions."

"I just want to know what he did."

"If you have to know," she laughed, "he didn't do a thing."

"Come on, Georgie, you're talking riddles. What did he do, why did they put him in jail?"

"Oh, that. I thought you meant..."

"O.K., what happened?"

"They say he got into a fight with a club member. He got two

months. Funny thing, he was a quiet kid, he kept to himself. Good
manners, never argued, never got drunk. He'd finish his shift and
go sit in the shade with a book. Arthur was a very shy boy.''

"Arthur? Arthur what?"

"Meller, something like that."

"Was he dark, sort of thin? I went to school with an Arthur
Meller, a dark fellow, sort of thin."

4

1939. Hospital Night.
Ralph Gilbert's Watch.

TWENTY YEARS ON the force. This is the first time.

I've kicked pushed tripped and punched the bastards, I've
slapped and roughed them up and clubbed them down, I've twisted
arms and choked necks till they damn near bust their gut.

I never shot one, not till now, not a civilian. This is my first time.

The others don't count. Nobody ever knew whose bullet hit who.
More than one of us fired more than one shot that time, including
the officers.

It was after the war.

That was a different kind of a thing. That was the army. I was a
soldier. It was like shooting the Huns, except these were our own
guys.

It was the first spring after the Armistice, a Friday, I think.

What difference now? No difference. It's another war now, so I
shoot one more, here at home.

During wartime you kill enemies.

1922. End of Summer.
Fred and Martin.

The last time Ralph Gilbert attended a religious service he was
overseas and it was compulsory. Still, if you asked him what he

was, he would look hard at you and snap, "Christian, of course."

Of course, what else?

During all the uproar in Europe (wasn't he there, hadn't he seen?) he knew what side he was on. Rumour and rhetoric blamed the trouble on an anti-Christ. Gilbert, a believer, agreed. Terror in Finland and the Baltic hells was Christ's revenge. The bloodspills were a sacred purge. The swarthy Balkan butchers, goddamit, were Christians after all.

When Il Duce's fascist legions strutted drumbeat by drumbeat in bombast and blood, Ralph snapped, "They stopped the Reds, didn't they?" You had to respect them even if they ate garlic and had a pope.

There weren't so many Reds right here in Montreal, as far as he knew—a handful, a few hundred at most in run-down halls around The Main, gritty places scattered here and there, and an old house on Jeanne Mance, the Labour College, where they trained agitators and plotted. They had meetings nearly every night, and most of Saturday and all Sunday, with speeches in half a dozen funny languages, and concerts of mandolin pluckers, mixed choirs and all-men choirs, and hunky dancers in wide pants, and seditious recitations and all kinds of incitement.

They sold propaganda and gave it away free. They marched on picket lines. You thought they were singing old-fashioned hymns, but the sons of bitches used the tunes and changed the words.

Agitators, anarchists and bums, Limey immigrants, Scotchmen, Frenchies, Jews and Polacks, Irish trash and Uker-anians, Russian Reds and Red Ruthenians—Ralph saw through them all, the Greeks, the Macedonians and the Bulgarians, the Swedes and Finns and the Norwegians. They all despised him. Their young women looked at him with loathing.

Among the men were real hot agitators, like Mike Buhay of the tailors' union, his sister Becky who sometimes retouched pictures for Rice the photographer, her friend the big blonde amazon Annie Buller, Albert St. Martin the anarchist court stenographer, the handsome scholarly lecturer Max Armstrong, and Martin Shaughnessy the longshoreman. Ralph knew them all, he had heard them speak, he kept an eye on them.

The Shaughnessy man was no orator; he didn't thunder or jump or wave his arms like St. Martin. The waterfront workers heard him out; they listened quietly as he spoke in everyday words laced with the wit and spirit of his lost homeland. Gilbert sized him up: not a big man but tough and stubborn, with wide shoulders and a short neck. A quiet type, slow-moving, deliberate, not easily scared.

There was the younger Shaughnessy, the son, not quite as muscular, not as serious, a bit taller than his old man. He was away somewhere, Ralph didn't know where. Stirring up trouble, probably.

*

On Fred's day off he sat at a table, writing home as rain soaked the golf-links.

"Well, Dad, I missed the train and I'm stuck here. Sorry I won't see you till my next free day. I got to bed late, helping a friend with a few quarts in the pub. I slept in. In a way I'll be glad when summer's over, not that I don't enjoy it here. I do, but there's lots of things I want to do in the fall, going to the Labour College, exploring Mount Royal, maybe with a girl, watching movies, going to the library or playing checkers with you. I want to make a desk and another bookcase for our books.

"The job's not hard, the grub's good. They're a friendly crowd, except the boss, the steward. Saturday, our big day when we were like rabbits with St. Vitus preparing the dinner before the dance, he went sniffing around and upset a hot skillet. It landed on his feet, grease and all, and he let out a squeal like a stuck pig, and before he fell down, waving his arms and howling blue murder, he knocked over a jug of special wine sauce the chef had been stirring and tasting all afternoon.

"What a mess! Chef didn't say a word, he just stood there with a carving knife in one hand and a meat cleaver in the other, shooting dagger-looks at the steward, who picked himself up groaning and swearing and limped out in a hurry. Everybody laughed, chef too, and also the girls, who don't like being goosed and felt up by this creepy bugger when they're carrying a full tray and can't free their hands to defend themselves.

"The guests here, they're something special, like another part of the human race. They're cool and prosperous, they breathe money. Their women float across the greens like swans in summer duds, smiling princess smiles, trilling princess gab. They're the important people, always seen in the best places. They belong everywhere and everything belongs to them. They're the upper upper upper crust.

"Do you remember my old high school master, Major Steele, the one that strapped me and got me expelled when I stood up for the strike? Well, he was here yesterday, golfing and guzzling. I guess he didn't see me or I'd have got fired for sure.

"How would you like me to sponsor you for member? Would you like that? I'll buy you a bag of clubs and a pair of fancy plus-fours and sick you at them. Can you imagine them wrestling bales and boxes into the hold of a ship?

"You know my job. Well, it used to belong to a fellow I went to school with, Arthur Meller. He's in jail here. I'm his first visitor. It seems a guest got plastered and hurt himself and when Arthur tried to help him the guy got sore. It was Arthur's word against the souse, a big-belly named Cormack, a sales manager and a real son of a bitch sober or drunk. Anyway, Arthur got two months.

"I told the fellows and girls we ought to do something for him and they each chipped in a dollar so the summer won't be a total bust for him.

"He doesn't know what to do about his mother. If he tells her, she'll be upset. If he doesn't write, she'll worry. He's really in a spot. I offered to see her, but he says no, he'll try to figure something out.

"That's all for now. See you next week sure. Cheers, Fred."

*

Martin replied before the week was out:

"Dear Son, I got your letter and am sorry you missed the train. I hope the beer was good. Too bad you work Sundays or we could do some real fishing, but that will have to wait till the fall.

"I'm sorry to hear about your school chum. It seems poor people always get more than their share of trouble, here as in Ireland. It's the same damn system. You know the old song, 'Its the rich wot gits the grivey, its the pore wot gits the blime.'

"I dont want to sound like a sermon, but you got to fight every inch of the way and keep your head up. Trouble is, working people dont all stick together or we would of had stronger unions and the commonwealth of toil a long time ago. But we'll learn. Thats what we need, more good union men, dont forget that, my boy, you got to keep fighting all the time, and dont let up.

"We learn from our hard times or we never learn a thing, even from your straw-boss, the steward. Its Gods truth Fred, we can run away but we cant escape. And dont get no idea your old man left Ireland for no good reason. If I didnt leave I would of been a dead Irishman and dead Irishmen is what the Black-and-Tans wanted. Thats why I came here. I'm still in the fight, as the union brothers can tell you.

"You cant stand still, Fred my boy, youve got to keep moving and pushing, and maybe you get pushed back, but you keep on trying.

"Well thats all for now. I'm proud of you and I know you'll give a good account of yourself in the years to come. Well Fred dont let the boss work you too hard. Goodnight for now and up the union. See you next time. Your affectionate Dad."

*

Martin, tired and lonely, lay on his bed. How can you tell your son that his mother's image haunts you, that you love someone who for six years has been dust?

1922. End of Summer.
The End of the Job.

On the evening before closing day, groups had sipped beers in the tavern. For others there had been more intimate farewells. A few stretched out lonely on a cot, reading.

Next morning Fred was up early with the kitchen people. From below, after a bell roused the sleepers, you could hear running water and bursts of laughter as workers came alive.

Chef was getting the farewell breakfast ready. The steward swept in, snarling, "I don't see why they have to have a bloody banquet. You'd think they were members. You've spoiled them rotten."

"It's just odds and ends," said the chef, "leftovers we can't save for next year."

"I'd throw it out first," the steward grumbled, then, over his shoulder as he stormed out of the diningroom, "I'd see them all in hell first!"

"We'll miss your sunny smile," Fred called to the retreating back.

After the meal, plates and pots and cutlery were washed and stored in cupboards, floors were swept and waxed, beds stripped in the guestrooms, windows boarded up, garbage stacked outside.

The steward made a final tour of inspection, locked the doors and walked off alone with his club-bag. Without the customary dinner jacket and black bowtie he looked shabby and insignificant.

The staff made their way in little groups to the train depot. Their summer was done, loves had been celebrated, friendships had flourished or died, youngsters had overnight become adults. Some would forever remember nights benign, whispers and kisses and eager young bodies blending. Would any ever meet again?

While they waited for their train a busboy sang, "Hail, hail, the gang's all here," and others joined in. The steward, sulking in a corner by himself, shouted, "Shut up!" but others joined in the song. Incensed, he threw a stone. Fred cried out in pain as it struck his foot. He hobbled over. "I don't work for you anymore, do I?" he asked. "I don't have to take any more crap from you, do I? You're not my boss now, are you, sir? Well, I have a farewell souvenir for you, something to remember us all. O.K., here it is."

Fred's fist shot out at his mouth, pulled back and struck the nose, pulled back again and slammed into the cheek.

"Police! Help!" cried the steward.

"Keep your dirty mouth shut or we'll shut it up for good," a caddy said.

When a railway cop appeared the chef explained that the steward had tripped over a valise. It was nothing, nothing at all. The steward scowled and wiped the blood from his face. The cop left.

A train pulled in and paused. They piled in with their luggage. The steward found a seat in another carriage.

They settled in and sat quietly, summer behind them.

Now they were unemployed again. They'd need to ration their dollars, and soon their dimes, until they got jobs, *if* they got jobs. When the grubstake ran out there would be no rent money for the furnished room, no new clothes, few beers, no restaurant meals, no midnight snacks. They could then line up for soup at the mission, could ask for charity or beg on the street.

But right now, dammit, one little binge, a hard-earned flash of fun before the famine. Hell, why not?

Goodbye, Pointe Claire! Montreal, we who are about to cry salute you! If winter comes, can we survive?

The country club was behind them, the train roared away from its own smoke. When it grunted and steamed to a halt in Montreal the waiters, the bellhops, the waitresses, the busboys, the chambermaids and the maintenance and kitchen help took an uneasy leave of each other. If they had a home, they went home. If not, they looked for rooms.

The next day or the day after or even the day after that, but not a minute later, they would start to look for work.

1922. End of Summer.
Arthur and Rose.

On the last day of Arthur's jail term he washed at 6 a.m., put on the coarse blue denim uniform, made his bed in regulation style, ate porridge with syrup, chewed a slice of bread and drank his coffee.

He waited. At ten o'clock he was led from his cell to the room where convicts' clothing hung on cords hooked to a ceiling beam. He took his city suit back to his cell and changed into it, ready to rejoin the world.

He was taken to the office where a turnkey dumped his watch, a dry fountain pen and some silver coins out of a cotton sack. He was given an envelope containing thirty-two dollar bills and a note from Fred that the money was a gift from "your fellow-workers to show their solidarity." Fred wrote that his valise and the stuff from his club locker and his pay-cheque were also in the jail office, and to remember to get them.

Arthur signed, collected his money and his cheque, picked up the suitcase and walked out a free man, more or less.

At the station he sat down on a bench to await the big black Grand Trunk iron horse which soon pulled in, hissing steam as the huge piston-pushed wheels ground to a halt. He settled himself in a day coach. Exhilaration mounted as he neared the city he had not seen all summer.

At last he hurried from the cavernous old Bonaventure station, hoisted himself onto a creaking wooden streetcar and rode home hugging his luggage on his knees.

When he finally stood at Laura's door and cranked the brass

bell, Rose brushed away happy tears. His aunt embraced him. They all embraced.

It was good to be home at last with those he had known all his life.

*

"...They're hangin' men and women for the wearin' of the green..."

For Martin Shaughnessy it was a stirring cry of the Republicans. His son Fred, in the Montreal of 1922, responded with quick longing for the Irish homeland. But he had by now grown more attuned to the new battle hymns and the labour ballads coming up from below the border—the martyred Joe Hill's skeptical Wobbly verses set to traditional Christian tunes from the British Isles, or the Negro spirituals of the U.S. South, or the emotionally charged words and melodies of militant socialists in Germany, France, Italy and Russia.

Fred was surprised to discover that the organizer-poet Joe Hill had written a song about Canada, *Where the Fraser River Flows*, for the 4,200 British Columbia men who went on strike during construction of a railroad grade and tied up the line from Hope to Kamloops back in 1912.

Four years now after war's end, the wartime songs were nearly forgotten: *It's a Long Long Way to Tipperary*, *Mademoiselle from Armentieres*, *Pack up Your Troubles in Your Old Kit Bag*...

In Montreal, vaudeville performers winked and sang, "He's not so great in a crowd," and paused. "But when you get him alone," and paused again, "you'd be surprised!" Thousands snickered.

Most of the new songs came from the States, inane ditties cranked out in Tin Pan Alley, but the old tribal songs still stirred deep responses. The immigrants from the British Isles and even their children clung to their folk ballads and music-hall favourites. The nervous newcomers fresh out of Europe cherished the melodies of their forsaken lands and sang the old lyrics and danced the old waltzes and polkas thumped out tirelessly by accordion-players and fiddlers at parties in the city and celebrations in the combination meeting halls-schoolhouses-social centres scattered over the western farmlands.

Arthur's mother and her sister, no longer greenhorns but real Canadians now, ridiculed and mimicked the sad little Yiddish songs of the Russian ghetto and the Polish ghetto and the Lithuanian ghetto, but their eyes would belie them and fill with sudden tears sprung from the echoes of ancient murmurings in distant birthplaces that had starved and insulted and driven out their parents.

Later, when he knew Gaby, when she sang for him or even for herself, her voice held few tears, her songs were spirited and lively, their tempo brisk and fresh and filled with the laughter of her ancestors. For this was *her* home, *her* province, this had for centuries been *her* country, this was *her* music. She was Canadian, or Canadienne, whichever way you said or spelled it, and she was a little bit Indian as well, which was better than not at all.

*

Neither of the women asked why he hadn't written home in two whole months—Laura because she wanted to protect Rose and because she told herself her nephew must have had a good reason; Rose because most of the unhappy summer had been a confusion of which she remembered little, neither whether he had written or not written, nor whether she had been awake or in a trance. He was relieved that the question was not raised.

Next day he went looking for work. When he returned after trudging for hours his mother asked cheerfully, "Well, any prospects?" and immediately regretted the question.

"What a silly thing!" Laura laughed. "What a silly thing, has he any prospects? The boy's just got off the train and you ask him has he any prospects."

"I was joking," said Rose. "Anyway, the important thing right now is supper. Let's eat. Later I'd like to go for a walk, all of us, a nice walk on Pine, where the rich live." But only Rose and Arthur went; Laura stayed home with Josh and Jessie. School was starting again next day and she wanted them rested and ready, her eight-year-old boy, her daughter of ten. On Saturday she was going to Kingston to visit Norm; she would surprise him and bring the kids.

Arthur and his mother, as they strolled west along the comfortable streets flowing south of the mountain, found themselves speculating about a world they saw and sensed only fleetingly and could never penetrate. They wondered what it was like behind the walls of Pine Avenue, behind the windows whose amber lights projected hazy shapes over plush lawns and screened out the city's poverty, its aches and wounds. Here, below this dark mountain, the city's noise was muffled by great trees, thick ivies, impenetrable bushes and excluding walls.

Rooted on rock on the tamed slopes of Mount Royal, the homes exuded an aura of feudal power, of wealth and ease and permanence.

Hints of autumn flecked a tree or a shrub in the half-light. The rustle of small animals, the sound of restive birds and the whisper of the breeze accented the night's peace.

"It would be heaven to live here," said Rose.

Arthur looked into his mother's eyes and smiled. Sensitive to each other's needs, detecting nervousness in the silences, they hesitated to unburden themselves. Should he tell her about the wild ride with Cormack, about the whore, the jail? Should she confess her own ordeal? What kind of mother would he think she was? Could she tell him it was only a summer melancholy when it was her whole life, that it was only weeks since she had heard Laura play a Schubert song, had at last gotten up from her bed and followed the music into the frontroom, smiling shyly, and alive again? She had been lost for light-years below the ocean's bed, awaking thirsty in the middle of the night and confused about where the tap was and why Max was not beside her. She had guilty memories of her child's poor toys, and seeing him founder on his first day's work. She had felt hurt when she heard him tell of boys who went to summer cottages. She had fretted for him when he couldn't find work. She had been scared returning to the shop at forty. And before that, watching Max at the end of the table near the kitchen stove, straining to read in the ebbing light of a winter afternoon, fleeing each morning to get away from her accusing eyes and throwing a quarter on the table. She had cringed under the hunted look he gave her as he wrenched a coin from his anguish. She had seen his brother coming to witness the break-up, with Max doggedly repeating, "I don't know, I don't know," and walking away with his valises. Then Arthur tiptoeing down the steps late at night with her and her foot-pedal Singer sewing machine and pushing the contraption down the street while awakened neighbours peered accusingly from behind curtains.

How could you tell your son what you had lost?

"It would be fine living here," Arthur broke the silence, "when we get rich. First I have to find a job, a position sounds better. Good pay, I mean salary. Thirty-five a week, raises, big bonuses."

"Forty, Arthur, forty-five."

"Forty-five and a half."

She laughed. "All right, we won't haggle over fifty cents."

"They'll make you manager."

"They'll make me boss!"

"A hundred dollars a week!"

"That house over there, Ma, I'll buy it."

"No, the other, the one with the fountain."

"All right, the fountain."

"It could happen, Arthur. You're intelligent, honest. Other young men like you..."

She was reminded of Max and a lifetime ago, before Arthur was born, and of their dreams for each other and their son. Her elation sagged.

Arthur sensed her sudden pessimism; it deflated him too. Fat salaries, promotions, rewards? Start at the bottom, boy, Horatio Alger's bottom. Work your way up from jail. No pay but a free summer holiday in your own cell, with free meals, free clothes, free time...He couldn't tell her that. He couldn't say, "I hope you're proud of me and my promising career. I'm on my way up. All I need's a job, Ma."

Rose broke into his reverie. "Was the club nice?" she asked.

"It was all right."

"Did you learn to cook?"

"Sometimes I helped frying bacon and eggs. Mostly I peeled potatoes and helped wash dishes. I mopped the kitchen floor every day. I served stuff from the steam-table—soup and such— for the waitresses."

"Was it hot?"

"It cooled off in the evening."

"Did you work all day?"

"Oh no, we got two hours off in the afternoon."

"Arthur."

"Yes, Ma?"

"You're too pale, you have no tan."

"I stayed in the shade, I like it better."

"You're as pale as the Count of Monte Cristo."

"Monte Cristo?"

"Don't you remember? All those years in the dungeon, the Chateau d'If."

"I read it in school."

She shuddered. "Prisons are full of horrible things."

He drew a pack of cigarettes from a pocket, fumbled for a smoke, lit up and puffed. Rose watched. He was still awkward about it. Well, he was growing up, he was really a young man now.

"Do you like them?" she asked.

"Like what?"

"Cigarettes."

"Oh, sure."

She smiled.

"You're laughing at me, Ma."

"Of course not, silly."

"Well, don't call me silly."

"All right, but you smoke too fast."

"You're not angry?"

"Why should I be? Of course not. But don't smoke too much, and not so fast, and don't blow the smoke in my eyes."

"I'm sorry, Ma."

"Silly!"

They laughed.

"When did you start to smoke?" she asked.

"In jai—" He broke off and added in confusion, "In July."

Rose stared.

"In July," he repeated. "At the club. Everybody smoked."

"Arthur," she said.

"Yes, Ma?"

"You're puffing too fast. Your cigarette is all red coal."

"It's the wind."

"Arthur," she repeated, "you said July. You were going to say something else. It sounded strange."

"I got my tongue twisted."

"Arthur, listen to me. You know what you started to say. Not July but jail."

He didn't answer.

"Tell me, Arthur."

He told her, about the cop, the whore, Cormack, the jail.

"You needn't feel ashamed," she said. She touched his arm, turned away, and added very quietly, "Now listen to what I have to say, not about you, about myself, my summer." She told him the whole story, as much as she could remember.

"Both of us," he said in wonder, "both of us hidden away. . . ."

She took his hand. "You're not ashamed of me, are you?"

"My God!" he shouted, "I swear, if I'd known, I'd have broken out of jail and smashed that sweatshop and. . . ."

"Quiet, Arthur, it's late. I'm all right now. Speak low, we don't want to attract attention."

Rain started to fall, lightly at first. He took his mother's hand and they hurried away towards their own street, ran against the pelting shower, reached their door and unlocked it, puffing and laughing in the vestibule like schoolchildren.

"The house is dark," she whispered. "Aunt Laura's asleep. We'd better be quiet." She giggled. "I'm soaking wet."

"So am I, a wet jailbird."

They tiptoed into their rooms and went to sleep.

**1922. End of Summer.
Ralph's Woman.**

On the afternoon when Veronica Sawchuk pushed Gilbert out of her bed she accused him of deception and bigamy. In an outburst of invective she denounced him for lechery, greed, insensitivity.

Only minutes before, her voice tender with affection, her lips brushing his mouth, she had been as happy as an adolescent bride. Now she shouted and moaned and threw an ashtray. He ducked and laughed uneasily.

She flung open a closet, snatched a voluminous dressing-gown and wrapped it around herself, clutching the collar high around her neck as though to deny him even a fleeting glimpse of familiar flesh.

After screaming him out and banishing the husband-impostor-seducer-cheat from her thighs and slamming the door behind him, she stormed into her kitchen, removed Ralph's bottles from a cupboard, one rye whiskey and a Benedictine, sat at the table and filled a glass. She'd never cared for liquor, she didn't like the harshness. The first gulps made her shudder. Angrily she kept refilling the tumbler until the raw taste didn't matter any more. She became so drunk she could no longer pour, so she drank straight from the bottle.

She burst into tears. When the rye was gone she dipped into the Benedictine, spilled half, drank a quarter of it and fell from her chair to the floor. Her face was ashen white. The liqueur bottle rolled across the floor, leaving a sticky trickle.

Two days later, late at night, when he let himself in with his key, Ralph found her body. On the table was an empty bottle, on the floor another, still with a small drink in its heel.

He checked the place quickly, professionally. He stuffed his belongings into a club-bag: pyjamas, socks, a shirt, razor, cigars, handkerchiefs, package of condoms, shaving soap, toothbrush. He turned out the lights, locked the door and slipped out.

Early next morning he telephoned police headquarters and said in a muffled voice that he was a neighbour, he was worried, he had heard shouting at night, he had not seen Mrs. Sawchuk since then. He hung up when he was asked for his name.

When he reported for duty he was sent to the Sawchuk address. "Check it out. A neighbour called, he sounded drunk. But check it out." Ralph forced the door, made notes and called the medical examiner, who reported death from acute intoxication. The *Star* gave the story eleven lines under a one-line eight-point-bold head.

On the following day, gathered at the graveside, were Ralph Gilbert, a priest, a cemetery employee and a man about sixty.

"You a friend?" the old man asked.

"No, I'm the police officer assigned to the case. Who are you, a relation?"

"Her father. I don't see her nearly a year. I live in Verdun. I'm widower."

"How did you find out?"

"Nobody told me. The least they could do, somebody could of tell me. I see it in the paper. It say she die from whiskey. I don't understand, she never drink at home, she hate the booze. Last few year she act funny, you know, like something wrong in her head. Every time I visit she chase me away; she say I don't look like her pa. So I stop coming. So I just put money in envelope and put it in her door every month so she can eat. I give landlord cheque every month. Sometime I go to her street, I wait for her to come out maybe to buy groceries, but she goes past and looks at me and never see me. So I go away...I don't know how she got queer like that. I don't understand."

"Was it because her husband died in the war, her Matthew?"

"I never hear of no Matthew. She never got married."

After the burial her father shook Ralph's hand. "Thank you," he said, and walked away.

In the evening Ralph ate at the upstairs Rumanian Grill on The Main. When he returned to his apartment he kicked off his shoes and sat in his underwear, brooding and sipping Benedictine.

She was a real woman, he reflected sadly. Often, when she had sat beside him, talking earnestly, she seemed entirely rational. Then, in the middle of a sentence, she would falter and become silent. He would wait for her to recover the thread of her thought; he would take her hand and hold it until she spoke again.

Ralph swallowed the last of the liqueur, put on his pyjamas and went to bed. He would buy a small bouquet and leave it on her grave. He sighed heavily and lay staring into the dark.

5

1939. Hospital Ward.
All Your Ancestors.

"ANY CHANGE, DOC?" the detective asks.

"No."

None.

But everything must change, even as you lie in this hospital. Nothing is static, Arthur. Silent energies of life and death contest each microscopic organism.

You are the sum of many forces, past and present. At thirty-four you are the seed of all your ancestors, all people you have known, all things you've ever learned.

For days and centuries you have been growing and becoming. Winds blew across deserts and typhoons over seas and snows beyond hills, scattering us throughout Europe and America, Africa and the Orient. Ideas were born in alleys, shook hovels and levelled palaces. You did not come from nowhere.

Joan of Arc was your mother. And Mary Magdalene, Rosa Luxemburg, Annie Buller, Emily Carr and the Duchess of Malfi. And a host of ancient household slaves and the forgotten heroines of the Paris Commune.

Columbus was your father. So was Galileo. And Shakespeare and Marx, Hippocrates, William Lyon Mackenzie, Toussaint l'Ouverture, Amor de Cosmos. And Spartacus, Louis Riel, Beethoven. All these were your fathers.

Their spirit crossed the Himalayas, the Andes, the Rockies, reaching this hospital where you lie, and this detective, who waits.

1922. End of Summer.
The Disenchanted and Others.

It was thrilling while it lasted. Now, in 1922, five years after those heady times, the summer soldiers have long since lost faith, withdrawn into hibernation and opted for unctuous oblivion.

After the fall of the Russian monarchy in the spring of 1917, a film at the big St. Denis theatre in the French district of Montreal drew thousands who came to see history change. No more Romanoffs, hurrah for Kerensky! Immigrant audiences cheered. Impassioned Russian orators appeared on stage after each show, gesturing in the spotlight.

People crowded into shabby ghetto halls to hail the revolution. A new day had dawned, the war would soon end.

People came to hear about the changes in the places they had fled before the war to find new roots. They'd left the mud and tears and come to Montreal and dreamed of finding fortune there.

Max Meller had taken Arthur to the St. Denis movie-house and Martin Shaughnessy had taken Fred, the one father a fugitive from Nicholas II of Russia, the other from the tsar's English cousin, George V.

The war was not yet over. The tsar had quit, but the generals remained. Kerensky was their man. It took a second revolution, in November, to change all that.

The distant storm-signals sounded new hope. Would they be

heard in the crowded sweatshops and the factories, mines and railway yards? Would the bosses hear in Montreal? Would life become a little easier for poor people here?

Immigrants from Europe and the British Isles met with native Canadians to hold rallies, listen to socialist talk, pass resolutions and print leaflets.

After a while, when the authorities lashed out at both the Russian Revolution and the Winnipeg Strike, the summer soldiers went A.W.O.L. They said they'd lost their patience, the damn revolution was taking too long and it wasn't pure, anyway. "We can't wait for the millenium. Phone us if it ever comes. We'll meet you on the barricades, if it doesn't snow. Right now we're busy. No, we can't spare anything. Some other time."

Some flung themselves into making money with a passion and elan they had never given any other cause.

Others turned their coats inside out and spat on their ardent memories.

Some grew fat and sluggish and stopped thinking altogether.

Others, like Arthur Meller's father, caught only a glimpse of the Russian spring, turned away, ate their hearts out and died in despair.

And some, not many but enough to go around—the calm, angry, inspired, patient, rebellious Martin Shaughnessys—they had little patience with the impatient, no stomach for recrimination and no time for tears. There were causes to defend, projects to launch and dreams to grasp, now more than ever before.

*

Arthur Meller in 1922 is a slender youth, nearing eighteen and of average height and weight, somewhat darker in complexion than most, with smooth dark-brown hair and eyes darkly liquid, large and intense. His nose is narrow and straight, cheekbones are high, the brow is wide and long, lips are full, soft, curving down at the corners.

He is a soft-spoken young man, reticent in manner, an attentive listener who responds hesitantly to friendly overtures before an uncertain smile slowly lights up his face.

He haunts the Art Gallery on Sherbrooke, the vaudeville show on St. Catherine, the Fraser Library, and attends occasional concerts, stage plays, dance recitals, readings. Once in a rare while, consumed with prurient excitement and shame, he climbs to the gallery of the Gaiety burlesque house in the heart of the bucket-of-blood to ogle the strippers and the high-kicking low-cleavage chorus line. Contrite after the sin, he craves cleansing. The cloister? He smiles wryly. It would disconcert his mother, though she has rarely set foot in the synagogue.

Such lapses apart, he seeks out the debates, open forums, lecturers, offbeat personalities, literary taboo-busters, political non-conformists. They offer manna for the mind and drink for the soul; they feed a rich ferment of wisdom, culture and rebellion.

His hunger does not discriminate but devours the spicy tidbits from a smorgasbord of reformed anarchists on Sunday and Hindu mystics Monday, a communist on Tuesday and a Wobbly on the Wednesday, then for Thursday a Christian socialist, with a free-thinking crusader for Friday and, to round out the week on Saturday, an other-worldly dreamer, supplemented in the following weeks by new eclectic feasts from a repertoire of vegetarians, sex-reformers, Fabians, back-to-nature disciples, health-faddists and even a man with a scheme to trick the capitalist system into receivership.

Arthur at eighteen is an iconoclast who canonizes the debunkers of sham. He thrills to the sheer physical sound of their words, the resonance of the rhetoric. The young idol-smasher genuflects before the pedestals of his heroes, venerating their metaphors, dazzled by their mystique.

If the platform star is an attractive woman whose faint smile hints of grand amours, he weaves extravagant fantasies that transform her into a goddess who has seen his face in the crowd and can hardly restrain her yearning until question period ends and she can slip away with him, fervently clasping his hand in the cab that speeds them through the night high into the Laurentians to a hidden mountain cabin.

In a more mundane mood he invents excuses for even the most prosaic radicals. His admiration is unstinting, his rationalizations overlook all but the most obvious faults. He idealizes many a bore, finds grace in clumsiness and stature in a pygmy.

Because racial slurs offend him and stir deep tribal hurts, he is sensitive to immigrants who are doubly damned as foreigners and Reds. At a Sunday public meeting an Italian orator struggles defiantly through a short speech in awkward English. Arthur is ashamed because he thinks the man sounds like an ethnic parody in a vaudeville act. To make matters worse, the man's pant-leg has been snagged on a garter, exposing bare calf and a red sock. Arthur is embarrassed for him, averts his eyes and guiltily tries to screen out the jarring jokebook accent and listen only to the earnestness of the voice.

When the oration ends in a crescendo of exalted words Arthur claps loudly and shouts, "Hear! Hear!" The man sits down and a platform colleague whispers to him. He looks down, loosens the pant-leg and smiles sheepishly at the audience. They laugh and applaud again. Arthur is glad, his eyes swim, but he is annoyed with himself for cheering.

He enjoyed a particular evening at the Labour College, a tongue-in-cheek lecture, "Formula for Success," delivered with straight face by a young man in caricature scholar's gown and mortarboard.

"To advance," he advised sternly, "work hard and bank money regularly whether employed or not. Choose your family. It helps to be rich. It is also an advantage to have attended a private school. You can learn to review books without reading them and to develop a smattering of knowledge about the arts.

"Cultivate a cultivated voice, excel at tennis and golf, own a stable of horses, sail a yacht, drive a foreign car, inhabit an exclusive neighbourhood and have a good tailor. Be calm, never sweat.

"And finally, make sure you're white, British and preferably Protestant."

*

Fred Shaughnessy is eighteen in 1922, unskilled and living with his father in Griffintown, an Irish working-class district in the southwest corner of Montreal, below the Bonaventure railway station, below the Windsor station.

Fred's grey-green eyes are alert, spaced well apart in a squarish Jack London type of face, with a wide and generous mouth and firm lips. He has wavy chestnut-brown hair combed back, and thick eyebrows. He has a sturdy torso and well-muscled limbs.

He is an outdoor boy, a brisk walker and vigorous swimmer. He likes rowing, fishing, winter sports. He enjoys a Saturday-night beer but doesn't care for hard liquor. He is quick to laugh, quick to show anger, quick to cool off and quick to befriend. He reads a great deal, attends public lectures and may argue with the speaker during question period.

Fred has marched with his father on waterfront picket lines. He recently joined the new Workers' Party. "I'm a communist now," he tells his old schoolmate, Arthur Meller.

Clean-scrubbed and healthy, he's a casual dresser. He favours blue. Efficient, well-organized and well-coordinated, the younger Shaughnessy is aware that he must control a tendency to be impatient and aggressive.

Fred likes just about every girl he has ever met. Most girls are fond of Fred.

*

Unlike his friend, Arthur avoided the free-for-all debates after lectures; he never asked questions or engaged in discussion from the floor. After all, he wasn't part of it, and he wasn't going to be. He was free and independent. He was sympathetic to the revolution, he believed in it, he admired its people.

"But someone has to be above the battle," he told Fred as they climbed Mount Royal near the derelict incline railway. "When you stand on a mountain-top the air is clean; you can see for miles around."

"Except on foggy days," Fred cut in sharply. "It also gets bloody cold up there."

He's being a smart-aleck, Arthur thought, but said nothing.

Fred resumed the attack. "Anybody who lives in an ivory tower sooner or later turns to ivory. They're dead."

Arthur complained, "You don't understand."

"Do *you*?" Fred asked.

"I understand," Arthur said patiently. "All I can see is that there are many different ideas in the world, and many different roads. I have to find out for myself."

"And have you found out?" Fred pressed.

"No, not yet," Arthur said impatiently. "I need time."

"How long will it take? Do you think you have forever? Do you think you'll find the answer up here, or under an ant-hill, or in a cave?"

"There's no hurry."

"Do you really believe that? Do you think the world and all the universe will stand still while you make up your mind? Are you satisfied just to wait and freeze on your lonely mountain-top till you turn to ice?

"Why don't you join us, Arthur? Maybe we don't have all the answers, but we're trying, not just to find the answers but to make them work."

"You're dogmatic," Arthur grumbled.

*

They met downtown after a day of looking for work and sat sipping draught lager in a Main Street tavern—a sloppy, noisy place, for men only.

"I'd like to read you a piece I wrote last night," said Arthur, "a kind of poem, free verse, it doesn't rhyme, you know. Well, listen to it:

> *Our world brings out the worst in us,*
> *So we become self-satisfied and smart*
> *And all puffed up with sly conceit.*
>
> *We plot new frauds at every dawn,*
> *We scheme fresh alibis and lies.*
> *Then when we have to face the truth*
> *The day we die, we once more try*
> *To fabricate a bigger lie.*
> *We wear false masks of innocence,*
> *We flatter those who flatter death*
> *And then, when we're laid out in state,*
> *Regret we cannot cheat some more.*
>
> *Is life a game of slick deceit?*
> *Must we indulge the petty graft*
> *And cover it with perjury?*
> *And then do we go on from there*
> *And perpetrate the biggest lie*
> *To cover up the greatest crime?*
>
> *We cheat, we steal, we double-cross.*
> *Is that the score? Is that the end?*

"That's as far as I got. It's not finished. What do you think?"

Fred considered for a moment. "It's pretty good for a start. I didn't know you had it in you. I'd like to see it again when you finish."

Arthur was piqued. Pretty good—was that all his friend could say, pretty good? He reached impatiently for the poem and knocked over his glass. Beer spilled on his pants, the manuscript was soaked. He crumpled it and threw it to the floor. Fred retrieved it and smoothed the sheet. "I'd like to copy it out, Arthur," he said, "I think it's great."

Arthur was mollified. "Do you really like it?" he asked anxiously, and continued, "Everything's a mess, isn't it? What's the use, Fred? If you complain, you're told to face reality. They say, 'You can't change human nature, that's the way of the world.' What's the use, Fred, what's the use?"

"Look, Arthur, pessimism's our worst enemy. Sure it's hard to live in a world of lies. Even a single lie can soil the whole universe. But grumbling isn't enough. You have to spike the lies. You have to give people a taste for the truth, and the guts to find it."

Arthur said nothing; it was easy for Fred, Fred had made up his mind, Fred was always so sure of himself, he always wanted action right away, he was too impatient.

"It's not enough to understand," Fred continued. "It's not enough to be indignant."

Why does he have to lecture me? Arthur groused to himself.

"We have to educate people," Fred pressed on, "and we have to organize them."

"I know!" Arthur exclaimed, "but it looks so hopeless."

"Just knowing isn't enough," Fred insisted.

Arthur wrung out his wet pant-leg. "Let's move to another table. I'll buy some more beer. I promise I won't spill it." He smiled.

"We're part of the world whether we like it or not," Fred went on, "with all the beauty and all the warts. Sure, there's lots to make you ashamed of yourself." He saw Arthur's frown of annoyance. "I'm not trying to insult you, I could say the same about myself. Everyone's done something they regret. If we're civilized, we try to change ourselves as well as our world. It's all part of making a revolution.

"Singly we're no bloody saints or supermen, we're no miracle-makers. But who knows what we could do when thousands

work together! When you have intelligence and heart and
conscience and guts on your side—especially guts—nothing can
stop you. Whether it's next year or ten years from now or fifty,
we'll win."

"I know it and you know it," Arthur said, "but who else, how
many? There's so few!"

"We're not the only ones," Fred replied. "The Russians tried
and won. Others tried and lost. But never mind others, what about
us? We have to stand up and be counted—me, and you too,
Arthur, now!

"We don't have to be frightened clams hiding in the sand. We
don't need to pull a shell over our head and think we're safe."

He stopped, swallowed beer and continued, "Open up, Arthur,
for Christ's sake! You're young, you're a man, you want to live
and holler for joy! Help yourself, help the millions of other poor
bastards like ourselves! Give us courage, Arthur, liberate the truth,
ventilate the dungeons!

"Life isn't a virgin, Arthur! She's a lusty lover rich in a million
wonderful ways, she's like a song drumming on our hearts. Let her
in, Arthur, embrace her, stay all night with her, marry her!

"Don't be a damn fool! Don't run away from her!"

*

In the autumn of 1922, when Fred and Arthur and hosts of others
were jobless, the country was hobbled by foreign and domestic
economic exploitation. Political corruption was a way of life and
intellectual timidity was rampant.

The Catholic Church was all-powerful in Montreal. Priests and
nuns seemed to be in charge everywhere in Quebec, cloaking the
province in black funereal robes. Protestants dominated the rest of
the country.

Class distinctions were rigid. Distances between dirt farm,
sweatshop and affluent Westmount were astronomical. The
foreign-born were reviled, women enjoyed few human rights,
Indians were exiles and the Inuit were not even mentioned.

Movies were silent, except for the pit piano. There were hardly
any libraries, museums or art galleries outside the larger cities.
Vaudeville and stage plays, films, operas and ballets, as well as
magazines and books, were shipped in from the States or England.

Arthur remembered that only half a dozen years earlier, when Santa Claus fluttered from the clouds and landed awkwardly on the snow of Fletcher's Field, he came in a rattletrap one-seater concoction of canvas, wire and wood plus engine.

In the Toronto of 1922, it was said, you could shoot a cannonball down Yonge Street on a Sunday and hit nothing. You couldn't buy cigarettes or a beer or see a movie there or a hockey game on Sunday. Other cities were a little better or a little worse, but Sunday was blue Sunday, true-bloody-blue Sunday across most of Protestant Canada, on the premise that if you were bored to tears for fifty-two Sundays (plus holy days) and survived a year's purgatory, you would be purified and die happy and henceforth wallow in films and smoke-filled, beer-drenched hockey games eternally in heaven.

*

They had been to an early Saturday movie and were having a coffee at Childs.

"*Sunt lacrimae*"...How odd, Arthur said, that of all the Latin plugging under Mr. Christopher at Montreal High, little else remained with them.

"Remember Chris? Poor old Chris, he'd be ashamed of us," he told Fred.

"'*Sunt lacrimae rerum*'...There are tears for the state of things"...

Fred nodded, grinning. "That's the only Latin I remember, apart from '*arma virumque cano*'...'arms and the man I sing.'"

"I can almost hear old Chris reciting with that rolling burr of his," said Arthur. "Whenever I see wretched people I think of those words—'*sunt lacrimae*'—like the time we lived on Hotel de Ville, on the third floor. We had a back gallery and we could look down to a wooden shack, actually an old horse-stable with a lopsided door and a little window without a curtain, just a cracked green blind.

"An old couple lived there. We hardly ever saw them in winter; it's a wonder they didn't freeze to death. Late afternoon, when it got dark, an old man pushed home a cart full of chunks of wood and pieces of coal and junk. Somehow they lived through the winter.

"In the spring and summer we saw a little more of them, but mostly they kept to themselves and stayed indoors. They came out to cool off on hot evenings. They worked a tiny garden plot for vegetables and grew a few string beans on their walls and morning glories around their door. They used every inch of soil, like Chinese peasants.

"While it was still light they weeded, watered their plants, sat on their doorstep. I never heard them talk. Sometimes, even on our third-storey gallery, I caught a whiff of the sweet habitant pipe tobacco he smoked.

"About ten o'clock they went in. You wouldn't see either of them again until morning, when he left with his pushcart. Would you call it a pastoral symphony?

"Late in the afternoon he came home. From the cart he took scraps of cloth, a battered pot, a piece of carpet, odds and ends to dress up the shack. The old bottles and the scrap metal had been sold to the junkyard before he got home.

"It doesn't sound too bad, does it? Two tattered, transplanted habitant paupers living the simple life, not complaining, getting by, counting their beads, observing their low place in the order of things, praying devoutly and dying a little more every night in their damp cabin pathetically patched with glossy colour prints of Christ's crucifixion, and Jesus pointing to his own bleeding heart, and opposite on another wall, a newspaper portrait of Sir Wilfrid Laurier sharing space with a demure bathing beauty calendar. Home sweet home...

"Well, one day in April, it seems, they got a letter saying that they had to get out and lose their belongings unless they paid up three months' arrears in rent.

"On moving day, May Day, the people's holiday, the landlord broke into the shack and found them hanging from a beam. They were taken away and buried and nobody came to pay their respects.

"Did they have family, children? Nobody came, nobody mourned. That's '*lacrimae rerum*' for you, isn't it?"

"Remember the Windmill?" Fred asked, "the one that used to stand at Peel and St. Catherine and wave his hands? He'd point to the sky and everybody looked up. Then he'd walk away and leave them all staring at the sky. One day he collided with a streetcar and got killed. There was a paragraph in the paper; they didn't even know his name, they just said the Windmill Man was dead. I suppose he didn't know his own name. I guess nobody lost any sleep over that poor bugger."

"The time we lived in Calgary, on the edge of the open prairie," Arthur recalled, "we kids used to catch gophers. We got a pail of water and a net. We'd flush the water down one end of their tunnel and hold the net over the other end. When the half-drowned creature came up we'd catch it in the net. We never hurt them; we put them in a grocery box covered with mosquito netting and fed them pieces of cabbage or potatoes or stale bread and told all the kids we were having a circus and they could see the wild animals for a penny or a piece of candy or gum. When the kids stopped coming we set the gophers free.

"Well, one day when we were looking for gopher holes we saw a family of Indians walking towards us. They came slowly walking single file, an old man in front, behind him a younger man, then a woman with a baby in a cradle-basket slung on her back, then three children, two girls and a boy between five and ten years old. They passed close to us but didn't look up or say anything and kept on walking until they got smaller in the distance and we couldn't see them anymore.

"I'll never forget their faces. They just stared straight ahead. God, they looked unhappy! A girl was crying but she wasn't making any sound at all, just tears running down her cheeks.

"Where were they coming from in their thin rags, when if ever had they last had decent food, why did they all look like corpses, why did they stagger on so stolidly? Their eyes were so empty!

"And only one of them, that little girl, only she of that whole family had tears . . . 'Sunt lacrimae'—goddam!"

The young men finished their coffee and walked to Dominion Square. From their bench among the trees they could see the Windsor Hotel all lit up, and the C.P.R. Windsor station, its great stone mass hugging Peel where the street dipped downhill.

"Another time, during the war, our teacher told us to bring twenty-five cents and chip in for a Victory Bond," Arthur said. One girl stood up and said no, she wouldn't give anything, she believed war was murder. They expelled her. I wonder, would old Chris have said, 'Sunt lacrimae'?"

"Last Christmas something woke me during the night. It came from my dad's room. He was crying softly. He said my mother's name and then he was quiet again. I decided not to go in, not to disturb him.''

Later that week the two friends were walking on St. Lawrence and came to the police station at Marie-Anne. Its two windows were painted white and fronted by black iron bars. An overhanging white globe read ''Police'' in bold letters. Fred muttered a curse about Black-and-Tans.

''Abandon hope...'' Arthur began.

Fred finished the line, ''...all ye who enter here.''

''That's Dante,'' said Arthur. He bent over, picked up a stone and hurled it at a window, shattering glass.

Fred grabbed Arthur's arm and walked him quickly around the corner. ''Don't run,'' he warned, and led him into a busy cafe. They sat near the back. Within minutes a policeman opened the door, surveyed the crowd, hesitated and left. The boys drank their coffee and presently left as well.

''Just what in hell do you think you accomplished with that?'' Fred demanded angrily.

''I don't know,'' Arthur growled. ''I was sore.''

Fred spoke grimly, ''Smashing windows won't close police stations or make them any nicer.''

6

1939. Wartime.
A Very Old Lady.

IRMA SITS IN her rocking-chair at a window of the flat in which she has lived for many years.

On an evening in the early fall the leaves are beginning to turn. The marigolds, the zinnias and the scarlet salvias flourish in the garden below.

Miss Gillespie is eighty-two and wonders whether they will come to her apartment to seize her books and whether she will be questioned and perhaps jailed because of the violence in the park.

She smiles uncertainly. Surely they aren't afraid of her. She has nothing they want. Besides, where would she run?

She rocks in her chair and pulls the sweater around her shoulders and sings in a barely audible voice:

> *The people's flag is deepest red,*
> *It shrouded oft our martyred dead.*
> *And ere their limbs grew stiff and cold*
> *Their life's blood dyed its every fold.*
>
> *Then raise the scarlet standard high,*
> *Within its shade we'll live and die.*
> *Though cowards flinch and traitors sneer*
> *We'll keep the Red flag flying here.*

Irma undresses, changing into a pink flannel nightgown, drinks a glass of milk, decides she had better wear the blue eiderdown robe as well, turns off her light and snuggles into bed. For some time she lies awake, wondering, worrying. Eventually she falls asleep, breathing softly.

1922. End of Summer.
Miss Irma Gillespie.

In her sixties now, she could not remember when anyone had ever called her anything but Miss Gillespie, never Irma, except her parents, but that was long ago. She had almost forgotten the sound of her first name.

The corner grocer was always patient and polite with the old lady who carried a shopping bag even for a half-pound wedge of cheddar or a few slices of cooked ham. It was invariably, "Good afternoon, Miss Gillespie, what can I do for you today, Miss Gillespie?" even though she bought sparingly. She never asked for credit, he told his wife. She never complained about the provisions, was never anything but the perfect lady. At the candy-shop where she picked up her daily newspaper it was always marked "Miss Gillespie" in full, not just her initials.

For supper she might boil two small potatoes, fry a pork chop and brew a pot of tea. She would spread a lettuce leaf on a dish and arrange slices of cucumber, tomato and potato around the rim, painting them with a dab of butter, and then set the chop in the centre. Other times it was cabbage and corned-beef hash or liver and onions. She was fond of mint sauce, which she prepared herself, and used as a universal condiment.

She held her teacup primly in the way her mother had taught her and took small silent sips.

She sat reading her paper on the balcony until dusk. She marvelled at the action photos of swimmers and tennis players, those strong swift creatures whose beautiful bodies poignantly reminded her of long-abandoned hopes.

As the day grew dim and the paper slipped from her hands, she dozed off. When she awoke it was dark. She went indoors, took a bundle from her shopping bag and untied it, carefully folding the brown wrapper and rolling the string into a small bow and setting them aside in a drawer. She neatly folded each leaflet and placed them all in her shopping bag. She drew on a pair of cloth gloves, adjusted her hat and went out on her rounds, slipping leaflets into letter-boxes and letter-slots.

One day, she knew, she would be caught. Would they fine her, lock her in a cell? Could they confiscate her savings, small though they were? If they did, what would happen to her, how would she live?

But she can't stop, even though she is afraid. "Shame on you, Irma Gillespie! Shame on you for whimpering!" she scolded herself. "You mustn't run scared."

She smiled, amused and flattered that a boy at the meeting just yesterday, a cheerful young fellow named Shaughnessy, a really nice lad, had said, "Thank you, comrade," when she put a quarter on the collection plate.

"Comrade . . . Well!" She laughed. "We never spoke that way in P.E.I., on the Island . . . Comrade, indeed!"

If she did not lose her meagre savings and if she lived long enough to greet the commonwealth, then all she'd missed—husband, children, joy and love—had not been in vain. Her tired old bones would be content.

Miss Gillespie dozed off and snored a little.

7

1939. Night Thoughts.
At Gaby's House.

WHAT A TIME to become pregnant!

It's two weeks since I checked with the doctor. I had been feeling funny and made up my mind to find out. I found out, all right. Now I know it and Arthur knows it. I told him right away, of course. You should have seen him; I had to laugh. First he looked stunned, then his face lit up like a happy drunk and he jumped up and kissed and hugged me.

"Easy, you'll suffocate it!" I warned.

He laughed. "I'll be careful. I'll be a good father, you'll see. I'd like a girl, but a boy would be just fine."

His mother and his Aunt Laura were here with me tonight for supper and then we went to the hospital together. We were allowed to look at him for a few seconds. He was breathing, that's all you could say.

Will our child be an orphan before it is born?

Rose and Laura came here to my place afterwards. We sat and talked and drank coffee.

Before they left, a little while ago, his mother said, "I wish I had your strength, Gaby."

I wish I had the strength she thinks I have. . . Poor woman, she's had one hell of a life so far.

I'm thirty-four years old and I'm going to be a mother for the first time.

I'm scared. But it's what we need, Arthur and me. We've been living too much for ourselves, *with* ourselves.

I should have told his mother about the baby. Would the news have made her happy or would it have upset her, right after seeing him so pale and motionless? I'll wait a few more days.

Next year the child will smile at me from its crib. Arthur will pick it up and hold it above his head and say, "Look at her grin!" and I'll say it's gas. We'll laugh like kids.

How proud we'll be.

If Arthur lives.

1922. Indian Summer.
Gaby and Arthur.

I saw her different places, mostly lectures. She's a girl you notice, not pretty-pretty but damn good-looking. She's round and slender, almost like a boy, but she *is* a woman, there's no mistaking that.

Her voice is low and very soft, with a French accent, not strong but enough to charm you. I like her blonde hair and her fair complexion. Her eyes are blue or grey or violet or green at different times.

I watched her at the Scott Nearing lecture, her chin tilted and her eyes concentrating on the tweedy speaker. She has a small oval face with fine features and a beautiful red mouth. Her ears are small and she wears little pearl earrings. I was glad there wasn't a man with her.

I saw her again at the St. Denis during intermission, standing by herself, reading her program. When she returned to her seat I noticed how gracefully she moved. She had an aisle seat and when the lights came on at the end I could see that she was glowing with pleasure. Anna Pavlova had just danced *Autumn Leaves*. I don't know what thrilled me more—the dancer or this girl.

I finally met her face-to-face when I went to buy a present for my mother at this new shop below the campus. There she was behind a showcase.

*

I was alone in the shop when he came to buy a gift for his mother. He examined the books, looked at the prints I had framed, stopped at the pottery and the costume jewelry and chose a silver brooch.

I had seen him somewhere. The Art Gallery, the Auditorium? Who was he, what did he do? Was he as young as he looked?

We chatted about the things in my shop. I told him about the artists who had made them. He showed interest but didn't say much; he was quiet and reserved, pleasant but very serious. He didn't try to flirt; I couldn't imagine him making a pass. I boxed the gift and he left.

A week later he was back, said hello and went over to the books. After a while he looked up and asked me, "Have you read it?" He was holding the first volume of *Jean-Christophe*. I nodded. His face lit up. "I'm reading it now, in English!" he exclaimed. "I wish I knew enough French!"

He turned up more often. He was so eager to talk about the book. Our conversations became less literary and more personal. How else can you discuss Romain Rolland?

I was drawn to this earnest young man with the handsome face and large brown eyes. I watched his mouth as he spoke and felt an awful urge to kiss him. I suspected that under his composure there was a great need for friendship and yet a hesitation. I think I have something of that in me too, but I am much more outspoken and I take more chances.

*

They met often, rediscovering each other each time.

There were Sunday afternoons on Mount Royal's lookout high above the crowded city and its harbour. There were the evenings when they sat on a rug in her livingroom and she read to him. They listened to records and took turns changing the old wax disks and winding up the hand-cranked Victrola.

They shared concerts and films, plays and musical comedies, lectures and vaudeville shows. They went on long walks and sat for hours in dim corners of obscure cafes, exchanging dreams.

At night they parted full of longing.

*

You shouldn't stay alone all day or sleep alone all night, Gabrielle reflected. The most beautiful things are those you talk about only with a lover.

For all her self-sufficiency, she knew what she had been missing. Now there was Arthur, to look at, to speak to, to kiss, to caress.

"...that thou none lovest..." The sonnet no longer accused.

*

She packed a picnic basket: boiled eggs, salmon sandwiches, potato salad, a bottle of Chianti in its raffia wrap.

They rode the high electric car to Cartierville. They walked to the riverbank and found a spot under the trees and sheltered by bushes.

They talked and kissed and clung to each other.

He tried to forget that his father had died here, in this water.

In the evening, after they had eaten and had some wine, they waited for the dusk.

There was no pretence and no desperation in their lovemaking, no pain and no regret, only the peaking of joy and then the serenity.

On the tram going home she leaned her head on his shoulder; there was no need to say anything. He had a memory of lying on a tram seat when he was very young and watching his mother leaning back against his father as the heavy car creaked its way home in the Sunday night breeze.

Arthur and Gabrielle silently entered the house, sat in her livingroom and sipped wine. A single lamp burned in a corner.

She moved closer to him. "Don't leave me," she said. "Stay with me. Stay tonight. Stay forever."

Again they kissed, touched, caressed. This time it was not tentative; they knew each other now. No more uncertainty. Now they were equals, equals and lovers.

Gaby kissed him on the mouth and rose. She led him upstairs to her bedroom. She turned off her lamp and removed her clothes. In the uncertain light from the street he saw only the roundness of her neck, the contour of a thigh.

"Arthur," she asked, and he could almost see her smile, "do you need all those clothes?"

He undressed and lay down beside her.

"Gaby," he whispered.

"Don't say anything now, just kiss me."

"Gaby, I want to tell you..."

"Later."

"No, now. Gaby, I love you."

"I know. Now kiss me, Arthur. I want you."

PART SIX

1

1939. Early September.
Fred in Hiding.

POLICEMEN CROWD into the Griffintown flat. They're looking for Fred. They find nothing, no plots, no propaganda mill and no Fred, only the father, the longshoreman.

"Where's all the books?" Detective Gilbert asks, pointing to a shelf on which rest a Bible, a French-English dictionary, an atlas, a cookbook and a fishing guide. "Where's the rest?"

Martin shrugs. "That's all. We don't read much."

"You're a liar," says Gilbert. "Where's your son?"

"I don't know."

The detective glares. "You're a liar."

Martin says nothing and stares back steadily from under bushy eyebrows.

Ralph Gilbert slaps him hard across the mouth and the old man falls to the floor.

The police leave; they're not interested in Martin Shaughnessy, there's no warrant out for his arrest, not yet. They want Fred. The last man slams the door, shattering its glass.

Martin picks himself up, bathes his face with cold water. He gets a piece of ice from the ice-box to stop the blood and gets himself a pint of beer.

"Sons of whores," he says.

*

Fred has been taken by car to an east-end house on a sidestreet off Papineau, where the grey-haired Armand Paquette gives him an upstairs bedroom, feeds him generously in the kitchen and brings home a bottle of brandy for their evening chats in the tiny library-den.

Armand plays Scarlatti, Chopin, Bach on his heavy Bell upright. Fred marvels that this shy widower can summon such quick beauty from brittle old fingers.

During the day, while Paquette is away tuning pianos in convents and parochial schools, Fred is left to himself and spends his time listening to the radio, and reading, and thinking.

*

Bombs fall on Europe, tanks flatten the earth.

Over the tracks of the caterpillar treads with their dappling of random blood and oil, the jack-boot automatons strut and shoot, shout and shoot.

Populations flee ancestral towns in panic.

Millions will die in the next six years, violently, horribly.

With infinite inventiveness the techniques of the kill proliferate.

*

Fred Shaughnessy, you Dublin scum,
Do you remember me?
I'm Major Steele, true blue,
Your high-school master, ramrod strict.
I paddled both your palms in Montreal High.
I'm Stinson Steele (Intelligence
In World War 1)
Back on the job
For the big new show.
I'll be delighted
To whack you
Any time you show your Irish mug again.

So, you've graduated,
You're a full-time Red.
How's the revolution?
Not so good, comrade?

Who in hell do you add up to?
You're a seamy crew of scruffy rabble-rousers,
A rag-tag band with bloodshot eyes,
And not a decent boot or suit of clothes
Among the lot of you.

You don't think you'll ever make it,
Do you, now?
You're finished. Period. End.
Like the Kraut says: Kaput!

Some day we'll hang you
With my old school tie.

*

Dear Major Steele, M.A. and S.O.B.: I dreamt last night you ripped my hands again to bloody pulp. Remember me? I'm Shaughnessy. I woke to nausea. I wondered what in hell you're fouling now, all spit-and-polish arrogant. Have you allowed one decent thought to penetrate your narrow mind?

You must be in your element today. This war is made for men like you, *by* men like you. Which side are you on, by the way?

*

Arthur, dear man, don't give them the satisfaction. For your own sake, for all our sakes, for your friend my son and for his mother who died on a doorstep in Dublin, live, Arthur!

The Twenties.
Apprentice to Revolution.

In the fall of 1922 I was eighteen, grubbing for jobs and not having much luck. The country club experience counted for little; hundreds more qualified than me were haunting hotels and restaurants.

My dad tried for me on the harbour, and they smiled hard and said they didn't think they'd need an extra Shaughnessy. They guessed one was as much as they could tolerate in any one place at any one time.

I managed to pick up a week's work here, there, a few days now and then, anything I could get. I washed floors and windows in a cheap hotel, delivered handbills and mowed lawns. For four days, 8 a.m. to 6 p.m., I guided a screaming buzz-saw in a back-alley woodwork factory. The boss took a dislike to me. "Don't pay him no attention," I was told, "he's crazy." When he threw a chisel I quit. I told him to shove his job. He slapped my face and shouted, "I love my workers!"

I worked the suburbs with a team hustling magazine subs. We got pinched for peddling without a licence. *Maclean's* paid our fines. My heart wasn't in sales and I got fired when I didn't make the quota.

I hawked ice-cream cones and chocolate bars in the aisles of the Gaiety burlesque. "Cools 'em off," grinned the candy-butcher boss. "Look at 'em, look at the jerks; they're all in heat. Go out there and cool 'em off before they bust."

They were a weird lot, glassy-eyed old men and feverish kids trembling pop-eyed like they were having a fit, hundreds of them, throwing looks like hot rivets at the strippers, hundreds of nervous males sixteen to seventy-five, like they were in shock, breathing hard, their eyes darting and crawling into and raping the taunting groins. Five shows a day from 2 to 10 p.m., and each show the buttocks heaved, the comics told dirty stories and leered, and the strippers jiggled their breasts and teased. Five times a day the boys and the patriarchs came there in fever, in shock and in shame.

At first it was fun walking in without having to pay to see all those flapping boobies, but after the first few shows I got bored; these women had been turned into machines. By the end of the week the whole business sickened me. I wasn't sorry when I left.

A neighbour advised my dad, "Tell him to try plumbing; it pays good money." If it was so good, how is it this fellow didn't try it himself, seeing he was out of work? I canvassed plumbers two whole weeks and all I got was a brush-off: "What experience have .you? We don't need learners." "We don't pay beginners." "We're not hiring now. Try us in December." "Come back in the spring."

I'm handy with tools. I wanted to be a mechanic, but it was hard to crack the trades. The craft unions were like fortresses, closed corporations. Newcomers were discouraged. The older men were afraid we'd work for less and steal their jobs. A few kids were let in when an old-timer died or quit. We were expected to sweat it out five, six, seven years as apprentices.

I'm built like my dad, only taller. Work never scared me, but I didn't want to slug it out like a workhorse for a bag of oats.

I found a job in a printshop; fair pay and a boss who didn't push. I swept up, wiped wet ink from type with sharp-smelling solvent, collated printed sheets, bundled handbills, cleaned the handpresses, learned to trim paper on the guillotine.

After a time they let me set type by hand and tie up pages with string and lock them into forms on the stone, ready to run. I liked it fine, I liked starting something and seeing it take shape and admiring the finished product. I liked the texture of fine papers. I began to appreciate a balanced layout of heading, body-type and artwork on a sheet. I still do.

A man should take pride in his work; it should mean something. "Fred Shaughnessy," I promised myself, "in six or seven years you're going to be a compositor, a good craftsman and a respected union man." I'd be able to boast, like the older men, that you're not a genuine typographical man until printer's ink instead of blood flows in your veins.

The fellows fooled around when the boss went out. They had a funny initiation for new boys; it happened on my second day. One of them sidled up close and right away I felt something dribble down my pants. I got angry at the dirty trick and grabbed him by the shoulder, but he only smiled like a fool and pointed to the floor. Others stopped work and laughed. I took a quick look down; there was no puddle and my clothes were dry. There was no trickle of wet, just a handful of cold metal linotype crumbs. I couldn't wait to initiate the next green hand.

I learned my trade on the job. I found out about other things on my own time. I read. I took courses at the Labour College: history, labour unions, economics, the Paris Commune, the Russian Revolution and so on.

I found books no teacher had ever mentioned. I heard lectures by the blacklisted American professor, Scott Nearing; Jim Larkin, the Irish rebel; and James Woodsworth, who was arrested in the Winnipeg Strike.

The college was a solid old house on Jeanne Mance, weather-beaten and comfortable, owned by the machinists, I think. Other unions rented space.

There was a janitor who lived rent-free in a basement cubbyhole. He used to come upstairs and talk to whoever he could corner, the same story over and over again about King George visiting the front. "He came right up close to me, he looked right into my eyes, the king passed right in front of me!"

The old soldier thrust back his shoulders and stood at attention, eyes bright. He saluted stiffly, sat down and stared at the wall.

There he was, surrounded by communists, radicals and Reds young and old but he looked blank when you mentioned communism; he thought it was something Catholics did.

He adored his king and the whole royal family. Earl Kitchener and Viscount Allenby were his giants.

Poor old lonely war-stunned soul! Were *they* his family? Did he have no other parents, brothers, sisters, friends? Were we new every time he met us? Were we real? Was *he* real? Was he still trying to focus on shadows from the smoking battlefield where sanity had exploded?

But what about the normal ones, the undemented? Why didn't *they* discern reality, why did *they* refuse to understand, what fears held them back? Were they annoyed with our intoxication?

*

Drunk we certainly were, gloriously drunk with new ideas, new friends, new sentiments.

We soaked it up, luxuriated in it, sang it, pursued the joyous adventure.

Those were the days, those were the nights; those were our brave defiant formative years.

It was our time of sweet euphoria.

We were young and burning with a beautiful bright fever.

We were bursting with dreams and drive and the urge to scale high mountains and the need to defy and defrock the old established gods.

*

I like being a printer, liberating words and spreading ideas. Metal type and the printing press can open eyes.

Of course the alphabet can either teach or muddle you; words can massacre the truth.

I wish I'd had a go at university; it would have helped. Maybe later, if I can save enough to put me through. I'd like to follow up on the things I only tasted at Jeanne Mance.

But for now I've got to learn my trade.

Maybe I'm dreaming out of my class.

*

I compare my father's life with that of other men—people who never went without and probably never will, who don't have to surrender a little more of themselves every day just to get by.

Men like my dad aren't greedy, but we resent having to scrabble at the heels of the rich. We don't ask a banquet and adventure every night, but we resent being broke. We don't ask for champagne, we'll settle for a beer. We don't belong to the charmed circle born into luxury, like a birthright, something they take for granted. My dad and people like us face a crisis at the start of every day.

*

Fred liked the brisk and self-confident manner of this organizer who came from Toronto in the spring of 1924 and spoke earnestly for thirty minutes to a roomful of young people on a sun-drenched Sunday afternoon. Fred liked the firm handshake and the crisp timbre of his voice.

The speaker gave his talk, answered questions and listened to discussion. He asked them to join the Young Communist League.

Fred chaired the meeting. He had joined the Workers' Party a year before and they had tried to form a Young Workers' League. It hadn't flourished; there had been too much talk. This time it would be different; there would be more fun, more interesting educationals and debates, and plenty of socials, picnics and hikes.

They would rent a room in the Labour College and hang pictures. They would have shelves full of books. They hoped somebody would donate a second-hand phonograph. They would get comfortable seats, a rug on the floor, soft lights, curtains.

Of the eighteen who came to hear the clean-cut young man from

Toronto, most were sons and daughters of socialist immigrants or native-born radicals, a few came with school chums, all were drawn by the promise of a whole new world of actions and ideas. They ranged in age from seventeen to twenty. The Toronto speaker himself was only nineteen, a handsome youth with a frank and open manner and an apt way with words.

They were eager to get started, to belong, to do things, float on air. They chose officers and elected Fred their organizer. They set up a clubroom committee and agreed to meet Wednesdays at eight. They urged Toronto headquarters to start a paper, a revolutionary beautiful inspiring youth paper to stir the imagination of the whole country.

Nobody put it in so many words, but they knew they were making history, they felt the future singing in their veins. They were right.

After the meeting Fred took the speaker home to meet his father and split a few pints. They fried liver and onions and hash-brown potatoes and spent the evening with visionary talk and beer before Fred saw him off on the C.N. night train to Toronto.

Their young guest was the kind of man the Shaughnessys admired. Leslie at twelve had gone to work in the English railroad yards in Kent, at thirteen worked at the big Ebbw Vale steel plant in Wales, at fifteen laboured in the Welsh coal mines and at sixteen was back in Canada, where the family had lived for a few years before the war. He worked in the Winnipeg C.N. shops as an electrician.

At nineteen a labour veteran, he had stood that afternoon in a Main Street labour hall near Prince Arthur and urged his peers to embrace his cause—"Communism, to which all roads lead," he had said—and form a branch of the league which, he declared vehemently, he was proud to serve.

Fred shook his hand at the railway station, said goodbye and promised to report soon. That night he was too excited to sleep. It had been a big day. He wondered whether he could put the Y.C.L. on its feet. Had he taken on too much?

He got out of bed and sat at the kitchen table, working on two outlines: a list of goals for their first six months and an agenda for their meeting to be held three days later. It had better be good, he told himself.

He got back into bed, optimistic and exhilarated. For the

umpteenth time he reviewed the day's events. He spun fantasies, imagining himself addressing a vast sea of faces in a crowd on Fletcher's Field, as far as the eye could scan, inspired by sonorous brasses pouring out a full-throated *Internationale* as marchers moved off under fluttering Red banners to take over the City Hall and proclaim the commonwealth of toil.

Fred dozed off with a beatific smile on his face. On the Toronto-bound night train Leslie Morris looked out into the dark and tried to sleep sitting up.

*

The years were crowded with dreaming and debate, meetings and conventions, door-to-door canvasses and political petitions. Laughter and elation, picket lines and protest marches filled their days. Lectures, study groups and literature sales preoccupied them. Shouted slogans, sing-songs and romantic myths inspired them.

The years witnessed their ardour and heard their pain as they coursed through 1924 and into '25 and on and on.

*

In Europe a White terror hunted revolutionaries. Pale-skinned northern Balts and tanned Balkan squires vied in bloodletting to surpass each other, to outbid the carpet-baggers of the post-war world, contesting for the patronage of the new emperors.

In Canada wages shrank, jobs dried up, farmers' children went hungry to bed.

Coal miners were shot on picket lines.

Lumberjacks signed up the camps, seamen organized the ships, needle-workers unionized sweatshops. New unions fought to break through into steel, auto, textile, furniture, footwear, asbestos and meat-packing. Strikes were lost and won.

In Canada the Chinese were *chinks,* the blacks *niggers,* the Jews *kikes.* Other immigrants were *hunkies* and French-Canadians were both *peasoups* and *frogs.* Eskimos and Indians were camouflaged and forgotten.

But we held solidarity rallies for India, for China. We hailed the British General Strike. We defended Sacco and Vanzetti. In this way we also defended ourselves.

*

Who were the protesters? Fred saw them as a variety of mavericks, reformers, non-comformists and revolutionaries—people basically at odds with a mad society.

Some had been rebels since youth, some were recent radicals, all were dissatisfied. Some were still searching and some had doubts about committing themselves.

Among the youngsters in the Y.C.L. there were few doubts. They had entered a world of exhilarating ideas and fervent emotions, they were inspired, they soared.

Wherever there was a mass meeting or a picnic or parade, you found the Young Communists collecting petition signatures, selling their *Young Worker,* pleading for money for strike relief, money for prisoners of the White terror, money for the labour press.

During the day they worked for a living. Evenings and weekends they spent in door-to-door canvassing, study-groups, hikes, socials, incessant discussions, leaflet writing and distributions. One campaign barely got under way before a new cause overlapped and demanded fresh dedications.

They came together in their free time in their clubroom or a member's parlour to chat and joke, nibble sandwiches and cookies, sip ginger ale or tea, tell stories, go to the movies afterwards and, before long, pair off.

*

Rose Meller continued working in men's clothing. She liked Gabrielle, but Arthur shouldn't have left home to live with her. "They're so young," she would tell Laura. "She's French; I think she's Catholic too; they're not even married. If there's a child..."

Norm Nelson came home from prison, subdued, grey-faced and restless. His first night home he pounced hungrily on Laura. When she became pregnant he slipped away without a word, to California. That's where a dollar multiplies like weeds, he'd heard. "I've got to live my own life once and for all," he told himself.

Laura, after considerable soul-searching, induced a miscarriage. A week later, she resumed singing for hire and playing the piano in silent movies to support herself and her two children.

Miss Gillespie dreamed of the north shore of Prince Edward

Island and distributed leaflets in Montreal.

Ralph Gilbert snooped in radical alleys and saw subversion in every handshake. He continued to visit his Veronica's grave and leave bouquets of flowers.

Martin Shaughnessy laboured on the waterfront, wished for his son's happiness, and doggedly attended union meetings.

Arthur worked in the wholesale houses of St. Lawrence-Main, read books and magazines and attended lectures.

Gaby's shop was attracting customers from Westmount and Notre Dame de Grace.

*

All new movements attract camp-followers, careerists and flash-in-the-pan joiners who soon become bored and move on.

One such was Bar-Kochba Narodzhinsky Adamson, 22, a tall Adonis with marcelled crown of chestnut curls surrounding a ruddy oval face from which black eyes flashed bright and seductive.

He arrived in Montreal trailing mists of glamour. He captivated the men with masculine camaraderie, the women with bold looks and electricity. He was fascinating, well-spoken, cultured and romantic. Everyone hoped to be flattered into his friendship.

He came from England. Visiting an uncle, he said. He'd been everywhere, Rome, Paris, Constantinople. "But you know," he told Fred, "what I really want is to be Canadian, like you. Canada is new and different. I plan to live here and work with you. I'm staying with my uncle, but I want to be free and independent. I don't share my uncle's views, he's a dreadful bourgeois, a Babbitt. Have you read the book? By Sinclair Lewis."

Fred had. He was also curious about the odd name. "That's a real monicker," he said. "How did you get it?"

The fellow laughed. "I invented it. I'm Harry Harris but I wanted a name that really says something. Bar-Kochba is Hebrew and means 'son of the people.' Narodzhinsky is the same, in Russian; Adamson is 'son of the first man.' Now I'm the son of all mankind."

During the final days of his charismatic Montreal month he was outfitted with a handsome suit and fine shoes by an elderly widow, borrowed twenty dollars from a druggist and a bottle of gin from a doctor, seduced a Y.C.L. girl on the very evening he proposed marriage, forged and cashed a hundred-dollar cheque in his uncle's name, lifted an expensive book from the Labour College library, stole the Y.C.L. funds (twelve dollars) from a desk drawer, and vanished.

Reports and rumours soon trickled in from the West where a youth of undoubted charm had passed through the radical communities of Winnipeg and Vancouver, leeched them and disappeared, into the States it was thought, to find his true fulfilment.

"He's just an amateur," Fred remarked. "Some day he'll graduate; he'll be a success. Isn't that what it's all about?"

*

Some strange characters drifted through the Main Street delicatessens, coffeehouses, *kibbitzarnias*. One such man introduced himself as Doctor Socrates from Constantinople. He was a fervent proponent of change, any kind of change. "All change," he argued, "must be for the better. Let's turn the bosses into slaves and the slaves into bosses. Let's change virtuous women into harlots and make sinners into saints. Fill the asylums with senators! Choose our rulers from the prison populations! Topsy-turvydom will set us free!"

"There's lots of important people crazier than him," Fred told his father.

*

Two new recruits turned up one Wednesday at the Y.C.L. clubroom. After the meeting, as they walked with Fred, one of them asked, "When do we get the girls? Which ones do we get? How long do you have to be a member?"

Fred was puzzled and tried to explain.

"Don't you guys practise free love?" one of them blurted out.

Fred snapped, "Why don't you practise screwing yourselves?" and walked away. They never came to another meeting.

*

On the last day of April, in the afternoon, the chief of police called in Michael Buhay, committee chairman and chief parade marshal, and warned him that disorders would not be tolerated in the First of May demonstrations. None were intended, said the marshal.

They faced each other appraisingly, agnostic Mike and the God-fearing chief, David and Goliath.

The chief heaved his hard bulk back into the swivel-chair behind the desk. He kept his antagonist standing. "There will be no street orations on or near St. Lawrence Boulevard," he decreed. "It is forbidden. I forbid it. They will be stopped." None were planned, the marshal said.

Mike waited to be dismissed, not a tall man but lean and tough, with the hard head of a soccer player, stubborn bright-blue eyes, a pugnacious curved nose and silky golden hair. "Anything else?" he asked quietly.

The chief snapped back, "I'm asking the questions." He paused and added, "No drinking will be allowed. No drunks." Mike nodded, "Of course."

The chief had been briefed. This man Buhay was a rabble-rouser with a voice like a church organ and a North-of-England fibre to his words. Socialist agitator, a declared communist, works in men's clothing, was once the union's business manager, lectures at the Labour College. "That's all, you can go," said the chief. He watched the man's back as he walked to the door, then he stopped him. "There's one thing more, there will be no big Red flag."

"What size would be all right?"

"Three inches wide, six inches long."

"Chief," said Mike, "suppose we compromise, make it a little bigger."

The chief glared. He could smash this Manchester son of a Polish Jew with one punch. He walked to the window and studied the sky. "All right, I'll permit four inches wide, eight inches long; that's final. Anything bigger, the bearer will be arrested."

Mike reported to his committee. "I think the chief figures on one small flag at the head of the parade. He didn't say and I didn't ask. We'll hand out small flags to everybody tomorrow and we'll ask them not to show the flags until they start to march. Agreed?"

They agreed. It was a grand May Day, with Martin and his waterfront buddies, and Fred with his Y.C.L. branch, with people from a dozen unions, with old-time socialists, all singing and marching in the afternoon sunshine, and young people swinging down the street, smiling and serious, buoyant and brave, hundreds and hundreds of them.

Policemen guarded every intersection. The chief was a red-faced martinet but did not interfere.

After the marching and the indoor evening concert and speeches at Prince Arthur Hall, Fred and his chums crowded into the Main Street cafe to devour sandwiches and coffee and to relish the splendours of their day.

Late in the evening, happy and exhausted as they prepared to leave after rehashing their triumphs, their marshal stood up, slapped the table-top so that the cups rattled, and chuckled. "By gum," Mike roared, "by gumalorum, it's been a great day!"

Gumbalorum? the delicatessen owner wondered. What kind of word is that? Polock? Why don't he speak English?

*

The Mellers listened to the concert and the speeches in the hall above the corner saloon where Arthur's Uncle Norm used to work. Mandolins played Slav dances, an Italian sang *Bandiera Rossa*, a Jewish choir recalled Old Country memories, a heroic living tableau depicted the Commune of Paris and speakers spun their inspiration in a half-dozen different languages. Fred delivered his first public speech.

"You know, he's very good," Gaby said. They sought him out as the crowd broke up. "That was a good speech, Fred," said Arthur. They didn't join Fred and his comrades in the crowded restaurant.

At home Gaby remarked, "What I like about Fred as a speaker is that he doesn't seem to make a speech. Do you know what I mean? He's direct and down-to-earth. He's friendly and he doesn't harangue. That's a good quality, isn't it?"

Arthur nodded, but his thoughts were elsewhere. Gaby continued, "We must have him over soon." Arthur murmured, "Sure, sure." Gaby glanced uncertainly at him, "You don't seem too eager." Arthur shrugged, "I wish he wouldn't press me to do something, join something." Gaby argued, "That isn't fair, he doesn't push. He tries to persuade but he knows when to stop, he respects our privacy." Arthur smiled. "All right, maybe I'm a bit edgy. Sure, let's ask him. Soon."

*

As tenants of the Labour College building, the Y.C.L. received an invitation to send reps to the machinists' yearly stag smoker. "Come help us celebrate with our union brothers."

The Young Communist League elected Nat Stone, a squat beetle-browed young man with the build of a bear and appetite to match. (A relative who worked at the delicatessen saved salami ends for him.) There had been some doubts, so they also elected Fred. It was implied that he would keep an eye on Nat.

The boys reported early, credentials in hand, and sat shyly smoking cigarettes until they were urged to "join the party." They proceeded to sample the cheddar cheese and the Danish blue and wash down chunks of sausage with lager beer.

There were free smokes and lots of free food and drinks, all donated. The blue fog of cigars hung heavy, the laughter grew louder, the singers more boisterous. The older men switched to whiskey with beer chasers.

"Let's try," said Nat, "just a little."

"O.K.," Fred agreed. "Just a little. We're not kids."

By eleven o'clock Nat was steering his friend homewards on silent sidestreets through the tipsy night. Fred walked on air and missed steps. Suddenly he made for a lane, leaned against a lopsided fence and threw up.

"Rest a bit," Nat advised. "You had a little too much. Maybe the cheese." Fred threw up again. "You'll be all right, just rest," Nat encouraged. "I'll see you get home O.K."

Nat grinned foolishly, pleased that he could hold his liquor better than the club organizer. He guided Fred to Martin's door, knocked and greeted the father cordially, explained the situation as one man to another and said it was a pleasure to help a friend. They undressed Fred and put him to bed between blessedly cool sheets. Nat declined a cup of coffee and hurried away; his own stomach didn't feel too stable.

As Fred sank into sleep, he thought he heard, from a great distance, a man chuckling.

If the stalwart Nat suspected that Fred had been chosen as his chaperone, he was amused that the tables had been turned, yet never once did he hint to anyone that Fred had represented the organization with anything less than dignity, honour and good fellowship, as befits a conscientious revolutionary.

When Fred apologized sheepishly to him next day, all Nat said was, "I don't remember a thing. I must have got tanked."

2

1939. Wartime. Night.
Arthur. The Hospital.

> *You lie mute and captive here. Yet eloquent.*
> *Where did you hide in the days of your youth?*
> *What were you thinking of?*
> *Arthur, goddamit, where were you?*
> *What did you do?*
> *And what were your fears of the challenging years?*
> *And now, when you finally move and cry out, are you too*
> *late?*
> *All you poor lost Arthurs!*
> *Your years have happened far away from you.*

WHILE YOU wavered and withheld and pondered and withdrew, the whole world thundered by, leaving you behind, imprisoned in nightmares and day-dreams and traumas and fears and trances and tears...

*

You are four years old and venture across the street from your father's house to the hospital of God, the Hotel Dieu on St. Urbain Street. You touch the fortress face of the hospital wall and are frightened by its rough cold sooty stone so different from the warm russet bricks of your father's home. You touch the hostile rock and feel its clammy flesh. And as though in retaliation, an ugly horrible smelly bellicose monster of a bully-boy brat confronts you and pushes your face against the wall and you run back home and upstairs stumbling terrified, bleeding, wailing to your ma.

Why don't you defend yourself?

Because nice little gentlemen do not hit back. Never?

The Twenties.
Arthur and Gabrielle.

Lenin died January 22, 1924 in a place called Gorki near Moscow, died in Berlin, Paris, London, Shanghai, and died in Montreal.

Fred phoned to tell the Mellers about the meeting. Lenin, he said, was one of the greatest men who ever lived. (Does he have to lecture me? Arthur thought. I know who Lenin was.)

The memorial was on a Sunday afternoon in the Monument Nationale. A small fair earnest blue-eyed man came from Toronto to speak at the theatre. The wisdom of Karl Marx and Frederick Engels, he said, spreading his arms wide, was mastered and expanded by Lenin, the brilliant Russian who was the first man in all history to lead a successful socialist revolution. What he achieved inspired the oppressed everywhere and in Canada too, Tim Buck said. Lenin's life enriched the world, his death reduced mankind.

The East Anglian cadences of the Toronto machinist rolled in waves across the vast hall and carried the radiance of his dream to a spellbound audience. Their applause rolled back to him, wave upon wave.

Gaby and Arthur were entranced by the man's deeply personal appeal, his magnetism and passion, but when he urged his listeners to "join Lenin's party" Arthur tensed and Gaby sighed. This, after all, did not concern them. The world also needs those prophets who sit above the battle, who, as Arthur said, keep score and pass judgement. Much as he admired the visionaries who threw themselves without reserve into the movement, he insisted that *somebody* on the side of the revolution had to be objective and critical.

Politics, he once told Fred Shaughnessy, even the most selfless politics, by its very nature compels you to take sides and assert loyalites.

"Politics at its best is naive," he argued, "at its worst corrupt."

"Corrupt!" Fred exploded. "Corruption is when the dirt piles up and you do nothing in case your hands get dirty.''

Neither of the Mellers joined. "I'm my own man. I'm a free agent," Arthur told Gaby. Yet they wished for the new society, believed in its justice, applauded its spokesmen, gave moral support to its campaigns and donated money. Gaby and Arthur were sympathizers, not doers. "Can you imagine me on a soapbox?" he asked Gaby. She smiled.

They built themselves a pleasant nest in Gaby's house. Memories of the poverty of his father's home nudged his ambitions and his pride. Gaby's shop was gaining a reputation as the place to buy authentic Quebec handicrafts.

Arthur was reluctant to rest on her laurels. He worked his way up through the dry-goods wholesalers on Main Street, from shipping helper to salesman to manager on the same grubby St. Lawrence strip where he had once been fired by fat Aaron Turner, in the seamy old buildings below the hill from Sherbrooke to Ontario, with here and there a high attic against whose window glass might be pressed the grubby face of a tenant or her child.

His employer was an anarchist (philosophical, the man stressed). Since we live in a capitalist society (he shrugged) we have to abide by its rules or perish. We have to do things we don't like, he said, like exploiting our help. Arthur sensed his boss felt few qualms about exploiting him but didn't argue with this philosopher who barely concealed his contempt for humanity.

Books, lectures, concerts and galleries filled their spare hours. Their home on the edge of the campus sported a bright modern rug on the livingroom floor. On their walls hung posters, framed prints, a few modest oil paintings. Small carvings and cut flowers in vases graced end-tables and window sills.

The Mellers were now collecting cookbooks and experimenting with recipes. They cultivated a narrow garden behind their house: neat rows of tomato plants, dwarf beans and peppers; straight lines of radishes, carrots and green onions; one cucumber hill; a row of cabbages; little clumps of chives, parsley, sage and mint; a screened frame for their strawberry plants; the spiky gooseberry bush Grandfather Lesage had brought from La Macaza; scarlet runners that gave colour and shade to their back-porch and provided food if the beans were picked before they grew too tough; and a healthy pear tree, one of only three on their street.

Flower-boxes in the front windows overflowed with petunias,

and rambler roses clung to a trellis beside the front door.

Some days, bemused by the lush green view from his bedroom window Arthur remembered the pathetic garden of the old couple who had lived on garbage in their shack on Hotel de Ville, and had one day decided to hang themselves.

3

1939. War Casualties.
Rose. Night Wait.

I CAN'T sleep.

Dear God, can't the doctors do something for him?

Laura gave me a pill, but it hasn't helped me.

I'm wide-awake and stark-white scared. My heart's trembling and my mind keeps racing and skipping, racing and stopping like a film projector out of control.

Click. There he is on our parlour floor on St. Urbain Street, where he was born. He's building castles, piling paper-faced wooden blocks, stopping to explore their coloured pictures.

Click. He's sleeping with his head on my lap on the high wooden country car racing us home from cool Cartierville to humid Montreal.

Click. Arthur sits proud and high and small on a powerful Clydesdale horse in the yard of the big stable. He smiles shyly, blinking his eyes against the Calgary sun.

Click. His eyes are angry and full of tears and he calls me a scab.

1925. The Strike.
Rose and Others.

"Mrs. Meller, I want you to know we appreciate your work. We're making you forelady of your section. It's a six-dollar promotion." He smiled.

"Thank you very much, Mr. Wolfe. I'll do my best to earn it."
She couldn't wait to get home and tell Laura.

Next morning when they punched their time-cards the workers
found a notice posted beside the clock. Stunned, they read and
reread:

"...adverse business conditions...management regrets...10
per cent off piece rates...7 per cent off hourly...your loyal
cooperation..."

Before they could reach the clock, three men and two women
were handed their pay and fired. Wasn't their work O.K.? they
asked.

"I don't need reasons," said Mr. Wolfe. "You're
troublemakers, that's all. Go organize a union in Russia, not here.
Now get the hell out."

At 10 a.m. the switch was pulled, the power was cut and the
workers picked up their belongings and quit, shouting, "Strike!
Strike! Everybody out!"

Rose and a dozen girls in her section waited in a worried huddle.

Within minutes the power came on again, motors hummed and
the boss came over to cheer up his frightened loyalists. "It's all
right, girls, everything's under control. Don't worry. We'll look
after you, we'll pick you up and send you home by car every day.
How's that for style? Just say, 'Home, James!'

"Now don't worry, the Bolsheviks are finished here. Thank God
and good riddance. Don't worry at all, the police will protect you.
You're safe. And I want you to know we sincerely appreciate your
loyalty.

"One more thing—Mrs. Meller's your new forelady, one of the
best. Give her your support. All right, now, let's get back to work.
Idle machines make skinny purses...that's Shakespeare."

The girls managed weak smiles.

"But the wage cut," one began. "How long will it last?"

Wolfe's face hardened for a second before he restored its
friendly mask. "Well, girls, it depends on the accountants, the
bank manager and some New York gentlemen who have invested in
our firm. I'd say six months at the most and we'll be back on Easy
Street. I can promise you this: there'll be a little bonus with your
pay at the end of the week. All right, ladies, back to the salt
mines!" He grinned benevolently. The women bent over the
chattering machines.

How, Rose wondered, would she explain it to Laura? But her sister was practical, she would understand. Life is a human right. If you earn nothing, the right means nothing. If you don't work, you don't earn. If you don't earn, you don't live. Everybody knows that. . . The strikers aren't reasonable. Don't they realize half a loaf is better than none at all? How can they hope to win against Mr. Wolfe with his rich New York partners and the bank, and the police?

Anyway, some of the strikers weren't very nice—ignorant greenies, socialists, even atheists. Picket lines and violence frightened her, like riots and revolutions. Only the week before the *Star* said a coal miner got killed in a strike in Nova Scotia. Why did the foolish man have to get mixed up in it? Why didn't he think of his widow and orphans? Are they better off now?

How would she tell Arthur? Perhaps he won't hear about it. He won't find out; it's only a small strike. She hoped the paper would not report it. She couldn't bear to have his eyes accusing her.

For a week she was picked up every morning at six. For a week she was escorted by policemen from the car to the factory building, to the elevator, to the shop, and escorted every evening by policemen into and down the elevator and through the lobby to the waiting car as pickets shouted and jeered from the sidewalk.

At the start of the second week she saw Arthur's friend, the young Shaughnessy, holding a cardboard sign on the picket line as she was herded by a cop into the waiting car. Had Fred seen her? But how could he when he was being shoved and slapped around by an officer?

For a week he had stood on boxes and park benches and made speeches about the strike. His father was on a union relief committee raising money. Mike Buhay was canvassing locals and union lodges, making blunt appeals and buttonholing ministers and professors, doctors and dentists. Irma Gillespie slipped strike leaflets into letter-boxes. Arthur considered offering his mother some money; a week off work would be difficult for her. But he was busy. They were taking stock at the warehouse and he was tied up every evening; there wasn't time for visiting.

Conscience nagged Rose when she looked down at the strikers with their placards. The pay had always been the worst in the trade and now it was cut even more. She saw them walking the length of the sidewalk, turning, walking back again, worn-out pickets handing signs to fresh pickets. She saw them—people she knew, girls she had chatted and laughed with as they ate their lunches—saw their stubborn faces on the picket line, their plodding feet, pleading eyes, weary backs.

Their shapes were a blur as she was hustled into the building each morning and hustled out and away each evening. She saw their grim faces and the taut looks of the cops.

During the long days in the workroom she watched the intense profiles of her section crew, heads bent, fingers guiding the cloth. Fast, faster.

She worried. How many more days running the picket-line gauntlet? And how much shame?

*

Wolfe sat in his office behind the closed door and sipped scotch with the chief of the goon-squad. The pickets would be taught a lesson. No guns or knives, of course, no clubs, just bruises and broken bones for souvenirs. Wolfe had spoken to Detective Gilbert and had met no objections. Roughing up the Reds was O.K., but don't get caught, and work fast.

"Is this your first strike?" the gang chief asked Wolfe, like a gynecologist checking: Is this your first child?

"Not exactly, I had a strike ten years ago. We lost. The bastards let me down."

"What do you mean?"

"I was a strike leader then. We wanted ten cents an hour more and the boss offered five. I said take it, but the dumb clucks said no, ten or nothing. After a couple of weeks the stupid jerks started to worry; they were running short of cash and wanted to go back, so I went to the boss and I said we'd take the five cents. So he said, 'That was two weeks ago. Now it's three cents or nothing.' I signed without even a vote. The next union meeting they fired me from the organizer job.

"You know what I did? I went right over to that same factory. I offered to flush out the troublemakers, so they hired me for the personnel control."

"Where was that?"

Wolfe lit a cigar and paused for effect, letting his match burn down, relishing the moment and regarding his visitor with amusement. "Right here, my friend, right here in this friggin' shop."

"Jesus, that's what I call a success story."

"You know what they say, only the strong deserve the prize."

*

Our Y.C.L.'ers are a good bunch, even if they are a little too spontaneous, Fred told himself. They leap-frog all over the agenda and everybody tries to speak at once. They're impatient and full of beans.

Now here's their chance to see the class struggle in action, face to face. Not just talk, but do and help and be a part of it.

At tonight's branch meeting a young striker will ask them for volunteers on the picket line.

*

Long ago as a schoolgirl in Charlottetown Irma Gillespie used to sing the hymn. Now at the strike rally she heard the Young Communists on the stage of the Prince Arthur Hall belting out the old English melody. The words had been refashioned in countless labour battles and had crossed an ocean to stir Jewish, Russian and Italian immigrants and the children of immigrant strikers.

She listened and she was comforted and stirred and lifted high out of herself. She looked around at the faces and her eyes misted to see their yearning and their faith.

"Hold the fort for we are coming; union men be strong!" The crowd joined the singers and Irma joined the crowd.

At home later, before she fell asleep, she whispered the song's fourth line, "To battle or to die." To die? Not now, she protested, not yet. I can't spare the time, there's too much left to see. But I'm old and tired and I need a rest. Later, after the strike, I'll indulge myself and go away for a holiday.

She would travel to a village in the Eastern Townships. The farmer would place her valise behind the seat and help her onto the wagon. The horse would trudge the mile or so and stop in the farmyard, where the farmer's wife would be waiting to greet her and lead her into a homey cabin all her own where she would be a sybarite for two whole weeks.

There would be a big bed and a fine old rocker, bright curtains and a thick hooked rug. The farmer's wife would cook delicious meals and serve them on the round oak table beside the cabin window from which Irma could see rolling fields and apple trees, a stream and grazing cattle.

She would sleep late or rise to witness the dawn, as the impulse moved her, go for long walks, sun herself, read, day-dream, doze in the rocker on rainy days, wet her feet in the clear brook as tiny startled minnows scurried away.

Irma sighed. It was late and she was tired. Tomorrow the picket line. She drifted into sleep.

*

The cars disgorge the thugs, who form a compact group before the building. A few yards away, the pickets walk, turn, come back, turn and resume their restricted route on the sidewalk. Directly across from the entrance are the parked autos of the city police. Detective Gilbert rests his rump on the hood of the first cruiser.

One of the hired thugs approaches the pickets, shoves through their line and screams, "Help! Police! They're killing me!"

Gilbert continues to lean his rump on the car hood. He signals to his men not to interfere and turns his back on the scene. Each thug selects an adversary and moves in, clutching pieces of rubber hose, lead-pipe and blackjacks.

Women shriek and men shout, skin is bruised and torn, bones break and blood begins to flow. Passersby are knocked down.

Gilbert finally turns, steps forward and shouts at the stragglers, "All right, everybody, go home! It's all over. Get the hell out of here!"

Wolfe looks down from his office window. Scum! Do they think they can tell *him* how to run his shop—these greenie kikes and commie bohunks?

Gaby, curious, has come to see the picketing. She has closed her shop and walked over. She smiles at the pickets as she passes. A thug brushes against her and knocks her to the pavement. Irma Gillespie, holding a picket sign, runs over to help. She is tripped and thrown down. She loses her grip on the handbag, it bursts open and her change purse falls out. Detective Gilbert strides over and kicks the purse into the sewer grill.

Irma cries out and Gilbert snaps, "Get the hell out of here, you old bitch!" She regains her handbag and walks over to Gaby, who is leaning against a wall, her head bleeding. Irma leads her away. Gaby hails a taxi and asks Irma to help. They drive to Gaby's house and go in. Gaby washes the blood from her forehead, lies down on a couch in the livingroom and soon falls asleep.

When she wakes she sits up, surprised to see Irma leaning back in an easy-chair and reading a magazine. She smiles wanly. Irma asks, "Did you have a nice nap? Do you feel better?"

"I'm all right now. I'm sorry I fell asleep. What's your name? Mine's Gaby Lajeunesse."

"I'm Irma Gillespie."

"Thank you for seeing me home safely, Mrs. Gillespie."

"It's Miss," Irma corrects her. "Will you be all right now if I leave?"

Gaby nods. "Stay a little longer. I'll make tea."

"That detective," Miss Gillespie says, "he kicked my purse into the sewer. I've been saving for a vacation. Now... Well, he's not a very nice man, that detective."

*

Next afternoon at quitting time the goons are absent; they were hired for only one performance. The police have been reinforced. No need now for free-lance goons. Two mounted men patrol the road, two motorcycle cops are parked at the doors, the squad cars wait.

A dozen pickets approach the building. Cops move in fast, swinging their billies, snatching placards and breaking the poles over the heads of demonstrators. Blood streaks faces, heavy-booted feet kick fallen strikers.

The front doors open and Rose and the others are swept up by a flying wedge of cops into the waiting cars.

A woman shouts from the sidewalk, "Don't scab!" She throws herself against the police line and is struck down. She lies on the pavement, sobbing. The cars swerve to avoid her as they speed their white-faced passengers away. Rose looks back—strikers are running, stumbling, falling. Police clubs are swinging, horses are rearing, motorcycles roar in pursuit.

*

At ten o'clock in the evening two girls knocked on the door.

"Please, Rose, can we talk to you?"

"There's nothing to talk about. Please go away," Rose pleaded. "I don't want any trouble."

In the dim light of the doorway she could see that one of the girls had a bruise on her cheek.

"Please, Rose, just for a minute."

"Leave me alone!" Rose cried. "Please go or I'll call the police!"

"Let us in, Rose. We need your help." The girl was weeping. "Please, Rose, please!"

"Go away!" Laura replied bitterly. "We've got our own troubles."

The girls left.

Late that evening, as she prepared for bed, Rose said to her sister, "You know I'm not against them; I just hate the shouting and the picket lines."

"I know. Now go to sleep."

*

Next evening, after supper, Arthur came with Gaby to see his mother and aunt and wondered why Rose looked so tense, especially when Gaby told them about the thugs and pointed to her bruised forehead. It was an uncomfortable visit and he decided to leave after half an hour. He pressed twenty dollars into Rose's hand.

"You'll need it while the strike's on. How long do you expect to be off work?"

It was then she blurted out, "I'm not on strike, I'm working!" and burst into tears.

"My God, Ma," he said. "*You*, a scab..."

Pale and trembling, she ran from the room. Arthur remembered another time when his mother had stumbled from a room, in her own home, when an uncle had come to advise and a bewildered father had walked away from them.

*

"Dear Arthur: I'm sorry I made you feel ashamed of me. It's a week since I saw you. I have to tell you what happened. I'd rather write about it, it's easier that way.

"Arthur, I have something to tell you. I hope it will make you think better of me. I've had a miserable time because of what happened to Gaby and what you said to me. I knew I was wrong, but people my age don't like to admit it, it isn't easy, I suppose I'm a coward, I never had to make such a choice before. I've worked in other shops, but they never had a strike, so I have never had to choose like this before.

"Well, Arthur, yesterday on our lunch break I talked to the women, all of us huddled scared like rabbits, eating our sandwiches. We could hear the pickets outside, more of them than ever before, labour people and ministers and even college students, singing and laughing. Up there in the factory we hid and sneaked the food into our mouths like dogs.

"Well, Arthur, I spoke to them, my fellow-prisoners. I just told them how ashamed I felt. I told them about Gaby getting hurt. I told them what you called me. I told them we were all wrong. I said, 'Go to the window and look at the strikers on the street, people like us.'

"They looked. Somebody down there saw them looking and shouted, 'Don't scab!' and we left the window. I told them about my raise, my bribe. I can't remember all I said, Arthur, I just kept talking. They were very quiet and very nervous, worried like me, and I think they were ashamed like me. Nobody said anything.

"The clock struck one and it was time to go back to the machines. I got my hat and purse and I said I wasn't going to stay. I started to cry. Nobody moved, so I went to each girl and asked her to come with me. I don't know what I said, but three girls came and stood with me, and then two more, then another left her machine, and another, and then the rest.

"Mr. Wolfe ran in from his office. He called me a traitor, an agitator. Imagine, *me* an agitator! We all walked out together and left him cursing and screaming.

"We all marched out, we walked right up to the pickets. We said we wanted to join the strike. They couldn't believe it. I said we were serious, we wanted to go to the union.

"Arthur, you should have heard them. They cheered and danced on the road. They lined us up behind the signs and we all paraded to the union hall. They sang and shouted. Everybody was so happy! I wanted to cry and I wanted to sing, but you know, Arthur, I've never liked doing things like that in public. But I was happy and so was everybody else.

"The only ones who didn't know what to do with themselves were the police. They got into their cars and followed us. They wanted to show they still ran things, so they wouldn't let us parade on the road. We didn't mind, we just marched on the sidewalk. You should have seen their faces!

"When we got to the union, people were laughing and crying. They hugged us like long-lost family. Only a few hours earlier they called us scabs.

"I had to write this letter before I saw you again. Come soon. And forgive, Your Loving Mother."

*

Two days passed. Picketing, meetings and delegations.

On the third day Wolfe phoned to say he would like to talk settlement. On the fourth day he signed an agreement.

The paycut was cancelled. The strike was over.

The picket placards were stacked in a back room of the union hall.

PART SEVEN

1

1939. Arthur's Night.
Escape Is a Trap.

YOUR EYES ARE closed. It is dark again, late... How many nights to daylight, how many days before dawn, how many hours to waking again?

Arthur, it's Fred, in hiding, waiting for you to come out of your white cage.

Listen to this fable. I think you will understand the plight of this man:

He hides in his room but cannot keep out the sounds of people clamouring pleading laughing greeting knocking on his door, shouting for him to pay bills, vote, come to a picnic, sign petitions, play checkers, protest, celebrate, sing.

He is annoyed and keeps his door locked and his windows barred and the shutters tightly fastened. People persist in rattling the doorknob and tapping on the walls in friendship or in anger as the case may be.

One night, when everyone sleeps, he steals from his room and moves away to the other end of town. People discover him there too.

He moves from place to place but cannot quite elude people or escape events.

He travels to another city, a far country, a distant continent, but is never at peace, for total strangers walk thousands of miles to knock on his door.

He seeks other hiding-places: cellars, mountain cabins, jungle huts, sanctuaries. Someone always searches him out.

He finds an almost inaccessible island in a brutally cold northern sea and lives completely alone, for himself alone, in a large cave alone, which he furnishes with skins and a stone fireplace.

He devises crude implements, catches fish and traps animals for his food.

He grows fat and sluggish and sleeps a great deal of the time. The air in his cave becomes stale.

A year, five years more, another ten years pass in this fashion. Once or twice he engages in desultory exploration of his island but finds nothing of interest, no challenges, no people, few animals, and only a few clumps of stunted trees.

He prefers it that way. He cannot bear to think of being driven out again to seek a new refuge. He assures himself that he is content and safe.

He grows fatter and slower and duller.

One morning of the short summer as he stands on a cliff kicking irritably at a clump of lichen, he thinks he has detected smoke on the horizon. When he is certain that what he sees is not a dark cloud and that it is coming closer, he turns in panic, puffing fatly as he stumbles into the cave where he lives alone without even a dog to keep him company.

He stands trembling inside the entrance. The danger is great and immediate. He shuffles and staggers, breathing hard and wheezing as he carries rocks and debris to close and camouflage the mouth of his cave from the inside. He dare not light a fire for fear that its glow will be seen outside through chinks in the barrier. His exertions have made him ravenously hungry and he chews on a piece of dried fish. His stomach growls all night. He can't sleep. He sweats.

Next day, although it is raining lightly, he hears songs and the laughter of men and women and even (he shudders) children playing, and the sounds of trees falling to the axe and houses being built.

He must devise a way to keep out the intruders. Cunningly he seals up the mouth of his cave from the inside with clay.

Nobody will learn of his existence, nobody can now disturb him.

Presently he dies from lack of air. Or from boredom. Or both.

1927 to 1928.
Fred's Diary.

Sept. 1. I remember Dublin places and people. It's all past for Dad and me; we can't go back to it. If anybody asked me what I am, I'd have to say I'm a Montrealer, Irish-born, Canadian now, I guess. I won't really know until I've seen the colours and textures, heard the sounds of the rivers, climbed the hardrock mountains and travelled the endless miles. I won't know about this place I live in until I've been to all the other parts. I won't know Montreal until I've seen Victoria. I won't know who I am until I've met the people in all those other places.

Sept. 2. As though he'd read my mind, Leslie wrote asking how did I feel about a Y.C.L. tour. I showed the letter to Dad. I'd have to give notice at the printshop. I'd be on the road six months through fall into winter and spring.

I feel guilty about Dad; he'll have to keep up the flat by himself. With what the Y.C.L. can pay I'll be lucky to send home ten bucks a month. National Office will buy my train fares and give me expense money for the first few weeks; after that I'll have to pay my own way out of the collections. I told Dad I hated to walk out on him but I couldn't let the Y.C.L. down either. I said I'd like to sleep on it.

Sept. 3. Dad always leaves for work earlier than me. When I sat down for my coffee there was a note on my cup. "It's a damn fine chance," he wrote. "Dont dribble it away. Go ahead, grab it."

Suppertime we talked again. "Take it," he urged. "I'll hold the fort till you get back." I searched his face; he was smiling broadly. I couldn't read any questions in his eyes.

Of course I'm excited. I've dreamed of this a long time. Since we first sailed into Montreal. Today I wrote Les and said I'd be ready in two weeks; when do I start?

Sept. 14. I'm going to Toronto to check my schedule with Les and take off from there.

Sept. 17. Christ Jesus! What a timetable! It looks like I'll visit every whistle-stop between Sudbury and Sointula, B.C. and then work my way back over a different route. I hope I can handle it...Canada, here I come!

Sept. 19. We crawled all night and stopped often, snorting steam. Was it a milk train? I dozed off and the bare white lights of a dilapidated little railway station slapped my eyes and instantly snuffed out. When I searched the dark there was nothing but black bush and black rock and swollen black shadows. I twisted into yet another cramped position; day coaches aren't built for cosy slumber.

I dreamed I sat at a rough table across from an old trapper in his log hut on the lip of a lake in the Rockies. The man stared at me, accusing without a word. I realized it was my dad and his eyes were wet with tears. And so were mine, dammit!

Sept. 20. When I stepped down in Sudbury the morning haze was streaked with smoke, and the rotten-egg stink of sulphur hung in the raw cold air. I waited but nobody came to greet me. I crossed over to the Chinese cafe, its bare light-bulbs yellowing the dark of the desolate place. I crouched half-asleep at the counter, my face unwashed and my eyes gritty as I sipped indifferent coffee and swallowed greasy toast.

I paid for the god-awful breakfast and asked directions, but the unhappy man just shook his head and walked back into his kitchen. I picked up my valise and the knapsack stuffed with literature and left. A milkman gave me a lift part way.

It was still early when I got to *Vapaus,* so I waited until an editor showed up. He took me in and fed me real coffee. The paper's name is freedom in Finnish. He said their Y.C.L. organizer went north to look for work and the branch just fell apart.

A hell of a way to start a tour! Well, no use moping. The editor got me a car and a driver. By suppertime I'd seen most of the dropouts and called a meeting for the same night.

It went off fine. I made a real short speech and answered questions. I taught them Joe Hill songs like *The Preacher and the Slave* ("You'll get pie in the sky") and the tramp song ("Nothing doing here for you"). We got along pretty good. Anyway, they elected new officers. First order of business after that was a Saturday night dance. We had more Finnish coffee and sweet white Finnish bread and sang some more.

I went to bed all worn out but feeling a lot better than the morning. The next few days I'm to make side trips to Levack Mine, Whitefish, Copper Cliff. Then back to Sudbury for the dance.

Sept. 23. Good meetings in all three places. Sold quite a few pamphlets. Picked blueberries near Copper Cliff, first time I ever ate any. Had too many.

Sept. 25. Back in Sudbury on Saturday. Those blonde Finnish girls are stunning. Good dancers too and make wonderful coffee. The dance was a success. It raised a little money.

I can't forget the slag heaps, the haze, the stench, the places where nothing grows any more.

Sept. 27. By train from Sudbury to Sault Ste. Marie. Other side of river is U.S., but I have no time to cross over. Maybe they wouldn't let me in anyway. Lots of immigrants in the Canadian Soo from Finland, Ukraine, Italy. Mostly in the steel mill, also lumber camps during winter.

Good Y.C.L. here. Put me up with very unusual family, nice home. Father owns bush camp, employs labour! Mother's an invalid, sounds more politically concerned than husband. Daughter in high school, belongs Y.C.L. Son doesn't; hopes to get army commission. "In this way I'll serve the revolution some day, win the army to our side."

He took me to a restaurant but not to eat. The waiter served us bootleg wine in plain teapots. The wine was sour, but I drank it to please my host. I'd rather have had a beer.

After my public meeting we had coffee and cake at the house. The parents excused themselves and retired, then the army boy said goodnight, and there we were, just me and the sister, hardly past seventeen. A sweet girl, enthusiastic, with sparkling eyes, bright face, red, red mouth. Eager to go storming into the world and defy all philistines and capitalist monsters. When I kissed her goodnight (gently, like an uncle, I thought) she withdrew shyly and damn near toppled me in a sudden crush. She blushed and said she was sorry, kissed me full on the mouth, led me by the hand to my room, pushed me in, closed the door on me and left me wondering.

Did she think I would seduce her? I mean, do I give girls that impression? Nonsense! Nonsense?

When I left her house next day she was at school. Damn!

Oct. 4. Travel overnight in punchy storm-tossed ship across Lake Superior from the Soo to the Lakehead, to Thunder Bay country. Only a handful show up in the diningroom, all men, middle-aged, morose, untalkative, probably drunk. Make a hog of myself, huge dinner, delicious. Ship pitches and I heave it all up during the night, my green face awaiting the grey dawn.

Find my way to Port Arthur address, small clean hotel run by dour Finn who refuses money from organizers and somehow manages to stay in business.

Oct. 5. Strange names: Nolalu, Intola, Kaministikwia, Suomi, Atikokan. Finnish, Indian? I'll be going to some of these places.

Port Arthur hotel room is tidy, comfortable, with good bed. I'll be in and out, making it my base while I attend Y.C.L. meetings, give speeches and take side trips.

During the day I roam the twin cities, Port Arthur, Fort William. Sustain my energy with powerful meals in co-op diningroom— down-to-earth low-cost eating places that cater to big-muscle lumberjacks, miners, millworkers in Sudbury, the Soo, Cobalt, Timmins, the Lakehead, all those places where men grow big hungers three times a day.

You sit at long tables piled with platters of solid grub. From breakfast to supper they tempt you with sausages, bacon and eggs, flapjacks and syrup, thick soups, slabs of beef and pork, potatoes, pickles, piles of bread and butter, and jugs of milk, golden mead and rich Finnish coffee. How odd that the Finnish stew they call *mojakka* should taste so much like the Irish dish my dad cooks up.

Oct. 7. Met Alf Hautamaki in union hall near hotel, a short chunky man, still sore because logging boss ordered him off camp property last week. No organizers welcome there. "I'll be there again," Alf vows. "They can't stop us." I walk him to his rooms and he invites me in for a drink. "Homemade but not bad." His gloomy face breaks into a smile. I only have one drink—dynamite! I agree to write short piece for his union bulletin. Later, at my hotel, they tell me he's utterly fearless. The union's his whole life.

Oct. 8. Was introduced to Harry Bryan today, in from Dorion for conference. Old-time socialist, early communist, militant member Bridge Iron Structural Steel Workers. Said he worked twenty-five years ago on Jackknife Bridge across Kaministikwia River at Fort William, founded in 1800 and soon a busy centre of fur trade, shipbuilding, commerce, farming, shipping. When it was owned by North West Company, and later by Hudson's Bay, it was a hell-raising money-grubbing burg. Now it's tired frontier; the hellery's tamed, but greed carries on.

Walked into a barbershop. The barber wore a skirt. First time I ever had a lady barber cut my hair. About thirty, easy-going, friendly but no nonsense, independent. I like her.

Oct. 9. Waiting for the train I saw a collie dog and whistled. She trotted over and I stroked her head and gave her part of a sandwich

I'd bought for the trip. She tried to follow me on to the train, but the conductor shooed her off. Just before Nolalu, forty miles west, I looked out the window and there she was, running behind the train. Followed me around Nolalu all day and sat beside me at meeting in the hall that night.

Next day I felt rotten, like deserting a friend, but I couldn't take her to the Pacific coast, so I asked a Y.C.L.'er to feed her and lock her up until after I left and try to find a home for her.

Oct. 10. Intola. Arrived late, by train. Nobody met me. Nobody in general store knew about any Y.C.L. branch here, nobody had heard about any school meeting. A kid showed me a narrow dirt road. I walked four miles through darkening countryside and reached the schoolhouse about 9 p.m. Saw light in window, knocked, and girl about my own age came to door, suspicious and holding oil-lamp to my face. "What do you want?"

Introduced myself and said I'd come to make a speech for Y.C.L. Was anyone here yet? No. Did she know why nobody showed up? No. Was she Y.C.L.'er? She laughed scornfully. "I'm the teacher here," she said but didn't bother to give me her name. "You may come in for a minute." She led the way into classroom and seated herself at table. I squeezed into desk-seat. She said nothing but looked me over coldly, finally spoke, calm and grim:

"This is my school. I don't like when it's used for sedition talk. All these Finn farmers around here are Reds. I can't help what they say to each other, God only knows what they say. But I won't let the children listen to foreign revolution talk in English. Outside school hours I don't have anything to do with any of these foreign people. I don't think they like me. Well, I don't like them either."

I tried patience, but it just irritated her. She had to complain, so she took it out on me. She complained about the low pay (twenty-five a month, if they had the money), the cramped quarters behind the classroom, the tough land, the harsh winter, the dreariness, but mostly the people. Her eyes glistened and her voice rose:

"It's rotten, it's boring and I'm trapped. They scheme in their foreign gibberish. They talk about me, I know; I can tell the way they look at me. What are they saying? Why do they hate me? What do they want from me? Why don't they speak English like white people?"

"You're imagining," I said. "They're farmers, they have no

time for plots. *They're* not your enemies and *I'm* not your enemy. I'd rather be your friend."

"I don't need your sympathy," she snapped. "Anyway, what kind of an Irishman are you, mixing with all these foreigners? No, thank you, we have nothing to talk about. You'd better leave. I have my reputation to think of. I don't trust your kind with your free-love ways and all. I know the type."

She picked up the lamp, raised it above her head like a weapon and motioned me from her presence. "Get out! I detest everything you stand for! Don't ever come back! Goodbye! Go to hell!" I left and she slammed the door behind me.

It must be lonely for her in this wilderness. She's made her own exile. I never met a girl with so much hate.

I walked back through the spooky night, wondering whether the wolves I heard were howling at each other or at me.

I hoped they weren't as hungry as me. I hadn't eaten since noon. I got safely to the tiny railway station and slept on a bench.

Oct. 12. Nipigon. In a low log cabin, north of Superior and south of Nipigon, with the farmer and his wife and three boys and two girls. I ate dark moose-meat steak for supper, and homemade bread, blueberry pie and Finnish coffee from a copper pot.

Oct. 13. Fort Frances, last stopover in Ontario. Saw my first paper-mill. Small crew in a big plant. Local Party member led me through on the night shift, showed me where wood chunks stew in vats and soupy processed pulp comes out in massive rolls ready for the newspaper presses. How white and innocent the paper looks!

Oct. 15. Winnipeg, a quiet place for quiet folks on quiet streets where only eight years ago crowds were stampeded by horsemen armed and riding hard to save the city from the General Strike. Scots, Ukrainians, Englishmen, Poles, Swedes, Germans, Irishmen, Jews, Icelanders, Welshmen. And French-Canadians, English-Canadians, Canadian-Canadians, Indians, socialists and communists, anarcho-syndicalists, reformists and revolutionaries, imported British Empire stalwarts and homegrown Tories and Grits—all still debating the strike.

At a big public peace meeting I spoke for the Y.C.L. about war and what it meant for the youth. I closed with the soldier's taunt, "You won't get rich, you son of a bitch, you're in the army now!" They were startled, they held quiet for a few seconds and then started to laugh and applaud.

After it broke up, Jacob Penner came over. He's a short, thin man with a long, narrow head, neatly clipped narrow toothbrush moustache and big mournful eyes. Born in the Ukraine of German parents, he migrated to Canada, joined the Social Democrats in Winnipeg in 1913 and afterwards the Communists. He spoke slowly and precisely, like a teacher or a judge. He was a baker; he'd organized the bakers' union.

Jake was friendly but formal. He gave me a warm quick smile and shook my hand. Speaking carefully, he said, "Comrade Shaughnessy, I wish to congratulate you on a well-reasoned and articulate anti-militarist address." He paused and his face turned sad. "But don't you think the—er—poem was a trifle daring? What is to be gained from shocking the people? Do coarse words win recruits for socialism? Think about it, comrade Fred. Apart from your little—er—lapse, young man, you delivered an excellent speech." He grasped my hand, pumped it firmly once more and withdrew.

Oct. 16. Still in Winnipeg. Met Matthew Popovich, also from Ukraine, college-educated, came here 1910, studied voice, sang in New York Metropolitan Opera, returned to Canada. Cultured, fluent linguist. Tallish, well-built, handsome, reserved; writer, editor, translator, lecturer, musician. Promotes building Ukrainian halls, social centres for choirs, string orchestras, folk-dancing, plays, all over Canada. Wife Lily also sang at Met, later in Montreal Russian-style tearoom. Respectable in black suit, white shirt, dark tie. Speaks softly, thoughtfully. People call him Pop, but I don't think he is comfortable with nickname.

Navis is another Winnipeg stalwart who worked the Pennsylvania coal mines; came here just before the war. He has a round, clean-shaven face and could pass as a bank manager or cherubic priest. He's cheerful and generous even when he can't afford it. Last night, after my "son of a bitch" blunder, invited me for a car-ride. Dentist sympathizer picked us up, five of us, drove to a quiet, dead-end street and parked. John Navis handed out corned-beef sandwiches from paper bag, passed around bottle of Spanish port, sighed, "Nectar..."

Oct. 17. After the tour I think I'd like to come back to Winnipeg to live, if she's still here. I walked her home one night and when we got to her street she took my arm and guided me up the stairs to her small apartment.

Neither of us said a word as she let me in, neither of us said anything as we sat, entranced in her livingroom, and neither of us said anything later, undressing. Afterwards, side by side and breathing softly as we drifted in spent wonder, she spoke, almost inaudibly, "I like you, Fred, I like you very much. I wish you didn't have to go away, I wish you could stay."

Oct. 18. From nice clean wide respectable Portage Avenue's smart shops and cool prosperity I crossed into Main Street's junky stores and grubby greasy-spoon cafes. Here the outcasts loiter, derelict men and women holding up derelict walls and staring into space, thirteen-year-old girls offering sex for the price of a meal.

They can't disguise themselves like movie Indians; these girls wear white women's castoff rags.

Are these the children of Indian chiefs?

Pride broken and bodies sick, minds pulped and horrified, the Main Street kin of eagles (and of sweatshop whites) stare from haunted eyes at passersby.

When they're alone at night, do they cry to themselves, these children? Can they?

2

1939. The Hospital.
Arthur's Night.

THEY BROUGHT YOU here at night. All through the long hours Gaby stayed, and after she was led away by your Aunt Laura and your mother you lay motionless. And Detective Gilbert sat brooding on his bench.

The next day passed, and the evening, and a new night. You are still inert.

In a house, hiding somewhere, is Fred, your friend. He cannot come to see you, nor can Miss Gillespie, nor Fred's father, nor Kravchuk the Mac-Pap, nor the others.

The hospital ward is silent. There is only the nurse now. And

Ralph Gilbert waiting.

It's late, the night is nearly over, you still sleep, we still wait. It is near dawn...How long, Arthur? When?

1927-28. Westward.
From Fred's Diary.

Oct. 30. Brandon, Portage la Prairie, The Pas...Souris, Dauphin, Neepawa...Gimli, Selkirk, Lac du Bonnet...Small type on a railroad timetable, tiny dots on the Western map...Mining camps, farms, villages and towns...French-Canadians, Ukrainians, Icelanders, Scots...Tomorrow I push into Saskatchewan where the West begins in earnest for me.

Oct. 31. Westward! Nearly two months of days and nights in meeting halls, schoolhouses, friendly homes, and cheap restaurants, drab hotels, dreary dusty day-coaches of steam-engines puffing me west through a thousand flat and treeless prairie miles. I've been speaking to hundreds of youngsters. It's a good feeling when they respond.

Nov. 1. There's a chill in the air, a hint of snow. The endless miles around Regina make me feel awfully small. I'm just starting out in Saskatchewan and there's twenty-odd cities and rural villages ahead of me. Montreal is far away, I'm in a new country, vast and without limit.

Everything they say on Dominion Day is absolutely true. It doesn't even begin to describe the rich waters and the prolific soil. And I haven't reached the Rockies yet.

But it's shocking too. Everywhere I go I see the rot of the sick city slums and the dying farms and all those bewildered and disappointed people. We were cheated by the myths we learned at Montreal High—about the Hudson's Bay Company and the R.C.M.P., about Louis Riel and Gabriel Dumont. About the C.P.R., the mining companies, the cattle kings, the politician kings, and about people like us.

Nov. 3. Saskatoon. Stayed with Jack Clarke in his cubbyhole office: desk, two kitchen chairs, filing cabinet, pull-out lounge, electric hot-plate. He's not supposed to sleep there, it's an office building; but he has to sleep someplace, so he pretends he's not there evenings or Sundays.

He came to Canada in 1911, worked as a logger on the west coast, went to Saskatoon, far from his childhood in the lonely Shetland Islands off Scotland. He hates to make speeches, so writes leaflets and edits radical farm papers, tells farmers about banks and mortgages, implement-makers, monopolies, plutocracies, oligarchies and the plunderbund. He's tall, blue-eyed, sandy-haired, speaks hesitantly, with a soft burr. He has the look of a shy, very earnest scholar, is none the less stubborn in defending his positions.

Nov. 7. We celebrated the Russian Revolution tonight in Regina. I was the speaker, compared the uprising to our Easter Sunday. We've had frost and snow flurries...Went to Moose Jaw for a day. I wonder how it got its name...I'll be stopping, the next little while, in southern parts of province, going by train, model-T Ford, horse and buggy, to Swift Current, Assiniboia, Moosomin, Fort Qu'Appelle, Weyburn, Shaunavon, Melville and the Bienfait-Estevan mining towns.

Sturgis, central Saskatchewan. A party member has died. His body lies in an open coffin in the parlour of the house where I stay. My bed is in a small room adjoining. There is a smile on his face. Walter Wiggins introduces me around the village. Long-time many-generation Canadians live here and everybody is some sort of radical: the barber, general-store owner, postmaster. Wiggins is an odd mix of personal reticence and revolutionary zeal. He has an open, honest face.

Never met Walter Mills, but people in Saskatoon told me about him. He came from England to homestead before the war. He was a small frail fellow and couldn't make a go of it; he and the wife, fighting the stubborn soil with one horse, and feeding themselves on the few potatoes the poor soil yielded. Scared by the loneliness as much as the arid land, they fled to Saskatoon. It was too late; the wife broke down and they locked her away in an asylum.

Near Alsask, close to the Alberta border. Stayed with farmer overnight. Ate chop-steak patties, very dark meat from a bear he'd shot. That bear will feed his family many weeks.

Nov. 21. Moved northward to Nokomis, Kamsack, Dunblane, North Battleford, Prince Albert. Fine bunch of young farm people, good Y.C.L. branches, good literature sales, good meetings.

I've learned to avoid repeating myself in speeches. If it bores me, I'm sure a bad speech bores my listeners. So now I try to make each talk sound new and fresh and spend more time preparing.

Learning a lot about farmers. They don't have an easy life. They learn to be stubborn and patient.

Everything's big here: the land, the sky, the loneliness, the defeats and the frustration.

3

1939. Fathomless Nights.
Doubt, Fear and Hope.

NIGHT, BRIEF NIGHT, long night, your night, Arthur—the hospital asleep, a nurse at a desk in an alcove just outside your ward. On the desk: letters for Arthur Meller, "Get well soon!" and telegrams. If you could read their letters...

You have shed old fears. You still have to wake from a bad dream...

We are nurtured on fears. You heard the bells and ran to the window, breathless to see the horse-drawn ambulance turn sharply on St. Urbain and pull in through the opening in the stone wall of the Hotel Dieu. You were scared when you saw the bodies carried in on stretchers.

Do you recall the day the coal caught fire and flames curled around the hospital walls as the fireman played his hose, a hero on a roof before he fell screaming into the flames?

Many things frightened you as a child. Now you're not scared any more, now you're angry. Your anger has conquered your fear.

*

Remember that winter of 1927-28? Montreal hungered and froze. Snowbanks higher than a man's head. The jobless everywhere. St. Lawrence gales whistling, seeping through clothes and into bones. Iron Quebec-heaters useless without fuel. Blizzards at night and damnation at dawn. Old men begging. Free soup at charity missions. Young men found frozen stiff in snowdrifts.

Rough on the rag-picker and even the cop on the beat, and also the streetcar conductor and the motorman, and the streetcorner hawker of papers, and people on picket lines, and those scrabbling for odd jobs, and the peddler and the pale floosie, the corner grocer, the cobbler and the Chinese laundryman, the neighbourhood tailor, everybody except the undertaker.

Bitter bitter bitter cold, stabbing cold, hacking cold and hunger, a foretaste of 1929.

Often, Arthur, you thought of Fred Shaughnessy trudging in the prairie drifts that winter. Nothing ever stopped Fred. You envied him.

Winter. 1927-1928.
Fred's Diary.

Dec. 10. Calgary. Whose bright idea was it to print the razzle-dazzle posters and paste them up everywhere, "Come Hear the Boy Orator!" Dammit, I'm not a circus act, I'm not a boy anymore, I'm into my twenties. What do I do now, dress in short pants, wear a Buster Brown wig and speak squeaky?

Dec. 11. I told the crowd the posters flattered me; I was a little too old for a boy, I have to shave every day. There was a crowd of a thousand in the hall and they burst out laughing and applauding. I said I'd talk straight and no frills, I wanted them to know what youngsters were thinking.

We're not children anymore, I said, we don't like to be treated like kids. We're workers even if we can't find work or learn a trade. We do a man's work for a boy's pay. We can't afford to go to college, we're lucky if we finish high school. If war broke out, we'd be the first to die in battle. Our parents would get our medals and the profiteers get rich.

They applauded. I got carried away and blurted out, "You won't get rich, you son of a bitch, you're in the army now!" There was a gasp, just like Winnipeg, and the applause rolled again and people actually cheered.

I really have to learn to control myself.

Dec. 12. Arthur Meller told me that when he was a kid here he used to wander out on the prairie to snare gophers and pick wild roses. On clear days, he said, you could see the blazing blue ice-peaks of the Rockies eighty miles to the west. Some nights the northern lights flashed like fires. In midwinter the warm chinooks brought sudden thaws after forty-below cold. And once in summer he saw the sky darken at noon when a cyclone funnel twisted across the city.

He told me about the Calgary Stampede, but I guess the Old Wild West is gone forever. The cowboys have been tamed and now they work for ranchers who work for meat-packers who work for themselves. Indians can't get any work at all; they too have been tamed—they learn to die slowly on reserves, but it's faster on skid road. Arthur remembered how an Indian had walked into his father's store in Calgary, pointed to a flannel workshirt and stripped himself down to his waist. Mrs. Meller was shocked to see the man's bare copper chest and withdrew in confusion. The Indian didn't say a word, he tried on the shirt, removed it and flung it to the counter, snorted and stalked out. That Indian had not yet been tamed.

Dec. 13. I've been on the move: one night a farm, next day a village, the day after that a city or a town or mining camp. I meet the secretary and usually stay at private homes. I wash up, rest up, have coffee. We talk about the affairs of the Y.C.L. and the movement as a whole. After supper we go to the schoolhouse or the hall, sometimes ten miles by horse or sleigh. I give my talk and answer questions. I invite recruits and sell pamphlets and books. Then we go back to the house for a snack and a sleep and an early start to catch the train to my next dot on the map. Alberta's one of the newer provinces. I'm seeing places I never heard of before.

I ought to write my dad more often. He must be getting lonely.

Dec. 14. The bitter cold! It's here to stay—freezing miles of blowing snow and lowering grey skies. I've spoken to young coal miners in Blairmore and Coleman, and farm kids in Red Deer and Sylvan Lake. In many districts most of the adults come from the same place: Ukraine or Finland, Germany, the British Isles. Some places they're all second- or even third-generation Canadian, including pockets of French-Canadians. In the bigger towns and cities like Medicine Hat, Edmonton and Calgary, it's a mixture of Britishers, Poles, Swedes, Belgians, Americans and a sprinkling of Jews.

Dec. 23. Camrose, Wetaskiwin, Vegreville, Vermilion, Cold

Lake, Smoky Lake. More far-flung prairie farms buried under snow and separated by miles of unending loneliness... I've bought a pair of high lined boots, a thick wool toque and heavy fur gauntlets at one of those general stores that sell everything from hardtack to hardware. Jesus, it's cold!

In Rocky Mountain House my meeting was at the tiny Canadian Legion hall. The editor of the skimpy four-page weekly wrote a long report of my speech. I suppose the visit of a Communist from the East was the biggest story his paper covered in months. He showed me the write-up before I left town; it was pretty fair-minded. There's no Y.C.L. here, and for that matter no Communist Party either, except for a wistful old man who gets a bundle of the *Worker* and peddles it around. He led me to a clothing store, introduced me to its owner and left.

Ben, the tailor, locked up the shop, handed me a tumbler of rye whiskey and some cheese in the room behind the store, where he lived. He'd been drinking. He assured me of his devotion to the socialist movement (he had once heard Eugene Debs) and started to cry. His wife, he blubbered, had packed a suitcase, emptied the cash-till, taken their baby daughter and run off. He showed a snap of the three of them in happier days, all smiling sweetly. A big burly man, he now sat in his long underwear and stockinged-feet, bemoaning his fate, picking marinated herring from the bottom of a wooden bucket. "Have some," he urged, but all I could find were a few onion rings, thin slices of carrot, some cloves and half a dozen skimpy herring cuts.

What in hell makes a man go out and buy a gallon tub of pickled fish? And where does he find marinated herring in a place like Rocky Mountain House? He must have sat up all night stuffing himself with herring and swilling raw liquor. Grief? Gluttony?

He showed me the note his wife left. All it said was, "Goodbye, lover-boy. Go mount a she-moose, not me. I quit and I resign. Your beloved former wife, Sally."

The Finns have this thing they call a sauna, a small bathhouse with tiers of wooden benches. They heat a pile of stones and when the stones get sizzling hot they pour cold water over them until they steam. After the sweating, if you're foolhardy like me, you roll bareskin in the snow.

Stuck in Camrose for a day between trains. In the evening a touring troupe put on a variety show in the hotel diningroom.

About forty of us paid to see them, hungry for a few hours recess from winter. The actors sang, mimicked and dramatized their hearts out and were thanked with a flutter of applause.

I stayed overnight with an elderly farm couple in their one-room hut heated by a cracked iron cook-stove. A worn carpet covered the dirt floor. They've lived here twenty years. The walls are caked clay, the roof is thatched. They have nothing but each other. Is that enough?

I've moved north, staying with a bachelor, about thirty. He farms and lives alone in two-room cabin. Apologizes as all he can offer is eggs for breakfast, more eggs lunch and supper, eggs three times a day, boiled, fried or scrambled. No meat, potatoes, onions, carrots, fish or bread, just hardtack. In the morning we have to crack a thick crust of ice in the water-pail to wash or make coffee or tea.

Another mix-up. After three miles of pumping near-frozen feet over a country road, I entered this prosperous house and introduced myself. They looked at me oddly and said to wait. They whispered among themselves, shook their heads, said there had been some mistake and sat me down in a hallway near the front door. Meanwhile, in the diningroom, ten people sat down at a loaded table. I wasn't invited. The redolence of roasted meats maddened me. Nobody offered me as much as a cup of coffee. A strange kind of farm hospitality!

After an hour I got up, walked into the diningroom, thanked them for a delicious meal, praised their hospitality and left, slamming the door. I plodded my way back to the village, where the storekeeper told me I had gone to the wrong house, my people had moved. These here were White Finns; their hero was Baron Mannerheim. The Red Finns called him "The Butcher Baron."

This afternoon I watched two coyotes running in a field. They look like dogs but seem kind of sneaky.

What happens when somebody gets sick and needs a doctor in a hurry fifteen miles or more from a telephone?

I've been in farmhouses where poverty mourns quietly and alone. One house I visited, the husband had gone away looking to earn a few dollars in the city. The wife stayed home with her two babies. In a whole afternoon she spoke to me only once, to offer coffee. I tried small talk. She hardly answered at all; she stared at her kitchen wall.

In Drumheller I spent four days, mostly in the union hall. They're a spunky bunch, scarred and toughened by the coal mines. Skitch Barnes is a miner, short, intense, spring-muscled, militant, a welterweight boxer fresh out of jail after a strike. I stayed in his house. Every morning he trotted three or four miles to keep in training. When I came down with the grippe he massaged and pummelled me with fists like hammers until I was near numb. The black rum I drank in the miners' hall and the plug tobacco I learned to chew probably killed the bugs.

Once a month during the long winter the Red prairie farmers have a social night in the community hall of the schoolhouse on Saturday night. They come bundled in blankets and buffalo robes, whole families huddled together for warmth on a large flat sled behind a team of big farm horses. Accordion, fiddle, mandolin or guitar offer melody and rhythm, mostly Old Country waltzes and polkas. Speechifying is awkward, so I cut it to ten minutes. Their applause is more for my brevity than my words, I suppose. Coffee, cakes and sandwiches are served. Liquor is forbidden, yet some men look livelier than others; their faces are ruddier. Long after midnight the overhead Coleman lamps are finally snuffed out and the celebrants leave for home, urging their teams into the wind and the snow. Soon I lie tired and content and blissfully half-smothered in my featherbed, bathed by the steady amber glow of the iron stove.

I'll be in Lethbridge Christmas Eve. I wonder what they've planned. I wonder what Dad'll be doing Christmas Eve.

Dec. 28. Spent Merry Christmas alone, another wrong address. National Office better revise their mailing list. I checked into a room in a cheap hotel; tomorrow would be time enough to find someone. I ate a late supper in the usual Chinese restaurant, returned to my hotel, tried to make myself comfortable and settled in with a bag of nuts, a couple of bottles of beer, some potato chips and a mystery novel to celebrate the holiday evening.

The later it got, the rowdier it got. The walls were thin and my ears told me this was no ordinary hotel. The guffaws, the grunts, the squeals and giggles got louder and wilder until, about 5 a.m., the revellers must have soaked themselves into a stupor.

I took off my clothes and got under the covers; at last I would have some rest. I was dozing off when the biting began. I leaped out of bed and turned on the light. My sheet was crawling with bugs. Merry Christmas.

Jan. 5, 1928. Warm sun, blue sky and moist green fields. Wild flowers in January. And me rowing a cockleshell of a boat in Queen Charlotte Strait, a few hundred yards off Sointula, a serene place on the western shore of Malcolm Island, fifty miles or so below the northernmost tip of Vancouver Island, where the strait joins the Pacific Ocean.

Coastal steamer took me from Vancouver, an unhurried overnight trip. This village was started as a cooperative community by socialists from Finland around the turn of the century. It has no autos and hardly any roads. The day the government man is due to make his regular visit, the Red flag over the post office is discreetly replaced with a Union Jack. The postmaster is Party Secretary.

Today, in the community hall's library (cramped quarters adjoining the billiard room), a scholarly looking man questioned me sternly about Karl Marx and Karl Kautsky. I felt like an ignoramus; I'll have to dig more deeply into theory and history.

I'm staying with an elderly couple in a wooden house on a rise above the waterline. A young woman lives here too, the schoolteacher. We walked the beach together; she identified shellfish and shells, starfish and weeds exposed on the sand by the outgoing tide. She knows a lot, she's read a lot, she's beautiful.

Last night as I lay in the dark, listening to the breakers and thinking of her throaty voice and her friendly face, she came into my room, sat on the edge of my bed, signalled me to be quiet, smiled gloriously and kissed me...Vancouver is a whole world and a million years distant...I'll be here two more days, almost three...She's magnificent.

Before I got here I travelled from Calgary to Vancouver through the mountains. The long train seemed at times to cling too precariously to the slopes, with furious waters pounding far below and ribbons of mountain roads snaking and climbing high above us. I've never seen anything like it before.

Then the snows thinned and at last I was in Vancouver. In the evening I went to the hall. It was decorated, festive and full of people and the New Year's excitement of accordions, tap dancers, bagpipes, Russian dancers, Ukrainian dancers, Highland dancers, B.C. Indian dancers. And recitations, elocutions, choirs, mandolins, acrobatics. A baritone sang *On the Road to Mandalay*, an odd choice, I thought, a little too much of empire

Kipling, but the singer meant well, he had donated his talent. He was in good voice too.

Vancouver sizzles with left-wing action. Longshoremen, lumberjacks and fishermen come and go. Streetcorner acquaintances argue about Lenin and DeLeon.

Trevor McGuire, whom I had met back east, led me to the waterfront to buy a pail of clams for supper. I got some beer and we ate in his room. Trevor's a good-looking fellow, tall and slender, about thirty-five, with a sort of absent-minded smile and quiet voice. He was born in Carleton Place, Ontario, was wounded overseas, had an arm crippled, was sent home to join a Win-the-War recruiting team. His ideas began to change, he joined the Socialist Party in Ottawa, and later the Communist Party, and became the *Worker*'s first business manager.

He made a May Day speech in Queen's Park in Toronto. He said, "The British imperialists arm their missionaries with a Bible in one hand and a bomb in the other." He was arrested and served six months for sedition. He wrote a novel, *O Canada!*, and it ran as a serial in the *Worker*. I was embarrassed when he asked what I thought of it; I hadn't read the book. He looks frail and seems to be ailing; his heart, I'm told.

New Year's Eve in Victoria. Crossed by steamer and arrived late in freezing rain. Street-lamps glistened, the sky glowed, a skin of ice glazed the grounds and the government buildings.

No Y.C.L. here. My hosts were Party people, a dozen middle-aged and elderly men and women with paper hats, sitting in a circle around the parlour fireplace, singing Old Country songs and drinking punch from a wassail bowl. I was introduced all around and taken into the diningroom to feast alone on a late supper, roast turkey and all kinds of holiday treats.

I see now why Easterners say this town's like a little bit of England, a retirement home for colonial civil servants. These old-timers were getting on in years and a little old-fashioned, but they were all socialists or communists.

After I went upstairs to bed I could hear them singing, "What'll we do with a drunken sailor?" and endlessly bawdy *Lydia Pinkham*. Not so stuffy after all.

I made half a dozen contacts next day, sold a few *Young Worker* subs and actually organized a Y.C.L. after a short meeting. I hope they stick.

Jan. 9. Back in Vancouver. More meetings, good meetings, a fine start for the new year. Tomorrow I cross again by boat, this time to Nanaimo.

Jan. 11. Shown around a sawmill on the island. Surprised to see so many turbaned, bearded workers, from India.

Massive logs travel up a steep runway from the water and onto platforms where men guide them into the ripsaw bite of gigantic circular saws. Nerve-wracking din. Everywhere in this huge vaulted industrial cavern the raw wood is ceaselessly remorselessly ripped sliced cut trimmed severed divided by screeching steel teeth.

Jan. 12. Former I.W.W. man, now communist, showed me yellowed copy of *Little Red Song Book.* It had the one by Joe Hill, *the* Joe Hill, *Where the Fraser River Flows,* that he wrote for a strike of construction gangs building a railroad grade between Hope and Kamloops. "I was in that strike," the old Wobbly said. "I met Joe once, in the States. I knew Joe pretty good."

In the East we know little about B.C. labour. They made their mark away back in the middle of last century, even before then. Here in Nanaimo I'm in the house of a man who went on strike in 1912 and got locked out by the company. The union pressed for job safety; they said they worked in the most dangerous coal mines in the world.

White and Chinese scabs were brought in to take the jobs of white and Chinese strikers. Canadian Indians were offered work. They sure could have used the money but they wouldn't scab.

Sympathy strikes spread across the island, the militia was brought in, artillery rumbled on the streets, hundreds were arrested and held without bail. The fight lasted two years. "A big piece out of my life," my host said.

Jan. 15. Vancouver again. Bill Bennett told me the story of Ginger Goodwin, the socialist union man. Ginger was a leader of the 1912 coal strike.

"Now here's a strange twist," Bennett said. "Ginger was examined and declared medically unfit for the army, but in 1918, when he led the smelter workers in the Trail strike in eastern B.C., he was reclassified and ordered to report for military duty. All of a sudden he was cured."

Well, Ginger disappeared and wasn't seen again till his body was found on the island, near Comox, with a police bullet in his head. Thousands walked out; it was Canada's first general strike.

Bill is quite a fellow himself. He was born in Greenock, in Scotland, forty-six years ago, "near the grave," he grinned, "of Mary Queen of Scots."

Bill's a short man with walrus moustache and friendly shrewd eyes, and looks a lot like Bruce Bairnsfather's wise old foot soldier of the wartime *Better 'Ole* cartoons. He walks with a limp, but it doesn't sour his good nature. He's a colourful speaker and down-to-earth writer with a touch of style and a sharp sense of humor. He was a poor boy of sixteen, an apprentice at barbering, when he joined the Scottish Labour Party.

He arrived in Vancouver twenty years ago and threw himself into the movement. During the long coal strike on the island he worked to raise relief for the men and their families. Five years later he helped organize the loggers and sawmill workers. He was in at the start of the Communist Party.

He's a rare man, a man of wit and warmth, he hungers for classical music, detests Wagner. He's unmarried and childless and adores kids.

Jan. 25. Two more months to go. I'll be working my way back through spots I missed before. I'll be making return calls to see how the Y.C.L. has managed since I saw them last. Then on to northern Ontario. In Sudbury it's been nickel; farther north, in Cobalt, it will be copper, and in Timmins, gold, and gold in Kirkland Lake.

There are northern place names I barely glimpse from the train window: Hawk Lake, Kenora, Vermilion Bay, Oxdrift, Wabigoon...Ignace, Bonheur, Upsala, Argon, Raith, Finmark... Clusters of dots on the map, as though scattered from a shotgun: Timmins, South Porcupine, Schumacher, Porquis Junction, Ansonville, Iroquois Falls, Cochrane, Kapuskasing...Arrowheads radiating from Kirkland Lake and Cobalt: Swastika, Larder Lake, Englehart, New Liskeard, Haileybury, Sesekineka, Temagami, Kenogami, Matachewan, Silver Centre...and the frontier towns of Rouyn and Noranda.

Feb. 25. Diaries are for old men's memories. I'm not old. A diary is for somebody who thinks that every thought or muscle-twitch is a big event. I'm not that vain. Diaries are for people with lots of time on their hands. I'm too busy.

Feb. 26. Home soon! I'll write Dad to buy two steaks and six quarts of beer. But first a few more visits, a few more meetings, a few speeches. No, Dad may be broke; I'll get the steaks and the beer on my way home. I can't wait.

Feb. 27. Odd things happen in the north country:

A motherly Finnish woman marries an elderly Ukrainian. Neither speaks the other's language, nor much English, but their faces light up when he comes home from the mine.

A God-fearing housewife of about sixty, straight-laced and decent, bootlegs good illicit liquor at a fair price in her kitchen. She won't bribe the local cop; she makes him pay for his drink like everybody else.

Neighbours, hard-rock miners, tap power lines on the poles on their street to get free electric juice. "How else can we meet the mortgage payments?"

Feb. 28. The Rouyn Party Secretary treated me to the steam bath. I was glad to wash the grit of the train from my pores. He sneaked up behind me as I left the hot shower stall and poured a bucket of cold water over my head. "You guys from the south are soft." I laughed, pretended it was great fun. B-r-r-r-r!

March 3. Moving towards Ontario by slow train on a sunny day, too soon for spring, but there's been a thaw and a quick freeze and everywhere you look in this corner of Quebec, on every bush, twig, tree-limb and weed-stalk, there's a skin of ice, and through all these transparent coatings the sun penetrates and makes the country glisten and sparkle from every dormant growing thing and from the acres of snow and the miles of electric wires strung overhead like music staffs along the railway right-of-way.

March 5. Cobalt. At night when I look out of my window on the third floor of the co-op roominghouse, the street is absolutely still, and dark except for one lone lamp-bulb on the tall pole beside this narrow house perched on a high rock in shadow, like a stage setting for some Martian fantasy.

March 7. She was thin, she looked sickly, she seemed depressed. Our paths crossed in this dying town, she too on tour, trying to sell, she said wryly, health books no healthy person wanted or could afford.

She was much older than me. I suppose that long ago she had been vibrant and attractive. Now she frowned and even her laugh had turned sour. This dried-out town must discourage her. She was lonely and so was I. But her bitterness spoiled everything she said. Her hunger was so fierce it scared me off. A friendly gesture could spell disaster for both of us.

She proposed a walk and I demurred. She suggested a movie and I said I'd seen the film. "Well," she said as she started up the stairs to her room, "maybe I'll meet you again some day. I just thought you'd like company. Or something. I'm still a woman, you know."

I feel bad. Should I have gone to her room?

March 10. This is my last entry. I'll keep this diary as a souvenir. It's my own discovery of Canada...The trouble with Canadians is that we don't know what we have...I've seen the country. It's mine too.

March 12. Tomorrow I'll be in Toronto. Then I'll go home to Dad. Afterwards?

PART EIGHT

1

1939. The Hospital.
The Years You Lost.

IT WAS YOUR time to decide. You chose to go, not as onlooker now, but part of it.

For years you had frowned and fretted. Within seconds, that evening in the park, you made another choice, to help an old woman you hardly knew.

All those wasted days meandering among shadows, until two nights ago...

What indeed had there been throughout those years for anyone to remember about Arthur Meller, except that you are an honest and a decent man?

A life can come to mind in quick bright proud images or tell no more than yellowed calendars awry on fly-specked walls in an abandoned shack.

What happened in all that time? What indeed did you say, do, learn, *become*?

Were you on pavements pounding resounding to the beat of running feet?

Did you sit in meeting halls where the walls bounced angry words around in an insistent tattoo of protest?

Were you in houses scarred by hunger and chilled with fear?

Did you witness in committee rooms the saddened eyes and trembling lips as they swallowed yet another bitter outrage, another defeat?

Were you a fugitive from the bullpen—the pogey, the mission soup-kitchen, the transients' jungle, the nightstick and the skid road?

Have you endured numbing frost and fear in clattering box-car, sodden trench, picket line or Spanish mountain pass?

Were those *your* years, Arthur? What did you get from them, what did you give to them, did you belong to them?

Every morning troubled you more than the day before. Every night was drearier, every day more futile. The future was a spavined hag who offered only lies on a treadmill.

But what did you *do?* What did *you* do?

Slowly and sadly your passion diminished.

You heard of deportations, arrests and beatings. You suffered in silence.

People sang at demonstrations and parades, mass meetings and marches. You brooded alone.

You read of executions and massacres. You grieved impotently.

You were distressed by wars and the threats of war. You ground your teeth in private.

You retreated into your lonely mountain cave. You shuddered by yourself.

Until two nights ago.

1929. Year of the Blight.
Arthur and Gaby.

Shortly before the big crash of October and before the ten-year Depression settled in, Arthur Meller was invited to make a modest investment in the wholesale drygoods house. In money terms it meant a tiny percentage of the profits plus salary. His employers good-naturedly reminded him that in business you don't give anything away. The promotion would cost a thousand dollars, in instalments. Total devotion would be expected, such as readiness to work evenings or Saturday afternoons if circumstances warranted (and they assuredly would).

It was tenuous security but more than most people enjoyed that year, and it seemed worth the penalty of spoiled evenings or ruined weekends as proof of his concern for the health of the firm.

Gaby's books and handicrafts sold well; her little shop attracted visitors who wanted "something different."

They saw Fred from time to time. He spent occasional evenings in their house, talking, listening to music, sipping drinks.

Fred realized that both his friends were deeply worried. They seemed dissatisfied with themselves. Gaby smarted under the English domination of her people, yet she was furious that they were exploited by rightist nationalists. Arthur still argued his right to stand "above the battle," but it was obvious that his conviction wavered. "Will the system rescue itself?" he asked. "Our world lives in fear and feeds on fear. We're told a war will overcome our fears. When I pass the campus I wonder, are they learning how to sell apples, how to beg? Will a degree buy an army commission? We're on a tightrope, Fred, and it's wearing thin."

Fred tried to soothe his friends. When he left, Arthur handed him a woollen sweater (It's getting cool," he said) and $10 for the Labour Defence League.

Gaby and Arthur Meller managed comfortably on the tightrope. And yet...Their house was pleasantly furnished. They ate well, dressed well, relaxed nicely, bought books and magazines, attended concerts, plays, opera, ballet, art shows, lectures. And yet...They bought a good inexpensive used car for excursions into the Quebec countryside. Then they bought a bargain of a summer cottage in the Laurentians. Considering the times, it was a good life. And yet...

2

1939. September.
Fred in Hiding.

I DON'T READ enough and I don't know enough.

I'd be a better speaker and a lot better organizer if I hadn't told that son of a bitch Steele that he was a son of a bitch and given him an excuse to throw me out of Montreal High. I should have hung on somehow.

I've learned a lot these last ten, fifteen years, but experience isn't enough, action isn't enough. I'm stubborn all right, but you need a cool head and patience. Maybe now I'll have the time for some real solid study.

Yes, I've read a bit, but not enough. I remember when I was younger I read the *Communist Manifesto* aloud and Dad listened and nodded vigorously. We got the *Workers' Guard* from Ontario and Gene Debs' paper, the *Appeal to Reason,* from the States, and later the *Worker* and *Young Worker* from Toronto. I enjoyed *Masses* and *New Frontier* with their marvellous cartoons and drawings and the stories and articles.

I read some novels of Dreiser, Jack London and Sinclair Lewis. I learned to sing the songs of Joe Hill. I'd heard of hardly any Canadian writers—they hadn't counted for much in school—but I liked the stories of Morley Callaghan and Frederick Grove.

We learned little about the country; it was only later I discovered Mackenzie and Papineau, Lount and Matthews, Dumont and Riel and the others.

I've got a lot to learn. I've got to start catching up. I need knowledge. And discipline. And a clear head. I don't intend to sit out the war in this little room.

The Ten Lean Years.
People of the Blight.

For many people the Thirties started in 1928. In the spring, after his tour, Fred Shaughnessy went to Toronto for a month and was immediately caught up in the inner-Party dispute. He was now a member of the Y.C.L.'s national committee.

In meetings and private conversation he criticized the Party's work as he had seen it on tour. He also accused them of treating the Young Communists like children and holding them back.

Some Party leaders had become ingrown and listless, he charged. They were content to follow familiar routines. They discouraged struggle. They resisted beefing up the Party to cope with worsening conditions. They scoffed at the idea that the country was in for a period of hard times and tough battles.

They're bloody opportunists, Fred stormed, they're avoiding the class struggle, they crave respectability, they're a bunch of milquetoast reformists, that's what they are!

He hated having to fight with Bill Moriarty, the Liverpool Irishman, whom he liked personally, and Mike Buhay, the booming "by gumalorum" Manchester Montrealer, whom he admired, and he was especially unhappy arguing with elderly Mrs. Custance, the prim and proper former schoolmarm who only nine years before had barely avoided prison when the Mounties raided a meeting that hoped to organize the Communist Party. Dear Florence, he reflected, for all her dedication and English background (or maybe because of it) she'd simply lost touch with 1928; her Marxism was too bookish and too mechanical.

Endless hours were eaten up in committee quarrels. Intense polemics consumed the days and nights. Factional groupings met surreptitiously on both sides, chewing and regurgitating the day's words, often into daybreak.

"What in hell do you want?" Jack MacDonald burst out, exasperated by his tormentors. A respected trade union man, dark-browed, vigorous, stocky and articulate, Jack was a founder of the Party and its national secretary. "Why don't you people listen and try to learn?" he demanded, and when Fred shot back, "From you?" he exploded, "I don't need lectures from a pack of half-baked leftists! I was a socialist before you were born! I'm no goddam social-democratic reformist either!"

Fred was distressed. When Fred had first met him, Jack had been cordial and hearty, but as the dispute grew his manner changed and he would stare hard through his glasses, so that you became nervous and defensive. But dammit, doesn't the man realize the world has changed? This isn't Scotland, we're in Canada now and it's 1928. Does he really believe we can avoid a crisis? Where is this prosperity he prophesied? Does he think Canada or the U.S.A. are exceptions? Can't he see?

It was a deep-rooted policy conflict, more than a clash of temperaments or personalities. Fred was sure that if Mac and his followers won, the movement would dry up and die.

Criticisms and recriminations, charges and counter-charges! Close friends who had suffered persecution together became impatient and suspicious of each other or openly hostile. Splits, resignations, desertions spilled over well into the following year.

One day MacDonald marched his followers out and left the field to Tim Buck and Tim's supporters. They'll just flounder and fall apart, Jack prophesied. Mac waited for the opposition to collapse, but instead, one by one and then in groups, his own disciples left him. After some painful soul-searching they threw in their lot with the new leaders. These old-timers weren't going to throw away years of devotion and self-respect. Perhaps, some admitted, they had been getting soft. They didn't relish the right-wing label.

*

In October, when the crash came, the lean days began in earnest for Martin Shaughnessy on the Montreal waterfront.

They were lean days too for his son Fred, who was lucky to get a couple of days a week in the printshop.

*

Lean days, mean days, cruel and obscene days. For millions.

Day after day the jobs dried up and the people went home to wait nervously for better times.

No need to panic now. You'll make out somehow. You'll move to a cheaper house, a flat, a room.

You're young, this is your country, you're no immigrant, you got good marks in school. You'll dress up in your Sunday suit, your dark-blue suit and nice blue tie, your polished shoes and neat grey hat. You'll go a-hunting and a-whistling for a job, tra-la. Smile, keep calm, speak well and low, inspire confidence.

(Be-gone, get lost, come back ten years from now, perhaps we'll have a war, the foreman said.)

No need to panic. You have savings, spend 'em.

No need to panic. You have friends and family, lean on them.

No need to panic. A penny here, a nickel there, go out and beg on the street.

No need to panic. Food vouchers are free, old clothes are free, free soup is free, and so is sweet friggin' charity. Line up for relief. (Be quiet now, don't push.)

No need to panic, steal.

No need to panic...smile.

*

Sometimes I'm reckless and buy a boiling fowl. We have soup and meat for three whole meals.

Mostly it's macaroni and spuds for Fred and me, or mackerel, or beans.

On good days it's hamburger. We eat turnips and cabbages, they're filling.

We dunk day-old bread in gravy. When I fry bacon-ends we save the grease and dunk our bread.

We Shaughnessys like our food. It's a long time since we had steak.

I don't get much dock work these days so I have plenty of time to go looking for bargains in different bakeries, in butcher shops and grocery stores.

Yesterday I bought us a treat, a pound of chicken livers. On the way home I met one of the union brothers and he invited me into a saloon for a beer. I didn't have enough to buy a round and I told him, but he pushed me in anyway. It was a hot day and after three pints he dozed off. I let him sleep a while, then I woke him and helped him to his house. When I finally reached home and unpacked the livers, they had turned grey and stank. So we had spuds and a tin of baked beans. The evils of drink!

I wonder about people with small kids. What do they tell them? "You eat like gluttons."

We live from day to day. We're never sure of our grub or even our shelter. We don't go to the dentist. You don't need teeth when there's nothing to eat.

You can get a tin of sardines for a nickel (Fish she is too damn small!) as an appetizer, for what? There's places you can buy a corned beef sandwich for five cents, coffee and one doughnut for a nickel, and even a full-course meal—soup, meat, vegetable, coffee and apple-pie—for twenty cents, if you have the money.

Young fellows stop you on the street for a handout. Girls offer themselves for four-bits. People sleep in parks, in lanes, in condemned buildings and in culverts.

Last week an old man knocked on my door and offered to scrub my floors or do any other kind of odd jobs around the house, a full day's work for a dollar. Not such a bad idea, I could use it myself, I'm not proud.

The streets look shabbier day by day. The city's sick and tired.

I must raise a few bucks somehow and take Fred over to Craig

Street for a second-hand coat.

He doesn't complain about the way we live but he sure gets sore about the system. When we're low on funds (which is most of the time) he'll walk a long way to save carfare, but he manages to put aside a few quarters for our weekend beer. It's just as important as food, he says, and I agree.

Everybody's on the move, it seems, like fugitives from an epidemic. They keep on the go; they're driven by a fever. They sneak onto streetcars without paying, they hitch lifts on the highways, they steal rides on freight-cars—young guys and even old men and even girls—riding the rods, riding the roofs, riding on flat-cars, riding inside. The railroad cops and the Mounties chase them, kick them off, beat them up and arrest them.

The youngsters stampede across the country from the east coast to the west, and when they get to the Pacific they turn around and push their way back east again, befuddled ghosts chasing a will-o'-the-wisp. And all the time the sharp winds slap their faces and sneer at the skinny ribs sticking out of their shirts.

Fred's made organizing trips that way, to Winnipeg and back, to Toronto, Windsor and so on. When he gets home it takes a couple of days to get the soot out of his system and clean his clothes. I try to scare up something special for the table. Also a few quarts.

Sometimes I leave the world and go to a movie. For a quarter you can see the show and get a free cup and saucer or a plate. We have a little radio and I like to listen. I like the comedy shows on Sunday night; I like the laughs.

Some saloons serve a free round on the house, but I can't see myself chasing free beers. I know fellows who try to guess the brewery salesman's route, keeping one tavern ahead of him. That way they figure on free beer all day.

Some Saturday nights we hold house parties for the Unemployed Association. We sell each other beer by the glass. It's against the law but what the hell! We have good times around the keg, jobless guys buying beers to raise money to help other jobless guys like ourselves and to forget our troubles for a couple of hours. That way we can start a little less discouraged on workless Monday.

*

We're not on relief, we Shaughnessys. Dad and I aren't 100 per cent jobless yet. But we won't wait till we're destitute; we've joined the Unemployed Association. I'm giving it a lot of time; it means being sent to Toronto, Winnipeg, other places, a week or two at a time, by box-car or the hitch-hike route. Dad wishes me a cheery "Good luck!" even if it's only an overnight jog, but I can see the lonely look behind the smile.

That sad brave decent grin of Dad's lights up his lips and spreads across his face, creasing the sides of the wide mouth and wrinkling the corners of the grey-green eyes. I want to kiss him but all I can do without embarrassing my dad is stretch out my arm, squeeze his shoulder, wave from the door and leave fast.

Jesus Christ! The tens of thousands of fathers and mothers who try to smile to the sons skipping out for the hunger trails! And the hundreds of thousands who can't manage a smile.

People sit around stunned. They've lost their jobs, then their savings are frittered away, then their homes and the last tatters of their self-respect. They sit scared. They get angry. Anger is their defence. Anger gives them hope.

The wonder is they don't all march on City Hall and tear it apart brick by brick, and chase the smug politician bastards out of their smug politician wits.

The employed become unemployed, the living become zombies and sit stunned. But how long? Can you imagine them forever denying their hunger and hiding forever behind the walls that barely conceal their shame? Just waiting, silently?

Sure, we could crawl into corners and bother nobody and spoil nobody's appetite. We could starve till hell froze over if we expected the powers-that-be to help. We could wait till we're old and grey and turned to dust. Imagine a whole country sitting and contemplating its thumbs and not uttering a single bloody word of complaint, not a single curse or solitary shout, just waiting meek, waiting mute, waiting comatose.

But we don't wait, we can't wait, we growl and demand, we demonstrate and we parade, we stop evictions and we hand out leaflets. We hold protest meetings, free-speech meetings, relief meetings, welfare meetings, anti-deportation meetings, pre-meeting meetings and post-meeting meetings.

We can't wait, we won't starve, we'll walk through fire if we have to. We don't give a good goddam. No cops or clubs or lousy scabs can stop us once we start.

We're expected to keep quiet, to wait patiently. We're harassed, beaten, spied on and intimidated. Every time you go near a meeting-hall there's a parked car and a couple of plainclothes bulls. Guys get picked up and taken to the station. If you have no money in your pocket, you're beaten up and charged with vagrancy and get thirty days. If you're not a vagrant, you're beaten up and get thirty days anyway.

Homes raided, offices wrecked, books seized, clothes ripped, teeth knocked out. You learn at first hand how the different jails compare—Bordeaux, Burwash, St. Vincent de Paul, Stony Mountain, Kingston, New Westminster, Prince Albert, the Don Jail and the local police stations. Neighbours are grabbed, deported overnight. British-born, European—it makes no difference, they're undesirables.

Sometimes you meet a half-decent cop who doesn't savage you before you're even charged, but I haven't seen many. Sometimes the prison guards don't treat you like dirt. They weren't bad at the Langstaffe jail farm a bit north of Toronto. I served two weeks there for disorderly conduct (a street corner speech on a soap-box). The keepers gave us outdoor work most days, but I spent a week in the big barn where the air was thick with dust from the threshing. Day and night I choked and sneezed and coughed up the strangling black mucous. The grub was dull, but we got enough baloney, stew, porridge and heavy bread. They didn't lock us into cells; we slept in dorms.

Most of the guards were all right, with the exception of a moody grey-haired sorehead who called me aside one morning. "Come here, Shaughnessy," he barked. He didn't invite me to sit; he kept me standing. "Why are you a comm-yoon-ist?" he demanded. Ah, I thought, a rare jailer, a thinker; he wants to share a dialogue.

"Well, sir," I started out, "I think we need to change the social system." He glared and scratched his armpit. I said, "I think it corrupts decency and changes people into animals. I think..." Before I could say anything else the gaunt old bastard knocked me down. He turned red in the face. "No friggin' Irish mick jailbird is gonna call me no friggin' animal!" he spat out. And that was the extent of our philosophical exchange.

*

Another time a magistrate with a red rose in his buttonhole sent me to the Don Jail because a Toronto dick stopped me and I didn't have any money on me and that made me a bum. This vagrancy got me a month. There really isn't much to choose from—Bordeaux in Montreal, the Don in Toronto.

Every morning the bell shrills into your nerve-ends at 5 a.m. You fight off sleep, you cling to consciousness. The panic bells pause and then you hear the iron beds creak and the men grunt and groan and cough and retch. Then the sounds of hard metal grating on concrete as the cots are straightened out; and the slapping of the sheets as men tidy beds army style; and the shuffling of heavy boots on hard floors.

Cell doors open at 5:30 a.m. and men stagger out into cell-blocks with pails to be flushed down a solitary bowl and rinsed in a sink. You line up to brush your teeth and wash your face over the same sink and gargle and retch and dry your face with a wet towel; one towel for how many? A guard unlocks a gate, you climb a spiral staircase to the dining-hall.

You file in and sit down at long, unpainted wooden tables, and long, backless benches. At 6 a.m. a signal sounds, a guard nods and you begin eating. Porridge without milk or sugar. Every morning. Two slices of pulpy bread, a tin mug of tinny coffee. And on the wall, in large black lettering, the warning shouts, "Silence!"

We eat quickly, sneak uneaten bread into pockets or under shirts, rise at a signal, file out and drop spoons into a basket as a guard counts them and us. We are led back to the cell-blocks, where we remain until 11 a.m.

Twice a week we scrub floors. Every day at 11:15 a.m. we eat gristly stew and dunk starchy white bread and drink weak tea without milk. On Fridays it's steamed fish. The sign on the wall says, "Silence!" For supper we get macaroni. The sign still demands silence. All you hear is the sound of spoons, of chewing and swallowing and belching.

At 5:30 p.m. we are locked into our cells. To think, to brood, to plan a new life? Every night at 8:30 the lights are turned off, except for a weak bulb burning bare at each end of the corridor.

Day is ended. Now we can dream and fantasize. Erotic visions? All the guys say the docs put saltpeter in our food to dull our sexual urges. Years later I learned it did little more than preserve the food.

The guards begin their periodic rounds.

Every morning at five the bells startle us into consciousness.

*

Some months later, when I'd got used to breathing clean air again, I went with three Y.C.L.'ers to hold an anti-war rally in Niagara Falls. Before we could get out of our car a bunch of hollering red-white-and-blue patriots surrounded us, pelted us with rotten fruit and chased us out of town. I guess somebody in Toronto must have tipped them we were coming.

The leader of the true-blue gang was a local character they called Ted Gill. Ted was an anti-Red who strutted around like a hero enjoying his fame because he had flopped over the falls in a barrel, probably humming *Rule Britannia* all the while. Anyway, we weren't arrested, just insulted, roughed up and run out of town with a howling escort honking car horns behind us.

They must have been drunk; one car went out of control and turned over in a ditch, two others collided and wrecked each other. Funny, there wasn't a cop in sight. None of the gang got hurt, as far as I could see. Too bad.

I wonder what makes them tick. I'm not sure but I guess people who live off these tourist traps hate you because they're afraid you'll wreck the merry-go-round and slow the money-flow.

Those guys who mobbed us were probably as poor as us. They weren't rich robber barons defending their money-vaults, they were jobless guys like us but they wanted blood, our blood. They thought a holy war would wipe out the native-born Reds, who were somehow in cahoots with the immigrant Reds, who were all secret pawns of a giant conspiracy.

The rowdies howled for blood sacrifices. If they howled loud enough, they would be rewarded with good jobs and free beer in the coming corporatist superstate. Cheers for Il Duce, heil Hitler!

You'll find the bully-boys hanging around saloons and poolrooms all over the country: small-time hustlers and shills, political pimps and petty parasites, bootlickers, blowhards. Some of them work, some live off their wits, and starve. Sober, they promote sordid little villainies to make a dollar. Drunk, they boast about their tricks. And always they wave the flag, always they're the loudest to bad-mouth "those hunky Bolsheviki union bums." They must have hearts of gangrene to hate so hard and stupidly.

For my part I don't hate them, I think they're just slobs and sons of bitches. They depress me, they turn my stomach. I guess maybe I *do* hate them. If you can hate ciphers.

The day after I got back to Toronto a strike broke out in a dress shop on Spadina. I went to have a look. A dozen women walked the picket line, young women of twenty, women in their forties, a few older ones too. A dozen cops stood watch beside the building.

Leaning from a third-floor window the white-faced boss ("I was a worker once myself!") shook his fist and shouted obscenities from an anguished face. "I pay taxes, I pay your salaries, I demand protection! I'm in danger of my life! They're giving me ulcers! Break their heads! Take them away! Kill the hoors! Arrest the Bolshevik bitches! Let them rot in jail!"

The police sergeant regarded him glumly and turned his attention to the women. "Keep moving." he scolded. "Get away from the door. No singing, no stopping, no profanity. Come on, keep moving!"

Nobody on the picket line was swearing, nobody sang, nobody loitered. They maintained the slow promenade—forward, then turn, then back again, then turn. Forward, then turn, then back again, and turn. Forward...*ad infinitum.*

Desperation, stubbornness, anger and guts—a little of each, but mostly guts. They *must* be desperate, these women, to walk out on strike at a time like this. The city's full of hungry people hungry for work, some of them frantic enough to scab.

But there's no other way, either they strike or their pay is cut, either they strike or the speed-up grows, either they strike or the piece-rate shrinks, either they strike or get fed to the crows.

Now they're angry. They'll need all their stubborn heartbreak anger to keep walking that picket line. They'll need all their stubborn courage to stick it out.

Twelve women. I worship every one of them.

3

1939. September.
Gaby's House.

AFTER I GIVE birth to his child and return here, I'll nurse our baby on this bed.

Only a few days ago Arthur and I loved in this upstairs room of our house near the university.

When I first knew him he addressed me as Gabrielle, solemnly, even in bed. I liked that name; it made me feel like a mature woman.

Later, when he became bolder, he called me Gaby, whispering my name like a caress or a gentle song and enveloping me with his shy adoration. Men had kissed me, men had slept with me before, but none had ever been in love with me.

Will we two love again in this house, Arthur?

Will your child ever see you?

The Thirties.
La Macaza and Montreal.

Gaby obeyed the impulse to see her family in the Laurentians and drove north to La Macaza. It had changed greatly in the dozen years since she had left home to live with her grandfather in Montreal. The pastoral serenity was gone. The main street shrilled with commerce. A poster damned *les Juifs*. She heard Mussolini praised and Hitler glorified. She was given a leaflet that warned of Red conspiracy and Russian Bolsheviks, of Jewish bankers and immigrant anarchists, gross monsters all. *A bas...a bas...a bas!*

Her uncle grinned. So she's married a Jew, is he rich? Her aunt grinned slyly. Is it better in bed? A cousin tried to drag her into a barn. She slapped his face. He shrugged. Who the hell was *she* to put on airs. He leered and walked away. Some other time, huh? She was practically a Jew already, he said.

She remembered the Jewish farmers, two immigrant families from Rumania: sons and daughters, parents, uncles and aunts, grandparents. They didn't fit the patterns of caricature; some had blonde hair and some were brunettes and one was a red-head. They were ruddy-faced, sun-tanned, sturdily built, hard-working and outgoing good neighbours. But now they were all suspect; the townspeople were warned to avoid them. These Jews, a village priest asserted, were all atheists. Had anyone ever seen them at prayer? He'd heard strange stories about blood rituals. Their forefathers killed Christ.

Wait till we have the corporatist state, a schoolteacher told her. Hitler knew how to deal with them.

The cordial Jewish farmers, now noticeably withdrawn, retreated into their farms, came to town only on unavoidable occasions, and took measures to protect their stock from poison and their barns from fire.

Distressed and angry, Gaby cut short her visit. As she drove to Montreal, she recalled with bitterness Arthur's memories of his own hurt as a child made to endure the taunts of French kids and the contempt of adults who sneered at the little Jew in their midst.

He had told her about the summer he worked near Peel and St. Catherine and ate lunches at the Northeastern cafeteria and how one day a youth carrying his tray from the counter was tripped and fell, spilling his meal onto the floor. The lout who had tripped him, an older man, kicked and scattered the food and sneered, "Goddam Jewboy don't know how to eat like a white man."

The victim got to his feet, looked at the others and hesitated. Nobody said a word, nobody protested, so he ran out of the place. "Jew!" the counterman shouted after him.

Another time, Arthur told her, he stopped at the display window of a new dairy store that had just opened on St. Lawrence, below Marie-Anne, just a few doors south of the police station he had once stoned. The shop was brightly lit, its interior gleaming with white enamel, its cheeses, butter-tubs and packaged foods attractively displayed, the owner in crisp white apron, proud behind his counter. A dignified, well-dressed couple paused at the window, gazed severely through the glass, and departed, the woman remarking in languid asthmatic tones, "It looks clean, for Jews," and the man, chuckling, relishing his riposte. "But for how long?"

When Gaby came home she told Arthur about La Macaza.

"What petty stupid vicious people they are! What they're not used to they don't understand and what they don't understand they fear and what they fear they hate. But it's more than just these stupid fools; it's the dirty politicians who goad them and don't care how they get elected. They need goats and they find some Jews, a dozen souls in all, not even prosperous, just farmers like themselves. They're Jews, they're different, they're easy to see and ready-made to be pushed around and blamed for everything.

"Oh, Arthur, will we ever learn to see below the skin and behind the language and beyond the differences?

"Of the millions of people in this world, there are hundreds of different races, nations, tribes. No two persons are identical, and yet all the millions on earth are marvellously alike—different but alike, like you and me.

"Of course we're different from each other," she spoke earnestly. "We're the result of many different outlooks, customs, places, lives and histories. For centuries we've been confused by all kinds of fetishes, all manner of outworn myths stamped into the beginning minds of newborn infants.

"Yes, we're different, you and I. My eyes are blue, yours brown. So. And another difference—I'm a woman, you're a man. So. I think it is very good for men and women to be together. And I think it would be very good for all the world's people to be together more. I think the human race must have new blood to make it more beautiful and help it live better."

*

Arthur woke during the night, troubled by Gaby's experience. He lay in the dark and remembered how as a schoolboy he had sent a letter to the *Star*. They printed it: an emotional, vivid protest against the lynchings in the States. How can men behave like such monsters? Why now do the ignorant vilify the helpless? Who prompts their hatred? Why are people incited against each other when they should be helping one another?

He remembered the country club dinner-dance, the drunken guest he had tried to help, the crazy drive to the village, the cop, the bootlegger and the local whore Angelique, racists all, and his own summer in jail. What a hell of a depressing time that was in '22! Boredom, time suspended. You lived a slow-motion animal-like routine. You lay in your cell, sat in the bullpen, choked in your claustrophobia, waited and welcomed the least diversion, sulked.

You reported to sick-bay and got aspirins for all ailments, real or imagined, attended compulsory Sunday services, performed countless useless chores or did nothing at all, ate unpalatable food and lived under rigid schedules and unyielding regulation.

You smoked forbidden cigarettes and improvised a lighter from a metal button spun by tautened string against the cell bars, so that the sparks ignited a scrap of cloth and you lit your fag from the smouldering punk.

Time preyed on your mind. Time and silence, waiting and more waiting; the restless young ones counting the days and nights, the old men not bothering to count at all.

They were all trying to escape, Arthur reflected, from one unbearable reality to another just as unendurable. The real and the unreal overlapped and blurred.

These captives had been abandoned and had abandoned themselves. When their sporadic defiances surfaced they hit out blindly, made brutal by cynical anger, cursed by futility.

Arthur wondered whether, after all, he was so much more intelligent than these lost creatures.

Button, button, where's the button? Button, button, where's the conscience? Where have I buried it?

He blotted out the awkward thought.

4

1939. September.
Fred in Hiding.

IN THE UPSTAIRS BEDROOM of the piano-tuner's house on the east-end Montreal sidestreet off Papineau, Fred Shaughnessy lies in bed in the comforting dark, day-dreaming, half-dozing. Below in the small parlour comfortably cluttered with books, potted plants, family photos, bric-a-brac and sheet music, Armand Paquette plays softly, as though offering a lullaby to soothe the restless fugitive sheltered in his house.

Fred dreams: The girl looks into his eyes..."You're too serious," he says. "You ought to smile...That's better now...You know, I think I've fallen for you. You know, I'm in love with you." She smiles now and draws him down to her...

Paquette ends the music, reads a few pages of a novel, turns off his light and lies down to sleep on a lounge near the piano.

Upstairs, Fred sighs, remembering the girl, and dreams of her slow smile and the eagerness of her loving.

The Thirties.
Fred Shaughnessy.

He was in love with her, drawn by her quiet grace and cool serenity, her soft slow speech and calm self-confidence, the sympathetic way she listened.

She was small, dark, plump and sensuous. She invited him to her flat after a meeting. Forthright, she encouraged him to stay late.

They saw each other almost every day. Fred spun fantasies: marriage, a house and garden, books and magazines, a cellar stocked with homemade jams and spicy pickles, vegetable bins, redolent crisp apples, bottles of homebrewed beer...Children.

Conscience bothered him. Would Dad come to live with them or would he refuse to give up his own place, would they be abandoning him to loneliness, neglected and proud?

The dream soon died. Fred and the girl were walking home from a meeting. A light snow fell as they hurried towards her rooms on Dorchester. A car pulled up, its window was rolled down, and Fred recognized Ralph Gilbert's familiar jowled face and the thin red slash of moustache.

"Who's the new girl friend?" the detective called out. "How about an introduction?" Fred ignored him, tightened his grip on the girl's arm and walked on. "Well, if you need any help, feel free to ask!" Gilbert shouted. "Happy landing! Don't forget to leave a piece for me!" He laughed loudly, cranked his window shut and drove off on squealing rubber.

At her flat, as they sipped coffee, she spoke angrily, "Did you hear what that man said? He made me feel like some kind of tart, some animal." He touched her face and kissed her mouth. She pulled away impatiently. "I'm sorry, I'm not in the mood tonight. You'd better go home. I'm too upset."

He tried to see her the next day and the next, but the flat was dark. A week passed and she was still absent. She failed to show up for committee meetings or the branch social. A month went by and he received a letter postmarked Ottawa.

"Dear Fred," she wrote, "I'm sorry if I've disappointed you, but the more I think about it the more I realize I'm just not strong enough for your kind of life, always struggling, always running, never enjoying any peace of mind, forever sacrificing. For what? A dream? Who'll appreciate it, that policeman? I'm young and I want to live. I want to have fun. I want nice clothes. I want a nice big house or a smart apartment, and all the luxuries, and fashionable rich friends. I want security. I'm sorry but I have to be practical. I guess I'm not the idealist you are.

"And Fred, I have to tell you this. I'm going to be married soon. He's a very nice man, a lawyer, he's doing well. I wish things had turned out different between you and me. Well, I'm human, and that's life. I hope you'll understand. Goodbye and good luck.

"P.S. Don't try to see me, don't write. It's better this way."

Maybe she's right, Fred thought. He shouldn't expect any woman to share his kind of life. Perhaps, some day, he'll meet somebody.

*

What kind of men were they, these Red Squad bulls? Fred wondered bitterly.

Physically they were cartoon caricatures: beefy, hulking behemoths, custom-bred for the job, staring down at you from fleshy heights, trained to intimidate, indoctrinated with contempt for dissidents.

What made the eyes so cold, the mouth so cruel, the jaws such predatory traps? He'd seen them in action in Montreal and Winnipeg and recognized the breed in Calgary, Quebec, Glace Bay. He'd felt their fists and heard them curse.

Sullen, foul-mouthed, violent. Hard guzzlers, heavy eaters in a hungry land, smart dressers among the ragged. Well-paid professional sluggers, threatening, bullying, marauding, vandalizing. Kissing the Bible and perjuring themselves in court without batting an eyelash.

He remembered with wry amusement the time he'd served thirty days in Hamilton after the cops bust up a Stelco picket line. He had slipped a copy of *Babbitt* into a coat-pocket, something to read on the bus. At his trial the crown attorney called a constable to testify that a communist book had been seized from the person of the accused.

Fred spoke up. The author, Sinclair Lewis, was certainly not a communist; perhaps, he told the court, the learned gentleman was confusing Lewis with the other Sinclair, *Upton* Sinclair, but *he* wasn't a communist either, he was a socialist.

The magistrate was scathing, "Don't presume to lecture the court, young man. Your book is patently offensive and it will be destroyed by the sheriff. But the book itself is not on trial, *you* are, and I find you guilty as charged. Thirty days."

Another time, when he travelled by bus to speak at a park meeting in Oshawa, he took a book of comic adventures by Jaroslav Hasek, the Czech humorist. Next day he read in a Toronto daily that "the speaker clutched a red-bound volume entitled *The Good Soldier,* by Schweik, apparently a Russian handbook for revolution."

Fred Shaughnessy, learning hard facts about the world at firsthand, was seen increasingly in free-speech rallies at street corners, addressing demonstrations of the unemployed, marching with strikers on their picket lines, preventing evictions of destitute families, leading delegations to government offices, defying prohibitions, giving courage, giving help.

He worked seven days a week and he was busy most evenings, organizing, speaking, writing, and warning about the tide of fascism, the threat of war.

He became known to his co-workers as a practical, tireless and effective organizer, a trouble-shooter you could send almost anywhere on short notice and be sure you could depend on him. When there was something in the treasury he might get ten dollars a week.

At home late at night in his father's flat, or away on the road, he liked to relax with novels, mysteries and adventure books to balance his intake of political studies. He read countless short stories; he was bewitched by the matter-of-fact magic of Indian legends and Eskimo tales. He browsed the bookshops and the old Fraser

Library on Dorchester. He bought a second-hand dictionary.

He read with fascination Douglas Durkin's novel, *The Magpie*, about Winnipeg at the end of the war, as he sat on the uncomfortable seat of the old railroad coach creaking through the night on its way to Toronto.

Fred had just finished two weeks in Winnipeg on the jobless-insurance campaign. As he read by the weak lights of the clattering train, yesterday's conflicts merged with today's and the old war projected prophecies for the new.

He was returning east on a slow cattle-train. There was nothing to do but sit and read patiently in the dubious comfort of the ancient car. At least this time you were inside instead of riding the rods. You read and day-dreamed and rested and looked out the window at the hundreds of flat snow-covered miles until you roared into Ontario and the landscape changed to bush, evergreen hills and red rock and lakes of hard blue ice.

He had been introduced to a cattle-dealer, a sympathizer, who wrote out a contract for him to take a carload of cows east. The dealer was a friendly chap and gave Fred two dollars "in case you get hungry." Livestock shippers were allowed free fare for a man to look after their cattle, but railway staff usually fed and watered the stock.

The night they left, two days before New Year's, Fred and four other contract-holders huddled in the corner of a railway shed, waiting for their train to be made up. Yardmen came in, warmed their hands, sipped hot coffee. At midnight a man with a lantern arrived, glanced speculatively at the little group and said they'd be leaving soon. Other railroaders came and went, reporting, handing over crumpled sheets to a man behind a battered desk, reeling off serial numbers on a telephone.

Finally the waiting group was told it was time. They lifted packs and valises, trudged across tracks while engines shunted freight-cars, and finally were directed into an old colonist coach lit by two oil lamps and with a coal stove at each end. Dust and grit covered everything. The men piled their packs on the seats, fed coal to the stoves, settled back.

The train moved, creaking and grinding, coming to sudden lurching stops and clashing as couplings made contact, and then they were off. They sat peering into the night until they left the city's lights and shadows and were moving through open countryside. A man unpacked a kettle and made tea. They drank, assessing each other. They read or played cards, banked the fires, changed seats, lay down and tried to sleep, listened to the clacking of the wheels.

In the morning when they woke their mouths were dry and their eyes gritty. They ate a little and drank tea and stared out over the snowdrifts. When their long freight paused at a station they learned that three cows had perished during the night from wind screaming in at forty degrees below zero through the open slits in the walls of the cattle-cars.

The frozen body of a young girl was found by a trainman checking a freight-car. She appeared to have been five or six months pregnant.

If there were no other delays, the boys would step down in Toronto in time to celebrate New Year's Eve.

5

1939. September. Wartime.
Irma Gillespie.

I DARE NOT leave the house; the detective's sure to be looking for me after what I've done. Does he know where I live? He must remember me from the time he checked my shopping-bag. I'd better stay home this week. Oh, don't be silly, Irma Gillespie, that was a long time ago. Still, I have to be careful, I'd better wait a while.

I'd love to be home on the island again. I'd dearly love to go there just one more time to walk the red soil of Charlottetown and lie on the beach at Dalvay and scan the infinity of water reaching out to the gulf and away.

Abegweit it was called, *Abegweet*, *Epageit*. "A cradle on the waves," the Micmacs said.

Its other name was *Minago*, *Minegoo*, the island.

It's too late to go there now; I'd be a stranger, nobody would know me.

It's comforting here, looking down from my balcony at the back of this house. There's apples on the trees in the garden, the red salvias are in bloom, the zinnias and marigolds, the petunias. The sun floods my room and the summer lingers and warms my creaky old bones.

My bones wouldn't be so sore today if I hadn't thrown myself in front of that detective. Old ladies like me aren't supposed to get violent at eighty-two.

The Thirties.
Irma Gillespie.

Miss Gillespie moved like a frail ghost along the dark street and slipped a folded leaflet through each letter-slot. Whenever she heard a car motor she stopped at a door as though waiting to enter. She was careful not to rattle the slot-lids.

For years she. has anonymously distributed messages to anonymous people. It is the sort of thing you cannot immediately check with certainty. When you work your way door by door along the sidewalk and slip a hundred leaflets into a hundred doors it is hard to say what effect they will have, except that you get awfully tired climbing exterior stairs, especially in winter. Often the leaflet will not be read, nor even looked at. Some people read and snort, some call the police. But for some it will trigger thoughts and inspire deeds to transform the world.

Irma could not precisely assess the results of her work, but she was fervently convinced that if only one new person accepted the message, her efforts had not been wasted. She had learned to be patient. She continued to move methodically from door to door.

*

When she was younger she used to find shy pleasure mingling with the Saturday afternoon crowds at the old Rachel Street market and shopping for the meaty tomatoes, the green onions and crisp radishes.

Fat strawberries were heaped in pint or quart boxes which were later emptied and tied together to make translucent lanterns lit from within by a piece of wax candle and swung like comets outdoors at night by children celebrating their own pagan rites.

Farmers piled produce behind their wagons on planks supported by trestles. You could buy slabs of bacon, leaf tobacco, butter churned only the night before, cheese and many other fine things.

Irma would move slowly among the housewives, wide-eyed children, fathers of families, habitant grandfathers trading gestures and makeshift words with Jewish grandmothers. Irma moved among them, warmed by the flow of life around her, loving the sounds and smells and sights of this pulsating place sheltered below the dependable body of Mount Royal, which rose only a short piece west across Park from Fletcher's Field.

She didn't know them but she loved these strangers. "If I have no faith in people the world will surely die," she told herself.

*

One cool October evening Irma had slipped the last leaflet under a door and was on her way home, weary but pleased, when she heard footsteps close behind. She was afraid to look. Was it that detective? Her shopping-bag held only a ball of wool; there was nothing to fear. She slowed her pace. The footfalls came closer, the man drew up closer, walked beside her.

"Hello there, baby," he said as she turned and backed away, remembering a day in Charlottetown, her books scattered on the ground. The man saw her tired old face. "I'm sorry," he said, "I thought—in the dark—I thought you were, I'm sorry, granny, I'm really sorry."

Irma regarded him sadly. "It's all right. But please leave me alone, please go."

The embarrassed young man stood uncertainly, turned and hurried away.

She walked home, climbed the stairs to her rooms, examined the ancient face in the mirror, then sat in her rocking-chair, whispered "granny," and wept.

6

1939. September.
End of Drought.

FOR TEN YEARS the larders were bare while hunger gnawed. People
were told to tighten belts. Malcontents refused to shut up.

A decade too much, a drought too long. . .

Now it's over. Factories hum, money flows, the world is waiting
for the sunrise.

High priests pitch voices in resonant prayer and praise the source
from which all profits flow.

A steady pelting fertilizing shower drenches the earth.

The downpour overflows rivers and floods lakes and fills the
desiccated wells.

It will not let up for six years, this deluge of blood.

Please pass the ammunition. More! Faster!

Before the Deluge.
The Epic Decade.

Martin Shaughnessy, a longshoreman: It's the system. It won't give
us any peace at all. It won't let us live. So I keep fighting to stay
alive. Even if it kills me.

A Kenora Indian trapper: This Depresion, it's no big change. We
always been hungry, we always been pushed around.

An Arctic Eskimo hunter: Nobody even knows we're here,
nobody cares if we die.

Ralph Gilbert, the detective: This Depression doesn't scare me
much. I live for myself. Let the losers croak.

*

His name is John Doe, born in Winnipeg sixty years ago, a
grandfather now, still paying for the house in the North End. He's
shop chairman in an overall factory but he's not at work, he's on
strike.

If they don't win an agreement soon, he'll lose the job and probably get blacklisted. And lose the house.

What can you do? You can't run away. He urged them to strike, and they listened, and they went on strike.

*

His name is John Doe, born thirty years ago in Calgary, father of two children, Jenny, six, John Junior, four, husband of Jean, who is pregnant again.

Doe, jobless four years, enduring on odd jobs and relief vouchers, gets nothing now. He's in the hoosegow serving 60 days because he stopped to listen to a street corner speaker and didn't move when the cop said, "Move on!" When the cop pushed he pushed back.

7

1939. September.
End of the Line—All Out!

FROM TUESDAY, October 29, 1929 to Sunday, September 3, 1939, for a decade of twilight and ten years of night, millions survived the pain of famine and the shock of fright. Millions did not.

Every hour of those convulsive years claimed victims. Many were maimed; many just sickened and died.

Now the real killing gets underway. It's formal, official, legal and planned. Now the delirium is tangible, real. The world's in a nightmare, insanity rules.

Dinosaur empires like mechanized dragons contest the earth.

*

The earth heaves, it groans and bleeds.

The Angry Decade.
John Kravchuk's Canada.

He was a big, clean-shaven man toughened by heavy physical labour. He weighed 180 pounds. His shoulders were broad and his stomach flat. Thinning blonde hair receded from his forehead. Grey eyes watched reflectively from a boyish, round face. A piece of an ear was missing. He moved with slow grace and dressed for comfort rather than looks.

He did not speak much; his words were chosen carefully and expressed thoughtfully in a soft, low voice. There was the suggestion of a Slavic inflection and an accent that lingered from his early years, first in Kiev, where he was born, then in Moscow, which he fled in his late teens after the 1905 Revolution, and then on the Manitoba prairie, where he lived for a while with his uncle's family, Ukrainians who had sunk roots before the turn of the century.

"My Uncle Peter was a kind man, a very patient man," he told Martin Shaughnessy. "He worked hard and so did I, but I had no complaints. Anyway, I was young and I wanted to see more, I wanted to meet people with new ideas, I wanted action.

"I left the farm and went to Fort William and from there I got sent to a logging camp. Hell, I didn't see much of the country there either, except trees and bunkhouse, bunkhouse and bush, but we talked and argued and got into fights and got drunk once in a while. I worked all winter, till spring break-up.

"Later I dug coal in Drumheller Valley and then I headed east and got work in Toronto in a fur-dressing sweatshop till I got fed up with grease and stink. I came here and got a job handling freight for the C.P.R.

"In Montreal I met a sweet Polish girl. We got hitched and after a time we had a little daughter.

"Then the war broke out. I was a socialist then, I was against the war, especially that kind of a war. I didn't enlist.

"My daughter grew up and when she was only eighteen she fell in love with a young doctor, a Macedonian boy. They had a nice wedding and moved away to Cornwall to start up a practice there. And so after a while she had a baby, a boy, and I became a grandpa. That's the story of my life. And now I'm thirsty."

John Kravchuk refilled his beer-glass and sipped slowly. Both men were silent. There was more to the story, but Martin had already heard it from Fred.

A few years earlier, when Jack's wife died suddenly, his daughter came with her little boy to comfort him and took him back to Cornwall to look after him in her own home. But after ten days the bittersweet memories drew him back to his flat in Montreal and he lived there alone until one day he sublet it, furniture, dishes and all, to a young couple he'd met in the Ukrainian hall. All he carried out with him when he left was a knapsack with a few shirts and socks, a change of underwear, a razor and a comb, things like that, photos of his daughter and his grandson and of his wife, personal documents and a book of verse by Taras Shevchenko.

Shortly afterwards he turned up in Madrid, fifty-odd years old and a volunteer in the Mac-Paps. He met other Canadians, including Fred Shaughnessy of Montreal, in the fighting at Fuentes de Ebro.

Jack was lucky, all he lost in Spain was an earlobe when he carried the bleeding Fred on his back to the field station. Fred couldn't walk, he was in shock, his foot had been shattered.

After John Kravchuk came home from Spain he sometimes dropped in on the Shaughnessys. He brought cheese and rye bread and Ukrainian kielbasa sausage, with a mickey of rye and some beer to wash it down.

*

"I always liked horses," Kravchuk reflected on one of these visits. "I was a farm boy, I knew how to handle them. But cavalry, that's horses of a different colour. They changed my mind.

"Three countries during my life I learned to stay away from horses. First Russia, when they used to gallop on the cobblestones under the fat arses of the tsar's Cossacks. Then later in Canada, the Mounties riding so hard they made sparks on the street. And not so long ago in Spain, the horses of fascists killing for Christ.

"I guess you can't hate a horse or blame him except at the racetrack. They ain't supposed to think. But the riders—all those bandy-legged bastards—they're supposed to have more brains than a horse.

"Anyway, Mart, this time Spain lost, and so did Fred, and me also, and you too, and Canada. Only the fascists won. Not just

Franco but Mussolini and Hitler and all those other bastards. Here too. They're riding high on their horses. Spain was just a rehearsal for the big war that's coming, sure, maybe this year, maybe later, but soon, soon.

"From the end of the World War right up to now there's been killing going on someplace, and crisis and hunger someplace, and fear everyplace. It's crazy, the system feeds on fear and blood.

"It makes people mean and tricky, it coaxes them to steal, to cheat each other, to claw like animals, to spit on your neighbour.

"You got no idea what it's like to be a hunky foreigner. We have to compete for jobs that just ain't there, we work like horses for peanuts when they let us work, and we also get insulted. If we complain, we're deported.

"We bohunks are a big chunk of this country. We have to fight harder than the others just to live. It's always open season on immigrants.

"But you know, we're not patsies no more, we don't like being pushed around. We organize, we demand, we hit back. We're stubborn buggers. Anywhere there's a picket line, an eviction, a jobless trek or a free-speech fight, you'll find us there, us hunkies, even if we don't speak English so good."

Kravchuk raised his glass and grinned. "Here's to the Polacks, Finns, Swedes, Yids and Ukes and all the rest of us, and here's to the Irish too!

"I picked up my English on the job and I learned to read at night school. I got books from the Fraser and the Labour College. When I earned money I bought my own. I've learned a few things. You know, this country's had real big battles from the start: between French and English, and them against the Indians, and lots of them against the fat Family Compact, and later the Riel uprising, and later again the coal-pit strikes and the printers and dockers and seamen and the city sweatshops, before the war and right after the war, in Winnipeg in 1919 and right down to now, Depression or no Depression, in steel and wood and autos, textiles, furniture, clothes—you name it, damn near everything and everywhere.

"And you know what? In every goddam case you start out arguing with a boss—and soon you're also fighting politicians and newspapers and cops and the courts.

"You know something else?" he said almost as an afterthought. "I've lived in Canada since 1906, and thirty years later they still call me a foreigner. But in Spain I was always 'The Canadian.'"

The Ugly Decade.
Ralph Gilbert's Canada.

Gunfire was no novelty; he had handled rifles, machine-guns, shotguns and pistols in war and peace.

Gilbert hunched over a table in the Fraser, killing boredom for an idle half-hour, alternately assessing the rump of a young librarian and leafing through books he scanned for diagrams and texts.

Too much detail, he concluded, too many words, too damn technical. Why can't they put it neat and interesting? Anyway, there's nothing in these books he didn't know already. To hell with theories and trajectories, he could take a gun apart and assemble it quickly and there'd be no parts left over. Better still, he could shoot straight and sure and right on the bullseye.

He liked the description he found in a dictionary: "The revolver is a pistol with mechanically revolving cylinder containing cartridges for firing several shots successively without reloading."

Neat and concise, it pleased Gilbert; it was a clean definition of an efficient instrument.

If you've learned to control your timing so that each motion flows smoothly into the next, your first bullet fired should find its mark. Hold your weapon steady, aim calmly, engage the trigger with an even pull. There's a small explosion, the bullet shoots out from the barrel and tears into its target of metal, wood or flesh.

Ralph returned the books to the girl, gazed steadily at her plump chest, winked and walked out into the sunlight. "I have a hunch," he thought, "that one of these days it'll be more than target practice."

Aloud he murmured, "It can't come too soon."

The Wasted Decade.
Twilight in Canada.

It's a country of infinite parts, lush lands and rich rock, fresh lakes, salt-water seas, massive mountains.

It reveals endless beauty in a million breathless places.

It was found by dreamers, staked out by courtiers and adventurers, exploited by merchants, truncated, dismembered, savaged and soiled.

It has been sundered, graded, catalogued and segregated into white and lesser breeds.

No country on earth can remain free when it is so divisible.

The Cruel Decade.
John Doe's Canada.

My name's John Doe, I'm not unknown. I'm sometimes called Anonymous.

My family tree is convict French and English, Irish, Scotch and Welsh, colonist, fugitive and child of tribes disowned by God, Slavs who share a troubled dream, paleface relatives of slaves, sons and fathers of the damned, daughters of despair.

I am the Everyman of the Depression hells, the bastard fool of poverty.

What I've seen and where I've been and what I've felt I'd like to forget, yet I plead with my kids to keep faith with their time. "Remember, remember, remember," I say.

Are they listening? Otherwise the years are meaningless, otherwise their truth is lost.

*

Statistics can't savour the stale smell of loss, the fear on city streets, the panic drought in prairie homes.

For the loser who pleads and the victim who cries out, there is neither patience nor pity.

The horses move in and the billies come crashing down.

*

We ache. We freeze in firetrap shacks. We fret in castoff clothes. We hate the stink of city slums. We're broke, sad, scared, desperate, angry.

Don't whisper, "Patience." Please don't.

I'm told a dozen different ways each day that I'm a flop, a has-been no-account, a cipher and a clod.

I've been blackballed from the human race.

I'm obsolete.

*

In our kitchen cupboard, I remember, we had a handful of onions and potatoes, a couple of tins of Brunswick sardines, a few pounds of flour and a half package of porridge. And not much else. There was no meat in the ice-box, not even stewing beef or soup bones. And there was no ice either. Ice... what for?

I started out at noon on a Monday in April and worked the restaurants and taverns around Peel and St. Catherine. It wasn't easy going inside a place and asking strangers for a dime; I'd never done it before. I got ordered out every time and once they threw me out. Now I know what they mean by the bum's rush. I kept at it all afternoon and collected eighty cents and a lot of insults. I worked the street near the tavern doors and the big hotels and I did a little better there. A drunk gave me a dollar. I took in two and a half bucks altogether.

I went home and told the wife and my two kids we were going to eat supper in a restaurant. She didn't think that was funny. I showed her the money.

"Where did you get it? Who did you kill?"

So I told her. She got sore and shouted, "We're not beggars! We're not bums!"

She started to cry. But we went to the restaurant and for a buck-fifty the four of us ate pretty good, soup to dessert.

Later, after we went to bed and I turned out the light, she said, "Don't do that again, never, we're not bums."

She was quiet for a while and suddenly she burped.

She threw her arms around me. She laughed.

Then she started to cry again.

PART NINE

1

1939. September.
Arthur's Long Night.

YOUR FACE IS LEAN, serene and cool, without a trace of fear.

The intravenous tube is neat, the bandage on your head is clean, and yet they seem inadequate to heal the flesh Ralph Gilbert's pistol tore.

You must have been afraid of him. And yet you weren't; you didn't run.

*

What things we feared when we were small! Strangers and ghosts and howling wolves, and glare-eyed owls and serpent's tongue, eerie bats and squeaky sounds and plunging falls from dizzy heights, bad dreams and flitting beasts and haunts, and flames and open graves and ghouls!

The first corpse you ever saw was the baby girl waxlike in the white box in the parlour of a neighbour's house. A crucifix hung on the wall, paper flowers lay near the coffin. You ran and when you reached home your mother shouted and forbade you ever again to see a dead body.

Do you recall when you were four your mother took you for a walk one summer afternoon along the slopes of the mountain? You saw a scared young cop hollering and gesturing at a scared boy hanging by his hands from the branch of a tall tree. You heard the crack as the tree's limb snapped and the boy dropped hard on the

273

grass and lay motionless, the dark trickle spreading from his head, dark as the grease from the incline railway track nearby. Your mother, pale and frantic, hurried you away, not letting you look back, over the fields and across the streets until you were safely home.

"Never climb trees," your mother scolded. "Good boys don't climb trees."

And do you recall the night when Haley's Comet streaked across the sky? Your parents drew the blinds. The neighbours prayed. The world was coming to an end. You hid under a bed.

As we grow old we learn strange wisdom from old fears. We close our minds and seal our hearts and live our lives in constant hibernation. We shelter no dangerous thoughts and utter no troublesome words. We have learned it is best to sleep and lie still and avoid any untoward act. We have achieved a deceptive animation that looks something like life.

The ancient fears and primeval superstitions are passed on by inheritance, inertia or decree in the hope that the children will continue to be zombies and forever reproduce zombies.

*

Arthur, you laughed away the medieval fears, but the superstitions of your own time were tougher to uproot. So you waited and debated and would not commit yourself. Until now.

You must have gone through hell these last few weeks.

Then, two nights ago, in the sad and shabby little park, you faced that bastard Gilbert and refused to run.

Decade of Discontent.
Arthur's Canada.

When I was called to the phone a pleasant voice said, "Hello, Arthur, this is Adrian Waterman. Do you remember me? Montreal High. Long time no see. Sixteen years? How've you been? Say, Arthur, d'you suppose you could slip out for a coffee? Oh, well, how about tomorrow? Let me take you to lunch. Tomorrow? It's a date. See you then. I'll pick you up at 1 p.m."

Adrian Waterman! Handsome Adrian, darling of the

literature-composition-elocution masters, dreamboat of the sixth form girls, romantic figure, poet laureate, Byronic virtuoso of the rotund vowel and incisive consonant, composer of odes and elegies declaimed before massed school assemblies, author of yearbook couplets pithily immortalizing all thirty-two schoolmates in Mr. Walter's all-male class.

Adrian Waterman the esthete was inviting me to lunch and I was flattered.

The Adrian I met next day was no longer a skinny, ascetic-looking high-school kid with pensive blue eyes, luxurious ash-blonde locks and elegant long hands. He wore his hair short now, and neatly parted. The face behind the bifocals was fuller, the torso more ample. The young man with the shy manner had become hearty, outgoing and very sincere. This confident fellow opposite me in the expensive restaurant wore a fashionably cut blue suit, handsome white shirt and maroon silk tie.

With tolerant amusement he reminisced about the old days, the teachers, the classmates. He sighed as he reflected, "Ideals were the dreams of our youth, a beautiful time. But you know, Arthur, whether we like it or not we grow up, we have to face the real world, and this world has no use for a poet." He smiled wryly and added, "Unless he's dead."

He flattered, "A mutual friend took me to your wife's little shop last week. A delightful place. And if I may say so, a very talented girl. Damned good business head. Very charming. I hear nice things about you too. You'll have to spend an evening with us, soon. You'll like the little woman."

The real world had treated him well. "If I say so myself," he confided, "I enjoy a rewarding career in insurance." He was also enjoying his poached salmon and his wine. "Is your omelette all right?" he asked.

"But I didn't lure you here to appraise cuisine, though it's good here." He chuckled and went on, "Actually, what I'd like to talk about, if you'll bear with me, is something else, but that can wait a bit." He smiled indulgently. "Let's catch up on personal histories first. Good. Let me fill you in on myself."

He ordered another glass of wine for me and continued, "We all change. I guess I've changed too. More than you expected? More than *I* expected."

He took another sip of wine. "When I was at college everybody assumed I had it made. You know, first McGill for my B.A. and on to my master's and then a doctorate from Harvard, and the return home in triumph to launch a distinguished career as a teacher, and sooner or later half a dozen slim volumes of poetry, perhaps a novel, a book of essays.''

He ordered our glasses refilled and conferred with me about dessert.

"I got the B.A. all right, and also the M.A. Then the market crashed, the Depression rolled in like a fog, my father's business collapsed. College degrees didn't impress employers and I couldn't find a steady job or any kind of job.

"Finally I tried insurance. I was married, we were expecting our first child. I was still writing poems and selling a few, but they paid pennies. I wasn't selling much insurance either. So, no sales, no commissions.

"Well, one day the branch manager took me aside. He was aware of my literary prestige, he said, and proud to have me working for him, but. . . He was going to speak to me like a Dutch uncle. He proceeded to lay down the law. I had to make a choice, he said sternly. With my education and my ability, he added, he was disappointed that I couldn't seem to face the real world. It was time I grew up and stopped indulging myself. He was distresed by my pessimism, my lack of drive. Was I going to be a quitter all my life?

"I would have to choose, either I wrote policies or I wrote poems! Which is of more importance, he demanded, to be a useful citizen selling solid protection to friends and neighbours and at the same time providing security and a little bit of happiness for my young family, or wasting my time spinning verses nobody needs and nobody wants? Even Shakespeare couldn't sell a sonnet today! I was depriving my wife and kid. What kind of virtue was there in that? What kind of a future did I offer them?

"He gave it to me straight from the shoulder, man to man. He gave me a week to make up my mind. If I decided to come down to earth, he promised me, he'd line up some good prospects and personally help me sign them up. But I'd have to work.

"After I'd made my pile, he joked, I could retire and write all the poems I wanted, like a hobby. 'But first,' he insisted, 'you have to be independent. Bread and butter come first; later comes the filet mignon.' He dared me: was I man enough to try it for six months?

Would I give my family a fighting chance?

"He sympathized with my problems because he himself had to make the same kind of choice when *he* was a young man starting out. In his case it was music.

"I spent a worried week searching my soul. Then on a Saturday afternoon I went to his office and said I had decided. 'I surrender,' I said, trying to be light-hearted about it, but he looked me in the eye and he answered me very quietly, 'No, my friend, it's not a surrender, *you're* not the loser. Far from it. You're taking the first move to make yourself a real winner. You've made the biggest decision of your whole damn life.' He produced a bottle of brandy and two glasses from his desk. We drank to my success.

"'Good luck and God bless you!' he declaimed fervently. He grasped both my hands in his and I swear there were tears in his eyes as I left to prepare for my new life, effective Monday.

"He was a rough-tough man, a realist, you know, very wise but also very sensitive. I learned a lot from him. He boosted my self-confidence, he made me strong. He was right, you know, literature could wait, music could wait; the bills couldn't, life couldn't.

"I opted for life. I never turned back and I never looked back.

"You could say I made good. There was a piece about me in the company magazine, a bit of praise for my sales record. 'What poetry lost, insurance gained,' it said. There were pictures of me and the wife and kids and our house in Outremont. Very flattering, very nice. I don't complain.

"But enough about me. Tell me about Arthur Meller."

I pointed to my watch and excused myself; I had to meet a customer and I was late. This matter he wanted to discuss, was it insurance? He smiled. How had I guessed? I told him Gaby and I carried modest coverage. Could we discuss it in the fall? I thanked him for an excellent lunch and said it would be nice to meet his wife. He drove me back in his navy-blue Packard. I shook hands, wished him luck and returned to my own reality. I didn't have the heart to ask whether he'd written anything lately.

I don't know what it was about that luncheon date that left me so depressed. Well, in a way I do. I saw Adrian Waterman as a man looking out from a clouded mirror. And I recognized my own image, hardly the same big success, but smug enough and spineless enough, looking out over his shoulder from the same mirror. The resemblance was shocking.

*

As he lay wide awake, edgy and dissatisfied, staring into the night, with Gaby beautiful and fast asleep beside him, Arthur imagined a procession of sheep and tried to count them to induce sleep. They had the faces of people he had known, neighbours and school friends, teachers he had admired and mentors he'd worshipped.

What were they doing here, these sheep crowding into his night, puffed-up and purse-proud, waving their diplomas, displaying business licences and stock certificates, mortgages and contracts, bankbooks and college degrees?

They marched in a garish disorderly parade, pushing each other aside to squeeze up-front. They shouted boasts, they taunted one another.

Were these the rebels of yesterday? Why did they go, where have they fled, turning their backs on conscience and their own best years?

Where were the poets whose songs dried up, throttled by their own hands? What silenced them?

The sheep with human heads seemed now to be dancing a stately minuet. How agile their rhythmic acrobatics, how glib the rationale!

How intransigent their recent zeal, how blithely they once fought, and yet how gracefully they switched their loyalties: the union militant who's now a sweatshop boss, the anarchist who scorns restraint and won't allow a union in his plant, the socialist who snipes at Marx, the son of immigrants who shouts, "Deport them!" if they strike, the profiteer who robs the poor and calls them cheats, the Nietzschean convert who detests the weak and turns his back.

The prancing sheep seemed to merge until there was only one, and this one appeared to Arthur to have changed from a sheep into the composite figure of an ambitious politician well-known on The Main as a stalwart socialist. He was a lanky, round-shouldered man with a small head on a long neck, protruding eyes and Adam's apple, hardly any chin at all, a flabby gargoyle face and a little belly that suddenly jutted above spindly thighs.

One-time union organizer and radical, he had transformed

himself into the very symbol of sensible civic pride. A public beach had been named for him, cleanliness next to godliness, conquest by mind over matter, the triumph of the safe and sane and perfect politician.

Beside this prodigal emerged another figure, in his youth a firebrand, now a suave medical specialist and in his spare time a dabbler with strong views on culture and morality. "All art is bourgeois, all art is decadent!" he had ranted as a youth. "Who needs it anyway?"

For a time he flirted with Marx, then paused to think, married into money, made some more in real estate, grew plump and proud as a prosperous surgeon (bones), turned sour on socialism, developed an interest (clinical, he pretended) in erotica, and bought himself a costly house crowded with expensive paintings, antiques, furniture and bric-a-brac with which he might part if he considered you worthy and if you could pay his price.

*

More and more, in that summer of 1939, Arthur grew aware of the alibi-makers. Glib and well-rehearsed they spoke their credos:

Under the system we have to do a lot of things we don't like, such as cutting wages, firing a worker, crushing the opposition. It's the survival of the fittest...All the workman knows is how to drink beer and knock up his woman...Socialism won't work, it's against human nature...Kids today want something for nothing...People are rotten...I worked hard for my success and I'm not parting with it...I was an idealist once myself; I soon woke up...The poor spoil property values...What's mine is mine, what's yours is mine too—that's socialism...The lazy bums think we owe them a living...Anybody can get a job if they really try...

Workers of the world, unite? But Kipling said, "East is east and west is west, and never the twain," etc....When I was young we had *real* revolutionaries. Not now...I was every kind of radical—single tax and socialist, anarchist, syndicalist, Fabian and DeLeonist. I've seen everything, been everywhere. It's all a bore...All those years I wasted...The revolution failed me...They deceived me...Gods with feet of clay...I know those bastards, I was one myself...The whole world stinks...

*

Among his schoolmates had been young crusaders who later caved in and became bosses in family factories.

Arthur dismissed them as weaklings, easily tempted. But had he too not succumbed? He brushed aside a tremor of guilt. He had not sold out; he had only held back.

He could not condemn the timid ones, but his anger burned deep against the brainy governors and erudite opinion-makers—the pillars of the state—those wielders of power who oil the gears and make the system work.

*

On a luxurious suburban plateau brushed by mountain breezes a spread of busy communities bustled with sales people. Arthur watched in loathing. Talented grubbers, he growled. They burnish parasitic skills from the day they first learn to draw dollar-signs, pursuing the symbol through high school and on to post-graduate degrees.

Esthetes consume a third of a lifetime nurturing creativity to stimulate the sale of sausages and cars. Composers make jingles to sell junk. Artists design sardine tins. Legendary actresses endorse deodorants. Millions gawk at garbage and applaud and buy.

What geniuses these hucksters have become! What *persuasive* prose they write! What bright *conceptualization*! What quick *communication*! What buyer *stimulation*! What sweet *manipulation*! What mindboggling nerve-tingling gilt-edged 100 per cent original *chickenshit*!

2

1939. The Hospital.
Gabrielle's Night.

"GABRIELLE," HE HAD WHISPERED in Cartierville as they lay close, sheltered among shrubs at the water's edge.

She recalls on this September night how serious he had been in the midst of their first exchange...Urgent young bodies, gentle hands, explorations ardent beyond dreaming...The ultimate tension and release and the serenity.

She smiles in amusement, remembering how she knew that when he first called her Gaby it was quick affection, but when he murmured Gabrielle he was utterly infatuated. She loved both names, both moods. And still does. She loves to watch his face when he speaks.

Now she looks down and sees the September casualty, mute on his cot in the hushed Intensive Care. She can detect no colour on the pale face. He is motionless but he is still alive.

The nurse tells her not to worry, there's always hope.

Gaby drives home, pours herself a glass of beer, takes it upstairs and sits on the edge of their bed.

1939. Decade of Dismay.
Gaby's Discontent.

Early on a Saturday evening in late February 1939 if you looked in through the snow-fringed front window of the narrow house, you could see birch logs burning slowly in a squat brick fireplace whose reflections dappled and warmed the livingroom.

Outside, to the northwest, the cold black bulk of the mountain brooded in its snows, but within, the room was cordial, a civilized place of crowded bookshelves and casual furnishings, low couches and deep easy-chairs, with bullrushes, bittersweet and cut flowers reaching out from ceramic jars on low coffee-tables. A friendly, restful room in which to chat in the glow of shaded lamps, or move around and admire an oil painting or a print, or sip from tall and frosted highball glasses.

On the deep shag of the plum-coloured rug, Gaby lies on her stomach, supporting herself on elbows, her face cupped in her hands, a mug of coffee close by on a low bench, smoke curling from a bulky ashtray.

At thirty-five she is a bit fuller, more rounded, somehow more physical than when she first came to live in this house of Grandfather Lesage. Her eyes are a deeper blue, her hair longer, her lips more sensual. Her limbs are graceful and her movements lithe. Gaby is as beautiful as ever.

Her feet are bare and she wears a loose red turtleneck sweater above the bottle-green corduroy slacks.

Arthur listens gravely to a new gramophone record, but he has had a drink too many and he is tired and fretful. How would Fred behave? Had Fred changed? Would Fred's visit mean an argument? Would Fred make demands, play on his conscience? Criticize, condemn? The record comes to an end. "To hell with Richard Strauss," he mutters.

"It's getting late. I guess you'd better stay home," Gaby says. "I'll drive over and pick up the Shaughnessys. Will you set up the bottles and the glasses and put out the cheese and stuff? Don't forget to order the Chinese food; the list is near the phone. And, lover, be a good host, don't get sloshed before your guests arrive."

Gaby and Arthur Meller have been managing nicely. He has earned modest bonuses at the wholesale house. Gaby's shop has become a respectable little showcase for Quebec craftsmen. The Mellers have improved their charming house on the edge of the McGill campus. They try out new wines and experiment with foods; they are mildly concerned about gaining weight. They go for long walks on Mount Royal and have joined a bird-watching club. They still follow the concerts and enjoy plays, and occasionally they entertain cosy groups of friends. Whenever they can get away, summer or winter, they escape northward to their cabin in the Laurentian hills.

When they learned that Fred was coming home from Spain they arranged a celebration. Martin would be there, of course, and a few of Fred's Party people, some of her own friends and Arthur's, and one of Fred's buddies from Spain, a John Kravchuk.

As she drove south towards plebeian Griffintown, Gaby accused herself irritably. How can we remain "above the battle"? What gives us the right? Who are we to be so *maudit* upper-class? Why do we take it for granted that we have a licence to live better? Does Fred Shaughnessy owe it to *me* to leave his foot in Spain? Can I assume that all I have to do is simper, "Thank you, Freddie, it was *awfully* generous of you"?

Fred answered the doorbell, grinned ear-to-ear and embraced and kissed her full on the lips. Martin, his father, more gentle, kissed her cheek.

She was overcome, she felt like shouting, she wanted to sing, she was afraid of crying and she tried to keep calm. But, goddamit, a dear friend was home again, *alive*, smiling and buoyant and full of beans. And *alive*, radiating strength and confidence, and a hunger to live, above all to live, above all *alive*!

All she could manage, finally, her eyes brimming, was, "Hello, Fred, you're back, thank heaven you're back! Welcome home, Fred!" And to his father, "It's marvellous to see you again, Martin, you look great. You both look wonderful. It's been such a long time, too long, too long. So much has happened! But we'll talk later. Will you be ready soon? Arthur's holding the fort, he's getting things ready. Are you hungry? I hope you're hungry, I hope you have a thirst."

"In a minute," Fred called from the kitchen. "First we'll have a quick one."

The flat had changed little. Older, of course, shabbier, the floor mat more threadbare, the woodwork in need of fresh paint. Yet it was still vibrant, spirited Shaughnessy territory, comfortable, tidy, easygoing, a masculine home for father and son, both bachelors. On the walls hung pictures, a May Day poster, an Irish Republican manifesto, the photo of a woman killed by random gunfire on her doorstep.

The celebration at the Mellers turned out fine. The people chatted and joked, sipped or swallowed drinks, told stories and argued genially, nibbled on snacks and filled up on Chinese foods, reminisced and dreamed aloud.

Fred chanted Loyalist songs. His friend Jack Kravchuk chimed in, rose to his feet and followed with a Russian dance. Gaby sang habitant tunes. A Jewish furrier belted out Wobbly battle hymns. Martin Shaughnessy the Irish atheist crooned a Negro spiritual.

The singers mellowed and became friends and got exuberant on alcohol and emotion and good fellowship and ideals.

After the visitors had left, Gaby and Arthur busied themselves cleaning up. It had been a grand evening, Gaby told herself. Fred and Martin and all of them had had a damned good time. Fred was still Fred, she reflected, calmer and, yes, a little too quiet at times, more contemplative than before he went to Spain, but after a couple of rum-and-cokes as eager as the old Fred, as quick to laugh, as cheerful and as spunky as he had ever been. Yet he had changed, he had matured and become deeper, warmer, stronger, more confident. The foot? No, Fred did not pity himself, never had. This was the old Fred; yet Fred was a new man.

Now Arthur and Gaby were alone together; the Shaughnessys had been delivered home to Griffintown. It was four o'clock in the morning. Gaby sat facing her husband, staring hard at the glass of milk in her fist. She spoke at last, quiet yet deliberate:

"You know, lover, I think we have to think. I think we have to get off the fence.

"We watch, we criticize, we even help a little. I give things for raffles, you give five or ten bucks. Should we call it conscience money? I don't know.

"What in hell are we *doing*, Arthur? We're on the sidelines, we're cheering. But other people take the knocks and lose their jobs and get beat up. Or lose their foot. Or their life.

"What in hell are *we* doing, *you* and *me*?"

3

**1939. September.
Fred in Hiding.**

EARLIER THIS YEAR, in February, we returned, 600 of us, all that was left, half the battalion, we came home from Spain, Mac-Paps.

September now, and the Spanish war long lost. Dress rehearsals are over. The big new show is under way.

Whose war? What for?

1939. February.
Postscripts.

Is it only a week ago that we sailed from Liverpool?

Here I am in Halifax, awkwardly hoisting myself up the steps of the train and settling in for the long trip home. Is it only two years since I left for France and then slipped over into Spain?

There were no bands to see us off as we stole away over an ocean and across the Pyrenees into Spain on the Iberian Peninsula, linked to ancient Georgia by distant eastern ancestors pushing west.

We trained in a hurry and became soldiers almost overnight and joined our piece of the convulsing battlefronts among the olive groves or on a burning hill, collapsing riverbank or city street. And Canada was far away.

Our enemies were robust, arrogant, well-fed, heavily armed and prosperous. There was little that they lacked. The finest families were on their side. They had the blessing of their Church.

Some days we won and some we lost and other times we won and lost and won again.

I learned some Spanish words and sang their songs and looked for mail from home. I drank their wine because the water was so bad. I made new friends. I mourned the dead.

When the bullet smashed into my foot Johnny Kravchuk carried me all the way to the first-aid station. Later, in the hospital, I had time to lie around and speculate and dream of girls in thin summer dresses and warm summer nights in Montreal.

*

Even before the war is over we are sent home. The International Brigades are disbanded, the Mac-Paps become the Mac-Pap vets.

I send Dad a wire from the Halifax dockyards and ask him to meet me at the train in Montreal before I go on to Toronto to check out.

He shows up all right, slightly sloshed, full of hearty piss-and-vinegar and bluff paternal pride.

He is two years older; it looks more like ten. His face is more sunburned and creased, his thick black hair more splashed with grey, his short sturdy frame visibly thinner. I see new gaps among his teeth when he laughs.

We chat on the train and relish each other. When it's time for him to go Dad hugs me, slips me a bottle of beer and a couple of corned beef sandwiches in a paper bag, and is about to leave when he frowns and gestures towards my bandaged foot and the crutches. "What about that? Is it healing all right? What do the doctors think?"

I say yes, it's healing all right, they're going to give me a metal foot, aluminum or something light, and I'll learn to walk again.

He nods, squeezes my shoulder and starts to leave but stops after a few steps and waves and shouts, "Hurry home!" then pauses and adds, "We need you," and waves again and stands uncertainly in the aisle and walks quickly away and out of the carriage.

*

Close to ten thousand have massed inside Toronto's Union Station. Hundreds more outside on Front Street stream towards the entrances.

Indoors the cops stand deadpan at all the entrances and exit doors, resolved to control events, discourage over-zealous reunions, hustle everybody out as early as they can and have this unappetizing chore concluded with as little trouble as possible.

A locomotive bell is heard, startling, coming closer, louder. The people press forward and the cops try to hold them back from the arrival gates.

Doors open, the men emerge, pause and move forward. They put up a brave front in their shabby peacetime clothes; they assert a stubborn dignity. But how can you march in smart military formation when your ranks are slowed and hobbled by men untrained for crutches?

Thousands cheer. Tomorrow and on the following days the men will be among friends; they'll be fed, get medicine, a little money to see them over the hump, and railway fares home. Jobs? They've come home to an unemployed country, but they're home, they're home!

A woman presses forward, pushes her way close to them, holds up a snapshot and calls out, "Do you know him? He's my son. Have you seen him? Is he alive?" How can they tell her they know he's dead?

The survivors move through a lane in the crowd. The cheers

bounce from the high vault of the huge concourse. The war veterans advance soberly, young men, middle-aged men, a few older ones, men with arms in slings and hands gripping foreign crutches, men with bandaged heads and healing scarred faces.

Cheers, songs, tears. Clenched fists saluting each other. Slogans and hurrahs. First names shouted as old friends glimpse one another. Wives and lovers. Waving. Or waiting uncertainly... Will he come home with me? Will she remember me?

Mac-Pap vets move soberly, slowly, seriously through the crowd. They near the exits; it's winter and they're home at last.

The poker-faced cops and the plainclothes officers have been standing frozen like gargoyles. Now they move behind the departing demonstrators as the Mac-Paps march towards the exits, and now the constabulary voices croak out like bored automatons, "All right, it's all over now!" and finger billies and repeat, "Go home. It's finished. Go home, it's over now."

*

Detective Gilbert of Montreal, in town to exchange information with the Toronto Red Squad, has already met Detective-Sergeant Phil Purser and other experts of subversion. And now, here at the railway station, he has also seen some of his old enemies.

He waits until the crowd thins out. He scans faces, registers them in his memory for future reference. There's the young Shaughnessy hobbling on crutches, grinning at his Toronto buddies, waving, calling out.

He stares at Fred and Fred's eyes recognize him and stare him down. As Fred passes, Ralph Gilbert notes the crutches, looks down and sees the bandage but no shoe below the fellow's left trouser leg. "Bloody fool," Ralph mutters. A cop beside him asks, "What?" and Ralph mumbles, "Bloody fools." A woman in the crowd says, "What?" and Ralph tells her, "Move on, get moving, fast."

Afterwards at police headquarters Ralph swallows quick scotches with Toronto colleagues, goes off by himself for a late-night steak and returns to his hotel for a midnight lay.

When he is through with his whore and has dismissed her he turns off the light in his Ford Hotel room and tries to sleep, but his nerves will not let him forget the cheers and the singing and the surprising size of the crowd, and the calm faces of the homecoming vets. And the unblinking cold contempt on Shaughnessy's face as their eyes met.

*

"We have to get off the fence!"

Gaby's outcry, at four o'clock in the morning, after Fred and the others had gone home, haunted Arthur all week.

"We've got to get off the fence!"

It seemed uncomfortably true that he had always been backing away, from the time he was a child...eluding a neighbourhood bully...running from ghostly pursuers through endless nightmare corridors...avoiding the mourners at the schoolgirl Elsie's funeral on that cloudy winter afternoon...giving up after one defeating day in the ice-cream parlour on Peel...holding back from Georgie on that summer night at the country club.

He had hovered too long on the sidelines, he had too long watched from behind a curtained window. The world's breathing had become muffled and distorted. All he could hear was the stutter of his own uncertain pulse.

*

"Spain is a warning," Fred said with quiet vehemence. "Step by step the fascists prepared for the new showdown: Mussolini in Africa, Hitler in Europe, Tojo in the east.

"Now that they've won in Spain," he told Arthur as they drank coffee in the Shaughnessy kitchen, "they've been encouraged to advance their timetables. The democracies sold us out. They sold themselves out too," Fred continued bitterly. "While Spain fought for her life, England and France blockaded her, starved and disarmed her. Hitler must be chortling; he always said the democracies were gutless. Now he knows. He knows they won't try to stop him till it's too late. We're heading for a new war, my lad, a bigger war than we ever heard of, a world war. We could have stopped it in Spain if we weren't sold out. I hope we still have time."

Fred stared into his coffee cup and for a while neither pursued the argument. Abruptly Fred turned to his friend and spoke earnestly, "Arthur, we need help. Come and join us, you and Gaby. I wish you'd think about it. Come in and join us, Arthur."

Startled, all Meller could say was, "Yes, I know how things are, I understand. I know how you feel. But please, Fred, don't push me, not just now."

Arthur had given him this kind of answer before, but this time Fred sensed a new disquiet in his friend, a hidden desperation. He dropped the subject.

When Arthur said goodbye he pressed two ten-dollar bills into Fred's hand. "Up the rebels," he whispered, smiled wanly, and left.

4

1939. September.
The Tenth Year.

IN THE LAST DAYS of the decade the buzzards float in lower and lower concentric circles of flight until they are only yards above the earth, until they are ready to land for the feast.

Hyenas play cards and sip aperitifs and file their teeth and look askance at the competitors.

Everywhere on and under the land, in the waters and in the skies, come predators: the rodents, vultures, vampire bats, the jackals, eels and killer sharks, the lice, the maggots and the ghouls.

Where do they all come from, these creatures who thrive on carrion?

1939. February.
The Summing-Up.

For all those ten tough years, Fred had been caught up in conflict. Now in late February 1939, he was home, resting in the shelter of his father's flat, still leaning on the crutches but already wearing a metal foot.

Inaction made him restless. He would have to move back into the swing of things; he would have to find work. Would the printshop take him back? He would have to learn to walk without the damn crutch.

What a decade it had been! What a turbulent, explosive, angry and embattled time for Fred and his comrades!

The country had been in deep shock, too stunned during those first months to realize how badly it was hurt.

Yet only weeks after the crash ten years ago, the Scottish-born Tom McEwen was recruiting for the newborn Workers' Unity League. The former blacksmith urged the newly jobless to join the unemployed associations. He pleaded for organization of the unemployed and the unorganized workers. He pressed for new industrial unions to replace the obsolete craft guilds run by heavy-handed pie-card artists such as the myopic Sam Gompers.

In 1929 during the first weeks of the epidemic loss of work, the Communists were already demanding work or full maintenance, proposing national non-contributory unemployment insurance, pressing for emergency measures.

Work and wages! Work *or* wages!

As the mushrooming sickness spread into the next year and the next and became chronic, the resistance grew.

City people banded together and shoved aside bailiffs to stop the evictions of neighbours from their houses.

Factory workers walked the picket lines for friends or total strangers.

Men and women clamoured for welfare vouchers.

Shy boys and young girls joined the shouting.

Civil-rights protesters defied the bans on public meetings, obstructed the invasion of labour halls, tried to stop the smashing of offices, the seizure of books, the bullying, the beating, the jailing.

Farmers tried to protect their farms. "Don't be hailed out, don't be froze out, don't be starved out," they shouted, "don't be sold out, fight!" It was natural to fight. What else could they do when they saw the labour of a lifetime blown away like dust?

Everyone who had to labour for a living was threatened. They were all under the gun, all penniless.

You had a choice. You could shut up and crawl into a hole to starve in silence. Or you could stand up and hit back.

The ruling circles were appalled when the victims failed to realize that nobody owed them a living. Why hadn't they saved for this rainy day? They've been eating too high off the hog, now they make demands. They won't work but they dare to demand: free doctoring and hospitals, free pensions and insurance, free education, teeth, glasses, food, clothes! Free this, free that... where's the money to come from?

The best families were even more appalled when the workless gave advice on how to run the world.

Nevertheless, people pushed resistance onto the market-squares and into welfare offices, city halls and factories. They pressed pushed hollered defended demanded resisted.

Communists? Some were, some weren't. What difference? They were all denounced, all rounded up and savaged and jailed. They regrouped, they came back, they fought again and again. They were hunted without pause and without mercy; it was open season on Reds. It was rough on radicals, especially if they had been immigrants lured here as cheap labour from some bankrupt tin-horn police state in the Balkans or the Baltic. For them summary deportation could mean a prison stretch, torture, and even death.

One way or another, one place or another, Fred had been caught up in the action of the chaotic decade. He had led free-speech fights and peace petitions, picket lines and hunger marches. He had struggled on a dozen battlefronts at home and in Spain.

Were all their efforts and their hopes to drown in a massive new worldwide hemorrhage?

Restless, discouraged and impatient, Fred sat in his father's flat in Griffintown, remembering and reflecting, anxious to be once more involved in the familiar movement from whose everyday storm and stress and euphoria he had been separated for two bloody years of war.

He had to become part of the action again, and soon, here at home. He had to find his bearings again. He had to become mobile again, foot or no foot. He had to convince people that Spain was the danger signal, that time was running out.

*

On a dismal snow-blown winter afternoon while Martin Shaughnessy was at his union hall near the ice-bound harbourfront, Fred lay back in the lumpy easy-chair of his father's parlour-den.

He had been asked to give a lecture on the Spanish war and he thought he ought to offer something more than mere description.

His awkward foot supported on a hassock, eyes half-closed and head thrust back on the upholstered chair, Fred scanned his memory.

Events of the critical decade crowded in, scattered pieces of a jigsaw puzzle whose logic, once the crazy parts were fitted into place, warned of war once more and new catastrophes.

Spain was a vital piece. There were others: Ethiopia, Manchuria, Austria and Czechoslovakia.

Beside Fred on a table lay scratch-pad and fountain-pen. He glanced at the window and the falling snow. The winter, he hoped, would soon end, the spring sun would ease the ache in his foot. He hoped the hurts of the other men would heal. He hoped that neither they nor the country would ever forget the wounds of war or the wounds of peace.

He jotted notes: "Climate of crisis. Season of fear. Mood of hate from the start."

Blood brothers. Storm-troopers in Europe, cops in Canada, thugs of a system gone haywire and scared to death. They relish their time in the sun, lording it.

Law and order. Even before the protests could be heard, armies of marauders closed in. Tons of cavalry joined marching foot police. Motorcycle cops and bulging plainclothesmen swung clubs and whips and feet and fists like robots, slapping, kicking, smashing heads and hurling tear-gas cannisters.

Fred made a note: "Nick Zynchuk, Montreal, jobless, evicted, tries to return to his house. Zappa, Red Squad cop, draws service gun, kills him, remarks, 'I was mad. He was only a Communist.'"

Statesmen said Il Duce ran the trains on time, said Hitler only wanted living room, said the jobless were the cause of the Depression.

Fred hobbled and hopped into the kitchen for a beer and sank back again in his chair to sip and think.

Wars, he would tell his audience, spill blood and sever limbs and break young hearts and end the best of lives. Can he really convince them, rouse them, get them to act? He must try to reach them. What can he say to warn them? How can he make himself heard above the tight-lipped silence? Fred wrote on his pad:

"First you work till you damn near die. Then you're out of work and nearly die of hunger. When you object you get bloodied and jailed and sometimes they try to kill you. If you survive all this, they send you off to war to open up new markets. Many of us perish. Then it starts all over again. That's the way the system works."

Was he sounding bitter, would his audience think he was feeling sorry for himself? But it has to be said, loud and often, before it's too late. England and France *can* stand up against Hitler *now* instead of brown-nosing and wheedling for a corner in a new Nordic world where there won't be Poles or Czechs or Jews or Africans or Russians or Chinese.

Fred wrote: "Urho Jaaska, lumber union organizer, clubbed to death by Port Arthur police at jobless demonstration."

Fred wrote: "In 1933 two of every five Canadians were out of work, a seventh of Canada on relief. In 1931, Toronto and Yorks, 12,000 lost homes. From 1931-33, 10,000 European-born and British-born were deported.

"From 1931-34, 10,000 arrested for loitering, littering, unlawful assembly. Also trespassing, vagrancy, begging, sedition. And disorderly conduct, resisting an officer. And obstructing, impeding, disturbing, assaulting. Plus other violations, fancied or real."

Observation by Fred Shaughnessy: "If I had kids, I think I might bend a few laws myself."

There was a knock on the door. A boy asked, "Wanta buy some homemade doughnuts? They're fresh, my pa just made 'em." Fred bought four, a treat for their coffee, and returned to his notes.

It would be great to get away from all this snow and ice and sun himself again on a Pacific beach, and walk and make love again with the girl in Sointula. He sighed, remembering Vancouver and English Bay after riding the freights west in 1935 with no damn crutch to inhibit him. He had seen the slave camps (twenty cents a day) and helped to organize the men; he'd been in the thick of the action, the marches and the meetings, the sit-ins, the protests, the demands.

He'd liked Slim Evans, served on committees with the calm and thoughtful leader of the On-to-Ottawa trek, had joined the trekkers riding gondolas and roofs and insides of freight trains rattling east, had stood on the Regina square on Dominion Day evening (remembering July First patriotic pageants) and had cheered and heard responding cheers and the gasp of outrage as the Mounties poured out from their hiding-places. He had seen them advancing, charging, slugging.

The trekkers were scattered but regrouped overnight in other parts of town, built barricades for shelter from the cops, and held their ground.

Fred noted: "After the fighting, one man was dead, a hundred had been jailed, forty were hurt by bullets and batons."

Afternoon gloom closed in on the Shaughnessy flat. Fred stood at the window, watching the snow, feeling the cold that seeped in from the frozen street. There wasn't a living soul out there. He switched on the table lamp, leaned back wearily and took another sip from his forgotten beer. It had turned stale.

He made a list and ticked off the items. He would have to show hard evidence and solid arguments; it would not be easy to convince this audience, a bunch of students from McGill. Rhetoric wasn't welcome with that crowd. Well, he had facts aplenty and arguments galore and he would break down their prejudice and influence these doubting sophomores. He would be concise, well-organized and rational. He would show that the danger is real, warn that they themselves would be conscripted for a brand-new war, plead with them to join the anti-fascist, anti-war cause and make it their own.

Facts? Christ! How many facts do they need to see what's obvious? Facts alone? What about conscience and humanity? What about the terror of these last ten years? Where have they been not to see it?

He would tell them: Twenty-three Arborg, Manitoba farmers arrested for resisting eviction. Three strikers are dead, thirteen wounded, twenty-two arrested in Estevan and Bienfait in Saskatchewan, and the R.C.M.P. fan out, hunting coal miners, terrorizing families. Hans Kist snatched up, deported, tortured to death by Nazis. Sluggings and muggings by Red Squads. John Doe's teeth scattered on a Winnipeg curb. John Doe's head cracked in a Calgary park. John Doe kicked in the groin in Quebec City. John Doe's ribs fractured in Saskatoon. John Doe bloody all over Canada.

Facts? I'll give them facts. If they're human at all, they'll understand, they'll know why:

In Stratford army tanks debauch the streets. At the Lakehead two organizers tour the striking lumber camps and are found in the slush of a brook next spring.

Fred switched on the radio, listened to the music and finished his flat beer. Separately and together, Fred wrote on his pad, the villainies are part of the picture:

Queen's Park free-speech battlefields in Toronto. Terrors and assaults in Montreal. Vindictive sentences by courts across the country. The Reichstag fired by Nazi torches in Berlin. Duplessis, the padlock law and Arcand's brownshirts in Quebec. Arthur Meighen, Colonel Drew, the fat-cat Leadership League. Fascism in Bulgaria, Poland, Hungary, where democracy is a dirty word. Hoods in Willowvale Park scream "Heil Hitler!" while Toronto Red Squad men grin and egg them on to disrupt a meeting. The raids of August 1931, arrest of the Communist Party leaders, a travesty of a trial, years in prison, the attempt to murder Tim Buck in his Kingston cell...All part of the criminal years, and of Spain.

Fred was tired; he had to rest. He'd organize his talk later, pare it, make it leaner, more muscular. Skeptical students would ask questions. Did he think he could change the world? Did he believe he could prevent a war? Did he really think anyone gives a good goddam anymore about anything?

Well, he'd try to answer patiently. It was important to tell them not to feel helpless. Fred wrote:

"If you're alive, you fight. Only the dead don't care. If you resist, you have a chance. If you're alive, you hope."

He made a list: "What we have done, what we have fought for, what we have helped to win.

"People in motion, people resisting for ten solid years...New unions and the birth of the C.I.O....The rout of Iron-Heel Bennett...The defence of prisoners and the release of the Communist Eight from Kingston Pen...Repeal of section 98 of the Criminal Code...End of the slave camps...Spread of the Youth Congress...The Mackenzie-Papineau Battalion against war and fascism...the *Clarion* is launched, Canada's first communist daily...Writers, actors, artists, dancers and musicians moving left and driven by a passion to break loose from British restraints and American seductions...And more, and more..."

Fred closed his eyes, thought for a moment, and wrote down

what he would like to tell his audience:

Class struggle is no longer theory. For millions it has become a fact of daily life, like breathing.

They should be told how people have resisted.

Spain was the symbol and the key. Six hundred Canadians died there. We tried to stop the Axis and prevent a new world war. Our fight in Spain was our fight for Canada.

He would try to describe to them how ordinary people became heroes, how for ten rough years you survived only if you resisted.

There had been plenty of drama, and conflict unlimited, and clashes and confrontations.

Do you know what it's like to feel your hunger grow twenty-four hours a day every day?

The battle sustained us, he would say. The resistance raised our spirits and gave us self-respect. Of course it was more than banners in the breeze. It also meant cranking an old mimeograph machine or a messy makeshift hectograph, and handing out leaflets door-to-door and at the factory gates to boss-watched men and women.

It meant canvassing for signatures, pleading for pennies from the penniless, seeking recruits to swell the ranks.

Resistance was artists painting posters and then pasting them on walls and hydro poles before police drove up.

It meant countless committee meetings preparing hall meetings, park rallies, parades and picket lines, conferences and congresses.

Resistance was starved workers and parched farmers in hundreds of towns and villages and burned-out city cores, planning, financing, organizing and creating.

It meant getting legal aid in a hurry before prisoners were railroaded or deported. It meant helping their families and raising a few dollars for the victims when they came home.

To resist meant you could be a victim yourself any hour of any day, that you could be pummelled, bludgeoned and blackjacked on the whim of any licensed slugger. Yet fighting back, protesting, chancing new brutalities, even when you knew you'd get beaten up again or go to jail.

Resistance meant you fought even when you were afraid. It meant guts.

He leaned back again, dozed off and dreamed of drift-fishing from a stubby punt in a Laurentian lake on a sleepy summer afternoon and being hailed softly by a luscious girl waiting alone in a green canoe.

When Martin came home he was amused to see the smile on his sleeping son's face. He retired quietly to his kitchen to prepare their evening meal.

*

Later that night, after he had washed the dishes, Fred returned to his lecture notes. There was much more he wanted to tell them, but there wouldn't be time.

If only he could make them sense the excitement he had seen in the eyes of all the fervent people he had known in all those fervent years! What a gallery of marvellous dissenters, greater and lesser rebels, heroes and ardent heroines! Communist, near-communist and non-communist doers and dreamers, socialists, utopians, freethinkers and believers alike! Straight people and maverick citizens, gifted thinkers who had barely finished public school, immigrants who loved this land more passionately than the native-born, businessmen detesting every hour of their grubby world, dirt-farmers trapped in the arid furrows of their barren fields and refusing even then to yield, inspired old men and singing youths and wide-eyed kids!

He will appeal to his young student audience:

Look, these are your countrymen and these your hope. Listen to the rhythm of their lives, hear and remember them. Learn from these prophets of a finer world!

He became aware of music swelling from his radio. He had never heard anything quite like it before. He put down the pen and the notepad and stopped to listen. He turned up the volume. The waves of sound were like a physical embrace.

There was a pause. An announcer said they would now hear the third movement of Beethoven's *Eroica*. Fred listened with growing awe to the scherzo's driving rhythm. My God, this is the music of revolution!

He leaned back, closed his eyes and listened intensely, gripping the arms of the chair. When the symphony ended he was surrounded by scores of people crowding around him, waving, wishing him well, smiling, singing and calling out.

"Do you remember me?" a farmer asked.

"Remember me?" said the miner.

"Remember us?" they asked—mothers, neighbours, soldiers, orators.

"Remember?" asked the pickets, harvesters and union men.

"Remember us?" they asked—students, teachers, poets, ministers. And actors, artists, doctors, engineers.

"Remember me?" a prisoner asked.

A workless man said, "I remember you."

Of course Fred knew them.

He recognized the *Eroica* in their eyes.

Then they were gone. He was alone. The flat was silent but refreshed. He must hear more music, he must talk to Gaby and Arthur about it, he must listen to their recordings, he must get his own record-player, his own records.

The gallery of heroes and heroines evoked by the radio were gone. He thought of the others he had never known, gallant legends or modest figures who had briefly crossed the firing-line in a blaze of dedication and then vanished into the shadows, perhaps weary in spirit and drained of health, or nursing some personal hurt, some failed endeavour.

There would not be time to fill in all the portraits. He could not expect the students to see what he had seen. He had been asked to speak about Spain. Very well, he must not distract with rhetoric about lesser heroes. He would stick to the facts, address the intellect. He considered a while and thought, yes, he could wind up this lecture with a punchline right between the eyes. It might amuse the audience and make a point.

He would tell them about an office factotum in the aging Queen Street shop where the *Worker* was printed. She made coffee for the staff and coaxed delinquent accounts. She was really a sweet soul, a widow forced back into earning a living.

Fred had business in the shop one day, months after Buck and the other Communists had been arrested. He chatted with the woman over coffee and as he was about to leave she asked, "And how is Mr. Buck? I haven't seen him lately. Isn't he with the paper any more?"

Engrossed in her job, involved as a meek automaton in adding figures, mailing invoices and looking after her rented flat, she had been totally unaware of the delirium tremens that had swept the country since the raids of August 11.

"Is Mr. Buck on holiday?" she asked. "Is he well? He hasn't come here in months."

Fred thought his listeners would get the point and maybe laugh a little. Bitterly, he hoped.

*

The lecture was a shambles.

A dozen engineering students invaded the hall, sang *God Save the King*, shouted and booed and threw rotten eggs. They climbed onto the platform and one of them made a mock speech:

"Comrades and fellow workers!" he clowned. "Join me in a toast. To hell with Russia and the Reds! To hell with Roosevelt and the Pinks! To hell with pacifists and punks! Three cheers for Chamberlain! Let's not forget that Hitler cured the kikes! And God bless Franco, he's O.K.!"

Fred tried to speak but he was pushed back and hooted down. He tried again and was bloodied and knocked to the floor. The bums booed and sang and threw stinkbombs and chased the audience out of the building and departed, laughing riotously.

The dejected sponsors of the lecture stood around helpless, apologized to Fred and spoke dubiously about another try some other time.

A janitor came in to clean up the mess.

Fred's hosts walked him to a tramway stop. He hauled himself up onto a streetcar and waved goodbye.

"Don't let it get you down!" he called out before the door closed.

He could have used some cheering up himself.

PART TEN

1

1939. September.
Arthur in Limbo.

WHEN THE GLOBAL kill of millions is a matter of logistics, the incidental death of one obscure civilian counts for somewhat less than nothing in the projections of the statesmen and the generals.

Yet even when you are almost dead, Arthur, you must not give in to them.

We must make ourselves heard if only with a dying shout.

You are deep in your sleep in this hospital; you have not regained your consciousness.

Slumped on a bench in the corridor, Detective Gilbert naps fitfully. He is bone-weary and his hungover head is heavy with worry, irritation and black rum-and-coke.

1939. Midsummer.
The Troubled Peace.

That summer, when everybody worried that there might be a war, but few really believed that there *would* be one, Montrealers went about their business, complained about the heat, worked if they had work, took vacations, looked for work, talked about Europe, which was far away, and Roosevelt, who was near at hand.

Gabrielle Lajeunesse, born in La Macaza and now living in her grandfather's house near the campus, is pregnant for the first time. If war comes, will they conscript Arthur? Are fathers privileged?

303

Jack Kravchuk, the Mac-Pap vet, is washing dishes in the Mount Royal Hotel. He hopes they won't find out he fought in Spain and fire him. If war came, should he join up again?

Rose Meller, Arthur's mother, works again in men's clothing and hopes her son won't be called if there's a war.

Her sister Laura makes a living playing piano, gives lessons and sings at clubs and celebrations. She is concerned because her boy is old enough to go to war.

Martin Shaughnessy is browned off. He's heard too many say, "We need a war, I need a job, a war would help to pay my bills." Well, anyway, the army won't want Fred with only one good foot.

Irma Gillespie is eighty-two and P.E.I. is far behind. She wonders, if she had married, if there had been a son, would she lose him now? The son? A grandson too?

Ralph Gilbert assesses prospects. When the war breaks out should he try again for a promotion, or switch to army intelligence?

Fred Shaughnessy can now use the metal foot without the aid of the crutch. What will he do when the war breaks out? What kind of war? How can they warn people?

Arthur Meller worries and debates within himself, worries and wrestles with his conscience.

2

1939. September.
Armand Paquette.

I CAN HEAR HIM moving about upstairs, my fugitive.

The house has been quiet for too long. First Elise, suddenly sick, suddenly gone. Then for a few years the laughter of my daughters, Margot, Jeanette. They grew up, married, started families, moved to Winnipeg, to Edmonton.

They don't write much. They rarely come east to visit; it's expensive. I guess they have their own life to lead.

I used to teach them piano pieces. I liked when they played their childlike duets.

It's good to have another person in the house. Shaughnessy is a fine young man, a serious revolutionary, intelligent and friendly. Poor boy, that foot gives him trouble, I can tell. I'll prepare a good supper for him tomorrow. Perhaps a little bottle of something.

He would like me to find out about Arthur Meller. Is he alive? Will he live? I dare not phone the hospital; the line may be tapped, the police would come here and take Shaughnessy away.

1939. Midsummer.
If War Breaks Out.

At 6 a.m. the morning was calm, clear and fresh.

Armand Paquette, the aging piano-tuner who lives alone in this modest house on the quiet sidestreet off east-end Papineau, stood in his pleasantly cluttered parlour, surrounded by books and potted plants, bric-a-brac and family photo groups. On the walls were framed prints: Rosa Bonheur's massive horses, an etching of a sailing ship, heroic heads of Chopin, Hugo, Sacco and Vanzetti.

On the piano rested sheet music, a tin of tobacco, a bowl of apples, a coffee cup and two slices of toast. He reached for the cup and swallowed some coffee. It's a pleasant street, he thought, old and comfortable, the people are poor and friendly. Yet it lacks something. Its spirit is poor, it's numb.

Armand dabbed jam and nibbled on his toast. He inhaled deeply the fragrance from trellised roses outside his open window.

These poor souls, they're steeped in muck. Some day we'll drain the swamp and make the country clean again.

He sighed and continued his soliloquy: The swampland poisons everything, thoughts and words and all we do. We learn to speak the jargons of deceit. We make futile gestures, white brushmarks on white ceilings, black dots on black floors.

Hollow men build altars in the market place, their voices like a piano out of tune.

They praise their way—take all you can no matter how—and make it law.

The thin man filled a pipe, puffed at it and regarded the sleeping street from his window. Peaceful now. But soon, when they leave their beds and go out, one neighbour will shove aside another or even strike him to snatch a few days' work, and the others will look on and say nothing.

Paquette smiled to himself. The morning's too beautiful. I mustn't sour it. It's not right to be so serious so early in the day.

He stood at his piano and tapped out a few bars of a honky-tonk song he'd heard on the midway of a carnival in Sherbrooke:

"Oh, they don't wear pants in the hootchie-kootchie dance, they don't wear pants..."

He was pleased with himself, he felt better, but shrugged. Damn, I'm much too old. He sighed.

The swamp, the swamp, its vapours sicken every unborn child.

The sickness is transmitted by a banknote or a coin. The germs induce greed and fratricide.

Today in this summer of '39, Paquette reflected, more than his own familiar district lived in fear. The whole world shuddered.

Somewhere he had read that an adult human contains in his body some eight and three-quarters pints of blood, without which life would be impossible.

If war came, he realized in horror, millions of person of all ages would be pouring blood into ditches, gutters, rivers, reservoirs—drenching the swamps and staining all the world.

3

1939. September.
Legends for Arthur Meller.

As TANTALUS OF ancient Phrygia bends to drink, the water in which he stands recedes. He straightens out and extends a hand toward clusters of cool grapes hanging within reach, but the ripe fruit eludes, escapes his fingertips. On the verge of tears he touches his wet hand to parched lips, but the hand is dry now. The sweet fruit hangs lower, swaying in the wind, and the moist leaves tease his cheek. Repeatedly he stoops to drink and the water vanishes. The drought is palpable. Repeatedly he lunges at the heavy overhanging grapes but grasps air each time instead of fragrant fruit. He suffers unending despair.

Sisyphus starts again from the foot of the hill, gasping from weariness and pain as he labours up the steep slope, pushing the rock before him. When he seems close to the summit but for one last push, the heavy mass slips out of his grasp and plummets down again. Then he returns to the bottom and starts once more to groan, to climb, to heave and push the infinitely painful burden of his futility...

Wu Kang of China, seeking immortality, does not scruple much about the means. Caught, he is condemned to chop a cassia tree. But each time he fells this tree it grows intact again. This way he spends eternity in pointless exercise, an exile on the moon...

The many daughters of Danaus pour water into bottomless vessels. They are forever doomed thus to expiate their guilt...

The Ancient Mariner, like Tantalus, is surrounded by water, a sea of it, and though his thirst is great he dares not drink the stinking stuff...

*

Some step off the treadmill and some defy the fates.

All it takes is guts.

1939. August.
Before the War Broke Out.

People were unsettled and perplexed. Anxiety was tangible. Fred hobbled from door to door, ringing bells, distributing leaflets, engaging the tenants in discussion.

People stood and listened, trying to understand, asking questions. A few slammed the door in his face. Some said not a word. Others snapped, "I'm busy, it's no concern of mine."

Some argued and blamed the Russians. A few grinned and praised Hitler. Others shrugged and said it was God's will. Most people were worried and scared; they knew that in one way or another they would all be dragged in.

Fred was patient and reasonable. He hoped he was getting through, but you can't always tell, people are afraid to speak up on the wrong side of politics.

How can you explain it in simple terms when it's so bloody complicated: the diplomatic doubletalk, the sellouts, the secrets, the military schemes? How can a few hit-or-miss words on a doorstep erase the confusions of a lifetime of prejudice, the obfuscations of generations of history classes?

Whom were they to believe? The radio oracles? Or him? Or those other oracles who commented on the first commentators? The newspapers? The politicians? Or him, Fred Shaughnessy?

When he returned home, dubious and disheartened, he tried to lose himself for a while in the narcotic fantasies of the radio. For five minutes he listened to a comedy show, switched to a mystery, then tried a musical, only to be plunged back into the world by news flashes and jolting new catastrophes.

His father was away at a meeting. Nervous and irritable, Fred shut off the radio after a crescendo of shrilling Hitler invective punctuated by staccato "Sieg Heil!" choral blasts.

Angrily he left the house and hurried down the street. His foot began to hurt and he slowed and stopped at a white-front hamburger joint, went in and stood at the counter to eat. The explosive tin-pan clamour of a juke box taunted him. He stormed out, slamming the door and limping home in a fury. He got himself a beer and removed shoes and socks and the metal foot.

He leaned back and sipped from the bottle. Presently he cooled down, shrugged and tuned in the panic radio, repelled yet fascinated.

Relax, he warned himself. Relax, don't let it rattle you. Take hold, try to figure it out, look for some key to this obscene insanity. Keep cool, my boy, keep rational. Relax. Have another beer. Smile. The beer's cool. He grinned sheepishly. Sip and relax. Stay sensible.

He listened, studiously calmer, to the rumours, opinions, suppositions, inventions and canards. He heard interpretations, official statements and wild guesses:

" . . . we interrupt this program. The news you last heard is entirely without foundation. You heard it here first. What you now receive is authentic. Uncomfirmed. Confirmed. Unofficial. Apocryphal. An unimpeachable source. Groundless. A hunch. Keep tuned. Keep faith. Keep calm. Keep quiet . . . "

Fred silenced the radio. The house became blessedly still. He clicked off the light and sat at the window, glowering into the dark street.

*

"If war breaks out," Miss Gillespie said to the corner grocer, "millions will be killed. They won't even understand why. The young will be the first to die. If there isn't a war, they could live another forty or fifty years. If there is, well, I just don't know."

"Will there be anything else, Miss Gillespie?" the grocer asked.

*

"We've got to fight. It's human nature," Ralph Gilbert told a fellow-officer in the squad-room. "We have to train tough soldiers that aren't scared to kill or die. We sure as hell can also use tougher cops and more of them. And a free hand to clean out the riffraff foreign element. And make the Reds wish they were never born. We need the muscle-power to enforce law and order, and I mean enforce.

"Anyhow, there's too much of the wrong kind. Know what I mean? Like animals. They breed fast. They smell up the place. They crowd us. They don't like our ways. They don't belong here. Or anywhere else in the world.

"Yes, we could use a war right now."

*

Gaby and Arthur went to a party.

When they were all gathered, a dozen or so, drinks in hand and settled on floor cushions and hassocks, chesterfields and easy-chairs in the spacious livingroom, their hostess, media director of an ad agency, jingled a brass dinner-bell and announced:

"I hope by now everybody likes everybody else. If you don't, you need another drink. Eat, drink and be merry, for tomorrow...But don't let anybody talk about w-a-r. Have fun. We who are about to try...salute you!"

All laughed and had another drink and animatedly dissected the war that could happen tomorrow or the day after.

The professor of geography, the clothing designer, the

photographer, the violin teacher, the advertising woman, the medical doctor and their escorts and spouses, and Arthur and Gaby. They wondered: What will I be doing a month from now? Next year? Will I get sidetracked? How long the duration? Will we win? How many of us in this room will be alive?

Conversation ranged nervously from dead-serious to forced-flippant. They fed snacks to a sleepy St. Bernard. They related anecdotes, recited jokes, laughed too hard, drank too much and flattered and flirted, nibbled hors d'oeuvres and sang sentimental songs, played brainy party games and strained to seem casual and fool themselves. Next morning they'd be cold sober and jittery.

A marvellous party, they said as they left, startling the serenity of the night. Under the banter it hadn't been unlike a wake.

Only the placid St. Bernard was unperturbed, dripping saliva from the corners of his mouth, ignoring the departing merrymakers as he stared from sad and bloodshot eyes.

Tomorrow they would try to cope with hangovers and with war.

Cheers. *Prosit.* Bottoms up.

We who are about to...

*

They came out of the neighbourhood movie-house into the August night. The sisters had seen *All Quiet on the Western Front.*

"I liked the part about Christmas Eve and the soldiers on both sides listening to *Silent Night* and dreaming of peace and their families back home. I cried," said Rose.

"I wonder these days," Laura said. "I wonder about us. I wonder will there be a war? And why? And who's to blame? You and me? I can't believe that. I don't know, maybe I'm too stupid. Is it human nature? I'll never understand. I hope our children can figure it out."

"We've almost forgotten the other war, Laura. That time it was the kaiser. He was a nephew or grandson or something of Queen Victoria. Wasn't the Russian tsar a cousin of King George? Anyway, this time it's Hitler. Whose relative is he?"

"We were young," Laura sighed. "We worried about our husbands being called up. This time it's our sons."

"I'm scared, Laura, I'm terrified."

"Who needs a war? You? Me?"

*

About nine o'clock on a weekday evening towards the end of
August 1939 Arthur sat in his friend's upstairs flat. Fred was in the
kitchen getting coffee. Martin was away at a union meeting.

A carefree living space, worn and run-down but clean. Pleasantly
casual, a rough masculine base sadly in need of a woman's
presence. A few pictures, a cartoon or two on the walls, fishing
rods in the hallway, beer empties by the door. The faded photo of
Kathleen Shaughnessy before her death at her door in Dublin. A
picture of Jim Connolly, "the Irish Lenin," with drooping dark
moustache and dark magnetic eyes. A newspaper clipping with
photo of Jim McLachlan, the Cape Breton miner, organizer,
striker, Communist, jailbird, bristling behind a walrus moustache.
The bookshelves Fred had built, filled with hardcovers,
paperbacks, dog-eared pamphlets.

Fred rejoined his visitor, smiling the old encouraging smile, but
eyes quizzical. Arthur offered a cigarette and Fred said no, he was
off the coffin-nails, he'd switched to pipe.

They drank their coffee, smoked in silence, listened to the radio.
Finally Arthur spoke. "I never thought it could happen. But all the
signs point that way. A month? A week?"

His eyes, full of pain, pleaded with Fred, moved to the sepia photo
on the wall. She must have been magnificent. Fred had her mouth,
her brow, the eyes. Arthur glanced at the metal foot. His friend
regarded him thoughtfully, patiently. Fred was a few years older,
more deliberate, and appeared to be just as confident as when he
had packed toothbrush, comb and razor and some clothes and
headed for the Pyrenees.

The lights flickered, went out. Fred hunted for a candle. "It
doesn't matter," Arthur whispered. Fred laughed, "Why do
people whisper in the dark?"

Footsteps sounded on the stairs, the door opened and Martin
stood peering behind a burning match. "The war hasn't started yet,
but we're blacked out already," he snorted. "I guess we got to
learn to see in the dark. That's nothing new, is it?"

The lights came on. Arthur rose. "Well, I better be on my way.
Goodnight, Mr. Shaughnessy, goodnight, Fred, good luck." He

descended the stairs, hesitated at the street door. Should he go back up again and confront Fred and cry out, "What the hell can anybody do now? What's the use?" Fred would say, "Plenty."

He stepped out onto the sidewalk, walked to his parked car and drove home.

The house was dark. Gaby had said she might go out. He let himself in, poured and drank a gin-and-vermouth and went out again. He walked to Park, went north between Fletcher's Field and the base of Mount Royal, out west at Rachel to meet the mountain road, and followed its winding climb until he reached the top.

At the edge of the lookout high above the city he leaned against the barrier over the sheer drop to the black space below.

Stars flickered. Below, lights glared from lurid signs and high-rise windows. Above him the mountain's giant cross burned steadily, dominating the city. Down to the left a slow trail of distant lanterns moved east on the river. Freighter or tanker or naval craft.

He moved back, away from the pale circle of night-light on the mountain lookout. He found a bench in a shadowed spot. He lay on his back, bemused by the stars. He closed his eyes.

He was on the grass before his father's house across from the Hotel Dieu on St. Urbain, awed by the vast low sky of night, mesmerized by sounds of sweet song and voices of piano and flute and violin. He was being lifted, gently, by his father.

"You don't have to whisper in the dark," Fred had said, laughing.

"You learn to see in the dark," Martin Shaughnessy had said.

Arthur dozed off. Blessed escape...

The beam of a flashlight on his face awoke him.

*

Soon after Arthur left, Gaby phoned. "Fred," she sounded anxious, "I have to talk to you. Can I come over? I'll take a taxi."

Fred's father met her at the door. She kissed him on the cheek. The old man glowed. "Do that once a year, Gaby, and I'll live forever." Fred greeted her warmly and poured three glasses of beer. They chatted. Martin finished his drink and excused himself, "I have to start early tomorrow," and retired to his room, closing his door behind him.

Gaby, awkward in her pregnant state, looked upset and helpless. "What's wrong?" Fred asked. "Is it Arthur? You know, he was here a little while ago, just before you phoned."

"I didn't know. Did he say anything?"

"Not much. I think he wanted to, but he only stayed a few minutes and left. I think he wanted to tell me something and couldn't get it out."

"Fred, I'm worried. I wish you'd talk to him. Help him make up his mind."

"I wish I could. I've tried before. I think sometimes I push too hard."

"He admires you, Fred. Make him listen."

"I'm fond of him too, but I can't *make* him decide. He has to do that himself. I'd like him to be a real part of the movement. And you too, especially you, Gaby. In a way, of course, you're both in it."

"He's troubled, Fred, it's eating him."

"I know. His pride, his spirit, whatever you want to call it—his self-respect, I guess. He bugs himself for not doing what he thinks he ought to do. Guilty conscience?" He shook charred tobacco from his pipe and emptied it into an ashtray. "I think you'd both be happier. You need a bigger anchor."

She frowned, smiled. "We need *something,* an anchor, a compass, whatever. I wish you'd speak to him again. Convince him. Please, Fred."

Sitting beside him on the worn cretonne lounge, she took his hands in hers and broke into tears. "Please, Fred, help us!"

Then suddenly their arms were around each other and his lips were on her mouth and his hands were caressing her face, her breasts.

Abruptly he left the sofa. "You know, my dear Gaby," he said softly, "I don't see how this is going to help anybody, least of all you or Arthur. I'm sorry, I got carried away." He smiled warmly. "You're a very lovely woman, Gaby, and Arthur's my friend."

She wiped her tears away and got up to leave. At the door she kissed him on the forehead. "That's more like a friend now, isn't it?" she said.

He walked her to the tramway stop, saw her safely aboard. They waved to each other and he turned homeward and limped through the worn, dark street inhabited by his neighbours.

Upstairs again in his flat Fred tried to dismiss from his thoughts the impulsive embrace with Gaby. He had promised her to speak to Arthur. He would, but when? Perhaps he ought to wait. Last time he tried, Arthur had declared, "I'm an individualist. I can't take orders, I won't feel free." Fred had impatiently retorted, "We don't order people around. And how free are you at work, Arthur? Are you your own man there?" Arthur had not replied.

*

The heavy, impassive face looked down on him, studying him from behind the flashlight beam.

"You know it's against the law to get drunk in a public place?" Then, after a pause, "Are you drunk?"

Arthur sat up. "No, I'm not drunk. I was tired so I lay down. I guess I fell asleep. I'm better now. I'll be going home. What time is it?" He looked at his wrist-watch. "My God, I had no idea."

The officer scanned the man on the bench. No, not a bum, well-dressed, respectable. What's he doing here? Had a fight with the missus, came here to get away?

"It's near midnight. You shouldn't be here; it's late, the mountain's closed." He took a cigar from his breast pocket, lit up, puffed and looked towards the river's lights.

"You have a lonely beat," Arthur ventured, and wondered why he was making conversation with this man.

"It's not bad, mister," said the cop. "I like it. I like the dark. I like the peacefulness. It's another world. Nobody bothers me."

"That's why I came here," Arthur said.

"You know, mister, I used to take my girl here before we got married. Now when I catch couples in the bushes I pretend I don't see and walk past. Let them have their fun. But when I finish my shift and go down to the city I'm different, I get nervous, I get sore at the world."

"You blame the world?"

The cop considered. "The way I see it, I got nothing against the world. It's the people I don't like. People spoil everything."

"Are there no good people?"

"Maybe a few, only a few. The rest are crooks."

"Don't you think the world could be better?"

The man was angry. "Why in hell should I worry about changing the world? I got a wife and four kids. I'm doing all right. I live for my own."

"And the others, what about them?"

"To hell with them. I live my own life. I'm a free man. What do you call it...an individualist? That's me."

"Every man for himself?"

"You know anything better?"

Arthur shrugged. "Well, goodnight, officer, goodnight." Under his breath, as he left the lookout, he whispered, "God help us!"

*

When he came home from his nervous night prowl of the mountain Gaby was asleep. He undressed in the dark. A coin fell from his pants pocket and clinked on a chair. Gaby woke.

"Where have you been?"

"Walking."

"What's the matter? You sound strange."

"Nothing. I'm all right, just tired. Go to sleep, Gaby, it's late."

He stooped and kissed her. She sighed and fell asleep again. He lowered himself quietly into the bed and kissed her head. She stirred but slept. He propped himself on an elbow and watched her face, pale in the dark, calm and beautiful. He lay back and stared into the dark.

*

On a late afternoon during that critical week Arthur paused on Dorchester before the dramatic facade of St. James Roman Catholic Cathedral, on whose high roof-edge Christ and twelve stone saints loomed as though drawn to the great cross on the crest of Mount Royal.

Arthur entered the huge basilica where worshippers, sparsely scattered among the pews, prayed or responded mutely to the hollow voice of a priest who seemed to call from far away, his words muffled by damp walls. It was a vast, sepulchral space made nervous by flickering tapers among the graven images and trembling silences.

He moved down an aisle, slipped guiltily into a seat, forgetting to kneel, or refusing to, son of an alien faith; or worse, no faith at all.

He glanced stealthily around him and was depressed by the metallic drone of Latin, the hopeless stare of old people with sad lumps of old faces and vacant eyes; the well-dressed woman of fifty with head erect and proud, her mouth taut, in her eyes a threatening flood; and a man of thirty, nervous, caught in some perplexing moral crisis; an Indian girl, about sixteen, stunned by her first sin; a ragged tramp; a streetwalker; a soldier; a farm couple; a half-dozen others who came for help or just to sit.

No, Arthur told himself, I need more than an altar, more than candles, prayers or incense, more than refuge or kind words. I need what only I can give myself, I need guts.

*

On the Friday evening of the Labour Day weekend, Gaby and Arthur Meller set out for their place in the Laurentians. His mother and aunt were going to spend the holiday with Laura's son Josh at a cottage near Magog in the Eastern Townships.

Arthur drove. Gaby made herself comfortable beside him on the front seat. As they sped northward in flight from headlines, they welcomed every rockface and cherished every stream. They drove steadily, turned off the highway onto a sideroad, then another, at the end of which stood their beloved cabin on the wide, blue lake.

They carried in supplies, piled twigs and logs into the fireplace, set a table on the screened porch, ate a cold supper of sausage meats, potato salad and cheese, washed it down with wine, and listened to the water lapping the shore and to the hum of cicadas.

Later, after cool highballs, but before it was time to turn in, he stretched out on the porch and laid his head on her lap and lost himself below the crowding stars, remembering his father's house and the wonder of the music and the great stone walls of the old Hotel Dieu.

Gaby bent and kissed his lips.

"Blessed, blessed peace, Gaby..."

She nodded gravely, stroked his lips.

All of the next day they pretended that Friday's firestorm over Poland had only been one incident; Hitler would not defy the whole world, there wouldn't be a war.

*

The signal varied. Pastoral, like woodwinds. Shrill, like a police
whistle. Pleading or imperative or beguiling. A piping little sound,
"Beep-beep," two notes.

Morning, a breathtaking spring day, golden sun on rich loam
acres, beads of dew trembling on green shoots.

Over a hilltop appeared Adrian Waterman, the lapsed poet, now
a lissome and tanned and spectacularly handsome young man, tall
and perfectly proportioned, an engaging smile on his lips. He wore
only a sort of classical sash around his middle, and the muscles
rippled as he advanced gracefully down the furrows of the field. On
Adrian's blonde head was the kind of broad-brimmed straw hat
farmers wear at work. In the crook of Adrian's left arm he held a
basket of small green seeds which he planted in the ground. When
he used up a supply he sat down on a rock and with a pair of garden
shears reduced green paper banknotes to tiny seeds and resumed his
planting along the furrows.

When he had seeded all the fields he didn't rest at all but
proceeded immediately to irrigate them, releasing rich red viscous
streams into the furrows. And all the time he whistled the two-note
incantation, "Beep-beep!" until the sky grew dark and the day
ended.

Now it was night. The green and golden world was obscured by
purple shadows. There came a rustling and a scurrying along the
dark furrows of the fields. The moon came from behind lavender
clouds and revealed a whimpering, quivering birth of life
throughout the countryside.

Where was the day's Adonis? Gone, succeeded by the midwife
whore who now controlled the night.

Fitful streaking light changed constantly—pale pink into
maroon, purple to electric blue, magenta to blood-red to
indigo—revealing a sprouting of new bodies—infants, children,
girls and youths—breaking out of the ground. And all these
newborn innocents were armed with rifles, handguns, bayonets
and bombs.

And all the while this florid whore, the fat-flesh Pointe Claire
Angelique, gave orders, organized, shrilled signals from a fife,
"Beep-beep! Beep-beep! Beep-beep!"

When morning came the sun hid behind clay-coloured skies. The hag had left. The harvester was now in charge, his gross bulk topped by a death's head mask, his robe of authority a bloodied cape. He took up a position on a high hill and introduced himself, "I am Jeff Cormack. They know me at the country club. Now pay attention!"

He issued orders for the newly born to form ranks in two adjoining fields divided by a shallow irrigation ditch.

Then he gave the command: Each army of the young will fall upon the other and kill. He warned, "Obey the rules!"

The fighting, he decreed, must be confined to within three feet of the ditch. All dying must take place no more than one foot from the ditch. No blood will be allowed to flow anywhere but the ditch. Whoever violates these rules will be compelled to fight and die (again and again if necessary) until they learn to respect the rule of law.

As the young people fell, venal old men and grotesque harridans threw stones.

The sound of the cash-registers was heard in the land, a tintinabulation, a *Te Deum*. "Beep-beep! Beep-beep!"

Arthur woke, listening. On the window sill a bird chirped, "Beep! Beep!" It was Sunday morning. He got out of bed and moved toward the window. The bird flew away.

After lunch, as they sat on deck chairs beside the lake, a boy guided a red canoe along the shoreline. When he drew near he called out, "They've declared war!"

Arthur had heard him but he called back, unbelieving, "They've what?" and the boy stopped paddling and said, "England's declared war. I heard it on the radio."

Arthur stared at Gaby, stared at the boy, watched a swarm of minnows dart away. "Are you sure?" he demanded, and the boy replied, "Sure I'm sure," and added, "I hope they'll let me enlist, I'm sixteen."

Gaby asked softly, "Have you ever killed somebody?"

"Never mind," Arthur cut in, "you'll learn."

The boy laughed, dug his paddle sharply into the water and sped away, glancing back once over his shoulder at the couple on the shore.

The day passed somehow. They sunned themselves, swam, read, said little to each other, ate supper and, in the evening, drank rum-and-cokes they didn't really enjoy, stared into the log fire and, at last, went forlorn to bed.

Gaby lay awake, thinking of her baby. Will its father die in the war? Arthur, also awake and silent in the darkened room, depressed and upset by the news, wondered whether Gaby and his child and he himself would outlive the war.

The rhythm of a plane in flight came closer until, through the window, they could see the coloured lights swimming in the summer sky.

"In the Laurentians it sounds like a sonata," he said. "Over Poland...tonight..."

Gaby drew him to her. She clung to him, kissed him and whispered, "Try to sleep." Eventually they both fell asleep.

Late on Monday afternoon, Labour Day, they closed the cabin and left for home. A restless wind ruffled the lake and the sky was overcast. The storm broke with savage lashings of lightning, thunder and rain. They travelled steadily into the premature night until the rain eased and the storm moved over to other areas. The road gleamed black, and wet leaves brushed against the car. Wet tires kissed wet pavement. Transport trucks rolled darkly on night missions. Roadside stands splashed light on glistening highway. Rain-soaked hitch-hikers waved listless arms.

Nine o'clock, ten, and at last they saw the city's lights and the welcoming body of the city, the excitement of the city, the songs of radios, the rumbling, friendly streetcars, bursts of laughter. The world's alive! And suddenly the newspaper headlines hitting out, berserk: war news, bombing planes, death from the sky, carnage in the streets.

Enlist! A dollar a day! No, it's more. A dollar-thirty?

At home, in the shelter of their house, in the safe citadel of their placid street beside the campus, Gaby mused, "This afternoon we sat by the lake."

"There's no such place anymore," Arthur said. "There's no such lake. It's a mirage. Summer's over."

Lost and forgotten was the long weekend. The war had come. For Arthur, Gaby, Martin, Fred. For Rose and Laura and Paquette. For Miss Gillespie and John Doe and Kravchuk. For all of them. For Ralph Gilbert too.

4

Wartime. 1939.
The Hospital. Before Dawn.

ARTHUR SLEEPS.

Unconsciousness? A coma? Death?

Does he dream?

There is a man running. Arthur recognizes him. He calls out to the running man, who is himself, and he begs him. "You've got to stop! You can keep running forever but you can't escape, you won't get away...Stop running...Stop...Stop running!"

Wartime. 1939.
Last Deadline.

Throughout the first week of the war Arthur struggled. He lay awake nights, thinking, accusing himself, demanding.

He went to see Fred and listened to his friend's sober assessment. But even Fred wasn't quite sure at first; he hesitated, perhaps we should keep out. He admitted there was confusion on the left.

"This is a power struggle of rival empires," he argued. "Canada should stay out of it." A few days later he speculated about giving "critical support" and trying to turn it into a genuine anti-fascist war. Then he questioned such a policy, "Can you trust a Chamberlain any more than a Ribbentrop?"

Finally Fred came out stubbornly and vehemently for opposition. "It's phoney. It's not our war at all. It's an imperialist war, between imperialist powers, for imperialist aims, on both sides. The men who sacrificed Ethiopia and Spain and who betrayed China and Czechoslovakia, they're running this show too. Let's keep Canada out of it! But we have to speak up. We can't ignore it. We can't pretend, we can't evade, we can't run away from it."

*

Later that night as Arthur sat in his livingroom after Gaby had gone to bed, he began slowly and very deliberately to make up his mind.

No, he agreed, I can't keep running. I know there's no magic tunnel to Paradise. I'm tired of keeping quiet. I'm not a vegetable. I'm tired of living like a well-mannered yes-man. The air in this town reeks of cowardice. I have to speak up. I have to break loose. Not ten years from now. Not next year. Not when I'm too old. But now, now!

Wistfully he told himself, "I wish I had the strength of a Shaughnessy...Perhaps I have."

Fred never gives up, Fred never loses hope, Fred has modesty and pride as well. Fred's a happy man.

Yet Fred isn't a saint, he's not a giant or a genius.

What kind of passion drives a man?

Morality? Intellect? Conscience? Love?

All these, but more. The man has guts.

At two o'clock in the morning, alone in his livingroom, Arthur Meller smiled, got himself a glass of milk, raised the glass in salute, and said the word out loud:

"Guts!" And again, "Guts!"

*

Gilbert drove the police cruiser south on St. Denis and west on Marie-Anne, south on The Main and west along Pine Avenue, south on Park onto Bleury and west on St. Catherine. He cut down Peel and swung to Dorchester and sped westward. Then startled and annoyed he saw it; he knew what it meant. *"A bas la guerre!"* He recognized the message; he had seen it scrawled on fences during that other war, his first world war. But this time it shouted in English as well, "Down with war! Stop the war!"

The angry slogan surfaced everywhere, as though to demonstrate that the anti-militarist passions of 1914-18 could bear fruit once more, a quarter century later. The words were chalked on windows and painted on walls.

He drove on, picked up the stoolie west of Guy, took him back to a dim sidestreet behind the St. James financial fortresses now resting in the night.

He stopped the car, doused its lights and demanded, "Well?"

The man reported, "They're going to have a meeting." "What for?" "Against the war." "Where?" The informer named the place. "When?" "Tomorrow night, about eight." "What kind of a meeting?" "Just a small one, ten or twenty Party people, whoever else they can attract at the park." "Who's speaking?" "I don't know." "What the hell *do* you know? Find out." "I'll try." "Don't *try,* find out."

Gilbert started the motor, but the fellow remained seated. "You forget," he said. Ralph reached for a wallet and handed him a bill. The man glanced, shrugged and slipped the money into his pants pocket, got out, walked to St. Catherine and took a streetcar to The Main where he bought himself a plate of chopped liver, a cabbage roll, a hot smoked-meat sandwich on rye, with mustard, a large dill pickle, a red pimento and a quart of beer. Unsatisfied, he ordered a hot corned beef on rye and another pickle and a beer.

When he left the delicatessen his conscience bothered him; he had spent too much, he'd made a hog of himself. But dammit, he hadn't been eating so good lately, and if there's one thing he can't stand it's hunger. Anyhow, it was his own money, he'd earned it the hard way. He could get hurt if they found him out. To hell with them, he owed them nothing. They could rot.

*

War was crowding the days for Gilbert—briefings, conferences, checklists of radicals, training sessions—but he found time to eat well, go to the burlesque show, seek out attractive and innovative bed-warmers and, on occasion, browse among the Fraser bookshelves.

In one book he was informed that revolvers are "at once a benefit to mankind and a menace to the peaceful citizen." And again, that "in most civilized countries the carrying of a revolver by unauthorized persons is a criminal offence." And further, that "the irresponsible person, who may be defined as one whose personal views, too often criminal, are held superior to the mandates of humanity and law, would be less a social danger if deprived of a revolver."

The moralizing both amused and offended him. It was the weapon itself that fascinated Ralph. He admired its mechanical simplicity and concise action but even more the amazing power it packed. He, Ralph Gilbert, veteran police officer, was authorized by law to employ that power as he saw fit. He was in charge, a senior man. He controlled this small lethal instrument, this titanic burst of energy. By God, it was a good feeling!

*

Fred for two weeks had been pressing for a meeting. Yes, he admitted, it would be difficult. No, he argued, it does not defy common sense, we just can't clam up, we have to speak.

"Sure, the air's full of hysteria and the papers feed lies and people actually expect Hitler will get his come-uppance at last after seven maniac years. We'll be unpopular telling the country it's not true, that the war's a fraud, but we have to blast this god-awful swindle.

"I don't want a collision with the powers-that-be. We have to avoid arrests, we have to preserve the organization. We're being forced underground and some of us are going to be interned or sent to jail, so we have to be careful. But right now we've got to make a stand, even if only a handful of people see and hear us. It's our duty and our right!

"First we'll have this open-air meeting. In a park or on a street corner. We won't advertise it, just word-of-mouth. We'll have one speaker, five minutes, more if the cops don't turn up right away. We'll hand out a short snappy leaflet at the start.

"I'm volunteering for speaker. I want to speak for the Mac-Pap vets. I insist."

The Party people discussed, argued, agreed and disagreed and finally decided on Fred's "lightning rally." A committee was struck to plan and organize: check the place, work out strategy, form a defence buffer around the speaker and, if the cops close in, arrange for Fred's escape.

Johnny Kravchuk would be there, and other Mac-Paps, and Armand Paquette the piano-tuner. Irma Gillespie would be present. So would Martin Shaughnessy.

Arthur Meller would attend, and Gabrielle; they had been told about it by Fred, who said, "It could be rough, Gaby. Do you think you ought to go? If you do, you better stay at the back." And Gaby had replied, "We'll be there," and patted her belly and smiled. "All three of us."

*

In the warm evening in the shabby, pleasant park the neighbourhood people have come to rest, to cool off, to talk and to watch their children skip, throw balls, play tag or run-sheep-run and hide-and-seek.

It's a small park, with shady trees, flowerbeds, footpaths. The people sit quietly on wooden benches and on the grass, and children run across the grounds and over the bordering sidewalks. Mothers chat, one ear to catch the conversation, the other alert and sensitive to the safety of their kids. All summer the neighbourhood's plebeians have come here to breathe for a few hours before returning to steaming, layered flats and sweltering rooms to reach out for the fringe of sleep.

It is evening in the park, warm but with a pleasant breeze. It is not quite dark, but a solitary soft light already glows from the lamp at the far edge and casts a dreamy haze.

The children play. Two small girls chase a boy. He runs and turns to taunt them but stumbles and sprawls on the grass. They pounce on him and the three wrestle and laugh.

Summer will soon end and the neighbourhood people cling to it.

They come to this park at Marie-Anne and The Main, old ones and young, to sit with friends or sit alone, to exchange gossip or speak fragments of thoughts or stubbornly voice convictions or obsessions. Shy people and bold ones, cheerful or morose.

They have come here to sit, the handsome and the homely, the dark and the fair, Greeks and Slavs and Britishers, Irishmen and Jews, Finns and French-Canadians, a few blacks and a handful of Chinese, to rest, to think, to talk, to laugh, to sigh, to dream, to dream...

Martin Shaughnessy serenely smokes his pipe. An aging man, he is alert and tough and knows what he wants and where he'll look for it and how he'll find it. His glance spans the park. He recognizes faces, two there on a bench, a group on the grass, an old man walking and chatting with a young woman, another leaning against a tree. Martin recognizes workmates, friends, a couple of jobless carpenters, a tailor, labourer.

Sitting prim on a bench is Miss Gillespie, conversing with two older women. Two boys play catch with a softball. When one of them misses and the ball rolls to Irma Gillespie's feet she bends over, picks it up and resumes the conversation as she tosses the ball back.

Gaby Meller and her husband enter the park and seat themselves on a bench. They appear nervous but determined. Gaby waves gaily to Martin Shaughnessy and then to Irma Gillespie. Should she and Arthur go over to meet Martin and Miss Gillespie? They decide to remain where they are. Martin smiles and waves and he too remains in his place. Irma Gillespie smiles and stays at her bench. Nobody, it seems, wants to attract undue attention. The Party people and their friends are anxious but behave calmly.

The scene is outwardly tranquil. People sit. People wait. The evening darkens.

Arthur wonders, what are they waiting for, when will it start?

A bell tolls deep and round and hollow and rolls low across the evening, summoning, scattering fragments of wistful sound. The ear mourns its memories.

Martin, gripping the pipe-stem in his teeth, rises slowly from the bench, removes the pipe and taps it on the palm of his hand. Tobacco ashes drop away and he rubs wet nicotine from his hand. He puts the pipe in his pocket.

Friends move briskly toward him, half a dozen of them. Another twenty or so come quickly forward. Others move swiftly into the compact circle surrounding Shaughnessy around the park bench.

Miss Gillespie and others in the gathering, and men and women attracted by the diversion, move over to see what is happening. A small band hurries towards Martin's group. A gap opens for them and then closes protectively. A man is seen climbing awkwardly onto the bench. He is helped by comradely hands.

Fred Shaughnessy, elated, starts immediately to speak. He says:

"I know what war is like. Last February I came home from Spain. I don't want any more war, least of all this phoney war. It's not my war and I don't think it's your war."

Three sedans and two black marias roar up to the park. Plainclothesmen and uniformed cops pile out. Gilbert leads his company, charging roughshod over flowerbeds towards the meeting's core, some eighty listeners.

There is shouting as Gilbert's men move in, running in the easy silent trot of trained pursuers. As they advance they fan out and draw clubs and blackjacks.

The fringe of the meeting wavers and falls away, but others turn

to resist. Those in the circle immediately around the speaker's
bench link arms to form a human shield.

A car pauses at the curb. The driver pounds his fist on the horn
and Fred's words are drowned. The drunks in the car laugh and
howl obscenities as their siren shrills.

Fred shouts, "It's a phoney war!"

The cops are close, the cops have reached the audience and have
started slugging with the cold precision of pistons.

Men and women try to defend themselves and are beaten to the
ground and kicked and clubbed as they lie there. A detective behind
a man twists his victim's arm and another detective in front hits the
helpless man, punching his face until it swells to bloody pulp. A
sobbing woman, her lips bleeding and tears streaming down her
cheeks, swings her purse at a cop and rips a gash across his face.

The siren howls drunkenly in counterpoint to the cries and the
shouts.

Arthur and Gaby stand to one side of the fighting, overwrought
and horrifed but refusing to run away.

A dull pounding of heavy feet on the adjacent street signals a
second wave of uniformed police advancing at a trot, beefy, fresh,
omnipotent.

Fred is still on his feet, still on the bench. He forces his voice
until it cracks, he rasps, he pleads. He must make himself heard,
people must listen, they must not let themselves be herded into
slaughter, they...

As the cops close in, protective arms pull Fred from the bench.
There is the bitterness of defeat and tears of frustration in his eyes
and a hatred that flares reborn from the day his mother died on the
Dublin street.

Friends try to hustle him away. He resists. He struggles to go
back. Jack Kravchuk, big and powerful, snatches him up like a
child, as he did once in Spain, in the Ebro River fighting, and
carries him off, running swiftly, determined not to be stopped.

Gilbert sees them and runs after them. The pursuer pauses,
draws his gun and resumes the chase.

Irma Gillespie, frail exile from her native Charlottetown, skinny
spinster in her eighties, should be at home sipping a cup of
aromatic tea and dozing off in a rocker in her livingroom. Instead,
the soft-spoken non-violent old lady throws herself onto the path
under Gilbert's feet and trips the son of a bitch so that he stumbles

and falls onto the chipped-stone path, messing up his handsome ruddy face as it hits against the stones.

As Ralph rises from his humiliation, bleeding and pale with fury, a brick scrapes his bruised face. He grips his gun, but by now Fred has been rushed out of the park and spirited away down a backstreet and into the shelter of an anonymous house.

Gilbert turns back, sees Irma and stares in amazement as he recognizes her. He raises his weapon in a terrible slow-motion arc until the muzzle points directly at the old woman who is now on her feet and hurrying away. Around her in the park the uniformed police and the plainclothesmen swing blackjacks and nightsticks.

The drunk demented siren continues to screech. There are few people left in the park.

Gilbert aims, considering whether to finish off the old bitch, merely maim her or just throw her into the black police van.

For Gaby and Arthur, shock succeeds shock like quickly changing images from a flashing slide projector: the hovering tension in the peaceful park, then the sober start of the defiant meeting, the police stampeding, and Fred borne to safety like a startled little boy, and now old Irma Gillespie breathless and stumbling in flight as Gilbert points his gun.

Gaby cries out, "Look, Arthur! Dear God!" and points to Irma, and Arthur knows the outrage in her heart and his own anger as that great ox of a man points his gun.

Arthur shouts, "Leave her alone, don't shoot, don't hurt her. Oh, God, no!"

He walks forward steadily and stations himself between Gilbert and Irma. "You must not hurt her!" he shouts at Ralph. "Do you hear?" He shakes his fist at the detective. "Leave her alone! Leave her alone!"

Now the trembling is gone. Now through his heart and through his brain flows a surge of release. He shouts. He is not afraid.

Gilbert faces him, waits, smiles, raises the revolver and very slowly presses the trigger. The explosion splits the night and then the park is still.

Arthur's head has been jerked back and a small round hole shows high on the left side of his forehead. It is about an inch and a half above the eyebrow. Blood seeps from the wound, but not much. He falls back slowly, his legs across the path, his shoulders on the grass. Gilbert returns the gun to his holster.

Gaby runs heavily to Arthur, kneels beside him and holds her hand to the wound. She finds a handkerchief in her purse and presses it over the wound. She does not scream. She holds his shoulders and kisses his face and her own is now smudged with his blood.

The park is silent and almost deserted, the lawmen are done, the people have been dispersed. Around the couple on the grass stands a ring of officers.

A policeman says, "We better take him to a hospital."

Gaby shakes her head. "No, you'll kill him on the way."

The policeman says, "If we don't hurry, he'll die here."

She gasps and bends over Arthur and cries out, "No! No!"

The officer says quietly, "You can come with us."

She searches his eyes and can find no anger and no compassion, only an official face. She moans, "I want to sit near him." The man nods.

A siren is heard, an ambulance draws up and its crew moves in on the double. Arthur is lifted to a stretcher, carried over and loaded in through the rear of the hospital van. Gaby sits beside her husband and holds his hand. Beside her sits a policeman and beside the driver sits Ralph Gilbert.

They speed through traffic, the siren keening. Gaby is silent. Gilbert and the policeman are silent.

When Gaby speaks again her voice is low, but it is filled with hatred and with grief.

"You bastard!" she says. "You murdering bastard!"

There is no reply.

5

1939. September. The Hospital.
Until the Day Break.

ARTHUR...?
Rest your hurt body on the pale cot in the silent ward where a

doctor touches you, checks the charts, frowns and mutters instructions to the nurse who has watched over you throughout the night.

In this room lie others who drift between living and death.

Outside in the corridor sits the sullen Ralph.

Somewhere hiding in the city are the shocked and angry ones.

At home Gaby waits sleepless. Within her, your child.

How many days, how many decades, how many centuries since you wandered late at night onto the lawn of your father's house on St. Urbain Street and lay on your back on the sweet cool grass and felt the stars kissing your sleepy face as the sounds flowed from the windows and your Aunt Laura and her friends indoors sang and sang and played their music?

How many songs ago, how many stars ago, how many humming blades of grass touching your cheek?

Your first day in this white room woke into sunbeams but you, Arthur, did not wake.

Night is here again, faltering before the third day's break. It is 3 a.m., 4 a.m. Soon...?

Do you remember, Gaby and you, "Until the day break"?

How many minutes, Arthur, how many days, how many decades to dawn?

Arthur?